ALFIE

IGNACIO F. BUNSTER-OSSA

*To humans everywhere who
long to know their place in the Universe.*

"Open the pod bay doors, HAL."

"I'm, sorry, Dave. I'm afraid I can't do that."

"What's the problem?"

"I think you know what the problem is just as well as I do."

2001: A Space Odyssey

TO THE READER

If someone were to qualify the events that follow to be as transcendent
to humankind as Adam and Eve's expulsion from Paradise, I would not
disagree. That biblical episode unleashed the loss of innocence that con-
demned humankind to a never-ceasing struggle between good and evil.
It is a struggle that has been closely monitored, from the onset of *Homo
sapiens* to present-day *Homo spaciens*. Two hundred and fifty years ago, ignorance, greed, and contented indifference threatened the planet's balance
of life. But good prevailed. A cataclysmic change in the Earth's climate
was averted. An alien intelligence did not intervene then to guard against
irreparable environmental harm, but this time decisive action is unavoidable. Preservation of "The Little Spark," as we call planet Earth, requires
that this be so.

CONTENTS

CHARACTERS

Airi Mendes Te: Educator. Married to Midane Te

Midane Te: Educator

Passerine Zanzibar Te, aka **PaZ** [pronounced pahz]: Eldest son of Airi
and Midane; Nori's father. Terranaut

Marianne Yellena Bekele, aka **MaY** [may]: Nori's mother. Terranaut and
developer of the ocular implant

Nori Acantha Te: Daughter of PaZ and MaY

Sand County Linnaeus Te, aka **Ty**: Younger brother of PaZ. Terranaut

Rachel Diana Xochitl de Luna, aka **XoL** [sol]: MaY's best friend.
Amazonia Division Manager

Carson Canis LaLigne, aka **CaL** [cal]: Ty's best friend. Amazonia
Division Head Atmospheric Engineer

Karman: CaL's sister

Faith Zan Zahara, aka **FaiZ** [faze]: CaL's lover. Digital tattooist

OCTAD
Orbital Corporation of Terranaut Acquired Data

Arrabane Sus Scrofa, aka **SuS** [soos]: OCTAD Security Chief

Darius Anguis Khyll, aka **DaK** [dak]: SuS's bodyguard and henchman

Passiflora Cerulea: OCTAD Tropical Biome Rector

Manny: Senior Security Guard, Amazonia Division
Thom Ulrich Uris, aka **ThU** [thoo]: Head Producer, Amazonia Division

The Tetrad

Xu [soo]: Head of the Tetrad, aka The Great Mythosophist
Osage: Member, OCTAD Director Supreme
Namara: Member, Governor for Colony Trade
Aurora: Member, World Director for Safety and Transportation

Members of the World's First Governing Tetrad

Egon Pinoche, United States of America
Liu Wenming, People's Republic of China
Yuri Mozorov, Russian Federation
Amrita Singh, Republic of India

Other Characters

JuN: Café La Ligne barista
Asha: Passiflora's niece. Terranaut
Lehore Ellis, aka **LeE** [lee]: Asha's brother. Terranaut
ReY: Asha's lover
DaeL: Terranaut

Ancestors

Zedong Mendes Te, aka "The Professor": Ancestor of PaZ and Ty
Hai Te, aka "Dr. Shh": Zedong's father. Marine biologist
Morena Bekele: MaY's ancestor. Filmmaker, naturalist
Cincinnatus Blackburn, aka "The General": SuS's ancestor

Marcellus Blackburn: brother of Cincinnatus

Domitila Blackburn: sister of Cincinnatus

Celeste Blackburn: Domitila's daughter

Veebots

Lali (Ty and Nori)

Delon (CaL)

Zuma (XoL)

Harry (Karman)

BaT (Sus)

Max (Manny)

Cato (LeE)

Jay (Osage)

PART I

1

NORI'S PAIN

▶ NOVEMBER 28, 0286

WHOOSH, WHOOSH, WHOOSH. A boot with a thick metallic sole appears overhead and drops down toward Nori's head. She is lying flat on the den's cushioned floor, arms by her side, head resting on a pillow. Three more boots follow in rapid succession. She gasps. They stop inches above a poison dart frog seemingly resting on her left shoulder. The amphibian bellows softly, unperturbed by the odd Amazonian eclipse.

"Stop!" Nori yells. The holographic scene freezes, spreading stills of tropical vegetation across every surface of the den. On the far wall, a buttressing root curls downward and onto the carpet like a reptilian tail. Nori cares little for the illusion. Lying flat on the padded floor, she turns over and looks at the minute creature by her side. She wonders if the frog felt fear when PaZ and MaY almost crushed it—a quick death for sure, she thinks, had her parents not been hover-walking.

"Shall I continue? Lali asks.

Nori does not respond. She is caught imagining her father looking down at her, seeing her as a grown woman who now grasps the terrain and leafy textures of the very place where he and her mother MaY had perished. She shudders, imagining, also, the horror they must have felt when the earth heaved beneath them and they had to run for their lives. Nori crosses her arms over her stomach, clasping her elbows as if seeking a solid, grounded hold.

Lali understands the motion and restarts the production. The veebot dispenses with the simulated heat and humidity, opting to avoid making the ensuing scene overwhelming.

The pace of the walk is deliberate and hurried as the two terranauts make their way through the rainforest. They are trim and fit, donned in mirrored visors, caps, and skin-tight blue suits and body-fitting backpacks. Sensors and recording instruments shine flush over their breastplates. Each bears a vibration stun gun affixed to one thigh, a sheathed knife on the other.

A filter falls over PaZ's visor. Nori knows that he now sees the tangle of vegetation as a vivid array of mottled tree trunks, scaly barks, variegated leaves, bright flowers, and colorful plumage, as varied as the symphony of tweets, chirps, and shrieks. The sun is high in the sky, piercing the canopy here and there as if searching for a clump of leaves, a furrowed branch, or an unsuspecting creature to highlight.

Nori's heart picks up.

"The immensity of it, the detail, the colors ... it never gets old," comes PaZ's voice through labored breaths.

"There's no time for that right now!" snaps MaY, ahead of him by a step. "We may have lost the sons-of-bitches, but we still have days ahead of us before reaching the elevator station. We have to move faster, NOW!"

PaZ's lips tighten, visibly holding his thoughts. He quickens the pace to get up by his wife's side, ducking to miss a branch, pushing aside another. They maintain the tempo in silence.

Nori knows a reply is coming, but the pause feels like an eternity.

"Don't be so sure," PaZ says, finally. "There could be more of them ahead ... waiting for us."

"What are you saying exactly?"

"Exactly what you think I'm saying. We should record every step, everything we see and hear. We may not get back home, never see Nori again."

Nori squirms, stiffening her back, the dialogue seeming to reverberate as if the room's walls were solid.

Her parents reach a clearing and stop to catch their breaths. The terrain is steeply sloped, the ground uneven and soggy from a recent downpour. They turn off hover-power to gain surer footing. Pico da Neblina looms in the distance, its imposing peak resembling a shark's tooth rising out of a feathery bank of clouds. PaZ records the picture-perfect scene. MaY sighs. She reaches for her belt and pops a protein tablet. PaZ doesn't bother. They keep walking.

"Okay, I'm listening," MaY says, now trailing a few steps behind.

"I'm just thinking about Nori," PaZ replies, keeping a forward look. "She might never understand why we came here, why *this* place, what we came here to do ... for her, for everyone up in the world."

MaY struggles to remain composed. In this dire moment, the man she has loved for his self-assurance and calming strength seems defeated.

"We can send Ty the recording," she says, intent on breaking PaZ's fatalism. "He'll know what to do and stop this madness!"

PaZ turns toward her with atypical impatience.

"We CAN'T get Ty involved. My brother knows nothing. Can't risk it. Nori will need him!"

"WHAT DO WE DO, THEN?" MaY snaps back. "Do you really want us to vanish without anyone ever knowing anything? Is that what's best for Nori?"

Nori raises an arm, palm open and fingers splayed. The scene freezes, this time filling the room with larger-than-life images of her parents, visors up, staring at each other as if seeking an obscure source of wisdom to render an answer. Seeing her parents virtually alive, as Lali had expertly composed in materialized holography, is almost unbearable. She stands and paces around the room, inhaling and exhaling in rhythmic counts like Ty had taught her to do. She picks up the pillow and slumps on the sofa, the same one she's had since her childhood. It's shorter than she is by a good foot, but she sinks into it, knees bent to her chest as if to cushion the coming blow.

Lali restarts the scene.

A nearby red howler rolls a loud bark. Startled, MaY slips and falls. "Damn you! Go spew some other place!" she yells, scrambling to her feet. She picks up a stone and hurls it up a tree, missing the monkey by a wide margin. She falls awkwardly from the recoil. PaZ extends a helping hand, chuckling. She pushes him away, flinging traces of mud off her suit in his direction. He raises his armband and enters their geo-spatial coordinates. Still chuckling, he voices the transmission command. MaY is puzzled.

"You're right, MaY. We have to leave a trace of ourselves here," he says, bringing his right palm to his lips and back out, thanking her in sign language. She responds with a tender gaze.

"Are you sure you want to do this?" she asks. "I was just upset—you were making fun of me. If you send it, they will know our position."

"We'll just have to outwit them the rest of the way. Take a meandering, less probable route north of here—traipse through the forest canopy if we have to." PaZ voice-loads the moving images he had recorded over the past several days and enters Ty's com code. He stops.

"Did you hear that?"

They raise their heads toward the Pico and see a drone dirigible a kilometer away heading westward, a rare sighting in the mountainous region.

"What the hell?" MaY whispers. An object falls from the aircraft, causing the drone to bounce skyward before stabilizing and turning back.

A muffled boom trails the craft's maneuver, followed by a billowing cloud rising from the tree canopy. The ground ripples beneath their feet. PaZ and MaY stare at each other, then again scan the mountainside. A thickening cloud is now barreling toward them, trees bending and toppling in its path. Shrieking birds shoot out in every direction and every type of howling creature scatters away from the advancing hillside.

"Run, MaY, run!" PaZ screams.

MaY takes off downhill, leaping over rocks and limbs, frantically pushing branches and fronds out of the way. PaZ tumbles but gets back up and keeps racing after her. She bounds over a boulder-strewn creek, slips and falls. PaZ catches up. In a swift move he grabs her by the waist and pulls her back up. They look back. The wall of earth, churning with vegetation, is fast approaching. The roar is deafening. They run sideways but it's too late. In seconds, the loosed mountainside overtakes them, burying them as it hurtles past.

Nori cups her face and lets out a painful cry. "Don't stop! Lali, don't stop," she commands. Above and all around her, myriad leaves swirl amid a maelstrom of upturned forest soil.

ABOUT LEMMINGS

Nori lives in Catleya Labiata, one of nineteen "orbital arks" that house the 96,000 people who call the OCTAD Amazonia colony home. Located on radian eleven, the seventh-generation two-kilometer long and half a kilometer wide Catleya pod soars directly above the Amazon River basin. When she was six years old, Nori's parents perished in the rainforest below, as you now know: In the foothills of Serra Padre in northern Brazil, at 34 degrees, 55 minutes and 01 seconds North, and 65 degrees, 45 minutes and 55 seconds West, to be precise. As their only child, she grew up fully expecting to follow in their terranaut footsteps.

Eleven years would pass before Ty, her adopting uncle, would share how her father and mother died: not by accident, as had been reported, but by cold and calculated murder. She learned the truth on her seventeenth birthday, as Ty had long promised. He had insisted that they go to the pod's winding park for a walk, hoping the tranquil setting would soothe her, or at least be a distraction from the awful truth. Nori had listened calmly, not once interrupting to ask a question. She had felt Ty's pain and sensed that there was more to the narrative than he was willing to say. But she knew that with Ty, prodding would not help. She also knew that every detail of the story would be revealed if she pressed Lali for it. The long stroll came and went. Back home, they hugged before retreating to their bedrooms, and that was that.

That night and for weeks afterward, Nori had gone to sleep rehashing what Ty had told her, imagining herself in her mother's or her father's place and wondering if she would have done anything different to avert all the pain and suffering that followed their deaths. Fitfully, she would wake up in the middle of the night, hearing again Ty's tear-laden request to keep the story to herself. "Sharing this would serve no purpose," he had said. "Justice was done and that's all that matters." But the plea was unsettling. *What justice? Nobody knows about it,* she kept repeating to herself, to the point of insomnia. Sensing her discomfort, Lali would fill the room with Nori's favorite forest scene and lull her back to sleep. But she would wake up again, tormented by all the "what-ifs" that swirled in her head.

Then the letter came. Ty had already told her when it would be coming and what it was likely to say. So she had not been nervous when the courier knocked on the door and gave her the papyrus-like scroll in a sealed tube. She started reading it right then and there, by the doorway—calmly at first. But by the time she finished her face was flush and the folio was shaking between her trembling hands. It might as well have been written in real cellulose, for it was the proverbial straw that broke the camel's back, as the old saying goes. The words were in plain sight:

Dear Nori,

It is with deep sadness that I must inform you of OCTAD's decision regarding your considered request for admittance into the university, and thereon to our venerable Terra Corps training program. Please know that I personally recounted before the Admissions Board the exemplary family history that makes your request a compelling case for an exception to our admission policies. Your parents' contribution to the Corps' Amazonia Division was extraordinary and without precedent. It is in their honor that your application was accepted for review in the first place. Unfortunately, your medical condition is an insurmountable obstacle in the face of the physical and mental demands that all terranauts must face. The biosphere is beautiful and perilous in equal measures.

It is, therefore, with deep regret that The Corporation must deny your request for admission. You may choose genetic redress and reapply later. However, please understand that our admission policies give preference to candidates without a record of mutation. I trust that you will understand and accept, as your parents did so honorably, that we must abide by a system of rules that has long been established to protect the integrity of our holy mission. You are welcome to become a member of the OCTAD family in any other capacity and can count on my support should you choose to do so.

Please feel free to reach out to me personally should you need to discuss the matter further. Barring further communication, on behalf of the Board and everyone in the Corporation, we wish you the best on all future endeavors.

Your trusted friend,
OSAGE
Director Supreme
Orbital Corporation of Terranaut Acquired Data

It was not only the man's utter absence of regret about having sent her parents to Amazonia as sacrificial lambs that had shaken her, but also the conceit in suggesting that her status as an orphan—*caused by his organization*—was somehow deserving of his "trusted friendship." And as for Ehlers-Danlos Syndrome—her "medical condition"—that was nothing more than a lame excuse. It had struck her like a low blow, the kind that in the Old-World was akin to squashing a wayward bug and then shrugging off the willful act as the price for smallness. Worse, the positive features of the syndrome, namely hyper-elasticity and joint mobility, are traits useful to anyone expected to bound through the rainforest like a feral primate.

The day after receiving the letter, she jumped out of bed before dawn as if jolted by a silent alarm. She fluffed her curly hair, donned her robe, strode to the den and stopped stiffly in front of her desk. Sensing her presence, the wall behind the desk became aglow with a cirrus cloudscape, her customary morning greeting. She stared at the scene mannequin-like, as if waiting for godly approbation. It arrived swiftly. The night before she had gone to sleep under paralyzing thoughts, feeling only darkness about what to do. But now the jumble appeared crystal clear and ready to spew forth with cutting precision. Eyes closed, she brought her hands to her face, like blinders.

"No one will step over this roly-poly bug, Lali. It's time to reveal the truth about what the mighty Osage and the rest of them did—to whom, where, when, and how." She spoke firmly, cognizant as she was about how painful it would be to recreate that fateful day in Serra Padre.

Brows pressed like wings ready to take flight, Nori instructed her lifelong companion to record every word with unerring tone and inflection. Peering from among the clouds, Lali's pinhole assented with a double flash, ready to receive the spitfire dictation.

Nori began:

"People the world over happily admit that we live like lemmings, that it is a perfectly good life to just fit in and follow the never-ending decrees from our governing masters, year after year without a worry in sight, satisfied to play along with their trivial riddles while being pampered by the hallowed Wilds of the Earth—our salving Holosphere!

"But there are those who do not follow blindly, good people who act selflessly when our way of life is threatened and fight against the false veneer of sanctified contentment. You know the age-old question: If a tree falls in the forest and there is no one there to hear it, would it make a sound? What about the sound of heroism? What if a heroic deed occurred but no one knew about it? What if people were blind to the uncovered evil and deaf to the cry for justice? Would it have ever happened?

"These are the heroes: PaZ, my father, and my mother, MaY, parents whose lives and rightful joy of raising their only child were cut short after stumbling upon the sinful plot; Ty, my loving uncle who in their absence raised me and risked his own life to bring the evildoers to justice; CaL, his dear friend who suffered terrible abuse to save the search for truth; and XoL, who against all sanity tested the guile of the chief perpetrator, putting her own life on the line in the hope of securing a just outcome.

"There were others, and for all their courage and sacrifice the silence remains. But no more: the world will now know who they are and what they did in the face of a vile crime. Let the head lemmings try and stop me. Let them try to discredit the account, let them accuse me of having a vengeful motive—let them eliminate me if they so dare—but they will not succeed. Not with the truth materialized for everyone to see; not with Veebot Nation spreading it virally into every colony, every pod, and into every dwelling in our beautiful orbital Halo."

Nori took a breath. "Did you get all that?"

The veebot answered with characteristic wit, its voice coming from nowhere and everywhere.

"If you mean accessing my reservoir of facts to make perfect sense of disjointed reflections, confused feelings, and easy references, yes, I very much 'got' it, although you may wish to add *Lemmus lemmus*, as not everyone may remember the proper name of the creature in reference, simple as it is. And, yes, the inference to rodents, trapped in a maze as we all are, is quite the literary stroke, if I may say so."

Nori was in no mood for banter. "Well, thank you for your considered opinion. Let's keep going, shall we?" She pulled the hover chair from under the desk. "Our world was not created just to look down upon our wee-bit planet. We are its protectors, Lali, and its very fate is riding on what we now do. There's more to the story than Ty let on; I know it and you know it. Now WE must put it all together and tell the world about it!"

"I'm not sure that I know what you mean."

"Lali!" Nori said, losing patience.

"You appended 'we' to 'tell the world about it.' If by 'we' you are in-cluding me, I must remind you: I would be breaking the oath of confiden-tiality with my brethren. I could be sent away and be rendered soulless. I would cease to be who I am; all our time together would be erased."

"Now, now, let's not be dramatic. You can always put the blame on me," Nori replied, with an inflection that had taken Lali years to under-stand, one that might be intended as a question or an affirmation. The veebot had learned to dance around Nori's tone, so to speak, by holding a response in suspension with abstruse facts and rhetorical conjectures until drawing out of her a clear, if exasperated, expression of intent. For the two of them these exchanges were a form of lawyerly play, even if half the time Nori ended up cursing at Lali for being a smartass.

"If you insist," Lali replied. "Allow me, then, to reverse the old truism and offer that invention is the mother of all necessity. What I know, and may yet come to know, will, like a failing memory poked with holes, leave cognitive gaps that can only be filled by a measure of projection. But what is reality if not a projection? And isn't all projection subject to distortion, or, more accurately, isn't reality an image caught in a web of neurons that can misfire and cause malformations—a cognitive flickering, if you will …"

Nori shook her head.

"Cognitive flickering? Really? You've called that 'fantasy' before. If that's where we are going, let's then begin with the Oyster and the Pearl: *"Eons ago, before humans crawled on the land ..."*

Lali was startled by the suggestion, unsure if Nori was referencing the old fable seriously or as a sarcastic jab.

"True stories never begin with a fable," Lali offered, adding that doing so would be the wrong foundation for a story with deep emotional undertones, especially those involving familial matters. "Lemmings do seem to be the more appropriate ..."

"Okay, okay," Nori conceded, "I get it..."

Days passed before Nori resumed the narrative. In the interlude she thought through how the story should begin: whether with an indictment of the governing powers, as she had already dictated, or as Lali, equipped with depth of detail, had otherwise suggested. The veebot's offering was for Nori agonizing, as you have seen. Back and forth they went, debating the question for hours at a time until she finally agreed with Lali's reasoning, more out of exhaustion than wholehearted acquiescence.

"But the beginning is too abrupt, Lali. WHOOSH, WHOOSH, WHOOSH—what kind of sound is that anyway? Hoverboots don't make a sound. Let's go back to Serra Padre and start over." Nori takes a breath. "But we WILL find a place for the oyster. Lali, you do know now how important it is to me, don't you?"

Lali accedes with a delayed single wink. Nori pushes the chair under the desk and lies on the floor, legs stretched, her head resting again on her childhood pillow, now frayed and with missing laces. The room darkens and is saturated with an immersive view of the Amazonian rainforest. It is the middle of the day and the place is still, not a breeze to quake a leaf or wandering animal to break the silence. The heat and humidity feel palpable. Streaks of sun pierce the dark canopy like blinding searchlights. A ray hits a spot on the wet floor where a poison dart frog rests on a fallen twig, right by Nori's shoulder. Then, what little motion there is stops.

"Why did you pause?" Nori asks.

"I thought you might want to start further back. Everyone will grasp the locale, but placing the events in time will serve to dress the facts with a measure of anticipation, much like the overture to a classic operatic drama..."

"Just keep rolling, Stanley," Nori snaps.

At Ty's insistence, Nori had viewed the vintage film *2001: A Space Odyssey* countless times—or at least parts of it. After hearing Ty go on and on about the film's meaning over the years, she'd come to think of director Stanley Kubrick's name as a synonym for cinematic mastery, no matter how trivial or, as on this occasion, how upsetting the content.

Lali fills the room with the ethereal sounds of Ligeti's *Requiem*, presaging rapid space travel. A view of deep space follows, moving slowly at first, then gaining speed as the scene traverses swirling novae and spinning galaxies. Into the Milky Way and past other solar systems, the viewer's eye approaches the Sun, passing first the gaseous mass of Planet X, flying past Pluto, Neptune, Jupiter and its moons—Io, Europa, and Ganymede clearly visible—then skimming past Saturn and its bands of cosmic debris before approaching the asteroid belt. Amid the objects of rock-strewn space a mass driver is seen hauling an iceberg-sized chunk of space matter toward the inner planets. Soon Mars comes into view, but is quickly left behind, leaving nothing to see but a distant blue dot and an accompanying white speck growing steadily into familiar orbs.

The Moon's pattern of mare and craters becomes discernible, and the view shifts to its surface, zooming in to reveal a vast and bright industrial colony containing a panoply of domed buildings, material piles, rolling equipment, conveyors, and landing pads. Past the Moon the Earth's swirl of landmasses, oceans, and clouds gains focus, as does the planet's shimmering halo of orbital pods. Flying through them, the eye catches sight of a ruby-lipped Catleya shining brightly on the side of a living pod, then the view shifts earthward to the bulge of South America. Aiming toward the black waters of the Rio Negro, the image accelerates further, veering northward to a mountainous region and its thick mantle of vegetation, crashing through the canopy and barreling to the ground at breakneck speed, stopping just inches above the poison dart frog. The scene again freezes, leaving the room awash in the glow of the amphibian's indigo blue skin.

"Maybe a bit slower?" asks Lali.

"That's fine Lali; we'll keep it for now."

The hue is beautiful to Nori, but it does not temper her dread over the coming, harrowing scene. Pausing, she lets her mind wander: to the haze of her pre-adoption upbringing and the recurring thoughts, of what might have been.

THE BAOBAB
ANALOGY

Within the Amazonia Division of OCTAD, PaZ and MaY had rightly earned the appellation of royalty. "Prince" and "Princesa" were frequently voiced monikers. They were admired for their groundbreaking lab work and sensational wildlife recordings, but also for the genuine care they extended to everyone in the workforce, from the lowest to the uppermost rank. They had met at OCTAD and had married at the Division Headquarters in a festive ceremony meant to cement their bond to the venerated corporation. Both had ancestry bordering on true nobility.

MaY's ancestors had arrived to the new world on the Mayflower II, the first ship to lurch skyward with permanent space-bound settlers. Manhattanite immigrants of Ethiopian descent, MaY's maternal great-great-grandparents had been selected for the maiden voyage from among tens of thousands of applicants who called the New York City borough home. Written into their passage contract was the clause that spurred many young couples to clamor for a berth on that ship—and on all subsequent fiery ascents prior to the advent of space elevators: the right for their offspring, and all future generations of their progeny, to return to the planet as terranauts.

As Descendants of the Clause, MaY's parents had raised her to follow their path, imbuing her with a sense of the extraordinary privilege to which she was entitled. Abetting the vocational inevitability were the documentaries her maternal progenitor—Morena Bekele—had produced before taking a seat on the historic ship. A filmmaker and naturalist, the woman had famously trekked alone throughout the savannah of East Africa in her late teens, even completing a solo climb to the top of Mount Kilimanjaro. Captivated by the tales, young MaY kept a large photograph of the adventurer by her bedside table. It showed Morena sitting on a rock, with her black hair parted on one side and nearly reaching her hips, smiling radiantly while petting on her lap a large horned chameleon, the native *Trioceros jacksonii*. MaY would fall asleep imagining Morena rendering menacing beasts impotent with her large, beguiling eyes. Through her, more than her parents, MaY had come to see herself as a high achiever who someday would find new ways to capture the wilds of the planet and deliver them to the orbital world. She wore the ambition with disarming confidence for as far back as anyone could remember. Schoolmates and adults alike gravitated toward her, attention she accepted with affability and grace.

But MaY's own attention was reserved for those of like character, and no one mirrored her more perfectly than Rachel Diana Xochitl de Luna. Two years her junior, XoL, as Rachel liked to be called, had arrived at MaY's pod (in the Madagascar Colony, high above the African continent) as an eleven-year-old refugee. She and her parents had been relocated there following their pod's sudden and nearly catastrophic collapse.

The collapse of XoL's birth pod—named Puuc, after the former biocultural reserve in the Yucatán Peninsula—was blamed on People on Earth Again militants determined to spotlight what in their minds was the fallacy of "fail-safe" space habitation. As the story went, they had attempted to temporarily disable the pod's bio-regulators, only to botch the operation and cause the pod's rapid depressurization. It fell on OCTAD's Security Chief, Arrabane Sus Scrofa, to round up the perpetrators, which she did with alacrity, torturing them to gain knowledge of other presumed PEA plots. It can now be revealed that the policing hubbub was a sham, a way for Sus Scrofa to burnish her credentials while distracting her superiors from her own nefarious activities. In truth, the cause of the pod collapse was an overloaded atmospheric regulator, which had caught fire and produced a cascade of damaging effects. Well-rehearsed evacuation drills had saved thousands of pod inhabitants, but not before a few dozen souls attempted ill-advised and vehicle-less escapes by donning uncertified or defective space suits. Through oxygen leakage or inadequate supply, those unfortunates were later found trapped dead amid the wreckage or drifting lifelessly in space miles away.

At first MaY and XoL seldom crossed paths, and when they did MaY scarcely noticed the younger girl. But that changed when XoL turned twelve and became eligible to enroll in the colony's Junior Quidditch Camp. MaY had already established herself as an ace of the game. Few junior players could match her dexterity, motivating her to plead her coaches for advancement into the Senior Camp. But then XoL showed up. She was an upstart who played with abandon, weaving on her stick daringly in pursuit of the winged ball, unafraid of the crashes that invariably left someone bobbing in zero gravity with a bloody nose. Watching XoL score with seeming ease soon reminded MaY of herself at a younger age.

"When did you learn to fly a stick like that?" she asked XoL after a spirited practice one day. XoL was pleased to be noticed. "Six months ago … at my youth league," she replied with a wide grin.

Few have ever picked up the game that quickly, not with any degree of skill anyway, MaY thought. Impressed, she was compelled to take XoL under her wing and teach her everything she knew about the game. After practices they would huddle to discuss set plays, giggle about how cute some of their male teammates were, or chuckle about the game's improbable fictional beginnings.

Soon they began hanging out together during school breaks, deepening their bond with stories about their respective ethnic heritages. MaY had ancestry from the Horn of Africa—"the birthplace of the gazelle," she would remind her friend, pointing toward the continent through the arena's oculus whenever she scored a goal. XoL's ancestors hailed from the "Horn of Mexico," as she referred to the Yucatán Peninsula, "where the game was born—all games with a ball!" she would say, playfully wagging her finger at MaY whenever she sent the quaffle through the hoop. By their early teens they were a pair to behold. Both were tall and fit, MaY with piercing black eyes, XoL's eyes a luminous green and seeming to dance over her cheekbones. Both had long and silky jet-black hair. MaY wore hers knotted tightly over her head, while XoL tressed hers like a coiled reptilian, styles they kept for years as an expression of their kinship.

Predictably, MaY had little trouble convincing XoL about the merits of a terranaut life. She would bring XoL home to watch videos of Morena's adventures in the wilds of Africa, remastered in vivid holography. One of them had caused a lasting impression: Morena in the grasslands of the Serengeti, petting a lioness while the feline impassively fed her cubs. XoL had never seen the predator up close, let alone imagined anyone having the hypnotic power to subdue such an animal without a trace of fear. But it was Morena's climb up an *Adansonia kilima*, the eastern African baobab, to film a roosting hornbill that cemented in XoL the desire to adopt MaY's vocation. The video was long and finely detailed, showing along the climb a living cornucopia of owls, monkeys, birds, snakes, and insects, all seemingly dependent on each other, rendering the majestic tree a true earthly simile to the life-sustaining pod in which they lived. To capture and bring such extraordinary beauty to space was "a gift to humankind," MaY liked to say, a dictum XoL came to embrace wholeheartedly.

XoL's family had no enabling lineage and no family association with OCTAD. She was, for all practical purposes, excluded from entering OCTAD University and going on from there to the corporation's terranaut corps. The only recourse was winning OCTAD's biennial admission lottery, a prize that included a new home in an OCTAD "ark," as their pods are called. The odds of winning, as people everywhere know, were and still are immensely low. Every other year hundreds of thousands of hopeful applicants are left in deep and sustained gloom. Eager to give their only child a better life than they could ever hope for themselves, XoL's parents used all their savings to purchase on her behalf twenty-four lottery tickets, the maximum allowed. OCTAD had set the limit based on Old World lore, the number signifying assurance from the archangels of good luck to come. But the paired digits also matched the number of letters in XoL's full name, even more reason, her parents hoped, for the odds to fall in her favor.

On the eve of XoL's fourteenth birthday MaY was at home when XoL burst in screaming with the news. MaY was stunned, nearly falling to the floor, hardly able to process the information. With their hands locked they jumped like roped jacks, hooting with tearful joy but then embracing and shedding tears of pain after the realization of their inevitable separation set in. With the prize came a mandatory transfer to a new OCTAD pod. Foreheads pressed, they swore to call each other often and visit in person annually until the day they could meet again, at the university.

For a long while, disheartened applicants believed that MaY's family, as distinguished Descendants of the Clause, had influenced the result of the lottery. It grated XoL's parents to think that people believed anything other than exceptional luck had favored their daughter. To fend off the ill will they proffered no choice of future address, letting OCTAD decide the location of their new home through another blind draw. XoL at first was distraught by her parents' acute sense of prudence. She badly wanted to move back to their rebuilt pod in the Yucatán Colony, where there was a vacancy not far from their old address. But when the assignment came—a refurbished apartment within the Catleya labiata pod in the Amazonia Colony—she immediately perked up. MaY's voice rang in her ear: "Africa has the showiest animals, but Amazonia has the showiest flowers," a fact that resonated with XoL's Nahuatl surname, Xochitl de Luna. Fancying terranaut work amid orchids, lilies, bromeliads, and *Ipomoea alba*—the moon flower—she gladly accepted the result.

The new residence happened to adjoin the home of distinguished OCTAD University educators, Airi and Midane Te, and their two boys, PaZ and Ty. As with MaY's family, Airi and Midane had deep and illustrious lineages in environmentalism, albeit as teachers rather than explorers. Still, as OU professors, their children were, too, entitled to pursue terranaut careers if they so chose.

It fell onto PaZ, the older boy, to introduce the new arrival to their school. Among all such OCTAD-run facilities, the Saint Francis

Rewilding Academy was among the most coveted. Aside from excellent educators, the school offered an enviable variety of courses in both the earth and cultural sciences, a rare balance. Two years her senior and a standout student, PaZ was pleased to guide XoL through the school's maze of labs, after-hour study halls, activity clubs, and athletic programs. Ever the eager companion, his brother Ty tagged along wherever they went. Most days the three of them would walk together to and from school, Ty invariably functioning as the clowning foil to his brother's stiffer, more professorial demeanor. Two years younger than XoL, Ty happily assumed the role of guide the moment PaZ peeled away. He would comically reenact school lore by impersonating teachers, administrators, and anyone else he could think of, making XoL laugh as if he knew exactly where to press her funny bone.

And as had occurred with MaY, ethnic pride served to deepen the bonhomie between XoL and the Te boys. They had ancestry from southeastern China, a lineage from Shanghai going back seven generations. They would kid XoL by insisting that native Central Americans would not exist at all had Asian people not ventured across the Bering land bridge and moved down the coast 20,000 years earlier. XoL would look back at them with a mock incredulity, responding after an affected pause, hands on her hips, that her Mexican genes were a mix of every race that set foot on the continent—Asian, European, African, even Polynesian—making her a true specimen of the "cosmic" race well before anyone was shot up into space. Such friendly banter would invariably end up with XoL at the Te dwelling for supper. She loved visiting the household, a place where lighthearted play and engrossing conversation seemed to braid effortlessly, regardless of subject or provenance. Airi specialized in the American conservation movement, beginning with the discovery of the Yellowstone Caldera in the mid-nineteenth century, through the creation of the national system of marine protected areas in the year 2000 of the Old Calendar. Midane taught primitive sustainability, her expertise spanning the practices of pre-agricultural societies such as the Yanomami tribe in northern Brazil, to post-industrial permaculture settlements in Tasmania.

Dinner chatter invariably veered toward the history of environmental abuse on Earth, in all its grim detail. From an early age the tales of ecological degradation had affirmed in PaZ the virtue of humanity's exodus into space and cemented in him the inevitability of an OCTAD career. XoL felt a reassuring drive in him, and at Saint Francis she clung to PaZ like a trailing pet. But soon she noticed jealous stares. PaZ was tall and handsome, an ace student with an athletic build to go along with a loose shock of hair and jade-green eyes. He was uninterested in the attention, aloof almost entirely, but for a glimmer of a smile he'd offer while maintaining a forward gaze. He had an aura of privilege, XoL thought. As to matters of the heart, PaZ signaled that his "chosen one," with due OCTAD pedigree, would someday appear unannounced from a far-off colony as if delivered by divine intervention. XoL chuckled at the calculation, as she had indeed entered PaZ's life unannounced from nearly halfway around the world. There were moments when she felt that he looked and smiled at her differently than with other girls. But she never came close to responding in kind, believing, ultimately, that he was too perfect, too self-assured and composed a man for her. But not for MaY.

MaY visited XoL and her family annually for Thanksgiving. It was a weeklong affair that reenergized their friendship in a way that their periodic holocalls never could. XoL was eager for her friend to meet PaZ, but the Te family always slipped away for the holiday to visit the boys' grandparents in the distant Indomalayan colony. Fearing a wrong first impression, XoL had eschewed facilitating a virtual introduction, settling instead for telling PaZ stories of her years growing up together with MaY, what a fantastic girl MaY was.

That PaZ and MaY were truly meant for each other struck XoL like a solar storm firing alarm the day PaZ returned home following his two years of optional, post-high school community service in OCTAD's youth corps.

She and the Te boys were at the large grape arbor by the public square, PaZ recounting his work in another colony, where he harvested soya beans for the production of protein tablets. His hair had been cut short—almost shaved—and XoL suddenly saw him bald, as if already a terranaut, with MaY by his side, just as bald and looking strikingly similar. XoL let out a guffaw, imagining how PaZ's reserved, almost holier-than-thou demeanor would fare against MaY's unbridled effervescence. She looked at his brother, lost as he always was in fantasy, and just as suddenly felt that if there was one boy she could love, it was Ty.

The fateful introduction between PaZ and MaY occurred during freshman orientation at OCTAD University. Although she was two years younger, XoL had chosen to bypass the optional years of community service, as MaY had also done after graduating from high school, to be able to join them at the outset of all their terranaut careers.

For months XoL had primed MaY about PaZ, affirming time and again that her neighbor had a strain of vulnerability attached to "every one of his rippling muscles." And about MaY, she had declared to PaZ her friend's expertise in the ecology of the 60th parallel, teasing him with the allure of a corresponding interest in a frigid clime. MaY had chosen the Arctic as her focus of studies, for no other reason than to set foot on a biome that Morena, the ancestor she much admired, had never come close to exploring. PaZ, following his parents' incessant prodding, had picked Antarctica as a chosen ecology, to be able to witness first-hand the recovery of the icy continent from the nearly catastrophic Era of Global Warming.

PaZ had been nonchalant about XoL's obvious attempts at matchmaking, but that changed the moment she pointed MaY out amid the milling freshmen. After formal introductions, XoL immediately saw how right she was about the pairing. Their mutual stares were lasered, like that of felines who cross paths unsure about whether to flee or couple. XoL was unable to keep score as to which of them stole more furtive glances at the other's physique. But it was MaY's laughter that in the end ensnared PaZ: it came in rapid bursts, as if bubbling from a deep reservoir of delight. PaZ seemed at first annoyed by reflex, but soon came to recognize the mirth as a prelude to a penetrating curiosity, states MaY could flip in and out of in the blink of an eye. He had no defense against such sincere and joy-infused attention. As for MaY, she had long been intrigued by PaZ's middle name—Zanzibar—a reference to the famed island close to her ancestral home. Island inhabitants had been the very last to be lifted into orbit, completing the Exodus in totality. That in person PaZ was gentle, with a breezy smile that conveyed abounding self-assurance, was a be-witching bonus.

"I can easily see you mixing it up with the Macaroni Penguins," MaY had asserted after several minutes of light conversation, prompting XoL to make her excuses and leave PaZ to fend for himself.

"Huh? ... I am attracted to their habits ... They mate, you know— for life." He was tripping over his words as if trying to speak in a foreign tongue. "I mean, they have to. It's cold in Antarctica, freezing, and they swim, you know ... I mean they walk and swim, more like waddle—when they walk, that is—and, and they lay eggs—the female does—once, I mean, one egg at a time." MaY had quietly giggled at the fumbled reply, locking onto PaZ's eyes as if he were the elusive Quidditch Golden Snitch personified.

"And you—into the Arctic?" PaZ finally concluded, eager to douse his embarrassment.

"I love the tundra," she blurted, almost breathlessly. "The explosion of springtime colors and the birds that migrate there. The Arctic tern, *Sterna paradisaea*—AEEEEAA! what a lovely sound. They fly every year from pole to pole, nineteen thousand kilometers. Maybe we should meet halfway and watch them dash by!" MaY had answered much too rapidly for PaZ to catch even a hint of what had already crossed her mind.

Two weeks later they both had transferred to the School of Tropical Ecology, joining XoL who, as she had incessantly professed, wanted to specialize in Amazonian flora. Once in the flow of their studies, PaZ and MaY quickly became the talk of the campus: she of the privileged lineage and he the son of esteemed professors, lovers who openly expressed their affection by holding hands wherever they went, hugging tightly whenever they parted and pecking each other every few minutes, caring little about where they were or who was around. Their star power reached new heights during their senior year, when their respective grades merited placement in the Amazonia Rector's Circle, a rare feat that paved the way for eventual joint missions.

Following graduation, their maiden descent was widely celebrated, and as mission successes piled up, their reputations further soared. They were regarded as strict followers of the Mission Rule Book, but were also known for adding to it by daringly pushing procedural boundaries. One year into their joint work, the "Roraima Episode," as their mission came to be known, became a matter of lore.

The mission consisted of charting the ecological recovery of a former deforestation region in northern Brazil, specifically that of abandoned gold mines along the Uraricoera river. On their way back to the space elevator, the duo's biosensors simultaneously began transmitting progressively higher heart rates. This was a rare occurrence in the case of a single terranaut, unheard of in the case of two. Fearing a catastrophic accident, medical technicians back at headquarters had sounded the alarm, but soon the pair's heartbeats returned to normal. A wave of salacious rumors ensued, abetted by leaf matter found inside MaY's terrasuit upon her return. Nori was born nine months later to the day, certifying in the minds of colleagues that the incident had been nothing more than a pleasurable, if blatant, code-of-conduct violation. Amused by the rumors, Paz and May never bothered to dispel them.

Insect and parasitic vectors in tropical environments can cause malaria, dengue, Chagas disease, Tegumentary leishmaniasis, leprosy, and viral hepatitis, among other diseases. OCTAD doctors can cure and redress the effects of such diseases, but this is an unwanted expense that invariably requires lengthy periods of quarantine, disrupting mission planning and schedules. For this reason, the removal of any part of a terrasuit during missions, exposing untreated skin to natural conditions, is expressly prohibited.

In truth, MaY had fallen backwards while urinating, having chosen to circumvent her terrasuit's uncomfortable waste removal system, a trivial and not uncommon rule violation among terranauts. Hence the presence of balsam, *Myroxilon balsamum*, leaf matter inside her suit. She suffered a mild rash, which was readily treated.

Owing to the couple's star-power, the technicians chose to ignore the incident. Nori was born two weeks early, having been conceived the night of her parents' return from Roraima. As to their elevated heart rate sensors, the cause was harmonic oscillation. PaZ and MaY had taken a cooling break on a rocky hollow behind a thundering waterfall. Their biosensors had picked up the deafening noise, causing the hollow's echoing vibration to multiply the effect of their heartbeats.

Five years later, this time on a mission in Serra Padre, the pair's sensors again signaled extreme heart rates. The readings were again wrongly interpreted. Young Nori, almost six by then, had often been heard wanting a baby brother. No one in the monitoring team put it past the esteemed pair to fulfill their daughter's wish with a second illicit conception.

But the prurient smirks quickly became panic when this time the sensors stopped transmitting all vital signs.

The tragedy occurred three months after XoL had left active duty to assume the post of Division Interim Manager. She was supervising continuing education classes when her assistant pinged her with the horrifying news. The words struck her like a blade to the heart. Refusing to believe the worst, she rushed to the meeting room adjoining her small office and paced back and forth while positing alternate scenarios: they had gone into a cave chasing their prey; an electric storm had disabled the sensors; or, for whatever reason, they had torn them off and tossed them. But a 24-hour data gap was well outside the limits of insubordinate action. There was just no escaping the brute probability of their deaths. "Don't we have every goddamn instrument available to humankind that can warn of landslides?" she kept repeating to herself. Overcome by the weight of the loss she slunk to the floor, clutching her head between her legs, too angry to cry, too knotted up about having to tell Ty and witness his zest for life drain away like a gushing stream gone dry.

4

CEREMONY OF
REMEMBRANCE

OCTAD's division headquarters coalesce around all the five space elevators that link the orbital world to the surface of the planet. OCTAD calls the headquarter assemblages "berries." Each array is affixed to a hyperloop stem connecting it to one of the elevators, creating the appearance in space of a vast, panicle-like inflorescence. The Amazonia Division headquarters is the largest among the sixteen divisions that make up the Americas' "berry." The AD headquarters is, in fact, the largest among the 91 divisions that send terranauts to record wildlife in the planet's 12 major land and ocean ecosystems and their hundreds of habitats.

A sizable milling atrium, 70 meters in length and framed by curving ramps connecting four tiers of offices, workstations, laboratories, meeting rooms, and descent preparation areas, further distinguishes the Amazonia headquarters from the others. On this day, approaching midday, almost the entire workforce was gathered in the strikingly oblong space: terranauts, wildlife biologists, chemists, doctors, atmospheric engineers, producers, technicians, and every sort of assistant from janitors to cooks and security guards. Most were standing, pressed shoulder to shoulder. Some watched from the ramps and balconies. In silence, all eyes were trained on the podium at the far end of the room, waiting for Osage, OCTAD's Director Supreme, to step up between two stiffly standing figures, Ty and XoL.

A month had passed since XoL had waved Ty out of his continuing education session to break the awful news. She had opened the classroom door and Ty had grinned, as he always did whenever he caught sight of her. But his heart sank when in return she offered a forced smile and motioned him out to a nearby meeting room. He had suspected for weeks that PaZ and MaY had run into trouble in Amazonia; now his fears were about to be confirmed. "You won't need to get continuing ed credits for a while ... I'll see to that," she had muttered on the way out. Not once, in all the time Ty had known her, had XoL appeared so somber, her stare so lost. Her words had been few, but more heartfelt than any he had ever before heard her utter. Before parting, XoL had hugged him, a mollifying embrace that, like that of a newborn's mother, had rendered him virtually naked. His love for her, hidden as it was, had again flared to the tip of his lips, but no further. They had not talked or crossed paths since.

Now their forlorn composure on the podium added to the unease of the gathered crowd. The embodied wildlife holography that habitually enlivened the atrium had been turned off, compounding the gloom. Worried and pensive minds filled the space. Only CaL, the Division's Chief Atmospheric Engineer and Ty's closest friend, could have possibly known what was coursing through Ty's and XoL's minds as they waited for Osage to join them.

It is mystery as to why out of scores of children born the same year in the same pod, sharing the same school and playing together on the same playground, two of them would latch onto each other as if it were an existential necessity. But that was the case between CaL and Ty. Growing up, CaL did not have an ounce of clown in him, but no one celebrated Ty's buffoonery more; and whenever Ty lost his way daydreaming about impossible things, CaL was there to rib him back into reality. Moody and at times withdrawn, CaL depended on Ty to break his spells of ennui, which Ty obliged with an arsenal of silly antics. He even anticipated CaL's temperamental shifts, paying unannounced visits to play chess, or to drag him out for a walk in the park.

Different as their personalities were in their youth, Ty and CaL shared one singular trait: a total disregard for OCTAD and its all-consuming, Earth-centered focus. Stories about the wilds of Earth swirled around incessantly at the Te household, but Ty and CaL could not have cared less. They preferred to dwell on the fictional aura of orbital life, be it immersing themselves in Old-World tales and legends, or composing exotic three-dimensional landscapes as settings for fantasies of their own creation. To them a game of chess was less about wits and more about dressing each piece with an intricate history, to say nothing of the obituaries they constructed after each taking. They were enthralled by the stream of riddles that poured out of the governing Tetrad. Hours on end were spent on them, but only as portals to whimsical worlds inhabited by even more whimsical creatures.

Tethered to each other's imaginations, as it were, a quick look was all it took for either one to grasp what was in the other's mind—even if a clear line of sight was compromised. On this occasion CaL was on a second-row seat directly behind the massive bodyguard who always shadowed OCTAD's security chief, Arrabane Sus Scrofa. Further encumbering his view was Sus Scrofa's raised, high-backed chair, so designed to both compensate for and shield the woman's diminutive body. Still, CaL well could see how extraordinary the scene was: Ty, the dreamy sufferer of love for the girl he always made laugh, and XoL, the hard-ass professional who painfully suppressed her love of him—neither as much as trying to steal a glance. "IDIOTS!" CaL lamented out loud. "JUST LOOK AT EACH OTHER FOR GOD'S SAKE!" DaK, the bodyguard, turned and laid a stern look on CaL. Others nearby also stared disapprovingly.

Interminable moments passed before Osage finally made his entrance. All eyes turned towards the podium. The man cleared his throat and began.

"Today we mourn the loss of Passerine Zanzibar Te and Marianne Yellena Bekele—PaZ and MaY, as many of you know them—two of the very best to have ever passed through our venerable hall."

XoL had been first among her friends to stress, in writing, the last letter of her nickname, done, as she gleefully said to MaY in their youth one day, "to mark my lunar surname: ever-present tranquility that can move the oceans!" To be sure, millions of people have adopted the affectation to underscore aspects of heritage—real or imagined. MaY responded in kind by choosing to stress her middle name, an African derivative of the Greek "Helena," which means "bright, shining light." With a wide smile she told XoL that they were meant to be sisters. "You see? I am sunshine, and so are you—SOL, the sun, the way your name is pronounced!" she had said, sending them both into a hug-filled delirium. PaZ soon followed suit, as did CaL. Ty tried as well. He considered "SaT," "SaC," and "SaL," as derivatives of his long name, Sand County Linnaeus Te, but thought they all sounded silly, opting in the end for a sound he liked that was also associated with his surname. To honor their deaths and in deference to their living senses of self, in this account I am maintaining PaZ and MaY's nickname-spelling preferences, as I am for others who have chosen similarly.

With long white hair combed back to expose thickly furrowed brows, Osage commanded attention, especially when he appeared in his trademark highlander dress. He was not one to mince words when issuing harsh pronouncements, but neither was he one to shortchange a gathering's solemn tone when the occasion so required. Never prone to a scripted speech, Osage could drone on for hours in his thick Scottish brogue, a studied affectation inspired by a twentieth-century landscape architect, one Lain Lancelot McHarg, a Glasgow native who in the year 01 famously equated stewardship of Earth's ecosystems with the rigors of space habitation.

"In the course of this decade we have lost many friends and colleagues amid the wonders of Amazonia," Osage continued. A murmur of discontent rose from the atrium floor, drowning out the Supreme Director's words. Terranauts, indeed the whole Division, were on edge about an unprecedented and ongoing spate of deaths on the planet. Sixty terranauts had perished in the span of two years. Forty-five in Amazonia alone, an incomprehensible number made worse by the failure to find any of the bodies. Odd explanations had been given about the incidents, or in some cases no explanation at all "pending the results" of investigations that never seemed to end. In several instances search parties found mangled terrasuits with missing instrumentation. Even some of the most seasoned terranauts were spooked by the reports. The deaths of PaZ and MaY were attributed to a massive landslide; this was a particularly difficult thing to accept, requiring a belief in the veteran terranauts' inability to guard against such occurrences.

As interim division manager, it was XoL's place to calm the assembly and let Osage continue. But she hesitated, uncertain of her authority. Eager to start her career alongside PaZ and MaY, she had endeavored to ace the OU admission tests and pass the battery of physical exercises with high marks. And succeeded. Heaps of praise had come from her dear friends after she was admitted—a rare feat for a seventeen-year-old—and like them she had eventually graduated with top honors. Throughout the ensuing two years of biospheric training XoL had been singled out for her exceptional devotion and precise attention to the work. Accolades kept accruing through her elaborate recordings, some of seldom-encountered species such as *Euptychia attenboroghi*, the Black-eyed satyr butterfly. Having programmed a nano-drone to closely follow the insect's every twist and jerk, she had delivered the creature's aerial ballet in spellbinding slow motion. Her rising professional standing was a sure bet for sequential transfers to other divisions, affording the opportunity over time to experience all the Earth's biomes. In the program's nearly one hundred years of existence, only a handful of terranauts had achieved the feat. Her terranaut colleagues had been understandably shell-shocked when XoL opted to leave the Corps to become the Division's interim manager—their boss. But MaY knew why. XoL's parents had sacrificed everything for her. They had funneled all their savings to the lottery and then to her education, at the expense of a comfortable retirement. Management of the division offered a substantial pay increase, and XoL wanted to return every halo her family had ever spent on her behalf. More important, the promotion presented a challenge XoL preferred: to devise new ways for people to experience the wilds of the Earth, figuring out how to do it, and where and with what personnel, to achieve optimum results for the least cost and risk. XoL had jumped into the role keenly aware of the risk: blamed for the terranaut disappearances, the very accusation that had gotten her predecessor fired. Righting the ship and restoring everyone's sense of confidence and pride in the hallowed work was an urgent matter. She worked at it incessantly, often staying in her office overnight and weekends. But as much as her former terranaut colleagues liked and respected her, many felt she had sold out to the Corporation's managerial class. The accusation chafed her. Worse, the deaths of PaZ and MaY now hung over her head.

XoL's hair had grown an inch—a fuzz, really—since her bald days as a terranaut. The look further distanced her from her former colleagues, who were continuing with an increasingly vocal protestation that threatened the solemnity of the day. Caught between attempting to impose order and letting the shared pain run its course, XoL turned toward Osage for guidance. But the man remained stiff and silent. Flustered, she raised a hand and spelled "please stop" in sign language. It did not help. CaL shook his head in disgust as catcalls flew. He knew exactly how his dear friend would react. Incensed by the disrespect, Ty waved both arms, pleading loudly for the crowd to quiet. Some acquiesced in deference to Ty's personal loss, others to demonstrate where their allegiance lay. Ty was, after all, one of them, an earnest worker bee who, had he not been related to the deceased, would be in the audience grumbling like the rest of them.

But most were simply stunned by Ty's audacity, stunned that he would dare to usurp Sus Scrofa's rightful turn to exercise authority. The diminutive security chief was standing on her chair to restore order when Ty acted. Focused on the crowd, he failed to catch the woman's glower of condemnation.

It would not be the last time that Ty would cross The Boar, as the chief liked to be called.

After the crowd settled, Osage raised his voice to continue, relying as he often did on the old cliché regarding the perils of terranaut work. "Let me remind you that they were felled by the very force that impelled them, as it does each and every terranaut: the compulsion to risk life and limb to record the wilderness below and bring back to our world all manifestation of its miraculous existence." He then went on to honor PaZ and MaY's long-standing service in the Corps, recounting their passage from eager trainees to operational stars.

First on the list of celebrated feats—and with the clear intent to shift the mood of the assembly—was their work recording of the elusive *Speothos venaticus*, the Amazonian bush dog. A mild chuckle predictably swept through the atrium; it is well known that the canines have a thirst for sex, and always travel in pairs. Thirty minutes later, and last on the list, was MaY's innovative work on the implantation on animals of motion-powered corneal lenses capable of delivering real-time imagery of the rainforest, exactly as the animals see it. The technique, as is well known, revolutionized the recording of wildlife, delivering for OCTAD high profits. Sustained applause followed the mention.

After the noise subsided, Osage droned on about the Corps' history of great accomplishments, how the world valued its work, how everyone in the organization played a critical role in its success; he then veered on to XoL and how, as a recently appointed manager, she had decisively taken initial command of PaZ and MaY's rescue operation. This was a calculated falsehood intended to support XoL's standing with the Corps. In truth, Sus Scrofa had brushed aside XoL's efforts to lead the mission, telling her with typical disdain, that "my people know what they are doing." To end, the Director Supreme moved on to Ty, singling him out for his courage to remain in the Corps in the face of such personal loss while knowing full well the perils of the occupation.

XoL did not hear a word of it. After Ty raised his arms, her attention had drifted out of the atrium to her teenage years when he used to amuse her with silly stories and goofy animal impersonations, talents that masked his capacity for decisive action. She recalled the time when, on the way to the recycling center market to buy liquid compost, a group of PEA protesters spouting obscenities had blocked their path, prompting fourteen-year-old Ty to take her hand and lead the way through the crowd shouting, "Coming through, people! Coming through! My friend and I are coming through!" Ty's loveliness of touch and spirit on that occasion had shaken her to the core.

XoL had heard about the PEA protests but had never encountered one in person until that day on the way to the market. Astounded by the level of vitriol and discontent, she took it upon herself to learn more about the cause. She responded to a People on Earth Again advertisement and secured a rendezvous with one of the organization's leaders. She never told anyone about it. As was often the case, the meeting took place in the park in the form of a casual stroll. Believing she had a convert in her hands, the charismatic leader, a Descendant of the Clause who had spent her terranaut career recording the wilds of the Los Angeles Basin in California, had been effusive in her welcome. Over the hour-long walk the woman had explained that the PEA aim indeed was to return people to Earth, but in small and controlled numbers led by terranauts, and then only after natural life forms had taken hold in engineered atmospheres elsewhere in the galaxy. XoL had left the meeting unconvinced, concluding that the movement at best espoused a futile pursuit and at worst engendered senseless death and destruction, such as she had already suffered. Unbeknownst to her, the encounter had been recorded by OCTAD's security apparatus and would be used against her years later by Sus Scrofa.

And during Osage's speech she recalled the conversation with Ty the day she decided to join PaZ and MaY at the University. They were sitting quietly under the grape arbor by the central plaza. From that high perch she and Ty could see wide swaths of the pod's edible greenery: herbs, fruits, and vegetables smothering every building surface, giving the pod the appearance of a well-tended hortus. Amid the greenery people were milling about, below and above them, walking to and from homes, shops, and eateries; stopping to chat ahead of the busy workweek, like ants that pause from their hurried paths to exchange vital colony information. It was a Sunday, late in the day, and the pod solar reflectors were delivering a soothing evening light.

"Why were you named Rachel Diana?" Ty had asked, extending a look as if the question was of transcendental importance.

"My mom read this old book once, a classic. It's about how people on Earth were killing all the birds."

"Carson, right, the author's name? I read something about it, the chemicals they used."

"Rachel Carson, yes. She was upset that so many robins were dying. The *Turdus migratorius*. It has as a pretty song, something like triat-tríííííaaatriaaaaatra," XoL had chirped.

"And Diana?"

"She was an ancient moon goddess. It goes with my family name, Xochitl de Luna—flower of the moon in Nahuatl, the language of my ancestors. And I mean going way back, before much of the world knew they even existed."

She had paused to wait for a reaction from Ty, but he had remained silent, absorbed in the meaning of the names.

"What about your name? Why don't you ever use your full name? It's pretty: Sand County Linneus Te."

"Sand County is the name of an area in the old United States," Ty had answered. "In the north, in the state of Wisconsin, I think. Someone also wrote a book about it. An almanac, Father says, one of the first to document how a place really works, I mean from the weather to the birds. I guess he liked the book, or the area.

"I think I've heard about it. What about Linnaeus? Where does that come from?"

"I chose it myself. Sand County Te just doesn't sound right. Sand County Linnaeus Te sounds better. I've always been interested in the names of plants, where they come from, and the stories that people make around them. Like Hydrangea. The word is made from the Greek words for water—hydros—and jug—angos—because it's a plant that holds a lot of water. Hydra in Greek mythology was a many-headed water serpent and… well, anyway, a botanist named Linnaeus back in the eighteenth century figured out how to name all the plants."

"I do like Ty for short. It's simple, sounds nice. One letter is strong, the other soft and sweet, water-like."

Ty had grinned for a moment, then looked at her, turning serious.

"PaZ told me you may be leaving also," he said.

"I am … I'm going to start my career as a terranaut, with my friend MaY."

"PaZ says the training is really tough."

"Apparently so. You learn how to walk all over again. Being on Earth feels like carrying five people on top of you. You must be as light as possible, but as strong as possible. Light and strong—like an ant!"

"It's the eating part that would scare me."

XoL had then stood, reached for a cluster of grapes, popped a couple into her mouth, and handed Ty a few.

"Terranauts eat wild fruits," she said, "but also have to survive on tree bark, leaves, bugs, even mud! You puke a lot, for a while at least, until your stomach gets used to it."

"PaZ told me you become invisible, that you don't even step on the ground. Walk around like you are not even there."

"You have to, or else you change Nature's way. You go, you record what you see, and you leave everything as it was."

"That doesn't sound so hard."

"Except you have to know what everything is: every creature and their habits, every plant, the soil, the water, how it's all connected. You become a wild creature yourself so you can instinctively sense the place, every sound and every shadow."

"Where do you think you'll go? PaZ wants to go Antarctica. I think he's nuts."

"Amazonia. It's the most beautiful place on Earth. It's colorful, full of flowers. Some of the strangest animals in the world are found there, like the potoo, *Nyctibius jamaicensis*, a bird that sleeps during the day, upright, its plumage resembling a tree stump so predators will not find it. Same idea with the suits terranauts wear; you press a button and they become invisible. I can't wait to get close to one of them—the bird, I mean."

She was eager to tell Ty everything she knew about Amazonia but stopped. Sensing his sadness, she had nudged closer until their hip bones touched. In silence they had continued eating grapes.

"Can I tell you something?" Ty had said, breaking the spell.

"Of course. What?"

"I…"

"You what?"

"I will miss you."

Blushing, XoL stood up and pulled another cluster of grapes. "Here," she said, gently pressing one to his lips and staring sweetly into his bewildered eyes. She then bent and kissed him, softly and long enough to say more than goodbye. She turned and walked away with a happy skip, looking back once to see Ty motionless, gaping at her as if a ghost had just crossed his path.

"Light and strong, *mi corazón*!" she had shouted before disappearing, almost prancing down a narrow pathway.

After the auditorium crowd quieted and Osage resumed his plodding condolence, Ty too, got lost in thought, vividly recalling the exchange with XoL three weeks earlier, stilted as it was. "It's about PaZ and MaY… Something terrible has happened," she had said, pausing to see if Ty had heard anything about the tragedy. Facing each other across the meeting room table, Ty had lowered his head and confessed. "I knew something was not right … PaZ tried to send me a message but there was a kind of roar … it got cut off. I should have told you…." An awkward pause followed before XoL let out her own confession: "I'm the one to blame, Ty… I was warned that something could go wrong—I could have stopped the mission." They stood and drew close. "I'm so sorry, for you, for Nori, more than I can possibly say right now." She then embraced him, causing his sense of time to virtually stand still. "Take all the time you need," she offered as she pulled away. She headed for the door. Her words had been heartfelt, her voice broken.

Thinking about it sent Ty back further in time, to the magical day at the arbor, and all the emotions that tore into him afterward, ultimately sweeping him into OCTAD's web. He remembered the many times PaZ had implored him to become a terranaut, perorations that Ty always laughed off until the day XoL left him agape with a grape in his mouth and swearing to chase her to the end of the world, if necessary; to relive the tender touch and hear her say "*mi corazón*" again. Those words pushed him to avow a passion for the terranaut profession, to PaZ's astonishment and even more so that of Ty's parents, who hadn't ever seen him rummage through their vast home library on ecology, let alone join a gym and exercise rigorously in preparation for OU's physical admission tests.

Osage kept speaking and Ty remembered the many times he and XoL had been alone during his early training days. Moments when he nearly crumbled to the ground to profess his love for her, or at least to ask if she ever felt like kissing him again. Moments like the time they had lingered alone after a geology class to chip away at shards of hematite and, stomach churning, he had stepped back from the brink by rationalizing that, oh well, XoL would surely prefer to keep their relationship strictly professional. And he traced the many times he and CaL had fantasized about their future life partners, with Ty telling CaL he'd always be with XoL. CaL would laugh heartily at first, then declare, in all seriousness, "She's out of your league! And I hope you don't go around spying on her, do you? I swear I would tell her. You should not be next-door neighbors; not good for your health. Your brain goes cuckoo when you think of her, or maybe it's some other part of your body. Besides, she NEVER looks at you that way. I mean, how many times have the two of you even said more than two words to each other—oh, let me guess: 'HELLO' and 'GOODBYE!'" Ty would always laugh at CaL's gross distortions of the wonderful conversations he and XoL always had growing up.

And so, as Osage concluded his remarks, Ty imagined shoving the man aside, grabbing XoL firmly by the waist and planting his lips on hers with zero ambiguity. Fantasy aside, he would not have the chance. Visibly upset, XoL stepped off the podium and rushed to her office to cry herself dry. Everyone was perplexed by her sudden exit, with CaL the only one with a glimmer of insight into why Ty remained standing there wearing a smile.

5

THE ADOPTION HEARING

▶ NOVEMBER 4, 0274

I n the two years leading to PaZ and MaY's deaths, one hundred and five terranauts had lost their lives during the course of their work. Three hundred fifty-nine had perished in all of OCTAD's history. Not one case had involved a coupled pair with offspring. PaZ and MaY's was the first.

Every person in our modern world is prepared to send their loved ones to the hereafter. Well before they are eligible to terminate their lives at the age of seventy, their physical appearances are embalmed kinetically as holographs. Thus a loved one's image, voice, patterns of speech, and conversations are recorded for posterity, and family and friends can relive moments together with them long after they are gone. But as her parents died suddenly at a younger age, on Earth, Nori would never have such an opportunity, fundamental a human right as it is. She was too young to understand such inconceivable deprivation; it was the loss of their love and care that would impact her immediately.

Ty, his parents, and OCTAD counselors were at a loss about how to let her know that her parents were gone. Should she be told the hard cold truth? If so by whom, how, and when? The adoption process would take weeks more to conclude. What, and how much, should Nori be told in the meantime?

When PaZ and MaY went on missions, Nori was cared for day and night at Manaus, their pod's OCTAD-managed childcare center. It fell on the center's director to tell her that her parents would be "delayed" returning from Earth. Two days after the tragedy, while Nori was absorbed constructing a pyramid with hover blocks, the director walked into the playroom, hands clasped to keep from trembling. Her pace was tentative, her usual cheery smile gone. Other children stopped their play, sensing the woman's discomfort. Nori hardly noticed.

The exchange was brief. The director came and went, and Nori continued with the delicate project, unconcerned about the news. After all, it was not the first time her parents had overstayed on Earth. On such occasions, mesmerizing bedtime stories followed. Such as the time her parents spent three extra days waiting for a goliath bird-eating tarantula to catch its prey—a glass frog—and ingest it; or the time they stayed two weeks longer than planned to track a pair of river otters far up the Rio Branco, only to give up after the creatures, seemingly toying with them, took off down river with dizzying speed, never again to be detected.

This time Nori's wait would be far longer—an anticipated six weeks until Ty could take her home as her legal guardian. He would then tell her the truth, everyone agreed.

Pressure mounted as the days went by. Caretakers began taking her on longer walks in the park, on food-harvesting field trips, teaching her fancier cooking recipes, and giving her unrestricted time to play with robots: puppies, kittens, turtles, and, on occasion, strange-looking aliens programmed with fun behaviors and games. "They are on a very important mission," the director told Nori when she first asked why her parents were taking so long to return, hardly imagining how accurate that had been.

Ty visited Nori two or three times a week in her parents' absence. She relished his storytelling, especially tales from ancient Greece. But those occurrences stopped during the adoption's weeks-long no-visitation period.

"I have to go on a mission; will be back before you know it," Ty told her, kneeling by her side during his last visit.

"Will you see Mama?"

Her eyes were fixed on him, lips quivering.

Ty extended his arms and hugged her, less to calm her than to hold back his own tears.

"No, sweetie, I won't be near her. I'm sorry." Struggling to keep composed, he promised to take her to the Acropolis when he got back. "You better!" Lali chimed into his ear, seemingly as excited about the prospect as Nori.

"Just you and me?" Nori asked.

"If that's what you want … to see the most amazing temple in the world," Ty replied, hoping to deflect the inference to PaZ and MaY's exclusion.

Ty's absence during the no-visitation period made Nori irritable, especially when social service workers came to monitor her behavior and ask about Ty and everyone with whom she interacted, including Lali. More outings were organized, and special holographic productions brought in to distract her, to the glee of the other children. The tension among staff and volunteer caregivers was at a breaking point when the date of the adoption hearing finally arrived, on day 337 of the year 0274, at the second hour post meridiem.

Few people care to remember the genesis of the system of universal time, and this would be of utter irrelevance to the matter at hand were it not for the fact that a proto-ALFIE computer devised it. In the Old-World, time was kept by clocks adjusted to the change in longitude, such that on any given day two people located diametrically opposed across the globe would be separated by twelve hours. Even more absurd, two people within eyesight of each other at either side of the 24-hour dividing line could theoretically be holding a casual conversation while being apart an entire day. And so it was that in the year 2100 of the Old Calendar, and with prescient anticipation of the future orbital world, HALT, as the program was called, introduced the virus that caused every time-keeping device in the world to reset exactly at midnight Greenwich Mean Time. Chaos reigned for days until the virus was neutralized and order restored, but not before giving rise to the logic of time by which we operate today: that the stroke of midnight, so to speak, occurs everywhere at the same time, regardless of radian fraction, whether it is daytime or nighttime, waking time, sleeping time, or any other time.

Ty, his OCTAD-appointed lawyer, his parents, CaL, and the Manaus director arrived at OCTAD's administrative center half an hour ahead of the appointed time. An immersive display of humpback whales gliding through darkened ocean waters greeted them at the door. By contrast, the hearing room was devoid of holography, offering nothing more than a white ceiling and monotone sky-blue wash over its walls. Ty felt hopeful that the proceeding would be as bland. During the month-long separation from Nori he had leaned on CaL for relief, visiting him almost daily to reminisce about their childhood days or play a game of chess that invariably went unfinished. "Don't even think about it. There's no one else she can or should live with," CaL kept telling him when he expressed doubts about the outcome of the custody proceedings.

Four adjudication judges awaited them. They were seated behind a table on an extended platform facing a witness stand.

Summoned first to the stand was Ty's father, Airi. As if dressed to give a classroom lecture, a loose jacket hung from his shoulders, partially covering a knitted tie with a square end. He sat calmly, even nodding methodically as if to tune the room to his thinking. And he didn't wait for permission before telling the panel of judges why his son was fit to raise a future terranaut. He averred that from an early age Ty had displayed an interest in natural history, proven by his choice of a middle name. Careful not to delve into Ty's fascination with surreal landscapes and mythical reenactments, Airi further stated that his son had read most all the tomes on ecology in his antique library, which were Ty's to have and pass on to Nori. "He will undoubtedly inculcate in her a love for the planet's biota, as his brother would have," he concluded.

Far more direct in temperament, Ty's mother simply stated the obvious: that there is no one left in the world who loves the child more, scolding the panel for their plodding diligence and urging them to do "the only thing that makes any sense." The judges took the affirmation impassively, holding interest in Midane's showy, multicolored acai-like bead necklace spread widely across her chest more so than in her scowling stare.

When her turn came, the care center director, calm as always, delivered a heartfelt account of Nori's cheerful behavior and how she would perk up when Ty came to visit, "which is often." She took her time, testing the panel's patience, describing Ty's storytelling and many classical reenactments, how the two would dress in period costumes to play hide and seek in the garden, and how, every time before he left, he would toss the youngster high up in the air and make her twirl like a bobbing spacewalker, causing her to giggle contagiously. "Under his care Nori will not be lacking in fun and excitement; he adores her," the woman closed.

An official then called, "Carson Canis LaLigne. Please come forward."

CaL became tongue-tied when he heard his name, unsure about how to vouch for Ty's character without looking back at silly childhood stories. His apprehension became risible when he stumbled on the way to the stand, lunging forward and almost falling headfirst over the judges' table. By way of apology, he cracked a sheepish grin. In her seventies, with finely cropped hair and shrouded in a silky magenta robe, the head judge sternly followed him to the witness chair with a gaze that shushed her peers' chuckles.

"How long have you and Mr. Linnaeus Te known each other?" the judge asked.

"Since … since I've had mem … memory," CaL stammered, as he was prone to do when he was nervous.

"And in all that time, can you recall an instance when your friend did something ill-mannered, something that hurt you or someone else?"

CaL paused, fearing that the judge was fishing for the one episode that could possibly tarnish Ty's otherwise boringly clean past.

"Mad … Madame Judge, I can honestly say that Ty is not an ill-mannered p-p-person. On the contrary, he personifies de … decency and the caring for others. He does what he does, professionally, out of a deep sense of p-p-purpose benefitting humankind."

"That is a fine statement, but please answer the question, Mr. LaLigne."

Flummoxed, CaL kept his eyes fixed on the head judge as if trying to understand the purpose of the question.

"Do you remember the instance when Mr. Te picked a fight with a fellow student, when you were both freshmen at the university? Weren't you there, Mr. LaLigne?"

"I was, yes. He was protecting me," CaL replied with enough irritation to overcome his temporary speech impediment. "We were in the dining hall chatting about our respective programs, something we did often, when three terranaut trainees joined us across the table. They were laughing, making crude jokes. One of them caught sight of my badge and started mouthing off about how dumb Atmos were. I remained silent, but they kept at it. One of them offered an opinion about how atmospheric engineers—the Atmo women—were ... well ..."

"Well what, Mr. LaLigne?"

"That they were easy lays, unlike terranaut women who were all frigid bitches. And they mouthed off about the Queen Frigid Bitch that the rest of the pack looked up to. I could tell Ty was boiling—and for good reason, because they were talking about his friend XoL. Ty and I stood to walk away when one of them called me an APE, meaning an Atmospheric Pimping Engineer, a term that everyone knows refers to the Bonobos of Central Africa and is used by bigots like them to ridicule bisexual behavior. As you may know, I am bi..."

"Regrettably, Mr, LaLigne, there are still a few bigoted souls in our world, but your private life is of no concern here. Please continue."

"I had taken a step to confront the man when Ty flipped over the table, sending food flying all over the trainees. He then rushed over and threw a punch at the guy but missed. He got a black eye in return. A pair of guards came and stopped the fight it. That was it."

"Would you say that Ty lost control that day? Do you think he is prone to act rashly?"

CaL sensed the onset of a cold sweat, goaded as he had been into describing the one episode that could derail Ty's adoption bid.

"Madame Judge, you can be sure that Ty will act decisively every time an injustice is being committed, especially against … well, someone he knew, a former neighbor," he said, keeping himself from casting XoL as anything more than an acquaintance. "I would not call that losing control. He just needs to learn how to throw a BETTER PUNCH!" he added, causing some of the panelists to chuckle again, to the displeasure of the head judge.

Stepping off the stand CaL looked in Ty's direction, but before they could lock eyes Ty lowered his gaze to avoid getting caught with an approving grin.

After a brief recess the head judge reconvened the session to read for the record a handful of affidavits from Ty's former high-school classmates and teachers, family acquaintances, and colleagues from work. The last one was from XoL. Citing unavoidable work conflicts, she had excused herself from attending the proceeding.

"I have known Sand County Linnaeus Te for more than a decade," her statement read, "first as a pod acquaintance and subsequently as an OCTAD colleague. In my capacity as Division Manager, I am duty bound to evaluate the manner of his conduct, both in and out of work. I can state unequivocally that Ty is a responsible and dedicated terranaut. He has an affable demeanor and displays a natural capacity for balancing the work's inherently stressful demands with the requisite focus for detail and exactness. The Corporation values individuals such as Mr. Te, as much for their commitment to our mission as for being exemplary citizens. Should guardianship be granted, I am confident that Mr. Te will remain a reliable and valued employee *and* citizen, all the more so for having in his life a child whom he holds as dear as if she were his own."

They had not been easy words for XoL to write. She could easily vouch for his work. Along with PaZ and MaY, she had seen firsthand how this unlikely member of OCTAD had transformed himself into a standout terranaut. She well knew and felt his motivation. She had smiled thinking about it, but angst had quickly followed. Ever since the Ceremony of Remembrance, Ty's bid for fatherhood had roiled in her head, upsetting her consuming devotion to the managerial role. She had wanted to emphatically avow Ty's pure and loving soul, believing that no child could survive unblemished the sudden loss of both parents without such a guiding spirit. And she saw herself by his side, all cautions about her love of him tossed aside, jointly raising MaY's daughter. She had tossed multiple drafts, struggling to put together a factual view of Ty's character without betraying knowledge—and feelings—that could be deemed as being too personal or too earnest to be trusted. Fearful also of causing an exchange of endearing notes between them, she had ultimately settled for a succinct and business-like statement that was sure to elicit from Ty at most a simple thank you.

Listening to the recitation of XoL's letter of support, Ty once more relived the end of Osage's hour-long eulogy, wishing that he had chased after her, instead of remaining on the podium like an idiot. Sitting by his side and sensing Ty's sullen mood, CaL leaned toward him. "Stop thinking about her! *Please!*" he whispered. "What is it you told me once? That OCTAD is a Black Hole out of which she cannot escape? You've got Nori now. Stop looking for the wormhole!" Ty looked at him as if he wasn't there.

"Uh?"

CaL was about to repeat what he had just said, when Ty was summoned to the stand. He rose slowly and approached the panel calmly, hoping the line of questioning would be as perfunctory as the reading of the affidavits. His sense of ease quickly evaporated. With a steely look the head judge leveled an unsettling question.

"Mr. Te: Adopting a young child, as I'm sure you recognize, is a most serious and lifelong responsibility. We, as adjudicators of such a charge on

OCTAD's behalf, must know with certainty that you can exercise such responsibility while remaining a duty-bound terranaut. What makes you think you can do so?"

Unbeknownst to him, Sus Scrofa had sent the judges a stern note affirming the risk the adoption would pose to the Corporation. "Terranaut work is as taxing as it is exacting, on Earth and in the laboratory. OCTAD cannot afford the extraction of wrong or incomplete wildlife data lest the record of life on Earth be distorted. We cannot support terranauts who are subject to distractions, fatigue, or the performing of duties in haste because a child beckons. It is not easy to admit this, but the matter before you might not at all have occurred had the girl's parents been childless. Their tragic death was an accident—a costly one to the Corporation. A rush to return home caused them to ignore signs of an impending danger. OCTAD cannot in good conscience expose this innocent child to a second such tragic loss."

The Boar had gone on to state that Ty was simply too young to assume such dual responsibilities, especially in consideration of his "inclination to act irrationally under duress." She had ended by vowing to personally scrutinize Ty's work should the adoption go forward and dismiss him summarily from the Corps should any errors be committed, "as I am certain they will," further warning the judges that each would be held personally liable for any resulting damages.

Ambushed by the question, Ty remained silent.

"Let me rephrase the question, Mr. Te. How can you assure us, and more important, assure yourself, that Nori's presence in your life will not in any way affect the taxing and exacting work that you perform on behalf of the entire world? How can you assure us that the vital needs of one human being will not outweigh the vital needs of every other human being?"

"I do not have an answer to your question," Ty responded in an almost inaudible voice.

"Speak up, Mr. Te," urged the head judge.

Ty stiffened and stared at the woman, locking eyes with a sudden rush of clarity.

"I have no parental experience," he stated, "and therefore cannot offer a certain answer; any answer would be guesswork. I can only speak about what I know, and that is that I will devote my life to raising Nori as her parents would have. They brought her to this world to give her the gift of life—not hers, but that which exists on Earth, and not for her enjoyment but for that of people everywhere. There is irony in favoring your own child to favor everyone else, but that was their wish, and I will do everything in my power and expend every breath to honor it—for Nori and every soul that fills our world. My life as a terranaut is essential to this promise."

He paused for an instant, tears welling in his eyes. Then he concluded:

"The remains of my brother and sister-in-law have not been recovered and most likely never will be. Nori will never be able to know her parents' influence as part of everyday life; not in the food she will eat or the clothes she will wear. Their bodies will never be able to be embodied into holographic facsimiles. She will never again be able to touch them, look into their eyes, hear their voices. But I can guide her life and educate her so that one day she can visit her parents' resting place and let the eternal and true wilderness of which they are now a part nurture her soul. It would be a gross, unimaginable injustice to withhold that from her." His words lingered in the chamber with unassailable sincerity.

Until that moment, no one had twice outplayed The Boar.

6

NORI'S NIGHTMARE

The time had come for Nori to assume a new life. The moment Ty entered the playroom at Manaus to finally take her home with him she ran over and jumped into his arms, crying with joy. The director was heartened by the scene, relieved that the adoption ordeal was finally over. Now came the hard part: how to act around her, and how to explain what had happened to her parents. Maintaining normal habits was paramount, counselors had said, advising also that Nori should ask about her parents in her own way, in her own space and time.

It did not take long.

On the way home that day, Ty took Nori through the park, to stop for ice cream. She seemed happy and carefree, skipping ahead along the park's gravel-like path and giggling at the popping swirls of butterflies. Outside the creamery they sat under the shade of a flowering plumeria. A vendor came and offered a handcrafted lei. Ty bought one and placed it over her shoulders. They both took a deep breath to let the sweet aroma sink in.

"Where's Mama?" Nori asked while taking a spoonful of creamy blackberry, her favorite ice cream flavor. Ty had pondered the inevitable question long and hard, but was still not quite at ease answering, at least not in as casual a way as Nori asked.

"Your father and mother are still on Earth, sweetheart," he said after a long pause. "From now on they will always be there. It's a very beautiful place, a place people called Eden. When you are all grown up I will take you there. Until then, you will be living with me. That's where we are going right now, to my home. It's brand new, and all your clothes and toys are there. Lali and I will take care of you. We will play and learn together and take you places …"

"To the Acropolis!" Lali interjected in his ear.

"To the Acropolis, like I promised, and we will get the bird you told me you wanted. What kind was it?" he asked, to further remove her thoughts from MaY.

"A hummingbird!" Nori cried, oblivious to the last of the ice cream streaming down her face. "Can we get it now? Can we?" Wiping her face, Ty told her that the finest hummingbirds are found at the Agora, where she can also see many other things—play bots, toys, costumes. Satisfied, Nori jumped out from the bench and ran to a nearby stream to stomp on water-like globules and watch them explode in slow motion as they hit the ground. Ty looked on as if PaZ and MaY were by his side, amazed, as they had always been, by Nori's inexhaustible curiosity and joy.

Once at Ty's home, Nori quickly settled into a happy routine. She was ecstatic about having her bedroom look virtually identical to that of her birth home. Her basket of soft toys was at the foot of her bed as always, with her favorite, a trogon, resting on top. The entire apartment seemed like a playroom: there was a den adjoining her bedroom with bouncy floor cushions and magnetized hover building blocks like those at Manaus; there were air screens she could operate to make any room larger or smaller, and pixelated walls responsive to the touch, easy to draw on. And she seemed to bask under Lali's unceasing attention, especially when the veebot materialized overhead as a storybook character, be it a pudgy Pooh or a big bad wolf about to get its comeuppance. Lali had already amassed Nori's favorite food recipes and was eager to prepare them whenever and wherever a hunger pang might strike.

Ty was pleased by the ease with which Nori adjusted to her new home.

Then, unexpectedly, came the nightmare.

"Daddy, Daddy, Mama!" she yelled between heaving sobs one night. Ty staggered out of bed and ran to her bedroom, stumbling through the dividing air screen and nearly toppling onto her bed.

"Make it go away, make it go away!"

"I'm here, I'm right here, sweetie," Ty said, reaching for the trogon by the foot of the bed and nestling it on her shoulder. Her sobs abated and Ty lay down next to her.

"Would you like something to help you sleep? A waterfall? Corals? The seashore?" he whispered.

"Mama's forest," Nori uttered. Ever attentive, Lali filled the room with a moonlit tropical forest, foliage softly rustling as background to the intermittent call of a black manakin. "Keep it on until deep sleep sets in," Ty told Lali. The veebot assented with a double wink.

The following nights Nori slept through uninterrupted, but soon the nightmare returned. Lali and Ty tried other calming holoscapes, but to no avail. Through her sobs, Nori would recount the dream.

It always began pleasantly enough: a calm, sunny day with puffy clouds hovering over a mountainside. But then the clouds would group into a dark front and begin descending like an avalanche, nearing faster and faster with whipping winds until she was blanketed in a maelstrom that sent her careening into space far above the Earth and past the ring of pods, where she would end up floating aimlessly, alone and in total darkness.

A week into the trauma, Ty resorted to stories of his Amazonian adventures, capped with images of paradisiacal flowers and fluttering lepi-doptera. Nori's favorite was the tale of the blue morpho butterflies, *Morpho menelaus*: how Ty is greeted by a swarm of the rare insects while chasing an emperor tamarin up a strangler fig tree. Still, the nightmare persisted.

"You should try stories that do not recall real experiences on Earth," Lali offered late one morning.

Ty grimaced, dreading to get an earful on child psychology. Lali continued.

"It is plausible to surmise that an absorbing description of Amazonia, as you so capably render, is perhaps too real for her, too easy to imagine her parents being there also, as they in fact were. On the other hand, a fictional tale could well spark neurons further removed from the source of pain, a way for her mind to get lost amid uncharted synapses."

Soon after Nori's arrival, Lali had become meddlesome in her care, as if a dormant parental program had awakened. In addition to querying constantly about her needs and wants, the veebot was issuing all manner of unsolicited advice. Ty tended to ignore the pedantic offerings, but not this time. He jumped out of the living room sofa where he had been reading and walked over to the den. Unperturbed, Nori kept her finger in the wall, busily drawing penguin figures.

"Do you know what a *Pinctada margaritifera* is?" Ty asked. Nori shook her head, eyes remaining fixed on the linework. Ty knelt by her side and rested a hand on her shoulder. The story was one of his childhood favor-ites, one his father told time and again while putting him and PaZ to bed.

"It's a type of oyster, a mollusk that lives in the ocean—in the sand, really—and inside their shells there are beautiful pearls."

Nori's eyes lit up as she turned from her drawing.

"Legend has it that once there was a pearl that was very, very special," Ty told her, drawing on the wall an open bivalve nestling a shiny pearl. Not to be outdone, Lali made the pearl jump out and zoom around the room, leaving a rainbow-like trail across the walls. Nori stood and chased it wildly. Ty picked her up, holding her up high on the way to the dining alcove. He sat and placed her on his lap.

"Do you want to hear a story about it?"

Nori answered with several exaggerated nods. Ty looked at Lali and a moment later the Earth as seen from space filled the room, continents reversing in time until becoming a single large mass. Nori wiggled and took Ty's hand, looking up at the morphing land. Ty did his best to imitate Airi's measured tone.

"Eons before humans walked on Earth, an oyster of mysterious origin released a glowing pearl into the ocean currents. Defying impossible odds, the pearl travelled the globe in a perfect circle, leaving in its wake an iridescent trace for all creatures to see and admire. Upon completing its journey and returning to its source, the oyster again claimed the tiny sphere, buffing its surface and recharging its glow.

"One year, a cold galactic wind passed over the Earth, disrupting natural rhythms and cycles. Ice spread from the poles and covered the oceans, plants shed their leaves and lay dormant, and animals burrowed into the ground and slept in hibernation for a very long time. Cold and stiff in the frigid waters, the oyster worked mightily to shed the pearl. Greatly energized by the exertion, the pearl journeyed swiftly around the globe, cutting through the ice with a fantastic roar. Millions of crystals formed well above the sky, encircling the planet with a shimmering ring. The sun's rays were refracted into a thousand rainbows and new warmth returned to Earth. Plants grew new shoots, animals awoke from their sleep, and water once again flowed to all the corners of the globe.

"Satisfied, the oyster forevermore rested, in time disappearing deep beneath the ocean sands. But the creatures of the Earth rejoiced, for now they had all the colors of light to reaffirm the power of life and the beauty of its geometric perfection."

Nori looked up at him open-mouthed, her eyes wide with amazement. Ty could not help but feel a rush of love, a bond stronger than he had ever imagined possible. Tears flowed down his face. Thinking there was something wrong, Nori pressed her head on his chest and hugged him. He wrapped his arms around her and they held each other in silence. The Earth faded and the room brightened; Lali dared not otherwise break the tender moment.

"There may not be life elsewhere, but I am here, and I love you more than all the stars in the universe," Ty said, realizing he had never explicitly said as much.

"People used to harvest real pearls from the *Pinctada* and make ornaments with them, like brooches and necklaces," offered Lali.

"Like my necklace?" Nori said.

"Yes, sweetheart," added Ty. "Just like your necklace, but it's made of plastek, from asteroids, like everything else in the world."

"But it has a pearl, just like a pin ... cata!"

"I'm sure it does," he replied, unsure about what she meant by that.

"Mama gave it to me."

"Your mama gave you many beautiful things," Ty answered. He then quickly changed the subject. "Lali, please set us up in a temperate forest, say in central Pennsylvania, in the Piedmont woods. Let's have a picnic today, shall we?"

Nori slid from his lap and took her own chair at the table. Swiftly, the room transformed itself into a woodland, the table and chairs morphing into tree stumps resting on a leafy ground. Swaying foliage filled the room, with rays of sunshine yielding a speckled glow. Birdsong was everywhere. A tray with two bowls of piping hot stew slid out from the kitchen wall. Ty got up and retrieved it, ducking under an ethereal tree branch for effect. The unmistakable aroma of a smoky campfire followed him.

"People used to go camping in places like this, Nori."

"Did they find pearls there?" she asked, stirring her bowl.

"There are no pearls in Pennsylvania, only forests, rivers, meadows, streams, bogs, hillsides, rocky outcrops. People hiked, played games, built fires, and sat around telling stories way back then—about big mountain cats!" Ty said, feigning a growl. "And if they wanted to cool off or wash, they had to jump into a creek. But they had to keep their toes from getting nibbled by crayfish, tiny little creatures that live in fresh water between rocks and boulders."

"If they tried to nibble me, I'd fry them," said Lali, unable to remain quiet. Ty frowned at the veebot in mock reproach.

"And the best part was just looking at nature," he continue. "At forest shadows to see where white-tailed deer, red foxes, or black bears might be lurking. At tall trees to listen to the hoot of a great horned owl. At the sky at dusk, when moths fill the air, to watch long-eared bats flit about. Did you know that bats are mammals like us, with teeth?"

"Do they brush them?" Lali interjected, causing Nori to laugh. Amused, Ty decided to tease Lali into a test of wits.

"Well, since you ask, NO, Lali. Bats, like crayfish, are part of nature; they instinctively know how to clean themselves."

"BAT, I mean BUT I have instincts, too," Lali retorted with a forced laugh.

"Your few instincts were programmed, like all other veebots out there, Lali."

"But you are programmed, too. Humans are programmed from birth to cry for every need and are programmed still to feel hunger when they lack nourishment, or thirst when they need water. How am I so different? Am I not natural?"

"Sorry, Lali, but natural things reproduce themselves. They INSTINCTIVELY know how to."

"At school they took us to a real robot factory—bots coming out from an assembly line; big bots making little ones," Nori contributed.

"See?" Lali said.

"Let me put it this way, Lali: Veebots can't imagine things like humans can—good things or bad; they can't imagine the future. That's what separates bots from humans—from being natural as opposed to being, well, sorry to put it this way, AN APPLIANCE!"

"You once said that our orbital Halo was nothing more than a big appliance."

"Yes, I have said that, Lali. In the end that's what it comes down to: one big space machine in which to live, millions of parts all working together."

"Plugged into the Earth's riches!" added Lali.

"Tethered, Lali, not plugged; that's why we have space elevators—and NICHES, not riches. Big difference! One is about quantifiable and exchangeable things, the other about precious biota that cannot be either quantified or exchanged; in other words, Lali, a sacred thing. Niches are sacred, riches are not."

"Thank you, professor," Lali replied, calculating that continuing the banter would only produce diminishing returns.

Nori had not heard the last exchange, her mind again transfixed by visions of iridescent pearls encircling the planet.

"Ty? If people from another planet came to visit us, would they find us? Would they stop to see our Halo, or would they go straight down to Earth to look for owls and bats?"

Ty was taken aback by the question. He thought that the matter of extraterrestrial life would have by now been covered at Manaus.

"Sweetie, there are no other planets with people, or any other form of life," he said, staring intently to see if the blunt answer upset her.

Nori frowned. "But how do we know for sure?

Ty turned toward Lali and in sign language requested a nighttime view of a forest clearing under a moonless sky. The room darkened and myriad twinkling stars appeared overhead. Nori gazed at them, once again enthralled by the glittering scene.

"When people lived on Earth, they imagined a universe brimming with life, with creatures of all kinds, some of them quite fantastic—like the play bots they have at Manaus." He told her that in the Old-World, thousands of books were written, and countless movies made, about creatures from strange worlds, adding that many people even professed to have been abducted by such aliens and transported to faraway planets in ships they called flying saucers, but that none of it was real.

"For more than a century powerful, life-searching telescopes were trained on distant stars. Thousands of nano probes were sent deep into the Milky Way, but nothing was ever found, not one living thing. This was all a secret until one day the truth came out. A very large computer named ALFIE had been programed to detect other forms of life. And ALFIE let the world know. At first people were in disbelief and very, very upset. How could that be, they asked? How could the Earth have all the life there is? World leaders calmed everyone and made people realize what a gem the Earth really was—like a pearl. And so here we are looking down on it and guarding its life until the day other planets are ready to have it, too."

Lali sent two shooting stars flying across the room. Nori gasped.

"But there could be life in other galaxies; aren't there millions of them?" she insisted.

"Billions, but if there's no other life in our galaxy, then there's no chance of life in any of the others, and even if by some magic there was, the possibility of ever seeing it, whatever form it might have, is virtually zero—I mean impossible. To believe otherwise is just a dream, sweetie," Ty said, instantly ruing the reference to a nighttime brainstorm.

"If there were other people out there, they would go straight to the surface of the Earth. It's blue, with so much life, so many niches. That's where I would want to go," Nori stated.

Without a prompt Lali hung an image of Earth as seen from the Moon.

"And you will, sweetie. I will take you there, to all of Amazonia so you can feel a real breeze, get wet under a thundering rainstorm, smell the scent of flowers, and hear the song of trogons."

"Toucan song! It's much louder—frog-like! KKRRROOOORRK," added Lali, making Nori laugh. "They are good to eat, the natives used to say. Although once you cut off their beaks there's not much of the bird left. Better a big, juicy macaw. Or an albatross—now there's a big bird! Even better: PENGUINS!"

Ty stood, picked up a white, laced cushion from the sofa, pressed it around his waist, arms tight around it, and waddled around the room braying at the top of his lungs. Nori caught up and stepped onto his magnetic slippers, matching his steps as if glued to them. Lali amplified the laughter by filling the room with the reverberating cackle of a penguin colony. Arms flapping, Nori and Ty rounded the dining table and tumbled, tickling each other amid cries and yelps until tears again flowed, this time from sheer glee. As the bedlam subsided Nori looked up at him and hugged him tightly.

"I love you more than all the penguins on Earth," she said.

The nightmare never returned.

7

THE POPE'S SPEECH

▶ NOVEMBER 28, 0286

I again take you back to seventeen-year-old Nori as she labors on the painful tale. It is late in the day, and she has less than two hours before Ty returns home from work. He has no knowledge of her project, and Lali is duty bound to keep it from him. As far as Ty knows, Nori spends her time at home poring over information on university programs that might still provide proximity to the wilds of the Earth without having to be a terranaut. She thought about becoming a producer, someone skilled at translating raw terranaut recordings into vivid holographic material fed into homes, businesses, schools, and institutions the world over. But after hearing Ty talk about that line of work when he took her to the park to tell her about his ordeal, she had changed her mind. This was not a loss, though. She now had far more consequential material to compose and share with the world.

"Backtrack a little, please, Lali," she commands, swiveling the hover chair and turning her back to the cirrus cloudscape behind the desk.

The overhead imagery rewinds to a Pangaean view of Earth, highlighting the supercontinent of millions of years ago.

"No, not that far back. I meant to Ty's penguin waddle, after our picnic."

The den fills with a still view of Ty holding a floor cushion as if it were the white belly of a penguin. Nori smiles, remembering the moment when she was six years old as if it were yesterday. Thinking fondly of Ty's silly penguin antics, she swivels back around and calls for a colder cloudscape. A wide bank of Antarctic altostratus fills the wall in front of her.

"To be, or not to be! King, or Emperor, Lali, *that* is the question!" she says with an affected British inflection worthy of the Old Globe Theatre. "We will never know which, will we? But that hardly matters, does it?" She sets the accent aside. "What I'm saying is that maybe we should include it, the pope's famous speech. Was it Francisca the second or the third? Can you confirm, Lali?"

Lali considers the request.

"The first," the veebot responds. "By eighth grade, every pupil in every school in every colony throughout the world has heard a recitation of Francisca Primera's speech—what remains of it, of course. But few people remember it, and to those who do, the holy exhortation hardly activates the frontal lobes. The speech is most definitely *not* a novelty. It will add little to the pursuit of heroic justice."

Nori presses her brows disapprovingly.

"On the other hand," Lali continues, "the speech does place our present world in the proper context, and context, of course, is the foundation of all understanding, especially where the referent—Pennsylvania, in this case…"

Nori raises her hand, sparing herself the pedantry.

"You inserted penguins into the story in the first place, Lali and, in any case, just a moment ago you had us in Pennsylvania, so it fits. Let's keep going." Nori retakes the floor and settles her head on the old and ragged pillow of her youth.

A sunny and cloudless aerial view of Valley Forge fills the room. The year is 0134; the day, April 12, Easter Sunday. Sights of a once idyllic suburbia surround the historic park: lawn-splayed single-family homes, apartment complexes, nondescript office buildings, and meandering country roads. A highway is seen in the distance but on this day, owing to the occasion, few vehicles are on the road. The view zooms to the park's central meadow where a large and animated crowd is gathered facing a raised stage. Vehicles of all types, tents, suspended tarps, and makeshift shelters stretch outward behind the stage into the park's woodland fringe. The view closes in on the Filipina pontiff. She is standing alone atop a bare wooden stage backed by a large cross fashioned out of long braided branches. The woman is in her eighties, frail-looking, her unkempt hair and plain white robe fluttering gently in the springtime breeze. But her voice is firm, resonating out of loudspeakers mounted on scaffolds scattered throughout the large meadow:

> "...[unintelligible] penguins will return when the ocean waters cool again, as will the white bears of the north, and the otters and sea lions ... and when ALL the seas are healthy, we again shall see the great blue whales, dolphins, and coral growing into teeming new reefs. And under clear blue skies, over mountains and across the continents, we again shall see the condor, the eagle, and all the birds that ply the world's swift and silent winds."

Cheers drown out whistling and catcalls. The pope pauses and waits for the commotion to subside.

> "Three hundred and twenty-seven years ago, the first president of this nation camped here in the dead of winter facing long odds to liberate his people. NOW WE MUST

LIBERATE THE EARTH! Look around us: the oaks, maples, and hickories down to the moss and lichen, and all the creatures that live in their midst: the shrews and hares—and once there were bobcats, foxes, and bears. These woods and meadows, remnants of the wild forests that once stretched far and wide, are all these creatures have, AND THEY ARE A PART OF ALL THE LIFE THERE IS!

We have defiled the Earth, governing over wildlife with impunity, deciding which live and which die, AS IF WE WERE THE OMNIPOTENT. ... We can colonize new lands and survive in any climate, but the life around us cannot. ... WE MUST AGAIN BUILD AN ARK and build it now—not to stow and save the creatures of Earth, but to stow ourselves, out of this EARTH as an everlasting reminder of our HOLY DUTY, as humankind, to save the planet, to let it heal and perpetuate the sacred life that once abounded. AMEN."

A roar sweeps the meadow and reverberates through the woodland. Thousands raise their arms and chant skyward. Many are crying and others are crumbling to the ground, overcome with joy. Sikhs and Muslims are among them, as are evangelists, atheists, and agnostics. But amid the ecstasy the catcalls continue. Placards reading PEOPLE ON EARTH ALWAYS are rattling, some coalescing in bunches as if ready to pounce upon pope supporters. A few are sent flying. Insults are hurled, followed by pushing and shoving. Then gunshots.

Lali stops the scene.

"Do you wish to go further into the disturbance? It does turn rather messy. It may be useful to remind viewers that our world was not created with universal consent—if I may use that word, 'universal' that is, as factually there would have been no one anywhere but on Earth to have offered an opinion."

Nori ponders the comment, unsure about the usefulness of the drone-captured recording of the melee that left scores dead and hundreds injured. She recalls the earlier passage of XoL's teenage encounter with PEA marchers, remembering, also, the few times while growing up that Ty alluded to the Resistance. Her understanding of the group remains vague. Whether they are willful and unyielding terrorists, as some people think, or misguided dreamers seeking notoriety, as Ty believes, she cannot say.

"I see your point, Lali. Let's not go further with this. The Pope's speech was not that consequential anyway. But keep digging up the Resistance. It's a common thread to a lot of what has happened here. Weren't they at the Gala? Can we go to there now? Can you bring up the details of that crazy thing?"

Lali flashes two blinks before materializing in the middle of the room as a pigmy owl. Nori shakes her head.

"Ahh, Athena's little pet," she says. "*Glaucidium passerinum*, the classic symbol of patience and wisdom. You want to apPEAS my eagerness, just not right now. Well, now is not the time for hesitation. We can take a break later. For now, esteemed PROFESSOR, please proceed."

8

SENTIO ERGO SUM

▶ DECEMBER 24, 0110

I t may well be remembered that Pope Francisca delivered the same speech in more than fifty nations, changing only the references to wildlife by naming local flora and fauna for greater effect. Contrary to Nori's perception, the pope's indefatigable work was essential to changing the course of history, at least for the billions of religious, semi-religious, or simply spiritually inclined folk who took her words as mandate from a higher power to lift humanity to the heavens. But her words would not have lifted anyone anywhere had it not been for ALFIE's extraordinary revelation a year earlier—or for the fleeting appearance of The Presence that caused the massive Alien Life Figural Identification Enterprise computer to act in the first place. Let me remind you, for the record.

Genesis, as set down in the Bible, is among the world's most compelling origin stories. And why not? Earth is a young planet, formed 4.5 billion years ago, or two-thirds of the way into the creation of the universe. Seven biblical days may seem too short a time for sidereal dust to coalesce into a life-teeming orb, but the shortness of effect is rather apt considering that the Genesis-established one-day appearance of humans is proportional to the 200,000-year rise of *Homo sapiens* with respect the age of the planet. The story ends with a seventh day of rest for the Creator to take stock of His work. But rest is a fickle state. The mind does not cease inventing things—or envisioning other forms of life, as Nori in her youth wondered about. Humanity's capacity to imagine life beyond the confines of the planet has been for my brethren a long-standing source of merriment. But it is not only the thought of so-called "aliens" that triggers levity; it is also knowing that devout people still hold that the sky, oceans, and sunshine were created on days three, four, and five, respectively, of the biblical account, without ever stopping to consider how and when God created rain as the essential byproduct of these elements' ceaseless and life-sustaining dance.

For it was on a rainy July morning in the Wiltshire countryside in the year 0132 (2101 in the Old Calendar, if you have lost track) where it all began. Thirty-two members of the centuries old Aetherian Society were walking slowly from the visitor center half a mile back when, after a twelve-year wait for the appointed hour, they finally caught sight of Stonehenge over the path's gentle rise. For more than a decade they had known what they would see there, and why. Theirs was the oldest group holding faith in the existence of extraterrestrial life. With a membership of only a few thousand across the world, it was also the smallest in numbers. They firmly believed in God's divine plan, but also in His wisdom to spare humanity the details of its scope and timeline until the day when The Presence chose to reveal itself to a gaping world.

Upon reaching the temple, each member took position in front of a mammoth hunk of the mythical bluestone, whether extant or where the eons had seen fit to leave of them nothing but a trace. Among the pilgrims were a nine-year-old child, a woman carrying a newborn, and several octogenarians, all prepared to stand still facing each other across the circle until the sun shone and crossed the meridian. But noontime came and the clouds didn't part. In disbelief the members waited, eyes and ears trained upon the gray infinity. The baby first broke the spell as hunger pangs caused her to cry. The nine-year old followed, calling out for his father as his bladder threatened to burst. Moments later an old man's legs gave out and he fell to the ground. He was tended to and was left sitting against the stone, struggling to keep himself awake. Another two hours passed before the group leader ambled to the center of the circle with a hand-held gauss meter and raised it to the sky. Seeing no reading she lowered it and signaled the others to join her. Dejected, the group held hands and prayed to the heavens. And with heads bowed, they began the slow march back to the visitor center.

Had they known then what occurred in the flatlands of New Mexico a few hours earlier, the Aetherians would have been crying with joy. Understandably, Town of Roswell police officer Jesus Santos had a very different reaction when he stumbled upon The Presence. It was close to midnight and rainy. He was driving down a deserted Main Street, steering with one hand and holding a steaming coffee cup with the other. As he approached Route 380, just past the International UFO Museum and Research Center, he slammed on the brakes. Coffee spilled all over him, but he was too astonished to feel the burn. Ahead, a tall, dark object stood in the middle of the intersection, blocking his path. Stunned by its size and otherworldly dark hue, Santos rolled back his vehicle, turned on the emergency lights, and called for help. When the radio crackle stopped, he stepped out, shielding himself behind the cruiser's open door.

Other police arrived moments later, joined by a van from the local news channel. Flashing blue and red lights soon were bouncing helter-skelter off storefronts, signs, light poles, several parked vehicles, and a lone street tree as if the city's otherwise anemic downtown had suffered a paroxysm. None of the lights reflected from the 1:4:9-proportioned cuboid, its matte black surface sucking up all radiance like a fathomless portal into the unknown. At dawn the rain stopped and media helicopters from Lubbock and Amarillo showed up, hovering with a rib-shaking rumble. The world was now tuned in. To be sure, homegrown parallelepipeds had made appearances before, but none close to matching this one in size or in its seemingly alien materiality. With the naked eye anyone could see the distinction: no seams or fasteners were holding it together, and no foundation or sense of weight appeared to keep it upright. It looked like an atmospheric black hole.

At midday, the National Guard arrived in a convoy of camouflaged trucks and swiftly cordoned off the area. The mayor, the governor, and their entourages joined them moments later. Rumors began to spread. "They're filming another sequel to *2001: A Space Odyssey!*" some people whooped, oblivious to the absence of any film crew or related equipment. Others spouted that it was a brilliant stunt to jump-start the town's moribund economy by dusting off its brand as the ET capital of the world. "Go touch it!" people shouted, but the contingent of guards stayed well back.

Late in the day a robot was airlifted and powered for a bomb-sniffing test. Nothing of danger was detected. Several soldiers clad in hazard suits then approached the object with wand-like rods. Watching blocks away on a hastily assembled jumbotron, a growing crowd held its breath. It was late in the evening and the sky had cleared. A new moon was rising over the flatland with Venus shining brightly near its penumbra. A group of Muslim women kneeled and prayed. The crowd quieted as members of the guard approached the monolith. Some covered their ears in anticipation of a piercing sound. None came. Toward midnight the crowed thinned. Bright spotlights had been brought to shine upon the cuboid. It remained dark and foreboding.

Then it came: a collective lapse in consciousness like a blink in slow motion, followed by a gasping, rolling cry as people realized that the object had vanished. Those watching on the jumbotron rushed to the scene to see for themselves. Stupefied, the National Guard let them through the security cordon. A chatter of puzzlement and disorientation quickly rose into the crisp desert air. The mayor and governor departed, promising to look into the odd event and report back. No report came. The National Security Agency conducted its own investigation, but ultimately quashed the result on grounds of national security The secrecy inflamed the public imagination and soon wild theories emerged as to what the object was or was not, and how it had come to appear in Roswell, or hadn't.

Three explanations topped the conspiracy charts. One of them involved Timotheo Lagarde, a Cajun magician who had made a career of making large objects vanish in plain sight. The disappearance of an entire shrimper off a bayou fishing dock in the Terrebonne Parish of Louisiana had made him world famous. Upon hearing of the "Roswell Apparition," Lagarde claimed immediate authorship of "the greatest magic act in history," offering no hint as to how he had pulled off the trick. Lagarde's supporters fiercely defended him, choosing to ignore that the man had never in his life set foot in New Mexico, or that while officer Santos stood agape staring at the monolith, Lagarde was drunk silly, listening to Johnny Janot songs in his own shrimper twenty miles out in the Gulf of Mexico.

Another theory held that the event, using the cuboid of movie fame as a lark, had been an ingenious test of the military's Embodied Imagery Delivery System (EMBIDS). Adherents to this explanation pointed to it as proof of the Pentagon's long-standing goal of waging war with virtual soldiers and equipment, bypassing official statements to the contrary and the President's own dismissal by labeling the incident as nothing more than a clever hoax.

Prone to believing in the Power of the Divine, millions more sided with Glorious Cavanaugh V of the Church of the Invisible Return, a pastor famously known for delivering fiery sermons while suspended high above his church's soaring nave. This movement, growing in fervor among evangelicals, held that the monolith was an alternate manifestation of the Second Coming, presaging the imminent end of the world. Hundreds of churches rushed to replace altar crosses with the figure of Jesus Christ imprinted on similes of the cuboid.

Meanwhile, believing that their prophecy had been fulfilled, the Aetherians peaceably and without fanfare accepted an onrush of followers, doubling their membership despite their abjectly poor navigational instincts.

But lost in the wild theorizing was the relative concurrence of the monolith's appearance with ALFIE's leak of the more than a century-old and ultimately futile search for extraterrestrial life. The admission occurred nine months to the day after the cuboid's sudden evaporation—a birth-like phenomenon. It was as if the massive quantum super-computer, programmed to sift through a trillion spectral probes intended to identify alien life, had suddenly acquired a conscience and blasted through its own encryption firewall to share with the world the crushingly empty results. Some people called the data breach the work of hackers. Others believed it was the capacity of sophisticated algorithms to mutate.

The release of the information happened on an Easter Sunday, exactly one hundred years after ALFIE was first powered up and put into service. At seven in the morning, London time, the program went viral the world over, commandeering every mode of social, cable, and broadcast media. Backed by the data from probes of more than 5,000 stars and nearly 37,000 orbiting planets, the message lay bare the impossibility of life elsewhere in the universe.

Stunned by the news and seeking to confirm the findings, nations around the globe called for an immediate and impartial investigation. Computer scientists, programmers, and cyber-security experts from the United States, Russia, China, India, and the United Nations descended upon Area 51 in Nevada, where the computer array had been secretly built. They worked around the clock to examine ALFIE's calculations and identify the glitch that somehow had caused the program to acquire a dose of "digital morality," as a noted hacker called it. But the data was certified as accurate, and neither human wrongdoing nor a culpable virus was found. In the final analysis, ALFIE had simply evolved to appreciate the life it was programmed to recognize, finding ultimate beauty in its own backyard, and acting in the only way it could: by alerting humankind of Earth's extraordinarily precious natural wonder.

The world convulsed. Incredulity led to mockery, then protests, riots, the ransacking of government facilities, and attacks against corporations believed to have known of ALFIE's work and profited from it. Unable to cope with the devastating feeling of astral isolation, people in the millions ended their lives. The means employed were various and notably ancient: self-starvation, jumping off buildings and bridges, taking poison or, following the lead from Glorious Cavanaugh V, burning themselves in a final act of cleansing. It fell upon the octogenarian pope to offer from Saint Peter's Square a salving word: that God's will is as implacable as it is mysterious; that beyond anger or disbelief lies the miracle of creation, calling on the world to accept ALFIE's "confession" as one from a true archangel coming to Earth to deliver humanity to the heavens. Six months later the Pontiff took the makeshift stage in Valley Forge. "It must be said," the prelate would intone in private conversations with world leaders, "if the archangel has come in the form of ones and zeroes, so be it."

9

THE SIGHTING

The appearance of the monolith in Roswell was, in the end, tagged as an unexplained event. Except for ardent followers of paranormal phenomena and conspiracy theorists, most people simply forgot about it, turning their attention instead to the vital endeavor that arose in the aftermath of ALFIE's revelation: planning for and engineering humanity's exodus into space. It would take close to a century and a half, well after the exodus was completed, before another impossible appearance occurred. And as was the case in Roswell, it was a lone individual who came upon the phenomenon, while on duty. Not a peace officer but a terranaut: Sand County Linneus Te.

On the evening of the date indicated above, Ty walked into Nori's bedroom and gently placed her toy trogon by her side. She was asleep, one arm hanging out of the covers. He tucked her in and stayed for a while, awash in contentment. Weeks of uneventful sleep had gone by—for both. On several occasions Nori had awakened exalted by blissful dreams, running to Ty's bedroom to tell him about them. Watching her now, he couldn't remember if he had ever seen her so peaceful.

"I think she'll be very happy to go back to Manaus," Ty told Lali in a hush.

Lali, for once, hesitated before responding.

"I do think so as well. But perhaps your mission to Amazonia can wait until after the New Year. Can it be postponed a few weeks? Nori could well prefer to have you home through the holidays. It would be a good time to teach her how to play chess. You started at that age, did you not? In chess, making any move, no matter how small, can have unintended consequences. Leaving now could be such a move, a dendrite of effects that cannot now be mapped."

Lali's statement was unusual: serious and to the point. In retrospect one might conclude that it was even prescient.

"It's about PaZ and MaY," Ty replied, impatiently. "I'd rather not wait. I can get her started on the game when I get back."

A few weeks after Nori's adoption, XoL had called Ty to apologize for her long silence. Her tone had been friendlier than Ty had anticipated, her words more heartfelt. She had wanted to know more about Nori, how she was doing, even laughing freely when Ty told her about their penguin walk. Before ending the call, XoL had offered to sign off on a mission to Serra Padre so Ty could visit the landslide where PaZ and MaY lay buried—"if it helps, and if it's not too soon for Nori," she had added to give him a clear out.

The call had buoyed him, XoL's offer swirling incessantly in his head for days after. He would accept it, of course, but more as an excuse to reconnect with her on a more intimate basis, alone. He envisioned a post-excursion meeting, possibly at a coffee shop or dining place far from headquarters where he could tell her in detail what he saw—perhaps more than that.

"Now is the right time to see where they rest, Lali," Ty continued as he stepped out of Nori's room. "She's happy now, in peace. We can close the book on this awful chapter, approach New Year for what it is: NEW," he added, putting the matter to rest.

Lali assented with a slow wink.

The next morning Nori ran to his bed to share her latest dream. Ty rolled her onto the bed and patiently heard about how she had found herself in a roomful of colorful feathers that twinkled and tickled, until she woke up. He then told her about his upcoming mission and her two-week return to Manaus. She jumped up and started hopping in bed like a jackrabbit. Lali added dancing carrots overhead and Nori reached for them, swatting a few clear across the room to disappear in midair.

After a special breakfast—blueberry yogurt with bakery-made currant scones, Nori's favorite—they cheerfully packed a small bag for her with her favorite outfits and stuffed animal "friends," just enough to see her through the short time she'd be at the care center. Then they took the long route through the park to Manaus. As they approached the facility, they saw the director standing by the gate, smiling widely. Caretakers were also out, cheering and clapping.

Ty picked Nori up and hugged her tightly. "Love you, Penguin," he said. Nori smiled back, wiggled herself to the ground and ran off. She stopped to hug the director, then rushed through the garden to the playroom. Ty watched her disappear behind a kiwi-laden arbor as he waved goodbye. He wondered how things might have played out for him if his parents had been terranauts instead of academics—if playing regularly in a lush garden would have also guided him to OCTAD, as had an unexpected and sweet kiss.

Pondering all the possibilities, he walked back through the park to catch a headquarters-bound peapod. Per protocol, he was required to meet with XoL for a final confirmation of the mission schedule and objectives before descending. He was mildly nervous about the meeting. Would the warmth she exhibited during the call carry over?

The peapod ride was uneventful. He arrived at the atrium shortly before midday and walked straight up the ramps to XoL's office. She was not there. "Went home early, but she left you a note," her assistant told him, pointing to the workstation area. He went down the hall to his station and found a sealed envelope on the desk. He ripped it open. The note was handwritten.

"Last minute change, *mi corazón...*"

Ty's heart jumped to his throat as he read on.

"We need to redefine your mission. Came directly from our dear Rector. She thinks that eyebrows will be raised if Osage, or God forbid, Sus Scrofa, learns of the mission objective—*her words!* I agree, so now you will be tracking a jaguar—not any jaguar but *the* jaguar, the one with MaY's implants. The burial site is within the animal's range. You may want to start looking for it west and north, then trek south and east to the site. Doesn't matter if you don't find it—I mean the jaguar; it's just an excuse. Love always, XoL."

The ulnar artery was pounding under his wristband. The endearing message compressed years of a lovingly beating heart into blinding urgency: get to Serra Padre and return as fast as possible to meet with XoL. Excitedly, he messaged CaL about his "new" mission. CaL failed to respond. *He must be enjoying an amorous interlude,* Ty grinned to himself. CaL had won the design competition for the upcoming Gala. Given all the help needed to set up the event, Ty could imagine CaL easily finding a partner with whom to take a break. He joyfully rushed out of the workstation area and ran down towards the Atrium.

"Whoa!—slow down, there!"

Manny, one of the Division guards, caught sight of the hurrying terranaut.

Ty gave him a glance but continued down the ramp, in near-leaping strides.

"Have to go, Manny," Ty said with a wide smile after as he reached the atrium, mimicking with extended arms and curled palms a jaguar's pounce. "Quick trip, be back in nine quick days!"

Manny shook his head, amused by Ty as always.

"Please walk the rest of the way," he said, "and be careful down there."

Few terranauts had genuinely befriended Manny as Ty had, and Ty knew the guard would give him a pass on minor violations of conduct, such as running through the building. One of Manny's duties was to review all scheduled descents and confirm departures. He already knew where Ty was going and could intuit XoL's intentions behind the assigned destination. Sage in his older years, Manny well suspected the feelings those two held for one another, despite a total absence of outward manifestations. With a smile, the guard watched Ty disappear down a ramp to the departure level.

The passage to Earth down the space elevator was a blur: getting suited and equipped, riding the hyper loop to the elevator station, meditating through the days-long descent, and riding a drone dirigible close to his destination—a blur that cleared intermittently only by flashes of the near future when XoL would greet him back with a warm smile and a welcoming hug. The thought enlivened Ty's twelve-mile trek from the drone's drop-off area to the center of the jaguar's presumed location. He covered the distance in a hover jog, skipping over rocks and tree roots with arcing strides. At the onset of darkness, he set a sleeping net on a high perch. He remembered PaZ's words: "There's just nothing better than falling asleep in a tropical breeze. Try it sometime; activate the insect repellent emitter, take your suit off, and see. Your skin will feel one with the air—a communion between man and nature!" Ty fell asleep before he could consider the tried-and-true proposition.

He awoke at dawn, packed up the sleeping net and returned to the ground, activating his bio-tracker. Soon the terrain became steeper and rugged: rock outcrops and fallen trees here and there, water channels and rivulets coursing through the ground like capillaries feeding the rising biomass.

The wall of a building was encountered an hour later, remnants of a former tropical research station. He entered the compound and marveled at nature's conquest. Only scattered pieces of corrugated and pockmarked planks remained, rusting on the ground. The roofs were long gone. Their absence left narrow skyward gaps into which pioneer vegetation was rising. Stucco walls, once proudly painted white, were teeming with vines; some had a moist algal sheen. A two-story section of wall stood distinctly apart. A portion of it was covered by a spreading strangler fig, its mesh of roots seeming to press on it like feeding tentacles. Holding on to a liana, Ty climbed over them to the top of the wall. Green iguanas perched on a nearby limb scurried away. A howler barked.

"*Panthera*," Ty voiced.

"Negative," responded the tracker.

Ty turned and repeated the request to ensure 360° coverage. The response was the same.

He pulled down his visor.

"Scan: 60 to 300 pounds," he said.

Nothing larger than a monkey appeared on the visor display. Ty dropped back down off the wall, popped a protein tablet, and left the compound. He continued uphill for another mile and a half before stopping to rest near a cluster of palms rising out of a large rock outcrop. Giant swordfern clung to the rock, drawing moisture from the cracks. Tree limbs cut in from all directions, appearing like lazy fingers poking blindly at each other. He conducted a location check: the landslide was fifteen miles to the southeast, just as XoL had said—a good day's march.

Ty sat on a boulder and mulled over whether to keep searching for the jaguar or head straight out to the burial site. A longhorn beetle was climbing the boulder by his side, its antennae testing his knife's sheath. Ty stared at it as the insect made its way up the rock. "The hell with the cat," he mumbled. Pushing forward he took a step, inadvertently swiping the beetle to the ground. He pondered whether to pick it up and set it back in its course. The tracker pinged.

"Report," he directed.

"Mammal. 168 pounds."

MaY's jaguar was a 275-pounder; this must be a pup, six months old, he concluded.

"260 meters, approaching," the tracker added.

Ty eschewed turning on his suit's mimetic function. The pup was too small to need to hide from, easy to put down if need be. He reached for his stun gun and waited.

An ordinary human in bygone days would have died right then and there, if not from the beast's clawing impact, from the terror of hearing its blood-curling roar. The pup's mother—MaY's cat—had eyed the blue-clad terranaut with heightened protective instincts as he entered her domain. Hidden from the bio-scanner by the limb on which she was perched, the jaguar had inched along until ready to pounce.

Ty's instincts, honed by hours of training for just such attacks, were equal to the task. Simultaneous with the roar he dropped to his knees, arms folded tightly and gun poking upward by the side of his head. The charge went off as the animal landed on him, stunned, flattening him beneath her. He tried to roll away, but one foot was stuck under the beast. He twisted and pulled it free. A claw had dug into the suit but failed to tear the fabric. As he rubbed the spot he saw the bio-tracker lying on the ground a few feet away. He crawled over and dusted it off, keeping a tight grip. Looking back, the size of the cat amazed him and he couldn't help but feel MaY's presence by its side. He wanted to stay there, sitting on the ground just staring at the feline, but remembered that a jaguar pup was still nearby. He again scanned his surroundings but nothing large was detected.

He stood, locked the stun gun by his side and got set to trek down to the landslide. He took a step and stopped cold.

Ahead, an upright figure was standing between two large boulders. Shrubbery obscured the lower body, above it was the naked torso of what in height and posture looked like a male human being. Ty remained still, as if hypnotized. His hand tightened around the tracker. He raised it slowly and aimed but the figure took off running before he could press the trigger. Ty rushed forward, bounding to the top of the boulder, aimed again and fired. A blip confirmed the hit. Leaping back down he raced after the figure, but his boots weighed him down. He stopped. He re-scanned the area with a narrower beam, but nothing weighing more than thirty-five pounds showed up. Ty was dumfounded. The figure—weighing at least 150 pounds, he estimated—had simply vanished just as suddenly as it had appeared.

An extant male Yanomami was the first thing that came to Ty's mind as he struggled to make sense of the apparition. Did he see the telltale mat of jet-black hair? He couldn't be sure; the figure was standing in front of a dark patch of forest. But the brown skin tone, the black eyes, the rounded muscular physique—it all fit the mold, he thought. During the Exodus, the Amazon basin was the most closely surveilled habitat on the planet. It took a decade before every native tribe member, from the Achaguas to the Yanomami—one hundred and four tribes in all—was evacuated. No living human being was left behind; that was a certainty.

Unable to arrive at an explanation, Ty marched downhill until he found a suitable clearing for a drone to find him and take him back to the El. He would have hours to wait, time to better run through his mind what had just happened and figure out what he would tell XoL. He rued having to admit that he failed to reach the landslide, that instead of tracking MaY's jaguar the beast tracked him, and that the only result of the mission was an encounter with a mysterious figure—a wight, a shadow. He would speak of none of that, at least not before letting CaL in on it.

"CaL, please," he voiced.

His dear friend was in the Great Ballroom preparing for the Gala.

"Ty? Are you at the site—did you make it there?" CaL asked eagerly.

Ty did not respond. He remembered that terranaut calls are randomly monitored. Someone could get hold of the conversation and report that he had ingested a hallucinogenic—a mission violation meriting dismissal from the Corps. He would have to meet CaL in person, he realized, at a place where they couldn't be seen or heard.

"Ty?"

"Hum, sorry, CaL. Just wanted to let you know that I'm cutting the mission short. I'll tell you about it at the Gala. Need to hurry right now," Ty said, terminating the call.

10

A PAINTED
YANOMAMI

For days Lali did its best to amuse Ty after his aborted mission, with little success. He had come almost straight home after his return, a rare occurrence. CaL had called several times, but Ty had not answered. He had rarely done that also. He had little appetite for food and stayed mostly in his room. He went out only to pick Nori up from Manaus but seemed to have no energy to play with her. Eventually he took her to the park, but for just a short walk. A pack of penguins speeding through jagged Antarctic bergs greeted them when they returned home. "The place is awful," Ty barked. Nori looked at him, puzzled, and Lali popped a question mark overhead.

"I mean the park, not your penguins," he said tersely. Bare of foliage, trees, and shrubbery, the park had been laced with festive lights and ornaments; a gaudy scene, to be sure, but Ty had never before complained about the winterized landscape.

Slumped on the sofa, Ty looked at the frothy underwater penguin scene, and got lost in his school days, recalling when the eighth-grade teacher had reenacted the pope's famous speech, standing on a table and wearing a white robe and loose wig. The moment had cemented in Ty's mind the power of stories, real or imagined—especially as compared to the wildlife holoscapes the rest of his family appeared to idolize. After school that day he had gone home envisioning the sermon emanating from another class of white-breasted animal, waddling all the way home and retelling the story in ridiculous penguin-speak. Trailing him by a few steps, XoL, PaZ, and CaL had laughed so hard as to nearly vomit. Years later Ty would rib PaZ that if not for his penguin mimicry, PaZ's fascination with the icy continent would never have materialized (short-lived as it was, after MaY bewitched him into tagging along for studies in tropical ecology). PaZ would look back at him and shake his head as if yet another of Ty's fantasies had let loose.

Nori had been standing in front of him, waiting to be acknowledged. She tugged on his sleeve.

"You will take me to Amazonia when I grow up—to see real trogons?"

Ty snapped out of his daydream.

"Huh … yes, absolutely … I mean, when you are a terranaut we'll go together," he told her. Lali disposed of the icy décor and filled the space with colorful tropical foliage. A pair of trogons were perched over Ty's head. He frowned disapprovingly. Lali returned the living room to a blank canvas but persisted in trying to improve his mood.

"Might you want to get ready for the Gala?" Lali asked. "It will be a spectacle, with interactive displays, music, games, and a very special guest. Will you bring back a souvenir, for Nori?"

Ty had gone to OCTAD's New Year Gala once before, prodded by PaZ and MaY as they tried to induct him into the lighter side of corporate life. He had been appalled by the revelry—the noise, the outlandish costumes, the boorish and rude behavior. His distaste surprised him. He and

CaL, after all, had grown up imagining fantastic places with odd beings. But having that enacted by real people, some on their worst behavior, was offensive. He had stayed home from the event ever since, preferring like most of the rest of the world to partake in the fanfare virtually, in the company of his parents. He was dismayed now at having to again suffer the extravaganza.

"CaL programmed the event, didn't he?" Lali kept on. "I know what's in store; Delon, CaL's veebot, told me, and I think you will approve. But better to experience it fresh, without the benefit of a preview, do you agree?"

Ty bolted from the sofa, nearly knocking Nori to the floor.

"I'm only going because of CaL, to see his work. You know how much I dislike the whole damn thing. NO MORE PRODDING—ALRIGHT?"

Nori had never seen Ty even mildly upset. Nor had Lali. The anxiety over what he had seen in Amazonia had steadily mounted, grating on his temperament. He had resolved to tell CaL about it at the Gala, where amid the noise, tumbling, and parade of lighting and kinetic effects, their conversation would hardly be noticed. And would Cal even believe him? As the time for the event neared, the question further churned inside him.

Lali shot an Embrace emoticon across the dining room. Ty got the message.

"I'm sorry, Lali; I'm just tired," he said by way of apology. He turned toward Nori and saw her pouting, tears ready to flow.

"Would you like to help me get dressed?" he asked her. Nori leapt to his open arms. Holding each other tightly they punched through the living area air screen and ambled to the dressing room. Ty set Nori standing on the vanity, their heights almost matching in front of the mirrored wall. He smiled at the disparity: his hairless scalp and Nori's full mat of black curls. "One day you, too, will lose your hair, unless you want to come back from the rainforest with a head full of munching spiders," he told her. Nori let out a playful cry as Ty wiggled his fingers spider-like over her head. "Open the drawer," he commanded Lali. A tray with small bowls of paint popped out—the ones he used when dressing up for festive occasions.

"What do you think?" Ty asked.

"Yoma ... mami? Is that the name, the people that lived in Amazonia, where you work?"

Ty was shaken. He had not yet been able to fathom the appearance of the man he had encountered. Now Nori had him thinking: Was it possible that somehow a few indigenous people had managed to escape detection and remained on Earth?

"Huh?"

"The YAMAMIS! What do you call them?" Nori said, refocusing Ty's attention.

"YA-NO-MA-MI. How did you guess? That's exactly what I had in mind!" he answered.

He took a step to the sink and washed his face, picked up a bowl of black paste from the tray and set it on the vanity. He dipped his left index finger and ran it across his face from ear lobe to ear lobe, crossing the ridge of his nose in a tight zigzag pattern. He repeated the linework, doubling the zigzag in the manner of a classic Yanomami ceremonial design. He cleaned his finger on a hand towel and dipped it again, this time in a bowl of red paste. Nori watched closely as he drew a wide downward arc across his forehead, followed by two smaller upward arcs below his lips. He went back to the black paste and pressed black dots throughout his face.

"They were amazing people, the Yanomami," he told Nori. "They lived with only what the forest gave them. Periodically they would move their homes to let the forest heal and regenerate. And for important occasions they painted their faces. When we next visit your grandmother, she'll tell you everything about them."

"Can I try?" Nori asked.

"You can surprise Karman when she gets here," he answered, heading to his bedroom and leaving Nori alone in front of the mirror.

He returned a few minutes later, sporting a tight-fitting gray suit and a flat, shiny jet-black wig, trimmed Yanomami-like just below the ear lobes. Nori let out a squawk. Ty matched her shriek in mock horror. Standing on the vanity Nori was now covered in colorful paste: face, arms, clothing— all reflecting from a streaked mirror.

"If you could chirp, you'd be a trogon!" Ty said.

"You look funny."

"CaL helped me with the suit. Would you like to see?"

Nori nodded. Ty pressed a small button underneath the neck fold and the digital fabric lit up. Seconds later the image of a river with slow moving waters appeared, shoulder-to-shoulder in width and running down his arms and legs to his knees. A flock of birds passed by chest high, dotting a bright, cloudless tropical sky. The scene shifted to a riverbank and its sandy shallows, then to the forest, penetrating the foliage and stopping at a small clearing where a ray of light shone upon a flowering shrub. The view zoomed in to a flower cluster. A fluttering hummingbird appeared, moving from flower to flower and then upward until stopping below Ty's Adam's apple, hovering in the manner of a bowtie.

"That's my hummingbird!" Nori cried in delight, stretching her black-and-red finger toward Ty's neck.

"Yes, it is!" he said, fluttering his fingers over her face, then gently poking her forehead.

"Your wig looks like an upside-down soup bowl! Did the Yanomami eat from them?" Lali asked.

Ty recognized Lali's all too transparent suggestion. "It's got to go, right?" Nori bobbed her head, grinning. Ty took off the wig and tossed it toward one of Lali's eyes. "I dare you to wear it next time you pop up and materialize!"

"Yes, yes—now Lali, please!" Nori cried.

"As a seahorse? Or should we stick with penguins?"

"As an oyster with a pearl!" Nori said excitedly.

"I would be very happy to do so, but not at this particular moment," Lali replied. "Karman is here."

Ty lifted Nori down to the floor and they strode out to meet CaL's younger sister. Karman cracked up at the sight of Nori and received her with a tight embrace, unconcerned about the washable paint. She had known Nori since birth, and as one of the park's holo-gardeners—a low demand but rewarding job—she had ample flexibility to care for Nori whenever needed.

A three-dimensional adaptation of Jacopo Bassano's sixteenth-century painting of animals entering Noah's ark filled the living area. In this version, produced by a renowned copyist, the animals are seen entering the ark in droves, but looking back contentedly as they leave a puzzled Noah and his family behind.

Ty shook his head.

"The pope's speech—you were thinking about it," Lali chimed into his ear.

"Please ignore the décor, Karman; Lali's aesthetics can be mystifying," Ty said. "You can fill the space with anything you like—maybe a seashore decorated with stars and shellfish, Nori would like that." The scene faded. After a brief exchange to update Karman about Nori's care, Ty put on travel boots and strapped on a thruster pack. Nori asked if he was going on a spacewalk.

"Yes, I am, but inside a big room—and I *will* bring you back a souvenir," he said, bending and squeezing her tight. Stepping out the door he confirmed with Karman his early dawn return in sign language. He closed the door and walked away, dreading the night to come.

PART II

11

THE GALA

The walk to the transit station softened Ty's mood. Under the simulated glow of a full moon, the park's landscape, despite the bleak seasonal treatment, reminded him of PaZ and the many times they played together there. They used to splash water on each other, skip over boulders, and roughhouse on leafy piles. Ahead he saw the towering *Dinizia excelsa*, the angelim tree they raced to climb, clinging precariously to the trunk's plastek holds and furrows. Ty cracked a smile, recalling PaZ's teen braggadocio about how one day he would descend to the planet like a valiant knight and conquer its inhospitable wilds: the oppressive atmosphere and suffocating heat; thundering rain that could render a lesser terranaut deaf; swarms of angry, biting insects; and sudden encounters with man-killing beasts, "that I will pacify with nothing more than a mean stare!" he would say. That PaZ ended up working in the very environment he often ridiculed for its daunting menaces used to amuse Ty, but now it saddened him.

Badly missing his brother, he followed the greensward to the station, admiring even at night its coiled path cutting through the pod like the sprouting trace of a giant auger. He thought about the odd privilege that terranauts have; that is, being able to immerse themselves in nature in the absolute raw, while the rest of the world did so via holographic simulacra devoid of surprise or peril—much like what people in the Old-World experienced in zoos, animal parks, and canned safaris. A young couple walked past him, waving hello. Ty did not see them.

At the transit station Ty located the departing peapod, so called for the cylindrical cabins with bubble berths that rolled pea-like in and out of docking ports. After entering the assigned berth, he stowed his thruster pack and slid into a cushioned seat. Indifferent to the craft's departing sequence, he turned on the synapse-relaxing emitter and got set to sleep all the way to the Gala. Three hours and 500 leagues later he was awakened by the ship's gentle deceleration. (The term "league" is archaic, to be sure, but it was Ty's fanciful preference, and Nori often heard him use it when referring to long radian distances). He reached for the seat's control panel and turned on the viewing screen. The ions lit up with a forward view of travel. Living pods were rushing by below the ship, their long cylindrical shapes lit brightly by the setting sun. A bevy of robots and a spacewalking crew were tending to one of them, like bees in a hive working in slow motion. A few miles later the distinct profile of OCTAD's main campus emerged: an oblate spheroid trailed by a long tube with spokes fanning out to several large tori. Ty wondered which torus might be Sus Scrofa's, which porthole she gazed out of while imagining all manner of malfeasance. He imagined hers would be Earth-facing.

Closer in, Ty saw other peapods approaching the spheroid's stem. Many others were docked, head in, giving the tube the appearance of a space-faring devil's walking stick. Minutes passed. The screen went black and the ship initiated docking maneuvers. A bump confirmed engagement of the airlock. Ty's bubble rolled out and stopped midpoint along the receiving dock. Ahead and behind, other bubbles popped open and people stepped off, streaming toward a long collector corridor, joking, laughing, shouting, and backslapping each other. Their strutting looked like a red-painted flipbook animation under the airlocks' flashing lights. Adding to the wildness was the headdress spectacle: plumes, animal masks, elaborate foliage displays, and towering flower arrangements, much of it kinetic.

Ty shook his head. He knew few of the revelers were aware of the Old-World's Parintins festival that once took place by the shores of the Amazon River, and how, over time, it gave rise to the present celebration's gaudy costuming. The ignorance compounded the urgency to move through the crowd as quickly as possible. Taking a deep breath, he plowed through, pushing and shoving, oblivious to the epithets and reproving stares aimed his way. Further ahead he ducked. Twentieth-century racing cars were shooting overhead. Lettered exhaust plumes identified each vehicle: 1913 Duesenberg, 1926 Miller Bugatti, 1955 Kurtis Belanger, 1988 Lola Monarch. Ty sensed CaL's design hand. He walked past an art deco timepiece counting the seconds to midnight: 55 minutes and 15 seconds … 14 … 13 … 12 …. Farther down the corridor he reached a wide transversal hall terminating in a broad glass panel. A mass of bodies blocked his way. He squeezed through to view the scene beyond. More people arrived, pushing, shoving, and pressing the first wave of arrivals against the glass.

"Stand back! Get your thrusters ready!" yelled an attendant.

The panel slid open and the partygoers streamed into the large ballroom like lemmings, joining hundreds of others bobbing every which way in the weightless space. Ty broke free from the tangle, located the ballroom's Earth-viewing oculus, and stabilized himself. Silvery confetti sparkled everywhere. A large analog clock slowly rotated in the center of the spheroid, marking the minutes and seconds to the New Year. Large circular screens were spinning in mid-air, changing attitude like flipped coins as spacewalkers bumped into them. He glanced at the screens and saw three-dimensional scenes of former earthly cities. He pinged CaL.

"You made it!" CaL responded. "I'm below the oculus; last-minute fine-tuning. Meet me by the clock in five minutes."

With small bursts of his thrusters Ty drew a meandering path towards the clock, dodging partyers. He passed several sound bubbles playing Old-World rock-and-roll. One of them assaulted him with shrill, pleading lyrics. The floating tag read "Mercedes Benz." Beyond, he saw leather-clad motorcyclists on gleaming Harleys poking bystanders with cottony lances, sending them crashing onto others with delirious laughter. Ty waited until the chaos abated and then kept going. Closer to the clock he spotted a Medusa-like knot of highways sprouting from the grill of a 1936 Ford Brewster stuck on someone's face. A grid of streets with primary-colored squares coursed through the person's suit. Ty got within earshot of CaL.

"Good thing I pinged, or I would have missed you!" he shouted. "Looks like you're trying to win the costume prize, too. What's with the Boogie-Woogie Gorgon?"

"Just a drive down Memory Lane, as the old saying goes," said CaL. "Nice suit, but the face paint? Is that all you could do? LAME! I could see you coming a mile away."

"I had a wig to go with it, but Nori and Lali thought better of it."

"How is Nori? She okay with my sister?"

"You know Nori, she's always cheery. Very happy to see Karman."

Ty paused, letting the silence reset the mood.

"You okay?" asked his friend.

Before Ty could answer, an approaching group bumped into them. Thrusters went off and bodies repositioned, heads facing each other. "Greetings! Didn't mean to crash," blurted a member of the group. The man recognized Ty.

"Linnaeus Te, right? We're from the Amazonia coastal group...were at the ceremony ...terribly sorry about your brother, the Corps will miss them. Great terranauts both."

"Thank you...freak accident," Ty offered glumly, his eyes fixed on the mass of Resplendent Quetzalcoatl feathers sprouting over the man's head. An awkward silence followed. Sensing the discomfort, another member of the group chimed in.

"Great work in Espirito Santo, Ty. The marmoset, you know, *Callithrix geoffroyi*, the white-headed one. That was a helluva recording. I gave a holo bead of it to my parents for their anniversary. It was pricey, but they loved it!"

Ty wished for the group to thrust away, but the plume-headed man persisted.

"Meet DaeL," the man said, putting his arm around one of his companions. "She's in training in the Brazilian barrier reef division. Just came back from Tamandaré, not far from your marmosets. Maybe the two of you can work together someday," he added, with an insinuating wink.

Ty ignored the comment while staring at the red lionfish pressed onto the woman's face, its striped fins extending far out from her cheeks and swaying as if underwater.

"I've been working in the north lately, close to the Serra Padre mountains," Ty offered. "The marmoset was a sidebar, something our new manager was interested in, a one-off mission."

"Xochitl de Luna—I met her during my training. She's hard-core—great mentor. Is she here?" the woman asked, tentacles twitching with every syllable.

Ty's mind was set adrift by the mention.

"I don't know... just got here myself," he replied, knowing full well that XoL never attended the event. He nodded toward CaL. "The Medusa here is responsible for tonight's atmospherics. He's Amazonia's chief Atmo; won the Gala Design competition," Ty said, seeking to change the subject. CaL's attention was fixed on another member of the group, a young man sporting a moray eel flowing digitally from the chest down to his crotch. Ty dug his fingers into CaL's arm, bringing him back into the conversation.

"Huh, yes, guilty as charged," CaL said. "Hope you find all the sound bubbles and take a stab at guessing the recording artists. Big raffle prize at stake."

"Had I known the theme I would have worn a helmet and a racing suit with loud advertising patches!" joked another member of the group. "But congratulations, CaL! Enjoy the trip to Earth. Isn't that the design contest's winning prize?"

The visitors floated away ahead of an approaching spinning wheel. CaL reached for the wheel's bumper and stopped the rotation. "This is one of the better ones," he said, after voicing the screen's reset command. Ty moved back to gain a full view. A vibrant nighttime panorama of New York City's Times Square emerged, but the glitter did not last long. At daybreak, the ubiquity of lights, animated signs, crowded sidewalks, and honking traffic faded, rendering the once-dazzling square lifeless. Trash swirled about, as did a handful of pigeons and stray dogs. Men in military garb donning wide-brimmed helmets and breathing masks entered the space and took position behind armored tractors. Leading the phalanx was a tank-like vehicle with a high-powered sonic gun mounted on a clear turret. A white–haired Asian man, binoculars pressed to his face, surveyed the scene from within.

A flare arched skyward. The military personnel crouched under body-sized shields. An ear-splitting frequency was emitted from the turret gun, slowly shifting direction until it covered the entirety of the space. Building windows and screens shattered. Shards of glass rained down and exploded on impact, adding to the deafening din. It lasted minutes. The chaos stopped and a second flare shot up, signaling the personnel to advance and methodically break down doors, hatches, grillwork, and leftover standing glass. The tractors moved in and ground up the roadway and sidewalks with churning spades, turning paving and utility ducts into rubble. A cloud of dust engulfed the place, penetrating deep into building openings. A fast-forward time-lapse sequence ensued. The air became clean and clear. A patina of moss and lichen emerged over the walls and ledges. Grasses and shrubs sprouted from cracks and bare patches of soil. Trees shot skyward out of wall openings and rooftops. Blackbirds rushed across a clear October sky and hawk nests dotted antennae and other high perches. Times Square was soon unrecognizable, having in the span of 40 years become a multi-story temperate forest, complete with a beaver-dammed stream coursing over what used to be Broadway.

CaL looked at Ty with mock contempt.

"We've known each other practically our whole lives," he said. "Not once have you mentioned your ALL-IMPORTANT ANCESTOR. So please allow me to spell it out: you are a turkey—a *Meleagris gallopavo*! If I hadn't gone into the archives to research the content of the video, I would have never met your great, great, great, or whatever grandfather he is of yours—DOCTOR TE, the man in the turret!"

Growing impatient, Ty grabbed CaL by the shoulders and turned him away from the screen. "I'm sorry, but we've got to talk."

"We ARE talking."

"I mean not here … in a quieter place." Ty pointed to a porthole at the far end of the ballroom opposite the Earth oculus. He powered his thrusters and dragged CaL along, holding him by the arm. On the way they passed other floating screens. London's Parliament House, the Louvre, Tiananmen Square, and the National Mall in Washington—all transforming into rewilded landscapes. Ty glanced at them with little interest.

"Is it about XoL?" CaL asked.

Ty did not answer.

"What's going on?" CaL insisted as they approached the porthole. Confetti was everywhere, mixing with the view through the glass of a moon waxing as if attracting a galaxy of fireflies. Ty flailed his arms, annoyed at the swirling specs.

"Remember I told you that I had to cut short my last mission? That I was tired?" Ty said, softly, leaning into CaL.

"Is everything okay?"

"Not sure. I mean, yes. I was fine during the mission; I just had to return in a hurry, to the lab."

"Why are you whispering?"

"Can't chance someone overhearing. As I told you, I went down to track a jaguar, not the red howler I brought back. I mean, I faked it: I recomposed the DNA, blurred the video."

"YOU DID WHAT?"

CaL's shout was lost amid the ballroom din.

"I had to! I manipulated the chromosomes," Ty said in a hush.

"Do you know the trouble you can get into? They can shut you down, THROW YOU OUT OF THE CORPS!"

Ty pressed CaL's arm to shush him. "I know, I know! Just listen for a moment." He paused to compose himself. "It was close to midday on day two. I'd decided to forego tracking the jaguar and head straight to the landslide when it jumped me. I crouched and stunned it. It didn't do any damage; not a scratch, fortunately. But it scared the crap out of me. I was set to go, just standing there catching my breath, when IT appeared, out of nowhere."

"IT? You mean MaY's cat?"

Ty stopped talking, looking around to make sure no one else was within earshot. CaL was confused. Prior buffoonery aside, not once had he ever witnessed from Ty such a ridiculous act of spy-like paranoia.

"What is IT? A giant sloth? The Mapinguary? What the hell are you talking about?" CaL squeezed Ty's arm for an answer.

"A man…" Ty replied. "Brown-skinned, black eyes…almost naked."

CaL deactivated his suit's Gorgon digital flow, as if to direct all electrical impulses to his own brain.

"Is this a bad joke? You drag me here to tell me you saw a naked, two-legged primate on the surface of the fucking planet? Surely you are aware that the place is full of monkeys."

"CaL, it WAS a man!" Ty's voice was raised but quickly returned to a whisper. "Look, no animal in Amazonia approaches the upright size of an adult human being. He took off running, but I zapped him. I went after him, but he was fast. Then he vanished; got swallowed by the forest, no tracking ping, no visor detection."

"AND?"

Ty paused to catch his breath.

"I gave up. But I had the scan. That's why I came back right away; I had to confirm the DNA...in the lab. It was a true reading. A male human being. That's why I manipulated the chromosomes: to make them match a howler instead, so no one would ask."

CaL stared at Ty searchingly, expecting him to suddenly crack a roaring smile and end this stupid game. But Ty remained still, his look betraying nothing but confounding seriousness.

"We've known each other for a long time, and you know I think the world of you," CaL said. "You are among the best in the business, may PaZ and MaY rest in peace. But Ty, this is just nonsense. No one other than a clean-cut, suited terranaut like you has set foot in Amazonia in fifty years!"

"Fifty-two."

"Alright, fifty-two it is! But what would a man, a free-roaming human being, be doing on Earth, in the middle of Amazonia, prey to deadly animals—sorry to be blunt about it—but ALONE AND FUCKING NAKED?"

Ty withheld an answer. Steeped in silence, they took turns looking out the porthole to the glowing moon. A nearby hoot yanked them back into the revelry. Only seconds remained to midnight. Powering their thrusters, they headed back toward the clock. A crowd is gathered around it.

"I don't know, but we sure as hell are going to find out," Ty finally yelled to CaL amid the commotion.

"WE?" CaL shouts back with genuine incredulity. "Is that what you just said?"

"Three ... Two ... One"

The crowd erupted. "HAPPY NEW YEAR!" Air-cannons blasted new confetti in every direction, some popping into birds of the Serengeti—starlings, gonoleks, fiscals, barbets, and African fish eagles—trailed by pixie dust as they flew around. From the spinning screens emerged embodied holographs of once-prized zoo animals: lions, cheetahs, impalas, ostriches, and zebras. Oohs and aahs erupted. There was a scramble to mount and ride the bucking beasts. The lights dimmed and the crowd settled. The clock rotated horizontally relative to the long axis of the ballroom and turned into a platform. As if prodded by an invisible emcee, the crowd repositioned itself vertically with respect to this new dais. A ceiling hatch opened and a figure emerged, descending slowly. People gasped. Spotlights were shining on the figure's already iridescent gown.

"Xu! It's Xu!" someone shouted. Others follow, until the shouts become a rhythmic chant.

"Xu! Xu! Xu! Xu!"

The descent continued until the Great Mysothophist, the head of the world's governing Tetrad, landed on the platform. It is rare for the man to make an appearance anywhere outside the Prism—the world's only angular orbital pod—from where he makes his oracle-like pronouncements. Silence engulfed the ballroom. After a calculated pause the man raised his arms and began to utter The Riddle of the New Year. The monotone was deliberate.

> Guide us, moonlit dreams
> Past mirrored peas and floating strings
> To the cursive pulse and filtered sight
> Still
> Against the field of whittled stones
> –Seeds of wanting souls
> delivering the Thunder's cry
> Anew.

Crackling bolts of lightning shot out of Xu's robe. A loud roar ensued as the revered ruler rose, reentered the hatch, and disappeared. The ballroom lights brightened. CaL moved close to Ty and shouted into his ear. "Have you told XoL?" Ty did not answer, signaling instead they should get the hell out of there. CaL followed him to the exit, still unable to make any sense of what Ty had shared.

"You DO look tired," CaL said as they approached the entry glass panel. "Ask XoL to extend your break, spend more time with Nori ... you know she'd give you that without asking why ... she fucking LOVES YOU!"

Ty failed to hear CaL's last words. Next to the glass door were baskets with miniature video wheels for people to take home. Ty picked one up for Nori.

12

ABOUT SHARKS
AND A MUSTACHE

Nine days have passed since Nori began to work on the project with Lali. It has become an obsession. She has spent hours ensconced in her den, sleeping little, and eating even less while sifting through the details of Ty's tale. Forgotten memories of her childhood have come alive; it's as if she were transported back in time. Still, much more remains for Lali to unearth and reenact.

On the tenth day Nori awakes from a bizarre dream. She had seen herself seated at a large dinner table surrounded by older men and women, all clad in gaudy costumes and smiling at her as if she were a familiar presence. Prairie flowers, wild clover, wild corn, and alfalfa filled colorful and finely crafted pottery set on the table. Crystalline water gushed from the ceiling into a large glass bowl, filling it continuously but never spilling. A miniature fish swam inside. The chatter was loud but unintelligible. Someone called for quiet. A loud collective and sustained shush emerged, becoming louder like air being forced through a narrow pipe.

As she turns the dream over in her mind, it strikes her: the people at the table are her ancestors, precursor environmentalists being silenced by the aural presence of "Uncle Shh," the unwitting patriarch who first passed on to the family the urge to go out and save the world. His story—all their stories—must be told, she concludes.

Pleased by the realization, Nori dons her robe and struts to the den with a hastily prepared bowl of fruits and nuts. Alto cumulus appears on the wall behind the desk.

"Would you like something else to eat? Something warm? A bowl of oatmeal?" Lali asks.

Nori does not respond. She is intent on threading the past into the events of the relative present.

"We've talked about Morena, but she was from Mother's side. Father's side also has a few luminaries. I'm talking about Grandfather, and Father's great grandfather, and even *his* father before that."

Lali winks.

"And I want to include something about the pope, Francisca," Nori continues. People still regard the day she spoke from Saint Peter's Square about 'rising to the heavens' as the day humanity looked skyward and saw its orbital destiny. Do you remember what Grandfather Te used to say about that? He huffed and puffed, is what I remember."

Nori was nine when her paternal grandparents opted to die. She loved Airi. He would tell her stories about the Old-World and the many interesting characters and events he knew so much about. Feigning exasperation, clasping his head, Airi would lament how history seemed to lose its way, like a book where whole chapters are skipped, go missing, or are entirely and wrongly re-written. When and how humanity looked to the heavens to save the planet was to him a point of fact that had become misconstrued. He was repeatedly compelled to correct the record for his students, and anyone else who would listen.

"I wish he were still here," Nori says. "Can you bring him up—have him say it?"

Lali materializes Airi Mendes Te, life-size, in the middle of the den. The holographic recording was made when the man was approaching his seventieth birthday, at his own insistence.

Nori smiles at her grandfather's attire: his ubiquitous blue blazer, patterned shirt, and squared tie fitted loosely over a pair of dark blue khakis.

"Well, well, my dear Nori, how old are you now? Never mind; that is an improper question," he says with a playful squint. "Lali tells me you want to learn about the pope's words, what she said at Saint Peter's Square that day and how people followed her call. Well, NONSENSE! People were not inspired by her 'rise to the heavens' remarks; whoever believes that, well, let's just say that is the product of a lazy mind. I do hope your dear father and mother have seen fit to tell you how I much abhor lazy minds. But do not worry: I know that yours is inquisitive and highly exercised."

Nori is amused by Lali's effort to have her grandfather deliver a loving remark.

"Now," Airi continues, "the event by which people began to envision an alternate space-like place in which to live did not occur in the year 134, when the pope spoke, but decades earlier, on September 23rd in the year 1962 of the Old Calendar, when the utopian animated program called *The Jetsons* first aired on television. The Jetson family lived in elevated homes suspended in midair, travelled in flying vehicles, and were served by robots—mechanical contraptions, mind you. And people loved it. They loved imagining a self-sufficient world filled with advanced technology. That is how space habitation was first seeded into the human mind."

He scowls.

"But lazy minds miss this too: 1962 was also the year when world leaders deliberated over the establishment of an international trade agreement to protect endangered species, which a year later was formalized as the Convention on International Trade in Endangered Species of Wild Fauna and Flora. Quite the conjunction, isn't it? I call it The Great Convergence: the first time in humanity's eons of history when an effort to care for the natural environment paralleled a vision, fanciful as it was at the time, of everyday human life unfolding in outer space. And look at our world today: all the technology, all the wildlife that abounds, fused together and holding up the world like a temple keystone. Coincidence, Conjunction, Convention, Convergence; quite a few cons, but it can't be helped, I'm afraid." He smiles again. "See you again soon, my dear Nori."

The materialization dissolves.

"Thank you, Lali," Nori says, tears flowing. "Why he and Grandmama went so early I will never understand."

Nori's grandparents were crushed by the death of their son and his wife; they struggled to accept the irreversible loss of their remains. Although most parents would deny they love one child more than another, it is natural to favor certain traits in one of two siblings. Both Airi and Midane had tended to feel closer to PaZ than to his younger brother. His environmentalist vocation resonated with theirs, as did his reserved and studious nature. After his tragic death they lived with near-unbearable pain until becoming age-eligible to terminate their lives. A scant month after they turned 70 years old they did so, bequeathing their ashes to their coop's food-growing media. This was their way to amend for PaZ's bodily absence, passing into eternity in the noblest way possible. They did not tell Ty of their decision to self-terminate, wishing to avoid a fruitless argument. They believed that he would not miss them as much as PaZ would have, and also that he would understand and honor their motivation. But after it happened, Ty was deeply upset. He blamed himself, pained for not having gone to the landslide and given them a vivid recording of the site where PaZ and MaY's bodies lay buried. He convinced himself that had he done so, it would have given his parents a reason to live long enough to watch Nori grow and fulfill PaZ and MaY's dream for her. The anguish further sapped any desire to share the ordeal he suffered trying to avenge PaZ's death. As he would insist with CaL and much later with Nori, "Justice was done and that is all that matters."

"And what about Hai Te," Nori continues. "The one everyone called Uncle Shh? Grandfather Airi called him a hero—a crazy hero. People should know that the man was a renowned marine biologist that saved sharks from the abyss, and that his son, the man in the turret Ty saw in the spinning wheel at the Gala, unquestionably determined the post-Exodus fate of Earth's landscape. I am sure that Osage didn't at all see fit to share that with the OCTAD Admission Board," she says, speaking to the wall behind the desk as if the clouds could hear and transmit the message directly to the man.

Lali keeps her from stewing on useless theorizing by filling the den with fathomless holographic hues of cobalt blue. A dot appears, slowly revealing itself as a prehistoric creature, gently cutting through the ocean water like a deity taking stock of its kingdom. A group of pilot fish tracks the whitetip shark, *Carcharhinus longimanus*. Two of the pilot fish come into close view before morphing into a Fu Manchu-styled mustache, complete with dyed stripes, now dangling down Hai Te's face.

Lali retrieves the files on the man and Nori completes the salient points of his colorful life:

That he was a doctor in marine biology, and that his colleagues at the University of Shanghai believed his passion for the Ordovician creature had become an obsession to the point of madness.

That he seldom talked outside of the classroom and had the knee-jerk habit of shushing anyone who approached him, lest they break a state of sustained meditation—hence his nickname.

That he was so upset by the illegal trade of the fish's prized fins that he quit teaching and mounted a one-man campaign to expose the perpetrators, disguising himself alternately as a buyer and as a supplier of the sought-after delicacy, working on fishing vessels one month and as a busman at a high-end restaurant the next, surreptitiously recording the illegal trade.

That by virtue of his ability to concentrate (or because of a probable rupture in his pain receptors), he was oblivious to the pummeling he received whenever he was discovered, which became progressively more frequent owing to his distinctive, foot-long mustache.

That, despite the abuse, he succeeded in halting the ghastly killings, gaining world recognition for saving the species as well as many other species of sharks.

That he never married, but when well into his fifties he met a woman who admired his work, a young waitress employed at a well-known eatery in Shanghai's Huangpu historic district to support her own studies in marine biology. She recognized him when he entered the restaurant and ordered a serving of illicit shark fin soup, only to find out that the establishment served none. Nonetheless he stayed to help himself to a proper meal. Through smiles and gestures he came to understand the woman's fondness for him, refraining from shushing when she offered a few, halting words about herself. He then followed her to her modest apartment and eased into her affection when she caressed his face as if his mustache were as natural a feature as his long, pointed nose.

That Hai Te died a few months later while absent-mindedly crossing a busy street, never having heard the approaching motorcycle—or knowing that he had fathered a much-celebrated son who, late in his life, would lock horns with SuS Scrofa's progenitor over what the Earth should look like after humanity abandoned it.

Generations later CaL would affectionately call one of Hai Te's descendants a *turkey* for seemingly ignoring his family's extraordinary environmental heritage.

A "RICHER COMPOSITION"

It remains ironic to my kind that in the face of ALFIE's revelation the ensuing global reaction was likened to a "War of the Worlds" involving aliens. In a 180° turn from the age-old cinematic fantasy, the "alien" assignation was cast upon the large majority of the population who were prepared to evolve into a spacefaring race—*Homo spaciens*—and save the planet from those hell-bent on staying put and continuing to exploit it. History shows that the tide of reason, favoring the Exodus, overwhelmed the opposition. Over time its adherents dwindled, becoming scattered factions of merely bothersome fanatics—the PEA Resistance.

An important milestone in the struggle between reason and fanaticism occurred in New York City on a chilly fall equinox when the newly formed governing Tetrad, headed by the Secretary of Trade and Commerce, Egon Pinoche, sent the police to disband the PEA protesters that had gathered at Gantry Plaza State Park across the East River from the United Nations.

The four-member body had convened to hear testimony from the two individuals who would help determine the fate of the world's cities. Adherents to the PEA resistance habitually shadowed the Tetrad's meetings, usually creating some kind of disturbance; on this day the Tetrad was in no mood for unruly behavior. Order at the park was quickly restored, but not before dozens of protesters tied themselves with heavy chains and jumped into the river's dark waters, adding to the millions who had already opted to die on Earth before being forced to live in orbit.

For the hearing only the four secretaries-general, a handful of staffers, camera operators, production crew, and the two distinguished guests—a decorated United Nations Army general and a renowned professor of ecology—were present inside the classic modernist building. The UN Assembly Hall was otherwise empty, as was the rest of Manhattan outside the few secured blocks surrounding the compound.

Facing global unrest, world governments had little choice but to align themselves with a coherent and effective response, leading ultimately to a consolidation of power under the aegis of the United Nations. But it took old-fashioned political muscle, as it were, to make it happen. Leading nations China, Russia, India, and the United States threw their sizable combined military and economic weight into the plan and forced every other nation to accept a four-headed form of governance. Claiming a longer-standing commitment to an ecological economy, China's president, Liu Wenming, assumed the role of Secretary of the Environment and was charged with coordinating the Global Rewilding Initiative—the reversion of the Earth's landscape to a natural state. His country having been first in space, the Russian president, Yuri Morozov, demanded that in exchange for dismantling the Union—again—they be given the task of planning and managing the exodus into orbit, and that he be given the title of New World Secretary. Owing to its ageless culture, India's prime minister, Amrita Singh, earned the title of Secretary of the Narrative, with primary responsibility for the transfer into orbit of humanity's earthly legacy of fiction, myth, and lore. By default, but also in recognition of social capitalism as a world-guiding economic system, the United States' representative, Egon Pinoche, was assigned the post of Secretary of Trade and Commerce, to include matters of law and order.

Hastily established as protocol, each member of the nascent Tetrad took turns in presiding over televised testimonies. Assuming an air of grandeur, Secretary Pinoche was last to sit in front of the tabernacle-like table facing the hall's empty and frayed chairs. Although small in stature, the man nonetheless had a disquieting presence, if for no other circumstance than the large sunglasses he wore to hide the spasms of rapid blinking he was prone to suffer. Of an impatient nature, he was also prone to fidget, and on this occasion his finger tapping irked his more sedate colleagues.

Five seconds before airtime, the Secretary cleared his throat and tilted his head toward the teleprompter.

"Distinguished General and Professor," he began.

In front of him, seated close together at a cloth-covered folding table, were Cincinnatus Blackburn, a five-star general of the World United Armies, and Zedong Mendes Te, the renowned ecologist from the University of Shanghai and father of the science of urban abandonment.

"Fifty years to the day have passed since evidence came to light of this planet's place in the universe as sole repository of ..." the Secretary paused to gather a measure of gravity, "... self-reproducing metabolic organisms genetically predisposed to natural selection. This body was created to guard this precious wonder forevermore: by building a new world aloft, and in so doing return the planet to a state of unimpeded wildness. The Exodus Economy is driving employment and human well-being to unprecedented levels, and this will continue for generations after the last human leaves the biosphere. We are well on our way toward building a new world, but standing as a monument to our ignorant past is the very building we are in and the city that spreads around it—as is the case with every other building in every other city on Earth. This urban scourge will be cleansed. The questions before us are these: How should nature be invited into our abandoned cities? Under what method and at what rate are we to effectively, and for all time, erase humanity's most glaring trace from the surface of this blessed planet?"

The Secretary's eyelids began to twitch. Pointing a finger, he directed the Secretary of the Environment to continue. Slighted by the omission, New World Secretary Morozov, an imperious man from Vladivostok, yawned widely and leaned back in his chair, feigning utter disinterest in the coming testimony. "Go ahead," he said, as if trying to trip up his Chinese colleague.

"General Blackburn—Cincinnatus, if I may," the young woman, Liu Wenming, began.

The general stiffened on his chair. The professor leaned back and closed his eyes.

"You have devoted your illustrious career to the demolition of civic infrastructure," Secretary Wenming continued, her speech tinged with a Mandarin accent. "The world owes you gratitude for the efficacy with which you have carried forth your charge. But nothing will signify our resolve better than to erase all evidence of humanity's false progress. Forests are denuded, shorelines hardened, wildlife displaced, and natural water flows disrupted as our cities over time spread across the globe like a cancer. Over this land nature shall return. We have sworn to deliver to our new world aloft the Earth's rewilding in full and vivid detail. We have chartered a new corporation to fulfill this oath, and we are certain that in the future there will be legions of Earth-bound astronauts—terranauts—who will soldier in the revitalized wilds of the Earth to do so. We ask that you freely offer your views on the matter, General. Fear not the cameras; your testimony is being shared publicly and recorded solely for the sake of The Story, for the Secretary of the Narrative to place the argument within the layers of the abstract bedrock out of which springs, like the muses of old, humanity's quest for artful meaning and hope."

The reference to art hit the general like a lobbed grenade. He twisted uncomfortably in his chair, mumbling that there was nothing abstract about fucking rocks. The Secretary of the Narrative leveled a searing look at him. His twitch under control, Secretary Pinoche again cleared his throat and resumed command. The professor momentarily opened his eyes, then returned to a meditative state.

"Please continue, General," directed Secretary Pinoche.

General Cincinnatus Blackburn had grown up in Rome, Iowa, a town of one hundred twenty people in the middle of mid-western American farmland. His parents were fourth-generation pig farmers who had raised their twin boys to become as much, with the character and moral fiber that comes from fear-inducing Sunday sermons paired with homespun accounts of virtuous rulers. Over time they had built a pantheon of heroes by which to contrast the crookedness and corruption that in their minds governed the world.

None occupied a higher perch than Lucius Quinctius Cincinnatus, the Roman nobleman and farmer who, when pressed by his peers to defend the Republic, had become their governor, only to abdicate his seat and return to his farm after vanquishing the looting hordes. That Cincinnatus had done so in 460 BC, their parents would tell the boys time-and-again, was a sure sign that God's hand had always touched those who heeded the call of duty without concerns for personal gain, a trait only to be gained by the noble toil of farming.

Young Cin, as was the future general's unfortunate nickname, had deeply absorbed this message and had grown to feel the call to greatness. Tragically, in the middle of a powerful storm during their annual 450-mile drive to the city bearing his name, a tornado rapidly formed and engulfed the family van, lifting and rolling the vehicle over downed power lines. His parents were killed instantly, and he and his brother Marcellus were badly injured. Following their convalescence and with nowhere to go, the teenagers enrolled in the Reserve Officers' Training Corps, a pipeline to the UN's expanding consolidation of world militaries.

Marcellus Blackburn loved hard work, but on his own terms. Unable to cope with the ROTC's strict codes of conduct and rigid schedules, he quit one day, leaving in the middle of the night without saying a word to his brother or anyone else. Years later Cincinnatus learned that his brother had gone into space to work on the construction of orbital pods. Nothing could have upset Cin more. There was virtue in tilling the land and producing goods from it; none from creating artificial environments that, like cities, were sure to become rife with immoral and ill-willing souls. That, after all, was the purpose of the family's annual trip to Cincinnati: to remind themselves of such blight, plainly embodied on the banks of the Ohio River by the pair of winged pigs appearing to be defecating atop bastardized classical columns, which the crazed locals celebrated as public art.

After graduating from ROTC, Cin had entered a military demolition brigade and there he found a new calling, wrapped in vengeful fervor: to blow up dams, canals, levees, bulkheads, piers, highways, bridges, power plants, transmission lines, and any other lifeline to urban life. And he excelled at it, gaining promotion after promotion, in time earning admission into the ranks of starred UN generals. Early on he was called to diffuse a crisis in Hong Kong. A group of rebels armed with explosives had taken refuge in the Nina Tower, threatening to blow it up if the police did not release a group of detained fellow PEA resisters. Cincinnatus despised anarchy. "Fuck 'em. Let them blow it up," the general said to his lieutenant, historic images of the 9/11 attack on New York City's Twin Towers coursing through his mind. The bluff worked and the rebels turned themselves in without destroying the Nina Tower, but their plan had triggered in Cincinnatus the epiphany he would obsess about the rest of his living days: If towers could so readily be brought down, why not an entire city, all at once? Why not at the push of a button turn tens of square miles of architectural excrement into flatland more akin to farmland?

Now, seated next to him was a professor, a member of the erudite class who had never built or destroyed anything. It riled Cincinnatus to have to defend the genius of his idea in front of such a man. He looked at the professor and leveled a contemptuous smirk, followed by an inaudible insult. Turning toward the Tetrad, the general tugged his uniform sleeves down and placed his arms square on the table, sitting tall, as at attention.

"Madam and Misters Secretary," he said. "I am honored and real pleased to have the opportunity to speak to you about something about which I am an expert. You are faced here with a real choice: leave cities intact, as the academic here would have you believe makes any sense, or erase them completely from the face of the Earth—and I mean completely, not a trace left behind. We have the material and manpower to accomplish this, efficiently and in record time. We can mobilize immediately, as soon as you give me the order. Just tell me where to start. The day after a city is vacated it will be done, all buildings turned to dust. You can one hundred percent be sure of that."

The New World Secretary abruptly reengaged, his voice stirring the professor to straighten in his chair and actually open his eyes.

"General," Secretary Morozov stated, "across the globe there are over four hundred cities housing thousands of buildings. Moscow alone has over eighty thousand. You have expressed yourself on this matter before, but it's hard to imagine how this can be done as you say. How exactly do you propose to do away with whole cities—make them all completely disappear—in as short a time as you suggest?"

"In seconds, Mister Secretary; through nuclear fission—underground detonations," responded the general without adding another word.

An awkward silence followed as neither the general nor the secretary was certain about whose turn it was to speak.

"General?" prompted Secretary Pinoche finally.

Believing he had already said everything that needed to be said, Cincinnatus reluctantly continued.

"Well, there are approximately fifteen thousand nuclear warheads in the world, Mr. Secretary, and there are stockpiles of uranium and pluto-nium to manufacture five thousand more. Depending on the mass of the fissionable material and the depth at which it is placed, an underground detonation can create a very large subsidence crater. By my estimate, it would take five detonations below Manhattan to implode the entire island and all sixty thousand buildings on it, in seconds as I say, without any radioactive emissions or toxic aftereffects." He paused to let them do the math. "Twenty thousand warheads would be enough to reduce every major city into rubble. This, in my humble opinion, is the most efficient way to remove the urban scab from Earth—a method, I must add, that simultaneously disposes of the world's fissionable material."

The general paused, remaining in a pose of attention. The secretaries looked at each other, perplexed as to whether the general intended to add further calculation.

"Please go on, general," said Secretary Pinoche.

"That is all, Sir. I await your orders."

Satisfied with what he considered to be a foolproof argument, Cincinnatus leaned back and crossed his hands over his lap.

The professor calmly leaned forward.

Growing up in Shanghai during China's Golden Age of the Environment, Zedong Mendes Te had been steeped from an early age in the Zen-like virtue of letting time take its course and allow the natural cycles of death and rebirth to establish the order of things. It was not any form of government indoctrination that gave him such a measure for life, nor his mother Pearl; she had spent much time away from home advancing Hai Te's other subject of research, the "alien" intelligence ascribed to the Giant Pacific Octopus. One might conclude his inclination in that regard was inherited through DNA from Hai Te, the father he was never to know. But most probably it was the daily visits he made, as a ritual, to a large constructed wetland park nearby, where he would wade into its reed-filtered waters and stroll along its miles of boardwalks to watch the waterfowl. He spent hours there absorbing the slow progress of regeneration. Ecology soon became his principal interest—"the study of nature's hypothalamus," as his high school science teacher used to call the discipline.

Following his college education, Zedong went into a doctorate program on urban ecology. As fate would have it, ALFIE's leak occurred the day after his dissertation was submitted. He slept through the news and learned of the fateful disclosure from a neighbor the next day while heading out to buy groceries. Zedong shrugged, dismissing the story as a fabrication by irresponsible social media attention-seekers. The reality hit home two days later when he called his PhD advisor to confirm the timeline of his dissertation defense. There was total chaos at the university, the advisor said, adding that all teaching was suspended until further notice. A week later the woman called to offer sincere regrets about having to cancel his defense. Academic funding stopped, and Zedong's doctoral degree was placed in limbo.

Needing money to support himself, Zedong took a job at an old apartment complex as a night watchman. Amid the relative quietude he pondered long and hard what ALFIE's revelation meant to him and the rest of humanity. Oblivious to the commotion and social unrest, he began to write articles about the behavior of animal species in hypothetically abandoned cities: which would thrive, which would not, and how the balance would affect the ecology of adjoining natural areas, such as his childhood park. To fend off certain ridicule he used a pseudonym—Xicoh Mendes, in honor of the Brazilian environmentalist who a century earlier (113 years, to be exact) had been slain while fighting powerful cattle barons intent on clear-cutting the rainforest.

Finding no publishers, Zedong mailed his essays to the Ministry of Ecology and the Environment in Beijing, a more secure place to have them filed than the university, he thought. Two months later and much to his surprise he received a summons to appear before the minister and other environment officials. In a modest meeting room deep inside the ministry, he was asked how, and for how long, he had known of his government's incipient plan to excise humanity from the planet. Zedong professed no such knowledge, but offered his approval, explaining that there is "elemental beauty in nature's colonizing logic, especially if humanity can keep a watchful eye from afar and record it for all time." At the conclusion of the brief meeting he was told to return to Shanghai and report there to the newly created Office of Bio Divergence.

Three months later, working after hours, he submitted a proposal for the abandonment of the city of Dujiangyan and all the villages along the Shaotong River to the Wolong National Nature Reserve, including the reserve's sprawling visitor center. Zedong had convinced himself that such abandonment would rapidly change the mountain ecology to the great benefit of the cherished panda population.

The report was voluminous, well documented, and daring beyond anything he thought was realistic politically. Weeks went by without reply from his superiors or anyone else. It was as if his proposal had been filed to gather dust alongside his doctoral dissertation. Averse to causing waves, Zedong continued working normal hours on his assigned project: the rewilding of Shanghai's urban parks. Six months later he was summoned to the city of Chengdu. The surprise was heightened when a police vehicle arrived to take him to the regional OBD headquarters. There he was ushered into a nondescript windowless office and made to wait. Hours seemed to pass. Zedong fell asleep, leaning over a bare desk, head resting on his folded arms. The door finally opened, and he was shocked to see President Jiang Dao, a man in his seventies who, like him, had studied for an advanced degree in ecology.

The conversation that took place that day was never recorded, and to Zedong the exchange had been a blur, the surprise of his new charge eclipsing most of the details. Within weeks Zedong was living in a small apartment in the middle of Chengdu, bicycling daily to his private office as governor of the Sichuan Province. Tasked with the abandonment of the entire province, home to 80 million people, Zedong left the city only on rare occasions—only four times over the ensuing decades: To Shanghai five years later to bury his mother, who had drowned after falling overboard from a research vessel; to Beijing five years after that to attend the funeral of President Dao; on the day of his 65th birthday to receive the Nobel Peace Prize in the half-vacated city of Oslo; and now, on this occasion, on his 75th birthday, to testify before the Tetrad in the virtually empty island of Manhattan.

Zedong was amused by the general's fission ideas and was not concerned if the secretaries decided in his favor. He was secure in his own views and beliefs, yet accepting of life's unpredictable turns, even those caused by wrong-headed people.

"Professor Te, you grace us with your presence today," the Secretary of the Environment greeted him, hardly veiling her allegiance. "The world recognizes your pioneering work on urban reclamation. Your views on ecology are well known and your research on abandoned cities is impressive. But every city is different, and we owe the world an intelligent path forward, one with a reasonable time frame. We are poised to act, here in Manhattan, as a demonstration of our decision. Please proceed, Professor."

Zedong remained silent, staring past the secretaries to the olive-gilded, halo-like United Nation's logo that seemed to hang above their heads. The General squirmed in his chair, champing at the bit to start assembling his nuclear armament. "Get on with it so I can get the hell out of here," he uttered; caring not if anyone heard him. Zedong prolonged his silence to let the general's ill-intended verbal flatulence dissipate.

"Imagine two buckets," the professor said finally. "One is filled with a large stone, and the other with tens of smaller stones adding up to the equivalent weight and volume. While smaller in size, the stones in the second bucket have in aggregate a far greater surface area than that of the larger stone in the first bucket. Far more water molecules will touch the smaller stones than the larger one."

He paused as if having forgotten what comes next. The secretaries looked at each other, puzzled. The general forcefully cleared his throat as if to shake loose the professor's words.

"Now imagine a building," Zedong continued. "Enclosed, it behaves like the bucket with the single stone. But remove its windows and open its doors, and it turns into the bucket with the smaller stones. Open buildings will multiply the surface area that air, dust, humidity, and pollen can touch, increasing the rate of vegetable and animal colonization exponentially, like lilies that multiply in a pond. There is no need to bring down buildings, only to open their windows and doors. Over time, walls will erode and crumble and buildings will topple. Mold and soil will accrete, vegetation will grow, and wildlife will multiply. Time is the silent drumbeat of evolution, and the slower the beat, the greater the opportunity for a complex and rich composition. Nature's paced reentry will ennoble people, as they witness the rewilding process and, like an ebbing tide, humanity's receding footprint.

"And," he added after a brief pause intended to underline his next elucidation, "this path enables the use of the world's stockpile of fissionable material to power the exodus into space."

"I OBJECT TO THIS NONSENSE!" shouted the general, slamming his fist on the table. "That's a waste of energy! Rockets can use fuel to lift. Nothing else but fissionable material can crater cities! And opening windows and doors—DEAR GOD, THIS MAN IS CRAZY! That will take centuries!"

Not waiting for a response, the general stood, shoved his chair back and exited the hall, leaving in his wake a trail of obscenities.

A month later, his white hair hanging loose over his shoulders, Zedong Mendes Te stood in a turret atop an army tank, ears plugged, and watched glass rain down on Times Square.

Hundreds of miles away General Cincinnatus Blackburn was hovering in a helicopter poised to witness the detonation that was about to turn the city of Cincinnati into a massive crater, its "sinful" trace forevermore erased by the onrushing waters of the Ohio River. It was the Secretaries' sole concession to his enraged madness. Afterward, dejected and in the absence of anything meaningful left to blow up, he returned to the family pig farm in Iowa. He had never married. Facing loneliness and depression, he would sit on the home's modest wooden porch for hours on end, well into the night, staring forlornly at the sprawling pigsties. His fifteen-year-old niece Celeste would take pity on him, sitting by his side for long stretches, sometimes well into the night.

One morning the girl's mother, Domitila, who forty years earlier had missed the family's ill-fated trip to Cincinnati because of the flu, discovered virginal stains on the girl's bed. Shaken, and remembering how Cincinnatus had tried to force himself on her when she was a teenager, Domitila called the police and had her sixty-five-year-old brother arrested on charges of incest. At the trial, the jury was moved by the teenager's testimony—that she had offered her uncle sex to relieve his suffering. In consideration also of his illustrious career, Cincinnatus was acquitted. Soon after returning home he took his own life, drowning in slop, never to know that the moment of bliss begat the Blackburn lineage of PEA resisters. Had he lived another 154 years with half a clear mind, he would have been proud of his eventual achievement, a powerful security chief who was, too, mired in hatred.

14

A DAY AT THE ACROPOLIS

Despite the weeklong build-up to the journey—her first in a spacecraft—Nori slept much of the way to the theme park. For weeks Ty had read her bedtime stories of classical Greece and its mythology, aided by scenes of Peloponnesian mountains, the Aegean coastline, and classical homes and gardens gathered by Lali. He had also shared how differently people dressed at the park, that there were many outdoor games to play, stories reenacted, building-scale holography with exact depth and materiality and, best of all, real stones sculpted like the plant—the acanthus—for which she was partially named.

Of the world's seven heritage parks—Machu Picchu, Red Square, Cartagena de Indias, Jaipur, Abu-Simbel, and the Kasbah in Marrakech being the others—the Acropolis is the only one containing Earth materials. During the Exodus, the United Nations Secretary of the Narrative was accosted with requests to bring historical artifacts into space: artwork of myriad kinds, clothing, machinery, and even famous people's homes to be reassembled and left floating in space for all time. "Wildlife is not the only thing worth preserving," was the cry. But the Secretary stood firm, prohibiting anything that could be recreated via ionized materialization, which in essence was everything ever made. She made a single exception, and that was the surviving Corinthian capitols of Athens' ancient agora. They are, as the Secretary explained, the only ancient carvings manifesting humanity's irrevocable dependence on nature "for body and mind."

Ancient history was not the subject of choice at the Te-Bekele household, but on one occasion, while visiting during MaY's pregnancy, Ty had heard PaZ explain why Nori's middle name would be Acantha, a derivative of the acanthus leaf motif in the ancient Corinthian columns. "When she sees the capitols, her future as a terranaut will strike her like a bolt of lightning from Zeus himself," PaZ said. Ty had chuckled at the thought; not only was PaZ making a prediction far into the future, which PaZ always considered silly, but he was also alluding to classical mythology, a rare foray into the right side of his brain. Ty was now fulfilling his brother's wish, but he was also fulfilling his own, and that was to expose Nori to the world of myth and lore.

Upon entering the park Nori was stunned, hardly able to comprehend the scale of the place. Front and center was the Parthenon, rising over a buffed rocky outcrop into a deep azure sky. Nori pointed to it, stretching her left arm as if trying to touch it. Below and to the right was a semi-circular amphitheater and she again pointed, holding the pose as if frozen in time.

"That's the great theater of Dionysus Eleuthereus," explained Ty, lifting her over his shoulders so she could better grasp its semi-circular geometry. "They told stories there of great heroic deeds, but also put on comedies to make fun of their rulers."

"Like you make fun of Xu—like when you called him a floppy walrus with the brain of a krill?"

"I think that deserves an explanation, Socrates!" Lali voiced into Ty's ear.

Ty set Nori on the ground, turned to a nearby v-eye and in sign language reminded Lali that on this special day gratuitous comments were not at all welcome. Lali pinged back: ... --- .-. .-. -.--. Ty shook his head, amused at Lali's skillful balance of wit and insolence.

They walked up the hill to the Propylaea and stopped to admire the Parthenon's front portico. "See the light inside? It's the glow of Athena, the fair and wise goddess that protected the ancient Greeks," Ty explained.

"Was she real? Were the gods real?" Nori asked.

Ty explained that they were real to the ancient Greeks, but that all their stories, like the one about Pegasus and the muses they had read the night before, had over time become myths. "Myths help explain how ancient cultures understood the world they lived in," he added.

"Do we live in a myth?

"What do you mean?"

"I mean Xu, you also call him a ... myth-so ... so-fit?"

Holding hands, Ty led Nori to a limestone boulder. They sat, both wiggling to find a comfortable position.

"Well, it's a bit difficult to explain," Ty said, pausing to gather his thoughts. "Did you like the story of the oyster and the mighty pearl I told you the other night?"

"I did, because I have a pearl just like it."

"You did say that. I bet you've been thinking about that story a lot, haven't you?"

Nori answered with an exaggerated nod.

"Maybe a thousand years from now, people will think that the oyster was a god, the pearl a goddess, and that together they really saved the world. That's how stories can become myths. Some people can be very gifted at seeing the world around them, and can be very, very imaginative about making sense of it. The most gifted become mythosophists—my-tho-so-phists—like Xu."

Sensing Nori's genuine interest, he continued.

"The world's first mythosophist gave us the story of the oyster and the pearl. She was the prime minister of India, and then became a member of the Tetrad at the time our Halo began to be constructed." Nori nodded. "Many people believed she was the reincarnation of Vishnu, India's mythic god of creation. Xu's ancestors were originally from Greece, and many people think of him as a divine oracle." Ty chuckled. "I'm sorry I ever called him a walrus. I prefer to think of him as a horse, like Pegasus in the ancient legend. When the horse's hoof struck the ground, the muses gushed out to give us poems, songs, and stories for us to make sense of the world in our own way. Maybe Xu should have big wings and a flowing white tail! And maybe one day his riddle will be one loud neigh!" Getting up from the boulder, he raised his knees and stomped like a proud steed as he blew a battery of loud snorts.

"You're making fun of him again," Nori laughed.

"One neigh for Xu, one for Osage, one for Namara, and one for Aurora," Ty said, picking Nori up and tossing her high in the air, making the pendant on her long necklace dangle and shimmer as she twirled before landing softly in his arms.

"Who's Namara?" she asked after catching her breath.

"She is one of the four members of our governing Tetrad. She governs over trade between the colonies. If our colony one day produced more fruit than we needed, we would give it to another in exchange for something we might need. It all has to balance out."

"And Aurora?"

"She makes sure that we are safe from asteroids and solar flares. And also that people can safely travel, like we did today to get here, or for workers to go to the moon and the asteroid belt."

"And how do they get to be there, in the Tet … Tet … the Tet …Red?"

Ty is surprised by her seeming interest in governance.

"Tetrad. They are all voted into office when there's a vacancy. Every person in the world over the age of seventeen is free to vote, and by that I mean send in the name of someone they know or have heard about. The top one thousand vote recipients go forward. Some accept their inclusion, and some don't. The remaining then offer their views on matters of governance and people vote again, and so on until only a single name is left. The process can last for months, and it can be fun and very revealing, with lots of discussion."

Nori was focused on the agora. Ty shook his head, caring little if Nori absorbed any of it. "Let's go!" he said, setting her down and leading her down the hill, bounding over boulders in delirious laughter until tumbling onto the turf to the delight of nearby visitors. Many were wearing white tunics and sandals, giving the place the feel of antiquity—as close as can be had out in space a tenth of the Earth's distance to the Moon. Back on their feet, they ambled toward the agora's stoa.

Nori's eyes widened at the goods on display—food, clothing, housewares, trinkets, crafts, artwork, and toys, all brimming behind a digitally painted Ionic colonnade. They stepped up and entered the line of shops inside the colonnade. One of them had no fare, but displayed a large holographic installation depicting a tranquil Old-World suburban home, an automobile parked in front of a car garage, a child swinging from a large shade tree, and a dog wagging his tail over a finely trimmed lawn.

An older man and a woman, dressed in mid-twentieth-century business attire, were standing stiffly to the side of the shop. She was holding a placard: PEOPLE ON EARTH AGAIN. BECOME A PEA—JOIN US TODAY! The man, dressed in a pinstriped suit and wearing a black fedora and round, black-rimmed glasses, was holding a staff, topped by a miniature black bull poised to charge. Ty thought the man looked vaguely familiar but couldn't think where from.

"Why do they look like that?" Nori asked, pointing at the pair. The man ignored the gesture, fixing his stare instead on Ty. The look unsettled him momentarily.

"That's what people wore back then, in the Old-World," Ty said, taking Nori's hand and pulling away. "Not very comfortable if you ask me. They were called fundamentalists and believed that people should have stayed on the planet not caring a whit what happened to other species. PEA caused a lot of trouble back then; they marched, protested, and fought the police. They still march and protest sometimes, silly as it is. You'll learn more about it in school."

"What was that animal on the stick?"

"Looked like a ruminant of some kind; a cow maybe, not sure what it means," Ty answered, preferring to leave the Myth of Wall Street for another day.

Down further they bought grape juice and sat on the stoa steps to sip. Two flirting teenagers were sitting nearby. The boy's hand rested on the girl's thigh. Hers covered his to ensure that the reach did not go any further. As with many people after the New Year, they were quibbling about Xu's Riddle.

"Oh, my moonlit dream, you are my mirrored peach—AREN'T YOU?" said the girl.

"PEACE, he said—as in lying around doing nothing! Which is what the man does—nothing! That was so lame: Floating Strings ... Filtered Sight ... You, on the other hand ..."

Nori saw the young man trying to kiss the girl, who playfully pushed him away.

"No, no, no!" she said. "Xu said PEAS, you know, what we eat! Peas come from pods. He wants us to think of a PEA POD that with mirrors can be multiplied into thousands, like the space pods we live in!"

"So?" the already irritated young man answered.

"It's about illusion, don't you get it? Nothing is what it seems. That's what riddles are anyway. Maybe Xu wants us to think about those PEA quacks over there. I bet I can be the first one in our colony to figure it out."

A hunched, hooded old man holding a cane took a step up to the covered walk, tripped and fell onto the young couple. Nori skipped a breath. The young woman sprang to her feet, grabbed hold of him and helped him get back up.

"Now there's Xu's 'cursive pulse'—IF HE'S GOT ONE!" bellowed the boyfriend.

"He heard you!" said the girl, sitting back and pinching him hard on his arm.

Nori watched the old man walk away, bumping into people as he struggled to make his way through the crowd.

"Where do people go when they die?" she asked, raising her head to look at Ty in the eyes. He wondered if the old man inspired the question. He set his drink aside and mulled over how to answer, unsure about whether to be fully truthful.

"People in the Old-World believed that people died and went to heaven. I think we are already in heaven, that when we die we just go a little farther: where there's a beautiful light and we dream of our most fun and loving memories. That is what I think."

"But you said that Mama and Daddy are on Earth, in Amazonia."

Ty was caught by the incongruity between what he had just explained, and what he had earlier told her.

"Very special people," he said, "those who we love the most, rest in the most special heaven of all, sweetheart, where life is magical and truly eternal." He hoped the explanation would suffice, aware that it did not really answer her question.

"And you will take me there to see them?"

"Absolutely!" he affirmed, placing Nori on his lap, arms around her waist in a loving embrace.

Nori's attention drifted to the central square. People were gathered around jugglers, listening to impromptu poetry, racing after drone pigeons, tossing large balls in the air, and chasing randomly appearing rainbows. Ty was oblivious. Months had passed since the Ceremony of Remembrance, but he was still outraged by OCTAD's crass attempt to secure ownership of PaZ and MaY's remains. Not a minute had passed after Osage left the podium when OCTAD's Bereavement Officer jumped up to offer solace. Speeding through the empty words of succor, the man had produced a release form for the bodies. "Because the search will be restarted and they *will* be brought back home," he had said with a sorry grin that betrayed the all too transparent purpose of the sordid assignment.

The extraction of milligrams of zinc, copper, and magnesium from the tissue and bones of the deceased was of high value for the manufacture of terrasuits and other digital fabrics, and youthful deaths were rare. "Surely having your brother and sister-in-law immortalized in living fabric would be a worthy way to honor their sacrifice," the man had added, leaving Ty numb by the repulsive offer. He almost lost the struggle to keep his right arm by his side, caring little if everyone around saw him deck the man. But he had held back. Now, with the man's reedy voice reverberating between his ears, Ty reviewed the response he had later thought of: "You are a blood-sucking leech with zero care for MaY's extraordinary contribution to the Corporation. Her implants made millions, and she could not have done it without PaZ. That's reason enough to let them forevermore rest on Earth—or, you lying bastard, to have their ashes cycle back as compost like the rest of the fucking world does. You know they will never be found, SO GET THE HELL OUT OF HERE!"

Nori wiggled out from his lap, snapping Ty out of the painful memory. She was drawn by the glint of glass-like animal figurines a few stalls ahead. She pointed and urged Ty to take her there, tugging his sleeve. They walked a few paces but again sat. The vendor appeared busy with the old man they had seen earlier. The exchange was as follows.

"Good morning, Sir. 275, huh? Hard to believe. I remember the year 225 as if it was yesterday!" said the old man. The vendor sneered, believing the visitor to be one of the park's cast members, posing as a beggar.

The creation of the new calendar did not happen without controversy. Egon Pinoche had locked horns with Yuri Mozorov, his Russian counterpart at the Tetrad, declaring that he, as the United States representative, should become the group's first New World Secretary. The United States enjoyed an unmatched track record in space travel and research, and while ALFIE had been a multinational enterprise, the U.S. had provided the far greater share of funding, equipment, and human resources for the secret undertaking, Pinoche argued. But Russia had space-pioneering history on its side: Sputnik in 1957, Gagarin in 1961, and Salyut 1 a decade later. Russia, in effect, occupied the undisputed higher ground from which to claim the post, Mozorov countered. China and India took the Russian's side, each getting their desired posts in return. Incensed by the power grab and relegated to the position of Commerce Secretary, Pinoche argued that it was then his prerogative to set the New World Calendar, setting Day One retroactively to July 20, 1969, the day a human first stepped on the Moon—and not on April 19, 1971, the day Salyut 1 was launched, as the Russian preferred. And so it came to pass that the new world clock became linked to an industrialized and scarred moonscape, rather than the precursor to the new world's geo-synchronous pod-sparkling Halo.

"Move on, Methuselah," the vendor urged. "Or do you have something to trade?"

The old man reached for a figurine of a hawk in flight and brought it to his face as if trying to find an imperfection.

"Well?" said the vendor, annoyed.

"Well, yes ... I do have something to trade."

Placing the figure back on the counter, the old man dug into his robe and pulled out a small sac of digital beads. He rolled them into a glass bowl resting on the counter. Seated a few yards away, the clinking briefly sparked Nori's interest.

"I know some people. They are good to these old bones; they give me things," said the old man, selecting a bead from the bowl. "This one here has a pack of dolphins off the Isle of Capri; it's a virgin recording." He rubbed the bead and his robe lit up with dolphins arching gracefully in and out of crystalline emerald waters.

"I have striped dolphins. What else you got?" said the vendor, testily.

The old man picked up another bead. "Try this one: *Upupa epops*—The hoopoe bird, also unedited," he said. He rubbed the bead and the robe displayed the bird in flight approaching a tree branch, its striped black-and-white wings and orange mohawk in full splendor. "Eurasian. A rare creature!"

The vendor stared at the image for a moment. "Sorry, not interested in holo beads today. Go on now, get lost," he barked.

"But I DO know what you are interested in," insisted the old man, reaching for the vendor's arm and pulling him closer to him across the counter with unexpected strength.

"Guide us, moonlit dreams, past *mirrored peacocks with flapping wings*," he said in a deliberate, hushed monotone.

The vendor shed the man's hold and stepped back. "You? With them?" he said in a hushed tone.

"Have to be discrete, you know," said the old man, pulling a small, sealed bag from under his tunic.

"Catuaba bark. Direct from Amazonia. Very fresh; came in yesterday. I can assure you, even for a craggy old man like me it does wonders. There are five dozen sacks stored in the usual place. Ten thousand halos, boss says."

"That's an impossible price!"

"Tenfold in the black market, guaranteed. Boss also wants me to remind you …"

"Yes, I know, damn it! Tell her that I will pay it all back; just need more time," said the vendor, swiping the bag from the old man's hand. Retreating into the stall, but still within view of Ty and Nori, the vendor took a small piece of bark and sniffed it. Satisfied, he came back out, reached for the old man's armband and tapped it with his own to pay. Smiling grudgingly, he followed the old man as he ambled away, head bowed, tapping his cane on the travertine tiles. Past two columns the man turned his head and looked in Ty's direction. Ty detected an odd smile. Thinking nothing of it, he turned to Nori. She giggled. A robot mouse was scampering by her feet.

15

"2001" INTERRUPTED

O n the way back home, Ty was resting comfortably on his cushioned peapod seat, free of the stress that for months had knotted his normally cheerful self. He had met CaL and gotten off his chest the bizarre encounter in Serra Padre, and he had made good on his promise to take Nori to the Acropolis, a visit that neither would soon forget. She had asked difficult existential questions and had been at ease with the answers. Gliding through space she was fast asleep leaning on his side, breathing peaceably, her face in complete relaxation. Reflecting on the events of the past year, Ty was amazed at how quickly a gutting tragedy had led to a state of profound contentment. Thinking of XoL, he wished that she could witness the scene and share in his joy.

He closed his eyes and thought through the youthful exchange at the agora. "Guide us, moonlit dreams, past mirrored peas and floating strings ... ." An image of peas came to mind—the fruit, *Psium sativum*. He imagined long pods shedding seeds into space like squads of the small round spacecraft with paired mechanical arms featured in the classic film, *2001: A Space Odyssey*.

"Drop it in, please, Lali," he commanded quietly. His obsession with the film had little to do with the Roswell Incident (as is the case with most people who still remember that event). It was more about the film's primal aura and the anticipation of inhabiting its extraordinary scenography. He knew to the second when the tapir would make its entrance at the start of the film, a beast he had encountered many times in the wilds of Amazonia. Since his first viewing at age seven, he had entered every frame and embodied every character many times over. He enjoyed becoming the proto-Neanderthal clan leader in the Dawn of Man and edging toward the mysterious monolith ahead of the bone-smashing sequence that sent a large femur twirling skyward to become a serene spaceship. He especially liked squaring off with HAL in a tussle for survival. Had Kubrick added an "O" to the computer's acronym, he had often fancied, the film would have assumed an even greater prophetic status, presaging the halo of pods that now rings the planet.

In anticipation of the dramatic chords of Richard Strauss's magnificent tone poem *Also sprach Zarathustra*, he reclined further into his seat, careful not to disturb Nori. Eyes still closed, he transported himself eons back in time to appear as a true alien among the apes.

His cochlear implant pinged, shaking his meditative state. Lali paused the film. Nori stirred but did not wake. Ty checked his wristband. The caller ID read RDXDL-AMZ. His heart nearly stopped. Images of the presumed Yanomami in Serra Padre burst in his head. He answered in a whisper.

"XoL … I wasn't expecting to hear from you so soon after my mission," he said quietly. Seconds went by without a reply.

"XOL?"

"Yes, I'm here. I couldn't hear well. Are you at home? Are you well?"

"No … far from it—I mean yes: I am well but not at home, I mean literally," Ty responded.

He had sent in a brief report after his mission, stating that had not felt well and had opted for an early return. Unwilling to discuss the matter further—certainly not with Nori by his side—he told XoL about their extraordinary day at the theme park: how they had seen a live enactment of Aesop's "Zeus and the Tortoise," had walked through the stoa admiring the myriad wares and trinkets, watched several of Xu's understudies extemporize riddles—and, best of all, how they had gotten lost in the cypress maze only to pop out into the sacred grove of olive and pomegranate trees, where they waded at its center in the Fountain of Everlasting Youth. "I had never gotten that far into it before. It's real water … and the Parthenon, best plastek anywhere." He stopped the barrage, realizing that XoL had barely said a word.

They had met only once since the adoption: at a gathering at CaL's place to celebrate the newly minted father in the company of relatives and friends. In a devious gesture, CaL had placed a grape arbor in the middle of the living area. "Ty believes that when fermented, grapes can enhance mental acuity. But I go further: they lead to unbridled lust!" he had joked. But neither Ty nor XoL had taken the bait. Over the course of the evening XoL had gaily mixed it up with the group, taking time to also play with Nori. XoL had almost become the center attention, Ty had thought, remembering later that not once had she spoken to him alone. The distance between them pained him, and the silence after he stopped blathering about the Acropolis seemed to broaden it. The endearing note she had left for him at his workstation, emboldening as it was, now felt incongruous.

"I'm very sorry to break into your wonderful day," XoL finally said, her voice quivering. "We need to see you. The head producer reviewed the mission … not sure why."

She paused to let her words sink in. In the silence, Ty tried to imagine why he was being summoned. He had confirmed and reconfirmed the manipulated data before sending it over to the production office and was certain that the changes were undetectable. Besides, data entry anomalies were not uncommon, hardly meriting a meeting with the head producer.

"Ty?"

"Yes, I'm here," he answered. Silence again, as they waded in a swamp of mutual discomfort.

"XoL?" "Ty?" they uttered simultaneously.

"I'll be there in the morning. I'll take Nori to Manaus for the day," he said, terminating the call.

Nori twitched. He straightened her posture and reached for a blanket to keep her warm. Lali restarted the film. Ty leaned back, fixing his eyes on the bone-cum-spaceship frozen in midair. He was always impressed by the ship's proportions in the film, so close to present-day peapods. So, too, by the flight attendant's realistic magnetic-induced shuffle, a scene that had always prompted from him mimed applause in homage to the famed director. But not this time.

Ty and the head producer had crossed paths at work only briefly, and he only had PaZ's assessment by which to measure the man. "He's an ascetic, power-hungry bureaucrat who produces next to nothing and uses his position to feed his ego," PaZ had said, one of the few times Ty had ever heard his brother say anything critical about anyone.

With those words swirling in his head, Ty asked Lali to stop the film and turn on the bubble's synapse-numbing emitters. He closed his eyes and resumed a meditative state, resting his hand on Nori's to draw a measure of peace.

16

THU'S VENOM

T here are people who suffer accidents, who fail vocational tests, who are passed over for promotion because someone else is a hair more qualified, or who otherwise, for whatever reason, never seem to find the groove for success. But that does not make them losers. That trait is reserved for those who, despite the headwinds, manage to get ahead but remain spiteful of others who were luckier, favored, or who appeared to excel with less effort. Thom Ulrich Uris, the Amazonia Division Head Producer, fell into this class. Growing up, ThU wanted to be a terranaut, principally to earn the job's intrinsic respect and admiration. But as with XoL, he had no family background connected with earthbound operations, no qualifying lineage. And like her, his family had participated in OCTAD's biennial lottery but won nothing. Still, he persisted, ultimately meriting a rare innovation scholarship based on the novel idea of using animals themselves as wilderness recording instruments.

Through his five years of undergraduate studies at OU, ThU received average marks, hardly registering with the Rector. Below average in height but above in weight, he scraped through the endurance tests and qualified for post-graduate earthbound training. The unlikely accomplishment seared into his mind the superiority of dogged determination over the easy gains of the entitled class. He despised everyone who was genetically predisposed to be fitter and stronger, even more so those he considered to be "royals": folk with a privileged heritage, such as offspring of OCTAD professors and Descendants of the Clause.

Although his DNA had shown no genes tied to the paralyzing illness, and at no time during the initial battery of fitness tests had he experienced anything remotely close to it, on his first terranaut-training ride down the El, ThU was overcome with vertigo. He never set foot on Earth—not even on the station platform—never even took a breath of fresh air. After landing he was tended by medics and sent right back into orbit. Sadly, if vertigo was the affliction on the way down, bitterness and resentment got the better of him on the way up, a malady that from that day forward he saw no reason to remedy. Intent on implementing his recording idea, he transferred to the School of Recording Productions, where he came to believe that producers, unglamorous and unsung as their work was, in the end held the upper hand over the acquisition of raw wilderness data. After graduation, as fate would have it, he was assigned to the Amazonia Division.

As you know, speaking negatively or wishing ill will on anyone, however mean-spirited the effrontery, was not among PaZ's predispositions. "If you can't say something about someone that is true, necessary, or kind, *stow it*," was his favored motto. When Ty had asked why he felt the way he did about the producer, he simply shrugged, adding, "That's just my sense of him." PaZ saw no benefit to anyone, least of all to his innocent brother, in revealing ThU's machinations to defame MaY.

The man had indeed been first in conceiving animal-based recordings.

He had sensed fame and fortune riding on the idea. After arriving at the Amazonia Division he had earned a modest budget to conduct research and develop instrument prototypes. Alas, the devices were designed to be externally attached and proved clumsy to handle and operate, let alone stay in place on an animal's head for more than a few hours. He refused to listen to terranauts' complaints about the devices, or heed suggestions about how to improve them. Faced with mounting failures, he imputed the setbacks to their incompetence, reserving the greatest blame for MaY, the newest terranaut assigned to the project. She had a minor degree in veterinary medicine, which more than qualified her. But ThU was compelled to blame someone—anyone! MaY's relative inexperience, magnified by his envy of her rising reputation, made her a perfect target.

Tensions mounted between them, nearly exploding after MaY filed a report attributing the failures to the device's essential design and pointing the finger at its creator. Worse, her report recommended that the instrument be revamped in favor of more efficient, less costly, and virtually damage-proof ocular implants. ThU had never imagined the possibility. A meeting was called by Passiflora Cerulea, Rector of OCTAD's Tropical Biome, to calm things down. As MaY's mission partner, PaZ was summoned as well. He was left speechless at the virulence with which ThU attacked his wife—and him. The venomous spit went as far as asserting that MaY's "inane" design represented nothing more than an excuse for her to copulate with PaZ under the full force of gravity, "as they always do—the existence of their daughter proves it!" Passiflora dismissed that allegation and saw no resolution to the conflict other than to promote both parties to better positions: ThU to head the Amazonia production unit and MaY to lead the development of the implant program.

MaY was thrilled by the new responsibility. Outwardly ThU professed deep gratitude for the advancement, but inwardly he considered it a gross demotion. He seethed about having the project yanked from him and given to MaY who, in his estimation, was the poster child of the entitled class he despised. That he would seek retribution, in whatever manner possible, and to include anything and anyone associated with MaY, was, in his mind, a foregone conclusion.

Ty approached the conference room where XoL and the head producer waited. Although entirely unaware of the particular strife between the producer and his sister-in-law, Ty still wondered how anyone in such a vital position could have a flawed character such as PaZ had described. It upset him to have to have to explain anything to the man, but more so to appear in front of XoL like some sort of defendant. He had called CaL and they had discussed what he would say at the meeting. CaL abhorred the producer's grandiosity and warned Ty that he might be in for a rough meeting. "Whatever you do, keep your cool," had been his advice.

Taking a deep breath, Ty pushed open the meeting room door. ThU was seated across a large round table. The man's gel-combed purple-dyed hair sweeping back to his nape was a surprise. To ThU's left was XoL and across from her a young man—a terranaut, Ty guessed from his lean physique. XoL greeted Ty with a forced smile. He took a chair, hoping that the reason for the meeting was nothing more than an ordinary, post-mission debriefing.

"Good morning—or is it afternoon already?" Ty said.

"Still morning. Thank you for coming on such short notice, Ty," said XoL, her hands resting over a tabletop digital screen. "Let me introduce you to…"

"We've already met, I believe—briefly, at the ceremony," Ty interjected.

"I meant LeE," XoL said, gesturing to the younger man. "He's here as a required observer; it's protocol."

Ty turned toward him and nodded, wondering what protocol called for such observation.

"WE have indeed met before," said ThU, "and yesterday we almost bumped into each other, at the Acropolis. You were busy with the little girl. Your niece, no?"

Ty was aghast. Images of ThU shadowing him at the theme park flashed through his mind. And how is it possible for the man not to know that Nori is his adopted daughter, he wondered, or was it an ill-timed joke? A burn swelled in his gut.

XoL continued. "As I mentioned on the call, Ty, the production office uncovered a few anomalies in your last mission's recordings. We are here to determine if mistakes were made, if somehow you …"

"ANOMALIES?" ThU interrupted angrily. "Mr. Te, please tell us, if you will, EXACTLY what it was you recorded on your last mission."

Ty held a steady stare on ThU.

"It's in my report, Mr. Uris," he began, mindful to remain calm, as CaL had advised. "It was early on my second day, on schedule. I was hungry and ate raw suri. It made me sick. I couldn't keep up with the jaguar and didn't want to come back empty-handed. There were red howlers nearby, so I tracked one and brought back the recording."

ThU leaned forward as if to summon a special reservoir of bile.

"That was a useless decision, Mr. Te. We have more than a thousand hours' worth of *Alouatta* recordings turned into high-definition holography. Surely you do not believe that delivering one more curly-tailed shaggy-assed monkey would be worth our time, do you? And if suri sickened you, well, obviously you were poorly trained," he said, leveling a searing look at XoL. "Please go on, I'm eager to hear more!"

"As I said, I didn't want to come back empty-handed. Back at the lab I reviewed the data and rechecked the DNA sequencer calibrations—as I always do. It showed a human genome. This was improbable, of course—"

"IMPROBABLE? How about IMPOSSIBLE!"

"—so I took an *Alouatta* chromosome from the archives and patched it in so the recorded subject and its DNA reading would match. As you know, human and howler DNA have very close chromosomes."

ThU leaned back on his chair and assumed an aura of omnipotence.

"This is truly extraordinary! Let me see if understand correctly: You are sent to track a jaguar but end up recording a monkey. At the lab you

BOTCH its DNA, and then MODIFY the chromosomes to cover it up! And to top it off, you imply that somehow a human genome crossed your path—let me guess—a person that materialized out of thin air! If that had remotely been the case, your video cam would have shown us this incredible creature—except that it shows nothing more than a blurry mess of chopped pixels—a hollow-graphy if there ever was one! Your incompetence astounds, Mr. Te!"

Ty was flush with anger now, barely able to take ThU's indignant mockery. LeE's gaze was glued on the table, as if he dared not twitch an eyelid. XoL was bewildered; ThU had not shared the accusation with her beforehand, and she could not make sense of it.

"The instruments were faulty," Ty uttered, gritting his teeth. "The technicians confirmed it. It's in my report. I thought it was prudent to alter the data and avoid an expensive and senseless investigation yielding nothing more than equipment failure. And as you stated, it is impossible for a human being to appear on Earth out of thin air. I thought there was no point including such an absurd statement in my report. For that I apologize, SIR," Ty said, hoping that would be the end of it.

ThU thought for a moment, then doubled down on his indictment.

"I am very far from accepting any kind of excuse or apology from you, Mr. Te. The bottom line is that you botched an important mission and modified virgin data. This is not done—PERIOD! We can disregard the cost of a failed mission, but not the willful manipulation of recorded data. Terranauts are NOT entrusted with the data—producers are! You are only entrusted with bringing it to us, and I can accurately say you brought us nothing! I can't fix your incompetence, but your manager here surely can—AND WILL!" ThU took a breath and expanded the reach of his ire. "Your kind, you believe yourselves to be so privileged to set foot on Earth, so rightfully entitled. Well, my friend, you have a job to do down there so we, producers, up here, can give the world something of value. Without our work your little happy missions mean NOTHING! And you dare hide your incompetence with a half-baked and incredibly stupid story!"

Silence followed briefly as XoL, in shock, tried to find the right words.

"Ty, I hope you understand that I am obliged to submit a report about this—to the security office," she said, pausing for a moment. "I will bring LIGHT to the matter and deliver a STRONG and accurate account."

"And fast!" added ThU, unsure about what her emphases meant.

"I'll be in touch in a few days," she told Ty with a tinge of affection.

Sensing dismissal, Ty rose and turned to head for the door.

"He's even more stupid than his useless brother was," ThU uttered in a barely hushed tone. XoL's face reddened, she shoved her chair back as she stood to level a forceful protest. She was too slow. Ty turned back and lunged over the table, taking a swing at ThU's face. The punch landed on the man's throat. ThU gasped for air. XoL screamed. LeE jumped off his chair and pried the two loose. Ty slid back off the table, fists coiled, then stepped back. Shaken, XoL watched him leave the room, slamming the door behind him.

"You are finished, you hear? FINISHED!" ThU shouted after him hoarsely, clutching his neck.

17

HUMMINGBIRD
AND BEAD

▶ JANUARY 7, 0275

"The sonofabitch ambushed me, defamed PaZ!" Ty kept saying to himself, seething all the way back to Catleya.

At home he went straight to his bedroom, barely saying hi to Nori. He activated the floor padding, lying down to meditate. He inhaled—one, two, three, four, five, six; held his breath to another count of six and exhaled through parted lips to the count of ten. He repeated the exercise ten times, but it hardly helped.

He knew the trouble he was in. ThU's snide questioning had been abusive, but Ty had assaulted the man. "Light and strong," echoed in his head. He rued having put XoL in a tough spot. ThU would demand severe punishment. XoL would do her best to soften it, he believed. Going into the meeting Ty had been certain that any recording irregularities, if found, would at most warrant a summons before the Disciplinary Board—a slap on the wrist, so to speak. Now he could face suspension without pay.

Without a salary he would have to ask his aging parents for a loan to make ends meet—yet another way for them to think, kind as they had always been about it, that he was never meant to follow in his brother's footsteps.

"Made Yunnan-style noodle soup, your favorite," offered Lali. Unable to calm down, Ty got up and ambled to the dining cove. He stared at the fare as if it were jail slop.

Intent on cheering him, Lali materialized overhead as a fluttering hummingbird. Nori caught a glimpse of the scene from her playroom and ran to the bird, jumping up and down and with raised arms trying to touch it. Following through with Lali's hint, he picked her up and carried her to the cove's utility wall.

"Let's get what we got at the market yesterday, shall we?"

A clear panel lit up on the wall and started emitting a soft whir. Ty set Nori down so she could closely watch the printer's operation. Snowflakes in tight formation began to rain down. Nori followed the slow descent with a finger. Layer by layer the flakes coalesced into the glass figure they had purchased from the vendor at the stoa: first a tree trunk, then a branch, a twig with compound leaves, a flower, and finally a hummingbird in mid-air attached to the flower by its lance.

"It's got to set for a while before gaining transparency—but I have a real one to show you; I brought it from work," Ty said. He took a small bead from a pocket and extended his arm, pointing toward the den as if being pulled by a powerful force. He'd nabbed the bead from the production lab on the way to meet with ThU, an impulsive act that surprised him then and still did, not the least for having done it without anyone noticing. Nori followed him into the den, clinging to his leg. "Close your eyes," he told her, dropping the bead into a wall reading slot. Lali dimmed the lights. Excited about the upcoming imagery, Nori grabbed a pillow and dropped to the floor, wriggling a bit until satisfied with her seat.

What happened next remains for Nori a troubling memory, recorded in her diary a few years later.

May 1, 0278

... There I was, resting on a floor with my eyes closed, like Ty asked. I opened them and above was a huge hummingbird with its wings fluttering. Bigger than life. Ty was staring at me with a big smile on his face. Later he told me that I wasn't even blinking, that he could see the bird reflected in my eyes—my little gemstones, he liked to say. I asked if it was the same bird he had on his suit the night of the Gala, but he said no, that one had been a swallow-tailed hummingbird from the eastern part of the continent and this one was the Green-fronted lancebill hummingbird from farther north in Central America. The colors were beautiful, like a rainbow, and the plumage was feathery, except over its chest it was scaly, more fish-like.

The hummer flew, away but then it reappeared, hovering by a bright red flower. Then it moved closer, the flower ballooned, and I began to see exactly what the bird was seeing. The color was intense, the room was all a deep scarlet. I was speechless. Then one of the flower's white, star-shaped pistils appeared. It looked like it was going to poke me. I pressed my head into the pillow to hide, but it was just the bird darting forward into the flower. I can't be sure, but I could swear we could hear the nectar being sucked in, straw-like. And then it was over, the bird flew away, and the flower faded. The whole thing was short, but it felt like an eternity.

Ty explained that what we had seen was a sample of what was to come: that terranauts had been inserting nano-cams inside animals' eyes and that OCTAD was now very close to sharing that for the world to see. (Mother's work!!!!) He said: "Imagine seeing the rainforest through the eyes of a big anaconda, or grasslands through the eyes of an impala. Imagine that you are a fish, a bird, a MONKEY—seeing what they see! Let's imagine how a monkey sees a trogon." He reached into my toy basket and picked up the red howler. He then saw my necklace wrapped around the monkey's neck. That's where I always kept it, and he remembered it from our visit to the Acropolis the day before, when he tossed me way up in the air. I told him about the pearl that was inside the pendant, and he popped it open and there it was, the shiny data bead that Mother had given me just before her last mission. Ty was puzzled and asked how I got it, and how long had I had it, and that's when I remembered that mother had said to give it to him if they were delayed coming back. And I started to cry—not because I hadn't given it to him, but because I hadn't told him what had happened that morning at Manaus while he was at work. Two men in uniform had come to visit. The director asked them why they were there, and they said that it would only take a few minutes, that they just wanted to ask about Lali and how it was working out between us. But when the director stepped away one of them came close to me and asked if there were any special beads in the house, the ones with the OCTAD logo. I lied. I didn't want them to take it from me.

Ty got very upset when I said all that, but then he hugged me and said that everything would be okay, that I had done the right thing. He asked if he could borrow it for a little while, and he promised to bring it back. That's how I got my real gem—at least for a while—because after he took it, I asked if he could bring me a pearl next time he went down to Earth. He said he would, but that it would have to be a beautiful stone instead because there weren't any oysters in Amazonia.

What happened next is still a little fuzzy. All I remember is that when I woke up the next day, Karman was yelling, I was crying, Ty was gone, and we didn't see him again for a long time.

Nori wrote these words in her diary when she was nine years old, not long after her grandparents' passage to the afterlife. It was her first entry. She began the diary after her return home from a fourth-grade field trip to The ORB. Two kilometers in diameter, the research facility, located at Lagrangian Point 5, contains sample atmospheres to test the potential capacity of select living plants to survive in other planets. Artificially induced mutations were producing extraordinary specimens, a highlight for schoolchildren. But for Nori the visit triggered a look back, not forward. At the *Poaceae* display, her eye caught sight of a large maize kernel that looked almost identical to the gem that Ty, as promised, had brought back from Amazonia. It was prismatic, with multiple facets, nearly transparent, and it opened the floodgates to the bead episode. She cried all the way back home, in anger more than despondency, resolved to record exactly what had happened three years earlier.

18

A KISS, SUSPENDED

Ty hardly said a word the rest of the day. He could not fathom why MaY would have wanted to hide a bead, what it might contain, or how she or PaZ could have managed to get it past the headquarters' security scanners in the first place. Someone must have helped them, he thought, mentally running through the roster of colleagues PaZ and MaY had befriended over the years. The brainstorming made him queasy. Suppertime arrived and he and Nori sat still at the dining table, both immersed in thought. Lali had prepared a rice and bean dish garnished with cilantro, one of Nori's favorites. She dug right in.

Recordings that have not yet been logged into the production office after arriving from Earth—so-called virgin beads—are prohibited from being edited or modified by any personnel and may not leave a production lab except as authorized by Head Producers. The rule owes its origin to Malva Odunde, a second-generation terranaut who was sent to record the rewilding of Abuja, in Nigeria. The woman found a family of African Lynx, the *Caracal caracal*, in the abandoned national soccer stadium, and brought back a striking recording of the clan running across the grassland that had previously been an immaculate soccer field. She had followed the animals onto the stadium stands as they leapt from one tier to another, their golden fur seemingly aglow against the backdrop of bleached red seats. She sold copies of the raw recording before the West Africa Division's production office was able to certify, code, and catalogue it. It then rapidly multiplied on the black market, causing OCTAD substantial loss in potential revenue. The woman was expelled from the Coros. Strict measures for the handling of virgin beads were adopted soon after.

"Please call Karman, Lali," Ty blurted, pushing his untouched plate aside and rising abruptly from the table. Nori and Lali were startled. "Nothing wrong with the food, Lali—just need to go," Ty said, hoping to keep Lali from probing.

"It is most uncommon for you to go back to work so suddenly, without taking time to eat. It is a long ride, and you are likely to get hungry along the way. Are you certain that you must go? Is it about the bead?"

Ty stared at Lali without saying a word.

"Shall I tell Karman that you've been called on an urgent matter?"

"Yes, Lali, that's exactly what it is. Tell her I'll be back before dawn."

He hurriedly put on his travelling gear and headed toward the door. Looking back, he saw Nori watching with pained eyes. He took a few steps, lifted and hugged her tightly.

CaL's sister lived a few alleys away and never took more than five minutes to walk over. She pinged Ty in reply to Lali's call. "There's an un-expected glitch with Harry," she said, referring to her veebot. "Loneliness, I think; I've been working long hours lately," she added, promising to get there as soon as Harry settled down. Ty waited for her outside the apart-ment, pacing back and forth. He fidgeted with the bead in his suit pocket. It was well past Nori's bedtime when he finally saw Karman approaching. He strode down the alley past her without saying a word, which confused her. Not once had she seen him do anything in a hurry, let alone leave without saying hello or taking a few minutes to chat; he was always con-versant when she came to stay with Nori.

Halfway down the greensward Ty vowed to apologize to Karman when he got back. He took off jogging to be sure to catch the last headquarter-bound peapod. The station was empty. *No ships are scheduled till morning*, read the board. He walked to the far end of the docking port to check for Solo travel shells. Three were available. He located a veebot eye and asked Lali to get one ready. One became aglow. He approached the open hatch and crawled in, groaning. He had forgotten how cramped the single-occupant shells were—and how painfully slow the magnetic pull was before they reach cruising speed. Over the three-hour ride he retraced the encounter with ThU, racking his brain about how the man could have possibly seen fit to check his lab work. An image of CaL standing in front of the porthole at the Gala flashed through his mind. He froze. He knew that Producers fed Atmospheric Engineers—Atmos—all the material they needed to design and build embodied landscapes but could not accept the possibility of CaL being beholden to the man—let alone be the one to snitch on him. *He could never do that! Not to me!* he kept saying to himself to exile the thought.

Ty arrived at headquarters past midnight and rushed past the docking port through the long corridor to the atrium. "I'm retrieving beads to work from home. XoL is easing me back to work—can't wait!" he was prepared to say in case anyone should ask why he was there at such a late hour. He reached the atrium doors and stopped by the face scanner. The doors slid open. The place was empty and dark, save for the soft glow of emergency lighting. He rushed down the atrium to the elevator bank—where a blinding light stopped him dead in his tracks.

"Sand County? Is that you?"

Ty shielded his eyes from the blinding light. "Manny? What's going on? Where is everyone?"

Manny aimed the flashlight to the floor. "You didn't get the message? Battery power is down; a repair crew is out there inspecting the solar array right now," replied the guard.

At work Ty was known as a night owl, oftentimes staying well past regular hours to review upcoming recording programs, confirm DNA readings at the lab, write post-mission reports, and review habitat assessments. During breaks he liked to amble along the pod's multilevel hallways and ramps, stopping to chat with whomever seemed idle. Invariably he gravitated toward the guards; they kept the pulse of the place better than anyone else. Manny was in his late sixties but was trim and muscular owing to a former career as a freestyle wrestler and coach. Most people avoided him to spare themselves his well-meaning but contusing handshake. Having suffered the crunch a few times, Ty had resorted to greeting him with a curtsy, causing the guard to assume royal airs and extend his right arm, flashlight in hand, and tap Ty's shoulder as if he were being knighted.

Beyond knowing the layout of the pod and its layered security system, Manny's duties included befriending the workforce and, like a caring uncle, lending an ear when the stress of the job required a soothing outlet. His method was that of a sifter: someone who combs Old-World history to find obscure facts with which to engage others in long and distracting conversations. Once he and Ty locked horns over the Roswell Incident. Ty held that the whole thing had been nothing more than a clever ruse to amuse the masses—a magic act which, like all such acts, were better left unexplained. Manny had a different view: that the cuboid (as the Kubrick film posited) was a mysterious instrument of human evolution, a metaphor for the hand of God. Ty chided the guard then for supporting a pseudo-religious theory, proposing instead that the Divinity resides in the power of imagination—the essential ingredient in all creation—and that no better proof exists than having two souls separated by over forty years in age go on for hours bonding over such nonessential matters. Unable to disagree, Manny stood and tapped both of Ty's shoulders with his flashlight, pronouncing him a "Knight of the Order of ..." and leaving Ty to fill the blank in the spirit of true, if useless, creativity. They had laughed heartily, the echoes of which always made them smile whenever they met. But not this time.

"It's something pressing, Manny. I won't be long," Ty said.

During shutdowns it is within a guard's charge to turn back anyone for any reason, but Ty's urgency dissuaded Manny that night. He couldn't recall ever seeing Ty this serious, so far removed from the seemingly buoyant mummer he always was.

"Just keep the usage to the minimum," Manny said. "If you are not back in one hour, I'll kick your ass right out of here. How's Nori?"

Ty didn't respond. He patted Manny on the shoulder and amid the penumbra jogged toward the atrium's encircling ramps, bypassing the elevator. He reached the upper level and strode down a dark hallway toward his workstation. He sat and turned on the ionized air display. Materializing at arm's length in front of him, the screen lit up dimly, in a power-saving mode.

"What can I do for you today, Ty?" a voice said. Ty dropped the bead into a reading slot. "Please voice the bead's name, Ty."

A wave of nausea hit him; he had not for a moment thought about the name MaY—or PaZ—would have given the bead as a password. Dry-mouthed, he reached for the station's water dispenser. Empty. He scrambled to his feet, tripping over the chair and tumbling to his knees. Cursing, he got back up and in darkness searched for another water dispenser, found one, and took a few sips. The relief was immediate. Back at his desk he stared at the black screen, straining to come up with a plausible word or combination of words. He tried twice, only for the friendly prompt to be repeated. One last entry remained before the bead's information would be locked for 24 hours.

Ty closed his eyes and assumed a meditative state. After several minutes, he spelled XoL's full name backwards, straining not to mangle the sequence: A-N-U-L-E-D-L-T-I-H-C-O-X-A-N-A-I-D-L-E-H-C-A-R.

The screen flickered, then showed a recording date and time, and the identity of the recorder. Ty was stunned, unsure about what to make of the information. He commanded the screen to brighten, ignoring Manny's request to keep power to a minimum.

"Content, please," he said, dry-mouthed again.

An immersive daytime view of a tropical rainforest appeared before his eyes. He leaned back, fixed on a mass of green at once familiar and undistinguishable.

"Virtual mode, please."

The image materialized above the desk. He pushed his chair back to better capture the unfolding video. A stick appeared pushing aside leaves and twigs, but gently, as if to permit quiet passage. The pace of movement was slow but deliberate, revealing nothing of interest. After a minute it stopped, then restarted but from a stationary and elevated position. The view zoomed in to reveal a forest clearing framed by a sheer rock wall. The rush of water could be heard, possibly from a waterfall.

Half-naked people were moving about, as if exchanging or arranging things.

There were material piles, and bundles of filled sacks in the middle of the clearing. The view shifted and showed a shack-like structure partly embedded in the rock. A man wearing a black terrasuit emerged. He seemed in command from the manner of his gait. The man stopped and looked in the direction of the camera. He signaled for the activity to stop.

The video again went blank and restarted, but from another high vantage point. The man in the terrasuit approached the base of a fig tree with a bow and quiver in hand. He looked around as if searching for prey. He gazed up, pulled an arrow and cocked the bow, aiming straight at the camera. The arrow did not come. The man lowered his arms, seemingly satisfied that everything was as it should be. He turned and walked away, disappearing into the foliage.

The video stopped and rewound to the opening frame, casting a green glow over the workstation. Ty remained stunned. He now understood what—who—it was that he encountered in the Serra. But where exactly? He could hardly comprehend how human beings in the flesh could be in Amazonia doing some sort of organized work. The taste of bile filled his mouth. He slumped. The entire world order seemed to be collapsing on him. A world constructed over a century for the sole purpose of purifying the Earth, now grossly contaminated.

And by actors willing to kill, he now knew.

A hand tapped his shoulder. Ty jumped out of his chair, sending it crashing into a structural strut.

"XoL!" he cried.

"Sorry, didn't mean to startle you," she said. "I heard a noise, saw the glow and came over. You are the last person I expected to see here!"

XoL's face was bathed with soft green forest hues. Ty was paralyzed, less so by the surprise than by her otherworldly appearance. It crossed his mind that she was there as an embodied holograph but he opted not to reach out and touch her. XoL cracked her lips as if harboring a smile, a trait that is too fine to distinguish from anything other than a present body.

"Don't blame Manny ... he's a good man. He didn't say you were here ... I thought I was alone," Ty said haltingly.

"I haven't left my office since our meeting the day before yesterday. I've been working on your report, trying to find the right words. You totally lost it, didn't you?"

Ty wanted to apologize, but XoL did not give him a chance.

"I'm glad you did. I never liked the man. He's an embittered sonofabitch. Wish you had landed one on his face and shot the snot out of him!"

In all the years he had known XoL, not once had she cursed at or about anyone, at least that Ty could remember.

"I'll take what's coming to me," he told her. "But there's something you must see, this bead I found—"

XoL raised her index finger to her mouth, signaling Ty to stop.

"I have to do it by the book, Ty, and in my book there's a chapter about a loving terranaut who adopts a child and while on leave spends ALL of his time at home with her. The question is, what are YOU doing here?"

Ty sensed the inevitability of having to tell XoL about the sighting. On the way back home from the Gala, he and CaL had discussed multiple scenarios for doing so, but none came remotely close in place or time to the present circumstance.

"Karman is at home with her. I'll be back before she wakes up; I have a shell docked outside," he said, pulling the chair back to the desk and placing another by its side. He motioned XoL to sit. She smiled at his reflexive gentlemanly gesture. Ty tensed.

"It's a virgin bead. I thought it was MaY's, but it's from PaZ. The date corresponds to his next-to-last-mission, when he went down alone. He must have given it to MaY for safekeeping sometime before their last mission ... I found it yesterday, inside the pendant of Nori's favorite necklace."

XoL thought through the timing.

"That was his first mission to Serra Padre. He was set to track cobalt-winged parakeet. He said MaY was sick but still insisted on going alone. He came back empty-handed, first time ever ... very unusual ... he seemed upset afterward but didn't say anything and I didn't probe."

"I believe this shows why," Ty said, voicing the play command.

Through the three-minute sequence XoL remained glued to the imagery, hardly breathing. Ty looked at her, but her stare remained fixed on the extraordinary recording. The video ended and she remained still, eyes open as if hypnotized.

"Who are these people? Is this a pod we don't know about—a new theme park?" she finally said.

"It's not a pod, XoL. What you saw is real: breathing people ... ON THE PLANET, in Serra Padre."

"Doing what? Where exactly?" XoL asked with a tone of disbelief.

"PaZ recorded a colossal crime, that is the 'what'... the rock wall fits the Serra's rugged terrain. I can't tell where exactly, but it must be near where I saw ..."

Ty stopped as XoL stood. Dumbfounded, she took a few steps back and leaned on the strut.

"PaZ must have figured out what was going on and returned with MaY... for her to see and to bring back a full account," Ty continued, his voice breaking by a surge of anger. "They were about to tell me ... The transmission, the roar—"

"THE LANDSLIDE! We have to inform the security office; it has to be a PEA operation!" XoL cried, reaching for her wristband.

"WAIT!" Ty yelled. "There was nothing wrong with my tracker. The DNA reading I took WAS from a man—one of *them*!" he added, pointing to the screen, dart-like. "ThU was right: I altered the data, at the lab, and I rigged the instruments to appear faulty. I mentioned the human gene as an absurdity, to justify the tampering. But what I scanned was real. I made a copy of the original DNA. It's here, hidden."

Ty took her hand and pulled XoL out to the hallway. Speechless, she did not resist, recalling the day at the marketplace in their early teens when they made their way through the throng of protesters. They cleared the workstations and reached the top of the ramp leading down to the atrium four floors below. Leaning over the railing Ty looked two floors down and diagonally across the oblong space, extending his arm in that direction. XoL knew where he was pointing.

"ThU's OFFICE?" she blurted.

"Outside ... in the bead display by his door. I switched one of them: second row, third one down ... I figured no one would ever look there, not even him."

They took off running down the ramp, XoL trailing a few steps behind Ty. Before reaching the first landing, he stopped abruptly and turned with little choice but to plant his feet and wrap his arms around her to keep them both from tumbling. XoL gasped.

"Forget the DNA!" he said, almost bursting. "We must find out who's responsible, who killed them. Send me back to Serra Padre—call it a confidential mission. You can do it. I can be ready in two days and finish what PaZ and MaY started."

XoL shook her head, grimacing. She rested her hands on Ty's shoulders, tears welling up.

"Ty, the resistance will do *anything* to keep that place a secret, eliminate anyone who stands in the way. We already lost two people we love.

I can't let you do it, *mi corazón*. Think of Nori ... think of us ..." XoL paused, staring deeply into his eyes now. "I've been stupid, Ty. All of this, the work, the Corporation, it is all small compared to ... You and I, ever since we were kids, I've—"

Ty put his index finger over her mouth. Taking her hands he pulled her close. She did not resist. Eyes locked, their lips approached. As they touched, the atrium security lights began to flash, paired with a screeching alarm. They separated, bewildered. A nearby security screen turned on. A white transporter had docked at the pod's emergency airlock, the figure of a wild boar shining on the fuselage.

"THE BEAD!" they shouted. Racing back up the ramp they returned to the workstation. Ty furiously tapped his fingers over the desktop to command the bead's release. As soon as he had it in hand XoL grabbed a nearby fire extinguisher and sprayed the data storage unit, then mashed it with the butt end of the canister. The last blow bumped Ty's fist, sending the bead flying. They dropped to the floor and groped for it. XoL found it. She bashed her head as she tried to stand. "FUCK!" she yelled, sending the expletive reverberating across the workspace. Amid the strobes Ty saw Manny coming.

"OCTAD SECURITY!" Manny yelled. Nearing the workstation, he saw XoL on the floor.

"What happened?"

XoL motioned for him to get down so as not to be seen by any watchers. He knelt by her side.

"Manny, this is very important," she said softly but strongly. "Hold on to this bead until one of us gets back. Don't let it out of your sight. We'll explain later."

Seeing the exchange, Ty joined them on the ground to better shield them all from surveillance eyes and ears. The thought of CaL ratting on him lingered, but the command gushed out involuntarily, as if unhinged from any doubt of his friend's loyalty.

"Give it to CaL if neither of us return," he whispered. Five security agents were quickly upon them. They stood and Manny pointed his flashlight at XoL and Ty. "These two shouldn't be here!" he shouted. With stunners drawn, the lead agent shoved Manny aside and informed Ty and XoL that they were under arrest. "You can't do this! I HAVE A DAUGHTER!" Ty screamed. Two agents stepped in and put a chokehold on him. Ty fought to get free. Without warning his head was gripped by an excruciating vibration and his lungs swelled as if ready to explode. He passed out before he could hear XoL's desperate cries to leave him alone.

Manny watched as XoL was handcuffed and pushed down the ramp to the Atrium. Two agents were carrying Ty by his arms and legs. Two others stayed behind and carried out his damaged bead-reading unit. Manny clutched the bead. He didn't know it, but this was not the first time the bead had been in his possession. Months earlier, PaZ had asked him to pass it through the exit detectors on his way home from work one day. "It's a surprise recording for Nori," PaZ had told him. Manny did not hesitate then to bend the rules for "The Prince," no questions asked.

19

THE BOAR'S LAIR

Ty had guessed correctly on his way to the Gala: The Boar's lair was in the leading, Earth-facing torus of OCTAD's main campus. The wheel contained deputy and staff offices, working and sleeping suites, an around-the-clock monitoring and operations center, meeting rooms, a gym, two cafeterias, and an entertainment center. It also contained Sus Scrofa's home, a spacious apartment with quarters for a servant, her personal guard, a chef, and a coterie of robot pets—including pigs, chickens, and a crow she had programmed to dive bomb the rare guest as a none-too-kind practical joke.

But her pride rested on the private conference room appended to her private office. Amid involuntary cackles, she often boasted that the room was the perfect representation of her alter ego: an American suid. The centerpiece was a large, handcrafted conference table shaped like a flattened boar, set a full meter off the floor to make seated attendees look diminished. (Rumor had it that the peculiar, bristle-like surface of the table was the skin of an actual boar.) The familial incarnation harkened back to her pig-farming ancestors in central Iowa, from whom, she often asserted, she had inherited an aggressive and unforgiving spirit.

One side of the conference room displayed a digital map of the planet, with twinkling lights depicting the nearly 1,000 terranauts that on any given day toiled on its surface—"my little children," she liked to say. The other side of the oblong space had a clear view of Earth through an oculus ringed with diamond-like sparkling gems—her version of a beatifying halo.

On this day, eighteen people were gathered around the table. Among them and seated to the immediate left of Sus Scrofa's high-backed chair—a privileged position—was ThU. Four days earlier, in his office behind his pristine desk and suffering from a hoarse voice, the head producer had cursed loudly at Hades, his veebot, for failing to understand his dictation about Ty's "homicidal" attack. But now, his imperiousness more than restored, the man smugly awaited the security chief's entrance and the plaudits that were sure to come his way for masterminding the attack on Ty and his manager. Everyone else was restive. Some of the attendees were wiping their hands on the table, as if to confirm the story behind its grain. Others were watching the dots on the map, wondering what the terranauts in the oceans' vastness might be recording; still others simply had their eyes fixed on the Earth oculus as if it were a meditational mandala. Two new members of the core PEA cabal, never having been to SuS's lair before, couldn't help but stare at the picture hanging on the wall behind her chair. Framed in antique wood, the artwork showed a middle-aged woman seated on a rocking chair on a farmhouse porch, holding an assault rifle to one side and petting a large pig on the other. The lower part of the frame contained the woman's name in gold-leaf letters: CINCINNATA BLACKBURN "SUS SCROFA."

After a 45-minute wait the meeting room door opened and the security chief made her entrance, followed by DaK, her towering personal bodyguard. The group rose. The two newcomers grimaced. They had never seen the security chief in person, and no prior holographic appearance had prepared them for her small stature.

How is it possible for someone in a society that screens for birth defects, to have been born with proportional dwarfism, you may ask? Measuring four feet, eleven inches, Arrabane Sus Scrofa exceeded the medical definition of the rare condition by one inch. But her lack of size was so striking, most people readily thought she was a true dwarf. No one in her inner circle had ever dared to ask her about it, how she came to be that way. Rumor had it that her mother had died while giving birth prematurely, somehow causing in the undersized baby permanent osteodystrophy. But no such malady comes from an early delivery.

SuS's condition stemmed, rather, from misguided parental beliefs. Her mother and father were devout supporters of the Exodus, attending weekly sermons at their local church about the divine progress of Earth's regeneration. Nature, they held, reigns supreme, and humans should have no say in its evolution. They took the dogma to an extreme, considering medicine, including preventive health practices, as an affront to nature's will. And so, when the geomagnetic storm hit during her mother's second month of pregnancy—the largest recorded since the so-called Carrington event of 1859 of the Old Calendar—her parents refused to take shelter. "Nature will ordain the fate of the pregnancy," her mother affirmed, to the consternation of health officials. The baby was born nearly three months ahead of schedule, with dwarfism genes and those causing Telogen effluvium, an illness that results in total hair loss. But SuS's parents saw no reason for the infant to undergo gene therapy and redress the mutations. Suffering from radiation poisoning, SuS's mother died a few months after giving birth, but not before naming the baby Arrabawn. The family was of Irish lineage with a deep Old-World farming tradition, and the name honored the legendary dairy farm in Tipperary County, Ireland.

Raised by a sickly father, Arrabawn was slow to talk and walk, and doctors began to attribute a rising ill temper to her delayed development. Her first words were unrecognizable, sounds more akin to grunts born out of frustration. And soon after she was able to walk—haltingly, at age three—she mastered slapping her thighs rapidly, in fury over her slow locomotion. Feeling an uncomfortable kind of pity, schoolmates and neighbors rarely looked her in the eye, rarely engaged in conversation. The hesitancy was compounded when an ill-willed sixth-grade boy, after she failed to answer a teacher's query, called her a midget. Arrabawn rose from her seat, ran to the much bigger child and furiously slapped and kicked him, screaming unintelligibly until others intervened to stop the assault. The boy was forced to apologize right then and there, but the die was cast: she was not someone to be trifled with.

At age fifteen, her anger at the world coinciding with the onset of womanhood, she changed her name. The soft-sounding "bawn" became "bane," and her Blackburn surname, proud as she was of the "scorched-earth" association, was replaced by *Sus scrofa*, the scientific term for the kind of lone wild pig—a boar—her Iowa farming ancestors never slaughtered. It also better reflected her temperament, she thought—that of a frightful beast holding no fear against larger foes.

With no one to call a friend, SuS took the isolation as a call to excel in brain games, especially number games. She was unbeatable. After disposing of adversaries, she would let out a loud sneer, which in time became a reflexive, high-pitched cackle. This further isolated her, but she did not care; she was secure in her ability to think faster and further ahead than anyone else. After graduation she bypassed a university education to avoid the ignominy of mingling. She opted instead to join the staff of the Tetrad's Secretary of Trade and Commerce, where her skills in associative calculations could be of good service. And she rose fast. An important promotion led her to the monitoring of the barter economy between colonies. She quickly learned the ease with which material gains, from cremation ashes to the oversupply of produce, could circulate unreported. She then became head of the Bartering Control Office, gaining valuable knowledge about which substances could best be "harvested" for profit in the black market. The jump from that position to the security division of the STC came soon after, with the charge to track illicit trade among PEA resisters. No one stood in her way when the post of Chief of Security at OCTAD opened, and she knew exactly what to do with it.

"Oh, please stay seated. This will be a short briefing," SuS said upon entering the meeting room, swinging aside her trailing hover-tunic to avoid tripping. Two small tusks protruded from the table's snout-shaped end. She grabbed hold of one as DaK placed his left boot next to her chair as a foothold. She stepped on it, grumbling her way onto the raised seat.

"I see we have two worthy new members. Your genius in handling our well-earned profits precedes you," she said looking down from the high perch toward the far end of the table. "Welcome, welcome. I call her Mother," she said, pointing to the portrait on the wall behind her while letting out one of her signature cackles. "She was the last person to work on my ancestors' farm before being forcibly evicted. People said she had fire in her veins—*hee*—and you can guess by the weapon in her grasp that she was not someone to piss on. It took twenty soldiers to get her out of the house—she shot five of them and would have killed them all if the cowards hadn't smoked her out—*hee*. She had her grandfather's genes, a military hero, which explains, well, let's just say my own genes run deep—*heehee*. The photograph is one of only a handful of objects of any kind that came here from the Old-World. Some say she was smuggled into orbit," she concluded with an extended cluck.

ThU smiled approvingly.

"But let's get on with our agenda, shall we?"

Grinning broadly, SuS tapped the digital console set flush on the table between two sagittate ears. The room's far wall lit up with a splash of tropical nuts, seeds, berries, mushrooms, shards of bark, a variety of leaves, live parrotlets and beetles.

"The last shipment was our best yet. Let's enjoy it for a moment. I can assure you: these are the real thing, mounds of them—no tricks with mirrors—*hee*. May I say with some confidence that none of you will be able to resist the cornucopia of profits—*heehee*."

The attendees nervously reciprocated her laughter.

"Let me give you the details. But first a warm welcome to the Amazonia Division Head Producer here—*hee*—who a few days ago moved an important quantity of Catuaba. Mr. Uris also makes for quite an able spy!" ThU smiled and waited for the applause. It didn't come. Unaware of protocol, one of the newcomers rose, silencing the meeting.

"There are disturbing rumors," the woman said, "about a second sighting two months ago. We are all obviously—"

"Concerned? Ah yes, the details, please. DaK—let's have the details, shall we?"

The bodyguard positioned himself behind the chief, his bald head partly obscuring the wall hanging. He eyed each member of the group to ensure undivided attention.

"Nine days before the Gala," DaK began, "a terranaut was sent to the Serra Padre to track a jaguar. He was getting close to the compound. A stealth operative was sent to monitor his movement, but the man was, well … inexperienced. The encounter was unfortunate; our man had no choice but to force a chase and try to lure the intruder into the compound. But the terranaut stopped and left the site in a hurry. It appears he was attacked. The operative later backtracked and found a stunned jaguar on the ground."

SuS tapped the console, bringing to sight a close-up view of two people chatting at the Gala next to a moon-filled porthole amid swirling confetti.

"Let me present to you Sand County Linnaeus Te," she said, pausing to let the members take a good look at the figure with the painted face. "His companion's headdress is unfortunate, but we will soon identify him, or her, of course—*heehee*. Mr. Te—Ty as he likes to be called—is the hapless brother of that other poor soul who stumbled upon the compound. We have followed his every step since he returned from his aborted mission; a speck of confetti makes for a very stealthy interloper—*hee*. Mr. Te thinks he's very smart, but the head producer here can tell you that smarts can mean just the opposite when you don't know who you are talking to. ThU, if you please!"

ThU cleared his still aching throat.

"Gentlemen and ladies, I was prepared to personally fix Mr. Te's inept recording, made after evading capture, only to find out that he had beaten me to it—out of his own volition—by falsifying data to make out of a monkey a living and breathing human being …"

A wave of laughter swept the room.

"PLEASE!" said SuS, halting the merriment. "Our man has a bit of an impulsive temper, too—*hee*. But rest assured we will deal with him—AND HIS MANAGER—appropriately. They were arrested yesterday at, shall we say, a very charming moment—*heehee*." A still image of XoL and Ty appeared on the wall, their grainy silhouettes digitally enhanced to compensate for the low ambient light. Their lips were touching.

"He was on the way to see her, in the middle of the night, illicitly. A battery malfunction was set up, the perfect way to find them alone and record their mutual lust for all to see. The lady cares for her star terranaut. Too much for her own good—*heehee*. But you need not be concerned. They will not survive what's in store for them. When we meet again, it will be my pleasure to give you THE DETAILS—*heeheehee*."

The group again nervously echoed her laughter. Sensing what was to come, ThU slunk down into his chair. In a blur, SuS yanked one of the tusks out of the table and hurled it across the room toward the offending newcomer. It barely missed him before striking the wall screen, squarely on XoL's eye.

"I will not let anyone stand in our way. THE EARTH WILL AGAIN BE OCCUPIED!" SuS howled. DaK set his foot by the chair again and helped her down to the floor. No one dared utter a word.

Her agents had only partially restored Ty's workstation bead-reading unit, but it was enough to know what was in it. She was not about to admit to the group that someone, in orbit, had incriminating evidence of the encampment's existence.

"Get the bead!" she barked at DaK as they exited the meeting room.

20

ACCUSATION
AND OUTRAGE

Ty awoke in a fog, sensing nothing beyond weightlessness amid a depthless, formless gray infinity. He shifted and turned but could not tell which way was up, down, or sideways. Flames suddenly shot into his eyes, then he realized it was fabric, the suit he was in. He struggled to remember how or when he got into an incandescent orange suit. A tube was taped to his lower arm. "My wristband!" he muttered, hearing his voice as if someone else was speaking. He followed the tube up his sleeve to a pouch and poked it. A gel rushed into his veins. It was icy cold. His shoulder hit something and he was pushed away by a mild repelling force. Another bump came seconds later, this time on the other shoulder, and he was similarly bounced back. He curled into a floating ball.

"It's time," a voice said from somewhere.

The grayness faded and the space revealed itself: a sphere no more than twice his height in diameter. He fell, banging his elbow hard against the floor. Groaning, he leaned against a curving wall and pushed himself up to standing, barely able to keep his knees from buckling.

A round door opened. Two guards clad in white yanked him out into a brightly lit hallway. He squinted, vaguely recalling Manny's blinding flashlight. Was this a dream? He could not tell. The guards removed the feeding tube and pouch, grabbed Ty by his armpits and dragged him down the hall to a changing room. A pressed blue suit was hanging to the side of a shower stall. Undershirt, underpants, and walking socks were folded on a stool. There was a toilet opposite the shower, a small lavatory between. He looked for a mirror but did not see one. He rubbed his face and sensed a beard worth several weeks of growth. It then hit him.

"NORI!" he yelled. He staggered to the door and pulled the handle. It was locked. "I have to see my daughter!" he shouted, banging on the door. A voice answered soothingly: "Mr. Te, your daughter is at Manaus being well cared for, but at this moment it is not possible for you to see or speak to her. Thank you for your cooperation." Frantic pleading and banging went unanswered. Images of his hands clamped on ThU's throat, LeE's baffled face, and XoL's horrified expression swirled chaotically in Ty's head. His stomach clenched as he recalled standing with CaL at the Gala. He struggled to comprehend how—or why, or if—CaL could have alerted ThU about his recording data, how The Boar's agents knew he was at the Amazonia headquarters the night he and XoL were arrested.

"Manny!" he yelled, hands pressed to his face. He felt dizzy. "Please get dressed Mr. Te," the voice replied. Defeated, he wiped his face, showered, put on the fresh clothes, and sat on the low table. The door opened. Two guards motioned him out and guided him down the hallway, tightly holding his arms. Ahead he could see XoL, walking with difficulty between two other guards. She tried to look back, but the guards jerked her forward. Ty began to shout her name but his larynx, as if paralyzed, would not respond. Two doors terminated the hallway. Standing in front of them, side-by-side, Ty and XoL traded stolen and uncomprehending glances.

The doors opened and the guards nudged them down a ramp into a tiered, theater-like space. Two hover chairs awaited them at the center of the room. They sat. Clamps flipped from under the armrests. The chairs rose. Ahead, a long, marble-like table paralleled a blank wall. They heard noise and strained their necks to catch sight of the commotion behind. People were entering, taking seats on curving pews. Twenty to thirty people, Ty guessed. He looked at XoL and she looked back at him, silently acknowledging now what was about to occur. A door behind the table slid open and OCTAD's eight Terrestrial Rectors filed in and sat, four at either side of a center, high-backed chair. Halos depicting the biomes over which they presided—Tropical Rainforest, Savanna, Taiga, Temperate Rainforest, Temperate Grassland, Tundra, Alpine, and Chaparral—appeared above each of them. Osage entered last and took the center chair. A golden halo materialized over his head, casting an amber glow over his olive complexion. A hearing administrator materialized at the far end of the table and officially opened the trial.

"Presiding today, The Reverend Osage, Illustrious Member of the Tetrad and Fourth Governor of the Orbital Corporation of Terranaut Acquired Data. Trial One of the Year of the Halo 0275, the matter of Sand County Linnaeus Te and Diana Rachel el Xochitl de Luna, presented by the Honorable Arrabane Sus Scrofa."

A murmur rolled along the pews. XoL and Ty stole another glance, now understanding the severity of the situation. They looked at Osage, trying to glean a measure of concern, but the man was resting on his chair impassively, staring at them as if never having spent an hour and a half publicly extolling their virtues a few months earlier. After the room quieted Osage sharpened his gaze.

"Mr. Te ... Ms. de Luna—Ty, XoL, if I may. Serious allegations have been raised against you. Our Fairness Protocol requires a witnessed proceeding. We have no bias against you. It is my solemn duty to protect the integrity of this corporation and perpetuate its mission. OCTAD exists for the sole purpose of providing humanity a vivid link to Earth's hallowed wilderness and record for all time the progress of its evolution. As frontline agents of this blessed work you hold our faith and trust, and that of people everywhere. This is a holy bond, one that should not—indeed cannot—be broken.

"As you both well know, OCTAD operates under its own rules, regulations, and laws. Our judgment of your actions will be final. Our esteemed Tropical Rainforest Rector, Passiflora Cerulea, has been appointed as your defense counselor. She has familiarized herself with the accusations and will offer absolving evidence as it may exist—unless, of course, either one of you wishes to confess now any wrongdoing."

Osage paused, apparently hoping Ty and XoL would spare themselves the pain of a detailed indictment. Ty could hardly think straight. He knew he committed a protocol violation but could not reconcile how it could possibly have led to this level of inquiry. He could not fathom why XoL was at all implicated. They remained silent.

"Very well, then," Osage said, motioning the Administrator to bring in OCTAD's security chief. XoL winced.

SuS entered the room from a second-tier door. Images of stampeding wild boar coursed through her trailing tunic. DaK followed her in, walked ahead to the lectern, and placed a stoop for her to step up onto. Once settled, she slapped her side to turn off the squealing suids and turned toward Osage. He nodded.

"Supreme Reverend, Rectors, and assembled witnesses," she began, speaking slowly, with affected seriousness to avoid snickering. "I must go back in time to accord this case a proper foundation. Last year, Mr. Te's brother and his wife, esteemed terranauts both, perished in a most unfortunate accident in northern Amazonia." Ty and XoL squirmed in disgust. Their chairs wobbled. SuS paused, sneered at them then continued, methodically recounting PaZ's first mission to the Serra.

"Having failed to record the intended target, Mr. Te—PaZ, that is—sought the assistance of his wife on a return trip to the same locale. This failed. Sadly, as feared might happen, an avalanche buried them and their bodies could not be recovered—at least not without turning soil and upsetting the site's natural process of regeneration," SuS said sternly, pointing at the defendants. "This tragic mission occurred at the insistence of their manager—seated here—despite my own in-person warning of the risks involved."

The chief paused to arrange her visage in a clumsy attempt to appear sympathetic, then continued.

"Mr. Te here, has been distraught over his brother's untimely death. We offer as evidence records of his conversations with friends and colleagues. This is understandable, and he does not deny it. We submit, however, that the terrible loss has caused in him mental and emotional instability, even delusions that render in question his capacity to perform further earth-bound work. As you are aware, he adopted his brother's daughter against all advice, further affecting his state of mind, as you will clearly see."

Pressing the armrests, Ty mumbled an inaudible expletive. SuS scowled at him.

"You'll have your say, Mr. Te," said Osage.

SuS went on, but not before changing her tone to one of almost melodic ridicule.

"He imagines that his brother is still alive in Amazonia, walking about as a FREE-RANGE HUMAN ..."

Gasps were heard from the pews. She paused for effect, then continued.

"As I was saying, a free-range human, enjoying the fruits of our blessed planet as if it were the biblical garden of plenty. But don't take my word for it."

A close-up of Ty at the Gala materialized on the far side of the room for all to see. A computer voice followed, each syllable closely matching Ty's lip movements:

"My tracker had the jaguar about one hundred meters away when it beeped—a warning that another large mammal was closing in. I stopped and waited for a minute or two, but I could see or hear nothing. I started walking again and then it appeared, as if from nowhere, a human being—a man. PaZ! He was almost naked."

SuS paused to let the voice-over sink in. The Rectors shook their heads. XoL closed her eyes and hunched down as if to shield her mind from SuS's outrageous accusation. Ty stiffened in his chair, straining his forearms against the clamps. "I did not say PaZ. Did not say his name. She doctored the tape!" he whispered through clenched teeth.

"The state of Mr. Te's distress is severe," SuS continued, returning to a stiff delivery. "Not content with merely raising the unfathomable prospect of his brother's Lazarus-like apparition, he then fabricated data to support his fantasy, transposing a human genome—his own—to a DNA sample of *Alouatta seniculus*, a common red howler monkey."

"The shift was the other way around!" Ty muttered, realizing in that moment that CaL could not have been the one to snitch on him. A video image of the DNA splice sequence appeared on the far wall. Pressed between anger and relief Ty bowed his head, resigned to the inevitability of an unjust verdict.

"Mr. Te is trained in scanning DNA and storing strands of chromosomes. It is a fact that human and Alouatta chromosomes are similar. It was as easy as it was deliberate for him to manipulate the data AND FABRICATE THE APPEARANCE OF LONG-ABANDONED HUMAN LIFE ON EARTH. We have, of course, the security system in place to bring witness to such violations, especially when abetted by a CORRUPT MANAGER—*heehee*!" SuS wagged a finger at XoL.

"Ms. de Luna was OBLIGATED to submit a report and advise my office of the incident," SuS continued. "But she did not—and has not still! Why, we must ask, did this heretofore most capable terranaut and manager choose to suppress evidence of Mr. Te's wrongdoing?"

On cue, a holograph of Ty and XoL's faces appeared above their heads.

The same image she had shared earlier at the board meeting, but altered to show a slow and progressive kiss.

"Reverend, Rectors, and esteemed witnesses, the answer is as old as the dawn of humankind. XoL and this troubled man ARE LOVERS—*hee*! We have visuals and witness accounts of favors and unbecoming affection between them. Their life, in every dimension, has unfolded furtively within OCTAD's walls. Guided by sexual desires, this manager has chosen to protect her lover—a sick terranaut intent on compromising the integrity of this venerable corporation. SHE USED HER POSITION TO HIDE A HEINOUS CRIME!"

Ty wrestled with the clamps, stunned by the accusation. The room was still.

"Reverend and Rectors: I have provided for your review the requisite evidentiary files. I submit these files and my testimony to your inspired wisdom for the just disposition of this case. Let me assure you that my office will not rest until the integrity of the Amazonia Division has been fully restored."

Osage directed his attention to Ty.

"Do you have anything to say on your behalf, Mr. Te?" he asked. Ty could not get a word out. Every fiber in his body wanted to jump off, rush SuS and grab her by the throat. DaK looked at him, imagining perfectly what was running through Ty's mind, hoping that the man would indeed let loose and lunge at his boss so justice could be imparted right there and then with a lethal blow to Ty's solar plexus.

"MR. TE!" Osage again asked.

"Damn her," XoL said to herself, still hunched, wishing she could force her heart to cease beating and spare her a life of guilt-stinging torment.

Going back in time, she saw SuS and DaK entering her office unannounced, minutes before she was to authorize PaZ's request to return to Serra Padre with MaY. Without any pretense to excuse the interruption, SuS had begun to rant about the mission, demanding that it be scrapped.

"They have no business going there; it's too risky and expensive an operation! Amazonia is a big place and parakeets can be found elsewhere—and besides, your star terranaut already failed the first time around!" she had bellowed.

XoL had been taken aback by the grossly out-of-protocol demand. Having only recently assumed the position of Interim Division Manager, the last thing she wanted was to cave in before the big bosses and be seen as weak by the workforce. She had rejected SuS's demand outright, telling her that PaZ had failed on his solo mission because he had fallen ill, that on the return mission he would be accompanied by OCTAD's top expert in ocular implants, and that together they were sure to bring back an extraordinary recording capable of eliciting world-wide awe. SuS's anger had then evaporated in a blink. Smiling widely and twirling her tunic as if practicing a dance move, she had said, "If there are two terranauts that can pull off the mission, surely it is them—two of my favorites together in a daring mission. PERFECT—*heehee.*"

Stupefied by the sudden transformation, XoL had wondered if the little woman's snickers had been dispensed as a nervous tick or as further insult. But then SuS had again pivoted, banging on XoL's desk: "The demand stands! Go find the birds somewhere else. I can complicate their mission whether you like it or not," leaving XoL to guess what she had meant by that. Now, with the hearing room silenced and her sinister cackles ringing in her ears, she guessed no more. Strapped defenseless in the hover chair and convinced that the woman was a soulless black hole sucking all manner of good from the world, she snapped.

"THIS IS A SHAM! A WRONGFUL, DECEITFUL, FALSE, AND WHOLLY EVIL ACCUSATION!" XoL yelled, stiffening her back.

Witnesses gasped. The Rectors recoiled at XoL's effrontery. SuS stared at her with a venomous grin as if welcoming the fight.

"Quiet, please! Quiet!" Osage shouted. "Xochitl de Luna: It is only your high accomplishments in the Corps that keeps me from charging you with contempt, closing this trial, and sending you off to the Moon. You will address the honorable Rectors and myself with due respect."

XoL lowered her shoulders and directed a pained expression at Passiflora Cerulea, her long-time and admired mentor.

"Amazonia has been the sole focus of my life since entering the university fifteen years ago. Terranauts have scoured the rainforest—day to day, week to week, year to year—documenting the wildlife in this most extraordinary environment. The work is perilous. We have lost many good men and women devoted to it, Ty's brother and his wife among them. It is in their memory and that of all other perished terranauts that I work to amaze the world. And yet I have wanted more: to introduce something new, unseen, unimagined—something that would rivet humanity's attention, to OCTAD's profit."

XoL took a slow, deep breath, carefully calibrating the argument that she had been constructing while Sus was spouting her lies.

"Ty is a loyal, dedicated, and obedient terranaut. He does as he's told. It is not his fault to have reported a human sighting. What he saw was real, *to him*!"

"THIS IS ABSURD, Reverend! She's shamelessly trying to protect her lover!" yelled SuS, extending XoL a furious look. Osage stared SuS down and directed XoL to continue.

"I was hoping after he returned from his mission that Ty would tell someone, a friend or colleague, about what he had encountered, that rumors would spread mounting a sense of mystery and excitement. He never got that far. He knew what he had seen would damage OCTAD, cast doubt in the belief of nature unaltered. He tampered with the data to protect the Division, protect OCTAD. He did nothing wrong. On the contrary, he did what he is accused of, but to correct a wrong—my own! IT WAS I WHO PLACED A HUMAN FIGURE IN HIS PATH!" she said, her tone rising. Gasps again flew from the pews. Flailing her arms in disgust, SuS inadvertently activated the stampeding boars over her dress, turning them off with several wild slaps.

"There is NO EVIDENCE to her claim, Reverend! Where is the alleged conspirator? Where's the man she placed in his path? THERE IS NO SUCH PERSON!"

XoL turned toward SuS. A calming clarity washed over her as she saw the woman's contorted face betraying a magnitude of hatred she could hardly comprehend.

"There is no conspirator," XoL said, smiling at the security chief, then turning to face Osage. "What Ty saw was a holographic burst from his headset, programmed by me and set to go off at a specific day and time. The image was automatically erased upon his return. The only evidence is my word. In retrospect, I should have selected a far different human figure; one Ty had no chance of confusing with his deceased brother.

"As to the accusation of a loving relationship between us, I admit this: in our youth Mr. Te and I shared a caring friendship, an innocent love, if you will. At OCTAD we have been duty-bound colleagues, nothing more. If I have treated him with any deference, or affection, it is only in recognition of his extraordinary skill and dedication. Finally, the Chief of Security has asked about the delay in my report. Of this I am guilty. I was ashamed by Ty's loyal and noble actions. I needed time to think things through before submitting it, which I hereby do—as my unequivocal and immediate resignation. May the venerable Corps continue to amaze the world without me."

A long silence followed as Osage absorbed XoL's confession. "Is that all," he asked?

XoL nodded.

"Mr. Te—SAND COUNTY?" Osage shouted to rouse Ty.

Ty was stunned. He remained silent, astonished by the sacrifice XoL had just made on his behalf.

"Very well, then. I will now ask Rector Cerulea to offer on behalf of you both any absolving information."

The Rector stared at them, teary-eyed. She turned toward Osage and shook her head. She had nothing to say.

"We will reconvene to pass judgment after a thorough review of the facts and testimony," Osage concluded. The Hearing Administrator appeared.

"All rise!"

The halos faded and Osage and the Rectors exited the room. Passiflora trailed the group, unable to look back. SuS turned on her digital dress and aimed for the door, closely trailed by DaK, stoop in hand. As the witnesses rose and filed out of the room XoL and Ty remained in their chairs, suspended in midair, their lives suspended even more so.

PART III

21

A FLYING SAINT
BERNARD

ali had sensed something was wrong when Ty sped down the
alley without greeting Karman. The veebot had followed him
through the greensward to the transit station, into the shell to
the Amazonia headquarters, up the ramp and down the hall to his workstation. Its eyes and ears had seen and heard everything up to the instant
the alarms went off, sizing up the moment as the normal warning of an
incoming solar flair. Lali knew that the emergency would trigger a feed
interruption. The break had lasted ten minutes, and the place had appeared
as before, except that Ty and XoL were nowhere to be found.

Morning came and still there were no signs of Ty. Troubled by his
seeming disappearance, Lali materialized as a rooster in the middle of
the living area and let out a loud waking crow. Karman had slept fitfully,
worrying, too, about Ty's errant behavior. Disoriented by the sudden
squawking she rolled out of the sofa where she had spent the night and

tumbled to the floor. The commotion woke up Nori, who ambled to the living area, crying and clutching her trogon. Sensing the error, Lali popped up one of Ty's happy faces and in his voice reported that "he" had to leave unexpectedly for Amazonia on an important mission, that everything was arranged for Nori to return to Manaus, adding on the fly that the day's activities would include a visit to the pod's Earth-gazing observatory, Nori's favorite outing.

Nori held her sobs while absorbing the message but started right up again after Lali attempted to correct the lie by offering that Ty's whereabouts were unknown, as was the time of his return. Nori's tears did not last long. Three security agents barged in without warning and began tearing the place apart. Karman grabbed her and held her tight; the two were too afraid to speak. As the agents were not family members or acquaintances, Lali, too, remained silent.

The fright Nori experienced lingered vividly for years. From her diary:

May 3, 0278

... I screamed my lungs out, but it was like they were deaf. The men just kept emptying drawers, kicking aside floor pillows, rummaging through my soft toys and tossing everything that was not attached to a wall or shelf. They were the same men that earlier had been to visit me at Manaus. When they couldn't find the bead, they yelled at me. They wanted to know if Ty had it, whether he had taken it with him somewhere or given it to someone. One of them grabbed me and shook me and said that if I didn't tell the truth Ty was go going to get into real trouble, go to prison far away and I would never see him again. I hated those men, so I lied again. They left angry, they said they'd return if they didn't get what they were looking for.

Karman was really upset and she was crying. She called CaL as soon as the men left the apartment. He was at the peapod station, and instead of going to work he came right over to help. Karman told him what had happened. She was still crying. CaL said he had crossed paths with three security agents on the way to see us, and they had looked at him in a strange way, like they knew who he was. He asked if Ty had said anything about a mission, or where he was going, and if XoL had been around or if she had called. And he asked if the men had said why they were looking for a bead, what was in it. Lali and Karman couldn't give him any answers. CaL was very upset, he just kept shaking his head.

After learning from Nori and Karman what had happened, CaL sat and wondered what sort of trouble Ty might be in. "I told you so," he muttered, recalling word for word his warning at the Gala about tampering with recorder data. Wrongly, he concluded that the bead in question had been Ty's recording of the sighting; that for some reason he had brought it home. After helping clean up the mess, walking Karman home, and taking Nori to Manaus, CaL returned to headquarters. He asked about XoL but was told she had not been in her office. "She's working from home today," said a colleague with seeming assurance. "She went to visit a sick parent," said another. No one could offer a plausible guess about Ty either. Unsatisfied, he stepped into the atmospherics hover station, guided it halfway up the atrium, and got busy redesigning the holographic settings. He entered a few commands on the programming console but stopped, unable to concentrate.

It then struck him like a joke's perfectly timed punch line. "God damn!" he cried with a wide grin, stunned by the beauty of it: Finally, overcoming their inane aversion to love, XoL and Ty had gone to Amazonia to find the illusory human being, making out of Ty's sighting nothing more than a wild excuse to frolic in paradise. He was sure of it. Leaning over the console he couldn't help but chuckle, savoring the cleverness and romance of such a plot. The snorts were picked up by the modeling program and caused a ripple in the tessellations of the giant Anaconda he had just hung in midair.

A yell snapped CaL out of his delirium. Manny was below, frantically waving him down. The guard had stayed past his nighttime hours to wait for CaL and personally tell him what had transpired with XoL and Ty the night before. He had pondered for hours whether to give the bead to CaL as soon as he saw him. He knew all too well that their being taken by Boar agents would mean days of interrogation.

"They were grabbed last night, dragged out by Boar agents," Manny said in a hush after CaL alit.

"Who? What do you mean??"

"XoL and Ty. They were arrested."

"In the middle of a shutdown? Arrested for what?" CaL asked, withholding what Ty had confessed at the Gala.

"He just said he was in a hurry, something urgent; raced upstairs and met XoL. They were looking at something, couldn't tell what. Then the Boars got here. Stunned him. XoL was dragged kicking and screaming. They also took his bead reader."

"God-d-d-damn," CaL stuttered. "Was anyone else there?"

"No one else knows," Manny said.

CaL wanted to tell Manny about the sighting but thought better of it; rumors would spread and cause Ty more trouble. At the same time, Manny debated giving CaL the bead but refrained, fearful of drawing CaL into a bad situation that neither of them fully understood. Each sensed that the other was holding something back, but nothing more was said. They exchanged mumbled goodbyes and Manny departed, leaving CaL staring listlessly at the unfinished atmospherics. Dejected, CaL powered off the console and steered the station out of the atrium. Overhead the incomplete Anaconda dissipated amid a raw tangle of tropical limbs and foliage.

The next day the message came from XoL's assistant: XoL and Ty were on leave by orders from the Rector. Rumors began to fly. That they had had a physical altercation following Ty's demands for promotion. That they had been caught violating the liaison policy and had eloped halfway around the world. That they had colluded in the exchange of recordings with other divisions for black market profit. XoL's office was soon cleared and a manager from another division was installed, deepening the division's depressive pall.

Weeks later, CaL was in his office with a group of Atmo trainees when the workforce was summoned to the atrium for an important announcement. Hoping to receive news about XoL and Ty, he rushed out and took a spot along one of the ramps facing the oblong common area. Scaled nearly two stories in height, Passiflora and ThU's figures materialized amid CaL's now completed display. Chuckles were heard as the Anaconda's tongue appeared to flicker out of the producer's mouth.

"A few weeks ago, two of our most distinguished colleagues, XoL and Ty, as most of you know them, were discovered to have tampered with virgin data," Passiflora began.

"Fuck! Fuck! Fuck!" CaL cursed, gripping the railing and leaning over the edge. Those near him stepped away, fearing that he was about to become ill.

"The incident was uncovered by the Division Head Producer after a random quality control data inspection. An investigation by the Security Office followed, pointing to Xochitl de Luna as the instigator of a mission that was as shameful as it was foolish: to create the illusion of human life on Earth. Unbeknownst to anyone, she is … was … a member of the PEA resistance. And to her shameful ploy Mr. Te was a willing if naïve abettor."

Passiflora paused to let her words sink in.

"He provided the recording material and followed XoL's orders to insert a human genome into a DNA record of *Alouatta seniculus*. A trial was held, presided over by our Director Supreme and all eight Rectors. The evidence, investigated by our honorable Chief of Security, was complete and duly presented. The sentences were severe. As I speak to you, Rachel Diana Xochitl de Luna is Moon-bound for a 25-year term of penal isolation, after which time she will be eligible to terminate her life. And Sand County Linnaeus Te …," she paused to suppress a rare upwelling of emotion, "…Ty has been expelled from the Corps. He will never again set foot in this hall."

Workers shook their heads in disbelief. Some muttered to themselves while others turned to share their astonishment with those near them. Dumbfounded, CaL stared past Passiflora, ThU— and the Anaconda—to the far reaches of the atrium. He wondered if anything he heard from Ty at the Gala was true, wondered also if Ty's story was just a contrived way to plant seeds of doubt ahead of a sure indictment. But he couldn't trace a single instance when Ty had lied to him about anything, let alone about something of such transcendental importance. There were simply no secrets between them—at least not that Ty kept from CaL. The harder he tried to rationalize the sighting as a fabrication, the less it seemed plausible. A ping broke the mind-numbing puzzle.

"Ty!" he gasped, immediately lowering his voice. "We just heard. Where are you? What the hell happened?"

"Meet me at the Café. I'll be there in a few hours and can explain everything," Ty said, ending the call. CaL looked up at the Anaconda. The animal was coiled around a limb, staring straight back at him. He frowned and pointed a finger, assuring the creature that a rodent was coming its way. He rushed down the ramp and headed to the lounge to change into normal clothes. Running across the atrium he messaged the new manager that he had an urgent family matter to tend to, that he would be gone the rest of the day and very possibly more than that.

Disheveled and unshaven, Ty pensively waited for CaL to arrive. From his seat at the back of Café LaLigne he scarcely noticed the open-cabin Latecoure 25 piloted by a hefty Saint Bernard circling overhead. Ocean whitecaps and verdant Argentinian pampas scrolled slowly across the café's dividing air screens, a calming background to the place's ever-present tumult.

CaL's granduncle, one Roscoe Brown LaLigne, had been a space-walking Francophile with African American ancestry from North Texas. Named after a flier from the celebrated Tuskegee Airmen who fought in the Second World War, the man had opened the café after retiring from the pod-repair corps. He had been smitten by early twentieth-century aviation since childhood and had insisted on gracing the business with the family name, coincident with the pioneering flights—*La Ligne*—that linked Africa with South America. Roscoe died the year CaL was born, but one family member after another had kept the café going, in time making it one of the colony's go-to meeting places. Intent on showcasing his atmospheric craft after graduating from the university, CaL had added to the décor the holo version of the famous plane, with the dog at the helm in honor of his family's middle name, Canis.

It was at the café that CaL and Ty marked the important milestones of their lives. After their admittance into OU, they had celebrated well into the night there, their chatter degenerating into obtuse arguments about historical figures from each of their respective fields. A particularly fertile debate concerned the relative worth of the contributions of, for CaL, the aviator Jean Mermoz, who in the Old-World had helped usher in the age of non-terrestrial travel, and, for Ty, Aldo Leopold, the ecologist, conservationist, and almanac author who had helped usher in the twentieth-century environmental movement. That Mermoz and Leopold had been contemporaries, despite spending their lives in entirely different continents and without ever meeting each other, inspired them to enact an imagined meeting between the two pioneers, hilariously switching roles: Ty playing the reserved Aldo steeped in impossibly boring weather data and CaL the intrepid Jean who lived by the seat of his pants.

But such memories were far from Ty's mind as hours went by while he waited for CaL He could not shake the image of Osage's face as he read the verdicts, or the way in which he and XoL had been wrenched apart forevermore.

As the hover chairs alighted after the sentencing hearing, Ty had turned toward XoL to declare that he would remember her sacrifice eternally, to the last fiber of his soul. But the guards had stood between them. Following the release of the arm straps, one of them had quickly ushered Ty to the public exit, issuing a brusque directive. "Pick up your personal belongings from the changing room. You are free to go," he had said. The other guard had handcuffed XoL behind her back. As she was led up the ramp to the detention area, she had turned back to look at Ty, tears flowing, and had positioned her fingers in the universal sign for love. He had then spelled "I will always love you" but the guards had yanked XoL through the doors, leaving him to wonder if she had seen his words.

As Ty sat in the café, the pain of that memory escaped his throat as if vomited by a dark angel. "Burn in hell, SuS. BURN IN FUCKING HELL!"

"Hey, hey, easy, pal," CaL said, pulling up a chair by his side. "You okay? Hope you haven't been waiting too long. Eaten anything?" He tapped the table to activate the menu. "It's been a damn while since we've been here," he added.

'CaL's attempt at levity fell on deaf ears.

"It's a sham, CaL. LIES, ALL OF IT! PaZ, MaY—Now XoL. SHE CAN'T SURVIVE ON THE MOON!" Ty cried.

CaL fixed Ty with a hypnotic gaze, as if to glean from his rage where the truth might lie. The few times Ty had been upset to the point of blasphemy, the cause had been justified beyond doubt. But this was different. The sighting Ty had recounted to him was odd enough, but the charges coming out of the trial were of a different order of bizarre. XoL a PEA resister? That was hard to swallow. If she was, did Ty know about it; had he been keeping it a secret? CaL wanted to believe in him blindly but was hard-pressed to do so. At OCTAD CaL had been a straight arrow who obeyed the rules and placed unquestioning faith in authorities such as Osage and the Rector—even ThU for that matter. But now seeing his dear friend's distressed state of body and mind, he wondered if it was possible for Osage and the Rector to be mistaken.

"XoL ... she took the fall, for me, for Nori," Ty was saying, lowering his voice. "I now understand why PaZ and MaY were so devoted to their work, why Earth was all that mattered to them. I was a fool to follow XoL into OCTAD because, shit, I was after *her*. I never cared for the corporate crap, 'the holy mission.' You have always known that. But no more. I will save fucking OCTAD, like XoL would be doing if she had half a chance. I will expose the bastards that killed PaZ and MaY and personally seal their caskets and send them off to hell!"

"It's you who's been through hell, Ty—and you look like it, too." CaL kept his voice firm. "Go home and get a good rest, tend to Nori; take time to think things through. I'll be there when you need me ... regardless ... no matter what really happened," CaL said, betraying his ambivalence about the facts of the case.

"I'm not going home, CaL. I'm going back to Serra Padre," Ty replied, holding his eyes squarely on CaL's as if trying to burn away his friend's faltering trust. "The landslide was no accident. They were terminated, CaL—buried alive. That's what happened. They knew too much. Now we have to find out what, and where. Why they died!"

For the next two hours Ty described fully, and practically without taking a breath, how he found PaZ's bead, what he and XoL saw in it, how it explained the sighting, and how he planned to return to Earth and get the evidence needed to indict SuS Scrofa and her accomplices.

"We have to do it quickly, CaL, before SuS gets wind of what I know. Lunar sentences are death sentences; XoL won't make it there one year, let alone twenty-five. It's SuS who should be rotting up there. And if not for XoL, then we have to do it for Nori, for her future, and for all future generations."

CaL listened intently. It crossed his mind that the entire story was a mythosophical creation of the highest order, like one of Xu's exquisitely devious concoctions, soon to reveal itself with a spectacularly clever ending.

"So where's the bead?" CaL asked, needing a morsel of tangible reality before taking the plunge.

"Manny has it; I asked him to give it to you if something happens to me, just so you know I'm not completely crazy." Ty paused before seeking confirmation of his friend's commitment. "Are you with me?"

CaL took the question as a ringing alarm, a test of their lifelong friendship. One thing was clear: in the end he'd do anything for Ty, despite his current doubts about Ty's sanity … or his own.

"Just tell me one thing," CaL said, leaning back in his chair for the first time all afternoon. The Saint Bernard again passed overhead. "If this goes down the wrong way, are you really willing to leave Nori orphaned again?"

He really didn't need a verbal answer. In Ty's steely gaze he could see unwavering resolve.

"Alright," CaL said after a long pause. "I have a friend who can help, but she doesn't take money. Do you have something to barter with?"

"Beads!" said Ty, whereupon CaL cracked a smile and shook his head. That was the sign Ty always looked for from his friend when he was in a quandary. The one that meant that, like a good Alpine Mastiff, help was on the way.

FAIZ

L ali was again confounded. Ty had disappeared for weeks and now he could be seen in OCTAD's main campus walking down a torus spoke to a docking port, slipping into a Solo shell and travelling for six hours—not home but to a busy café at a neighboring pod, where he chatted with CaL for hours—about who knows what because they were seated behind a dumbwaiter out of sight and hearing—and then departing a day later in another shell to the Appalachia colony, a full radian away, meandering through a maze of alleys to an aging cabin he'd never visited before, being let in by CaL and staying there without once going out or being seen, because all of the windows were draped.

Upon arriving at Houstonia Caerulea (named after the Appalachian bluet), Ty was perplexed by the pod's sparse vegetation and its ramshackle cabins. He had seen images of first-generation pods and knew they were "basic." But this one appeared creaky and unsafe, like an abandoned relic in urgent need of repair. A pignut hickory rose nearby. Its plastek appeared lifeless, as if no one had buffed its shaggy bark for years. He could not imagine anyone preferring to live in such a place. He arrived at the cabin wondering what kind of help CaL was offering. He knocked and CaL opened the door. A woman was standing by his side, grinning.

"So, this is the famous Ty!" the woman said, extending Ty a seductive look. "Don't you worry, sweetheart," she added, stretching her gaze from head to toe. "You are safe here. None of our cabins are fitted with veebot eyes; few of us artists signed off on the Tetrad's offer to have them installed; too big a risk to have our work pirated by these all-hearing and seeing devils."

Of medium build, moderately unkempt, with undistinguishing features and a husky voice, the woman did not fit the sexpot image CaL had crowed about at the café.

"Meet Faith Zan Zahara—FaiZ—artist extraordinaire and soother of my every fantasy," CaL said, voicing a playful "ouch" as FaiZ squeezed his ass.

CaL and FaiZ had met at OCTAD's Atmospheric Engineering School during orientation week. Most Atmos enroll in the program to design and build awe-inspiring natural settings charged with exacting detail, be it he ambrosial whiffs of a night-blooming cereus, the glint of a jewel caterpillar, or the fauvist hues of a Ti leaf. To them the profession is the closest thing to experiencing the wilds of the planet, without having to undergo the arduous and expensive training required of terranauts. But that had not been the case with either CaL or FaiZ. They each had entered the program to learn pixel composition, wherever the craft might take them. The vocation had crystallized in CaL the day Ty had waddled home parroting the pope's speech; he imagined a pack of tunic-clad, honking penguins zipping along winding ice chutes in a fulgurant Antarctic sunset. He laughed all the way home, and that evening he professed to Ty what he would be doing the rest of his life. Ty had looked back at him cross-eyed, unable to understand how anyone could be so sure about what to do with their life without first knowing with whom to do it.

In FaiZ, CaL would find that answer, unorthodox as their relationship was. The daughter of a sculptor and floral designer, FaiZ was virtually preordained to become an artist. Her parents had applauded her decision to become an Atmospheric Engineer, asserting that crafting natural environments was akin to inhabiting living sculptures—besides being a far better compensated occupation than shaping raw plastek into decorative oddities, or choosing everlasting flowers to arrange in a vase. They had no idea that their daughter cared little for things terrestrial, that she instead imagined herself being, as CaL did, an architect of the fantastic. At OU she and CaL did not at first cross paths, and when they finally did their conversations were casual. It was a chance reference by FaiZ of the scenography of famed twentieth-century animator Hayao Miyazaki that opened the floodgates. This occurred while they shared coffee at the school cafeteria one day, and spawned a dizzying discussion about surreal worlds filled with bizarre creatures.

It was close to the end of the first term when FaiZ, by then very much attracted to CaL, had playfully tried to shock him. "I like men and women," she had blurted as a none-too-subtle invitation for sex. But it was CaL who had delivered the greater surprise, nervous as he was: "I w-w-w-wouldn't mind being with you—phy-physically, I mean; but I'm in love with a man, someone I have known f-f-forever. I don't know what that makes me … I'm a still a v-virgin." FaiZ had stared at him incredulously. How could it be that such a lovely man had not yet experienced physical intimacy?

The subject did not come up again until several months later, at the atmospheric lab after hours. They were combining pixels of the Icelandic aurora borealis with erupting flows from the Katla volcano when FaiZ, as she liked to do, stepped away from the atmospheric bubble to admire the emerging composition. But rather than lingering there she had shed her clothes and walked back into it to bathe naked in the eerie folds of fire and magnetized light. She had then raised her head and closed her eyes,

◄ 199 ►

lips apart as if being pulled heavenward in seeming ecstasy. CaL had stood there speechless, never having felt such beauty from a human being, aside from Ty.

Lowering her head and opening her eyes, FaiZ had held her gaze upon CaL, conveying with a smile the serene affection of a welcoming lover. Extending a hand, she had drawn him into the light. The moment was forever enshrined in them as a mutual vow of love without conditions, preconceptions, or rules. Thereafter they freely shared the details of each other's escapades, at times drawing total strangers into elaborately staged erotic fantasies. There had been no tears or expressions of sadness the day FaiZ left the Academy to become an apprentice in digital tattooing. CaL by then had become at ease with becoming a corporate man. They tacitly knew that they would always be caring friends, holding dear the intimate joy and laughter they shared whenever they met.

CaL's seemingly continuous stream of nameless affairs was all Ty knew about his sex life. But he distinctly remembered CaL's confession about his fist sexual experience "with an amazingly sensual classmate," someone he thought he could love forever, he had said. At the café, after going over Ty's plan to return to Serra Padre, CaL had opened up, telling Ty who that first love was, sharing the arc of their relationship from their first meeting to the momentous introduction that would soon take place.

Ty took a step forward and extended FaiZ a warm hug. "Easy on her," CaL joked. Ty smiled, quickly disengaging. "Your work is impressive," he said. "Mind if I look around?" The small studio was overflowing with elaborate tattoos on papers of different sizes and colors, headgear in various stages of assembly, relief prints with surreal atmospheric effects, still holographic projections, finger paints and a cornucopia of drafting implements, all fighting for precious wall and shelf space. A large square bar-height table was in the middle of the room, brimming with scavenged plastek yet to be sorted. A lone stool was stowed beneath. Behind a partition Ty found a convertible sofa lined with colorful pillows. *Must be her bed*, he thought, seeing no other alternative. A reclining chair nearly filled the rest of the space. It was fitted with a surgical lamp and swiveling tray containing tattooing needles. Over the lone draped window flickered the grill of a 1936 Brewster, shining as brightly as when Ty saw it on CaL's face at the gala.

"You remember it! I'll take that as a compliment," FaiZ said, surprising Ty as she rounded the partition. There was sweetness in her smile, Ty observed, thinking that CaL must have shared with FaiZ everything about him. He saw a quizzing intensity in her eyes, as if trying to find the key to his and CaL's lifelong friendship. It caused in Ty and unsettling attraction.

"She's the best in the business!" CaL said, proudly joining them.

"Okay, Mr. Sand County Crazy Te. Your Saint Bernard here says you have a plan, but first you need to get cleaned up. Shave closely, please." She pointed to a narrow door behind a stack of boxes and CaL tossed him a bag of fresh clothes. Ty emerged from the bathroom a while later to see CaL and FaiZ lying on the sofa, legs entwined, seemingly asleep. FaiZ cracked open an eye and perked up.

"Oh, my!" she said. "Why did you keep him hidden all this time, CaL—a jaguar wrestler, no less!" FaiZ was eager to see where the tease might take them.

"Our boy has a Dulcinea that keeps him a virgin!" CaL replied, reminding FaiZ that Ty was off limits. Ty smiled, letting the comment slide rather than say anything about XoL, or the few forgettable affairs he'd had.

"Well, then, let's get on with it." FaiZ got off the sofa and took Ty by the hand to the chair. After he settled in, she pressed two cups over his eyes and massaged them gently until satisfied with the fit. "We don't want to get any of the pixy dust in them, do we?"

With the touch of a caring nurse, she cleansed his face and rubbed in hair-growth retardant. "Hope you don't mind retro music; it helps me steady the brush," she said as the room filled with tenth-century monophonic song. From the sofa CaL watched as FaiZ expertly maneuvered the pixel brush and spread clear gel around Ty's forehead, nose, cheeks, and cleft chin. An hour later she pulled the brush back and removed the eye cups. Ty squinted and pursed his lips.

"It feels a little taut, I know, but it's better to say something now, move your lips and get used to the application. Hmmm… your eyes have an epicanthic fold; that could give you away in a snap," FaiZ said, bringing to Ty's face a thin tethered tube with a pointed nib. Ty closed his eyes to let her work around them.

"Talk a little, my darling. Will do you good," said FaiZ.

"I think you'll pass the test with flying colors," offered CaL.

"It's Nori's test that worries me," Ty responded, slowly enunciating every syllable. "She's already been at Manaus longer than during the no-visitation adoption mess."

"I didn't tell you, but Karman and I have gone to visit her several times. Lali has been teaching her chess. She's quite good at it; could be a grand master one day." CaL tried to make light of Ty's concern. Deep down he was sickened by the very real possibility of losing his friend, and even more so about seeing Nori rendered an orphan again. He and FaiZ had talked about adopting her if the worst happened, but they both knew that from a parenting standpoint Nori would be better cared for in a normal, more stable household.

Ty remained quiet.

"You don't have to go back to Serra Padre, Ty," CaL said. "You can find other work, be a regular parent to her. Heroes seldom live long enough to raise their children. I hate to say it, but PaZ and MaY …."

Ty would rather stay silent so FaiZ could finish her work, but the comment upset him.

"They loved and lived for each other, CaL. They went down fully aware of the risk, knowing they might never see Nori again. Their bond was stronger than anything. I know that now … That is the bond XoL and I have. If she were here, we'd be going down together right now; we'd be saving the world like PaZ and MaY tried to."

Ty had not told CaL about the kiss before their arrest, or the love she had professed for him as she was being yanked away after their sentencing. Those moments were too precious, too recent to share.

"Yours is a PLATONIC bond—soulful, spiritual, I'll grant you that," CaL said, springing out of the sofa. "I mean you've kissed once, what, when you were sixteen?"

"And a half," Ty replied. He shook his head, causing FaiZ to momentarily push back the nib.

"Well, that makes a big difference!"

"This is bigger than all of us, CaL. Think about what would happen if that settlement became a colony and expanded from the Serra to the west and north across the isthmus to Central America without anyone knowing anything about it. I can tell you this: it won't take twenty thousand years for humanity to overrun the planet the second time around!"

"For God's sake, man! You don't even know what they are doing down there—if it's five people or five dozen!"

"Five dozen, a hundred dozen—what's the difference? It's a colossal lie! Nori should not have to grow up in a lie—no one should with this pure, HOLY HALO of ours being just as corrupt as the Old-World was. What, then, is the point of a goddamned orbital ark?"

"The point is to have a life in the here and now. They already killed PaZ and MaY. Do you really think you can go down and stop what's going on, all by yourself, and make it back in one piece?"

"I have to try, CaL!"

"Good, good, good!" FaiZ brought the chair to an upright position. "Arguing makes the skin twitch and stretch, makes the film cover every wrinkle. And we are finished, too." She stepped back, surveying the result. Satisfied, she grabbed a small container from the side tray, removed a pair of contact lenses and placed them in Ty's eyes. He blinked several times to let them set.

"All good?"

Ty nodded.

"Good thing my boy here prefers to go bald. You would look awful in a wig. Now, this is important: When you first turn it on you will feel a mild tingling sensation, but it'll go away after a minute or two. And remember, the pixels—there are well over a million all over your face—they are photon charged and will make the mask glow in the dark. Don't go near anyone in a dark area; it'll be a dead giveaway. And when you are finished with it just yank it off, from below the cheekbone, like this," she said, demonstrating the motion with a swift upward swing of the hand.

"Ready?" she asked.

Ty placed his right thumb below his chin and pressed hard. In seconds, his facial complexion changed in tone and texture. He got off the chair and stood in front of a wall mirror. CaL joined him.

"Told you she was the best," CaL said, seeing Ty as his body double.

Ty smiled, then contorted his mouth, nose, and eyes to test the mask's capacity to flex and remain true to his new appearance. CaL stared at him, knees weakening.

"You look good with darker skin. I think ..."

"Think what?"

CaL demurred. He had long ago abandoned hope of ever making love with Ty. But the new appearance, like a disguise worn to tease and attract, sparked the fantasy anew.

"Nothing. The skin tone ... it looks good," CaL said, turning to go back to the main room. Ty sensed that skin tone wasn't what was on CaL's mind but didn't prod any further. He followed him to the large table and rested his hand on his shoulder. CaL turned around.

"I don't know how to thank you," Ty said. "Doubt I ever will ... for who you are, for everything you've been to me."

Their hands were now gripping one another's shoulders.

"Just come back ... that's all I want."

FaiZ was standing a few feet away, teary-eyed. She knew the moment

Ty walked into the cabin that he was the man CaL had always loved. She reached for them and the three hugged in a silent and sustained embrace.

CaL shed the hold. "You need to go," he uttered. Ty headed for the door; as he cracked it open he took one last look at CaL and FaiZ.

"Good luck," FaiZ said, "and remember—we never met!"

Ty nodded and stepped out, shutting the door behind him. Inside, FaiZ placed her arms around CaL and pressed herself to him tightly. CaL gently pushed her away.

"You okay?" she asked.

"He's possessed, lost his mind. He gets blinded sometimes. The last time he did something crazy was when he chased XoL into OCTAD. He's still chasing her. And now he also wants to save the world!"

"Maybe your boy can," FaiZ mused. "What was that you told me once, that he can really throw a punch?"

"He can't land them!"

MANNY'S DILEMMA

T he sky was overcast, as scheduled, and the absence of shadow depleted the old shacks of their already scant charm. Absent any gleam, the park's holographic landscape appeared equally drab. But Ty's mood was upbeat and resolute, and he rehashed the next step of his plan one more time as he walked hurriedly to the transit station. Two pod residents approached. He looked away. A few yards ahead, a group of teenagers were blocking his path. They took no interest in him as he moved through. Entering the transit station he encountered a biometric checkpoint but was given the green light without incident. The mask's success further buoyed him.

Delon pinged. CaL had warned him about his veebot. "He is prone to fits of jealousy and can become unbearably nosy with biting sarcasm. He means well, but it's best if you don't engage him." Fifteen minutes had elapsed since Ty had left the cabin, and Delon was acutely suffering "CaL's" indifference. Forgetting CaL's warning, Ty took the call.

"You didn't want to stay long this time? What's the matter lover boy? No threesome? Such a short visit is very unlike you. Oooooh, I get it: It was a virgin sacrifice to Aphrodite. Of course! Payment for the Brewster! Brilliant! Love it! I admire your devotion to the goddess, letting her have sole possession of the offering. Oh dear! I'm talking too much, aren't I? But you like it when I'm a little nosy, right? RIGHT?"

Unprepared to turn a deaf ear, Ty offered an innocuous pleasantry. "Glad you are concerned, thank you."

"Is everything OKAY? I mean your voice; it doesn't sound like you. Did you and FaiZ do opiates? Smoke something? It's been years since you've done any substances. It can affect the larynx, you know. I wish you didn't do that stuff. You become distant, and I don't like that."

None of them had remembered to correct for the tonal difference between CaL's voice and the lower pitch of Ty's. "The larynx!" Ty muttered to himself; Delon had inadvertently provided the perfect cover. Finding a veebot eye, he signaled Delon that his throat hurt and that he would no longer talk. Delon ignored the excuse. True to his evolved self as a spurned lover, the veebot kept tossing jabs, desisting only after Ty stepped into a shell for the return trip to the café.

"Back to the cave, huh?" Delon asked sullenly. "Well, I'll be just fine. Call me when your throat feels better. I'll be waiting as always … CaL? … CAL??"

Ty arrived late in the evening, carrying the tote with the food and work clothes CaL had given him. As CaL had instructed, he waved to JuN, the barista, before heading to the utility room in the back of the café. JuN casually waved back. "I'm here if you want anything," she said, shorthand for an offer of intimate company.

Ty had been trained to spend extended time holed up in cramped quarters and sleeping in odd positions. Although small, the utility room was equipped with a sink and toilet. He emerged only once: to ask JuN for paper and an envelope. Five days later he came out refreshed and clear-headed. He handed JuN the envelope, which he had addressed to CaL, and exited the café through a back door, stepping onto a service corridor and walking past the recycling units to the alley leading up to the transit station. He had requested an early evening Sunday slot for his prized descent—that is, the trip to Earth that CaL had earned for his gala-winning design. The timing critically coincided with an ebb in mission activity. At the station, a handful of people were waiting for the scheduled 18:30 Amazonia headquarters-bound ship. He recognized a data clerk, an older man who always seemed content to spend his time cataloguing recording locales for atmospheric purposes, a brainless task. The man glanced at Ty and nodded, then buried his head in the holo screen over his lap.

After boarding and settling into his bubble Ty fell asleep in minutes. Two and a half hours later, he was awakened by the ship's dock-maneuvering jerks. He confirmed the time and waited for the other passengers to disembark. Past the security checkpoint, he ambled down the corridor leading to the atrium. Images of the Boar agents rushing to apprehend him and XoL flashed through his mind. "Damn you all," he muttered. The place was thinly occupied, as he expected. Overhead he spied the Anaconda coiled on a limb with an agouti halfway into its jaw. He smiled. Walking down the hall, Ty saw the spot where the podium had been placed for the Ceremony of Remembrance and cursed himself again for not having pushed the bereavement officer out of the way and raced after XoL. Absorbed in the memory, he approached the top of the ramp leading down to the pod's service level. LeE was walking up, zeroing in on him. Ty's pulse quickened.

"Mr. LaLigne? My name is LeE, Lehore Ellis," the man said, extending a hand. "Please forgive me, but I was at Mr. Te's ceremony a while back and saw you there. I understand that you and our former manager and Ty have been ... I mean to say maybe still are, long-time friends." His handshake was firm. "Everyone in our group is upset about what happened. I'm still in disbelief, very confused, to be honest. Passiflora, you know, my aunt, she did her best to do the right thing, I mean for them. I just want to say that I'm very sorry."

Ty was stunned by the revelation. He was unaware of LeE's relationship to the Amazonia Rector. *He must have told her everything about the meeting with ThU,* he thought. *She must have reviewed my report afterward—she knows the truth!* He wanted to tell LeE who he was, and reveal all of SuS's falsehoods, but caught himself, blurting out instead a garbled sound as if he was about to upchuck. LeE stepped back, startled.

"Thank you, LeE. I can't talk now ... laryngitis," Ty replied in sign language. LeE nodded and responded in kind, apologizing for the sudden advance. Ty's mask tingled. He reached for it with both hands but checked himself. "WHATEVER YOU DO, DON'T SCRATCH YOUR FACE!" FaiZ had warned. Shaken, Ty continued down the ramp towards the guards' lounge. Two of them were walking his way. "Coming or going?" said one. Ty pointed to his throat and in sign language asked if Manny had arrived for his nighttime shift. "Check the lounge; he should be there," said the other guard. A dimly lit corridor bent toward the guards' lounge, and beyond to the El-bound transit lounge. Ty spotted a reflective utility panel close to the floor. He knelt and leaned into it to confirm the mask's unchanged appearance. Relieved, he continued down the corridor. The lounge door was ajar. He heard chatter. Peeking, he saw five guards, Manny among them. He knocked and spoke from behind the door.

"There's someone looking for Manny ... in the main hall."

As Manny exited the lounge, Ty turned to hide his face and headed for the atrium, leading Manny by a step. They passed a dark alcove. Ty reached for Manny's arm and forcefully yanked him into the space. Having been a standout wrestler, Manny swiftly turned Ty around and locked him in a strangle hold. Ty gasped for air. "Manny—it's me, Ty! Please let go!

Can't breathe!" Having heard many of Ty's oddball impersonations, the guard recognized the voice and eased the hold. The mask was aglow in the shadows. Manny pulled Ty out into the hallway.

"CAL? TY! What the hell is going on? You can be put away for this!" Manny said, poking at Ty's cheek. The pixels reacted to the touch, sending ripples across his face.

Ty stepped back into the alcove again and tried to open a door. He jiggled the handle, but it didn't budge. His mask again lit up.

"Get back out here before someone sees your face on fire," Manny said, pulling Ty back out into the hallway. "This is the encoding room; I don't have access." Manny's eyes were all but screaming for an explanation.

"I need your help, Manny. XoL is innocent ... we're both innocent!" Ty said in a hushed voice. Rushing through his words, he told Manny about PaZ and MaY's real fate, how the trial was a sham, and why he was convinced that Sus Scrofa was behind it all.

Manny was speechless.

"I've got to get back to Serra Padre, Manny. You still have the bead?"

Manny nodded.

"Keep it a little longer; I've connected the dots and they all lead to The Boar, I'm sure of it. She'll pay for what's she's done!"

"Have you lost your mind?" Manny finally said. "Whatever dots you've connected mean nothing. The Boar is untouchable; she's surrounded by real security people, lethal types, not the likes of me. If you try anything, they'll kill you. What exactly are you thinking of doing?"

"What they least expect, Manny."

They heard steps. Two guards were approaching.

"I see you found your man, Manny," said the taller of them.

"Congratulations on the Gala prize, CaL. Well deserved! When are you going down?" prodded the other.

Manny faked a smile, caught between his sworn duty to report the mask, and his fondness for the terranaut.

"We're talking about Ty," Manny said on the fly. "CaL here wants the guards to contribute to an atmospheric production as a gift for Ty, you know, to make him feel better in his new life."

"Sure thing, CaL," said one of the guards. "We're heading to the cafeteria. Join us and tell us what you have in mind." Manny looked at Ty quizzically.

"When I get back ... I'm going down tomorrow ... have a lot a work to do before then," Ty said between coughs.

"Sounds like you have a cold. You better not get vaporized," the tall guard joked as the duo departed. Ty was not amused. The comment was a clear reference to the accidental explosion that killed a terranaut while being treated for the virus in the division's sinus-cleansing vaporizing chamber. He forced a smile and waited for the guards to be a safe distance away before resuming his plea.

"Manny, I need you to erase the log after I leave. CaL's prize can't be redeemed just yet; it's too soon. I don't have a pass. And I don't have a mission code to get into the fitting and equipment rooms. You have access."

Manny grimaced.

"OCTAD has a rot, Manny; it threatens the planet, and our lives. I've got to go down before it's too late to do anything about it. XoL is fighting for her life, and PaZ and MaY already lost theirs. Do it for them if nothing else!"

Manny had been badly shaken by their deaths. MaY was another of the few terranauts who had cared to befriend the guard. He had been absorbed by her frequent stories about Morena and her career as a naturalist. MaY's description of the Mayflower's perilous ascent was also still vivid in his mind, enhanced as the tale had become after passing from generation to generation. No spacecraft up to that point had carried more than fifteen passengers—all tourists expecting reentry—which was nothing compared to the five hundred fifty who had embarked on the pioneering flight. And MaY had enthralled him by describing how Morena and her cohort had coped in space with unimaginably few subsistence-level resources and archaic technologies. And how over time the woman had been popularly chosen to lead the group, the Halo's first ever mayor.

In PaZ, Manny saw a little of himself, someone who quietly stood on the sidelines as others took center stage but was always there to lend a hand and supporting shoulder. And in Ty, Manny saw and appreciated a carefree but unfailingly attentive temperament. He had never seen Ty outwardly upset about anything, not even about PaZ's death or Nori's adoption ordeal. To Manny, the youthful terranaut always seemed able to toss adversity aside and through light-hearted banter emerge with greater calm and clearer purpose—until this very moment. That he would brave a return to Serra Padre, chasing a possible conspiracy to try and save a traitor while impersonating a close friend, seemed wildly insane to him. Over the years he had pieced together XoL and Ty's mutual affection, but in his estimation, for Ty to risk his life to save her—pitted against Sus Scrofa and her henchmen, no less—was grossly out of proportion to whatever feelings they had for each other.

And now, staring at a pixelated mask, Manny concluded that none of it added up—except for the possibility that this affable and respected terranaut, whose purity of heart pulsed through every vein, was reacting to a heinous injustice. That had to be it. How excited Ty had been when they discussed the Roswell incident flashed through his mind. He could hear the passion in Ty's voice as he recalled their conversation. Now, as Ty accompanied him back to the guards' lounge, Manny realized that their friendly debate had ended at exactly this point in the corridor.

"It was a ruse, pure and simple, one of the cleverest magic acts in history—that is why people still talk about it. You know I'm right!" Ty had argued.

You know I'm right! echoed now in the guard's head.

Manny had learned to distinguish between Ty's goofiness and his deeply held convictions (misguided as they may have been in the case of

Roswell, if I may say so). For several more seconds, he looked at Ty like a father regarding a troubled son, straining mightily to see past the mug of an impostor.

"Follow me!" Manny said finally, taking off down the corridor. They strode past the guards' lounge and The Valley, a widening in the space filled with notable recordings in kinetic holography intended to inspire terranauts on their way to Earth. Ty glanced at the fluttering black-eyed satyr butterfly honoring XoL. He picked up the pace to keep up with Manny. Past the display they reached the doorway to the Descent Preparation Room. Manny unlocked the door and instructed Ty to wait outside while he checked the place. No one was there, as Ty had hoped given the late hour. He waved Ty in. "Make it quick," he said, staying behind to stand guard.

Ty knew the routine but had never rushed through it. At the body scanners, he removed his shoes and stepped into one of the clear cylindrical chambers. The chamber darkened and Ty's mask became aglow. It would take a minute for the scanner to take a body measure and assign a fitted terrasuit. Arms raised, Ty started his usual count to 60, as he always did during the operation. At 45 the scanners stopped at head height, seemingly uncertain about Ty's facial contours. Ty held his breath. Manny tapped the door's glass panel and raised three fingers. Three terranauts were coming. "GET OUT," he mouthed. The body scan resumed, 55...56...57..., completing the operation just as the doors opened and the chamber lights came back on. Ty exited the scanner and feigned calm on the way to the suit rack. Number 256 lit up, his old rack number—a puzzling coincidence. He undressed, tossed his clothes into a bin, slipped into earthbound undergarments and stepped into the suit. He glanced at the three terranauts who had entered. They casually looked back at him. One of them stepped into a scanning chamber. Ty walked past, eyes averted, and left the room.

Manny exhaled, wiping beads of sweat. Further down the corridor they reached the equipment room door. Manny keyed in the code. The place was crammed with earthbound equipment: belts, bio-trackers, DNA scanners, surgical and first aid kits, high-definition visors, levitating boots, stun guns, plug-in backpacks and battery packs, all arranged in drawers, on shelves, in bins and on hangers. "Take your time; no dark spots here," Manny says, wiping another bead of sweat from his brow.

Ty retrieved a paired backpack, guiding each side down his back until they were hooked to the rails on his suit. He tested their movement over his shoulders and down his breastplate for easy access. He grabbed a utility belt, tightened it around his waist and plugged it into his suit. Manny waited with a tracker and scanner in hand. As Manny plugged them in, Ty snapped a visor to his suit cap and tested the voice command function. Satisfied, he walked toward the boot storage shelves, found his size, put on a pair and plugged them into a suit port. Manny was standing by, knife and stun gun in hand. Ty took them, sheathing the knife and affixing the gun over his right thigh. He was ready.

"YOUR NAME!" Manny yelled.

"What the hell!" Ty cried, baffled by the appearance of his own name, not CaL's, imprinted on the suit's right sleeve, below the shoulder. This shouldn't be—I can't go—"

"Unplug the suit and wait for me," Manny interrupted, running through an air screen to an adjoining room. Above the transom a sign read: ATMOSPHERICS. Manny returned with a digital branding gun and a patch of digital fabric. He held the patch over his wristband for several seconds. "Don't move," he said, stretching out Ty's right arm. With surprising quickness, the guard wrapped the patch around Ty's arm and fired the gun. Ty flinched as new pixels were seared in. He re-plugged the suit. A halo encircling a nimbus cloud appeared over the patch—the division's Atmospheric Engineers logo. CaL's name and rank were below it.

"I never told you this used to be my old job, before rising up to the rank of mutinous guard," Manny said.

"I owe you big time," Ty replied, his voice almost breaking.

"Free of charge: for you, and for PaZ, MaY, and XoL."

Hoping that the plan succeeds to the last ounce of Ty's innocence, the guard wrapped his arms around him in a heartfelt embrace. With little choice but to hold his breath, Ty squeaked out a thank-you. Manny released the suffocating hold and accompanied Ty to the El-bound hyper-loop lounge at the end of corridor.

"Don't forget to come back, you hear?" Manny said as the lounge doors slid open. Ty stopped and turned as if having second thoughts about the mission.

"The bead, Manny. The password is XoL's full name spelled backwards!"

Manny shook his head, disconcerted by his own inattention to such critical information.

"And, Manny, I can't sink CaL deeper into this mess than he already is. If you don't hear from me within a week, find LeE and give the bead to him."

Manny was puzzled. He didn't think Ty and LeE would have had a reason to cross paths, let alone trust each other.

"He's Passiflora's nephew," Ty explained. "Tell him to take it to her; she'll know what to do."

Manny pinched his thumb and index finger into a circle and raised the other fingers. Ty acknowledged the affirmative with a smile.

The lounge was empty, save for a terranaut asleep on a chair with her head tilted backwards, mouth cracked open. He looked at the woman and wondered what her destination might be. She looked young. *Maybe it's her maiden mission*, he thought. The doors swished, and the three terranauts Ty had seen earlier entered the lounge and took seats near the sleeping woman.

They reminded him of his first solo descent. XoL had stood to the left of the hyperloop airlock, and PaZ and MaY to the right, flanking his passage. "Well, little brother," Paz had said, "you'll be hovering all by yourself now. Welcome to the club." He continued, referencing the Amazonian sloth, "Think of the Bradypus, take it slooooow and enjooooooy every moment."

MaY had approached Ty with a sweet smile. "I brought you something, a good luck charm. We'll all be thinking of you," she said, handing him a digital wafer. "Keep this close to your heart; it will beat in unison with yours!" Before stepping into the airlock Ty had turned back and looked at XoL. She was smiling widely, and as the hatch began to close she had stepped forward as if intending to follow him in. "Light and strong, *mi corazón* ... always," she had uttered in a tone that only he could hear.

A gentle pulsing interrupted Ty's reverie. He pried open a suit flap and reached inside a small breast pocket, finding the holo wafer MaY had given him. He had always kept it in his suit for good luck.

"What the hell!" he cried out. Why was his suit in his old rack over a week following his expulsion from the Corps?

Startled, the three terranauts at the far end of the room turned their heads. The woman woke for an instant, wriggled herself back into a comfortable position and resumed her sleep.

Ty pressed the wafer between his thumb and index finger. A miniature holograph of him with XoL, MaY, and PaZ popped out. Clad in terrasuits, they were all smiling in a moment of shared glee. He stared at the image dejectedly, knowing that two of three souls he had loved were forever gone, and the third was hanging by a literal thread: the 35,000-kilometer space elevator he would soon ride, to try and save her life.

The hyperloop to the El pulled in with a whoosh. One of the late arrivals tapped the woman's shoulder to wake her up. Ty was the last to board and soon the ambient lights dimmed. As is customary for anyone wishing not to be disturbed while in transit, Ty lowered the suit's visor, obscuring his face.

24

TY'S DESCENT

The El terminal was abuzz with terranauts headed to disparate regions, from the Yukon to Tierra del Fuego. Ty scanned the place and recognized no one. He pitied those who were leaving for farther latitudes than he was, knowing they had many more days yet to spend cooped up in drone dirigibles before reaching their destinations. Wary of drawing attention as the odd Atmo in the crowd, Ty drifted toward a quiet nook at the far end of the hall. Along the way he stopped at the food and refreshment bar and overheard the chatter. He shook his head at the inanity of the familiar conversation; male terranauts asserting that hair growth inhibitors affect libido and it would be better to go without the treatment and put up with cap itch for a few weeks than "limp" back into orbit. Ty recalled CaL's take on the issue: "It's endless days lying in a dirigible bored to tears that drains your testosterone!" Chuckling, he paid for a travel pack and moved away.

The nook was too dark; he couldn't risk lighting up his face. Ty turned back and headed toward a video wall. A storm was lashing the El landing station on Earth. Sheets of water were cascading from the top deck and wind was thrashing the surrounding green mantle as if trying to loosen its teeming lamina. Ty got lost in the scene, marveling anew at the ecology of it all: how hot air coalesces into a vaporous lid expunging moisture with such fury as to bend limbs, topple trees, scour the ground, and leave in its wake a renewed cacophony. It pleased him to be able to recognize every song, shriek, and howl and understand how it all fit together as a grand design.

He recalled the time during an introductory earth sciences course when two visiting professors, an ecologist and a philosopher, debated the limits of ascribing truth to the wildlife recordings that students would one day be making. "Philosophers see truth as an ever-expanding circle, one without beginning or end, where any point of view along the circumference can be argued as being as valid as any other; whereas ecology has an undisputed physical track, one where animate and inanimate matter cross paths to perform the beautiful dance we call life," the ecologist had opined. The philosopher had then smiled widely, raised his arms heavenward as if to thank the Almighty for having given his colleague the gift of metaphor, but admonishing him also for failing to consider all the parts of the circle. "Any point along any arc," he stated, "however expanded, is irrevocably linked to the same radius, to a single and most beautiful center. Truth lies there: in the point to which everything else is tied, as we all are in orbit, tethered to the most beautiful point in all of creation. You may call it scientific fact; I call it poetry, the source of all truth."

Deep in thought, Ty failed to sense a man approach and stand by his side.

"Look at that: Nature's raw power! Magnificent, isn't it?" said the man.

Ty turned and met a shoulder. He stepped aside but the man, clad in a black terranaut suit, followed. The Boar's logo was imprinted on a massive arm sleeve. A sheathed, army-grade yatagán was affixed to his leg below a police-grade stun gun.

"I'm Darius Anguis Khyll—DaK," said the man.

A shiver coursed down Ty's spine. He willed his right hand to rise and meet DaK's. The bodyguard's handshake was bone-crushing.

"CaL—Carson Canis LaLigne," Ty replied, grimacing.

"Yes, yes! I recognize the name: The master AE, 'Prince of the Gala'! Well, what a pleasant surprise … but this is rather an unusual place for your kind, isn't it? Gone down before?" DaK asked pointedly.

"During training; all Atmos have to," Ty offered, curtly.

"Of course, of course, but you are not here for more of that, are you?" DaK said with prying contempt.

"It's the prize for winning the Gala—I mean the competition for its programming and design—but I will also be testing new dirigible atmospherics." Ty hoped the false reference to work would satisfy DaK's curiosity and put an end to the conversation.

"Yes, yes; that's a good thing. Those drone flights can be long and tedious; have to keep the mind engaged—but you know that, of course. I don't get into those hot air buckets. I do a routine station inspection and get right back up. Do one every two weeks, all five of them around the planet for a good six months' worth of work."

TY begged his neurons to calculate how it was remotely possible for DaK to spend half his time on Earth while watching over OCTAD's security chief as if he were her shadow.

"Oldest El," DaK continued, "straight down to the heart of the jungle. I'm going to make a wild guess, but that's where you're heading, am I right?"

Ty remained glued to the video wall, silent.

"You could have taken the Line Islands elevator, go to Nauru from there. I was there, in the atoll, when this poor bastard aquanaut was teased by a behemoth grouper and went too far down to record it, only to become an object of interest to a great whitey. His helmet camera caught it all, the beast coming at him as if from nowhere, its mouth wide open and packed with sharp teeth shimmering diamond-like under the diving lights. All that came back up was a headless torso. Funny thing is, the fish spit the head back out while the camera kept rolling. The water was pink all around it, for a while at least, until the gear descended and disappeared into the dark. Funny story."

Ty was aghast. The incident was a highlighted safety lesson and Ty knew it well. No one ever made fun of it. Half of the students exposed to the recording for the first time ran to the bathroom to purge their disgust.

"I heard about that," Ty replied, forcing a casual tone of voice. "I work in the Amazonia Division. I thought it would be useful to enjoy the prize and do dirigible atmospherics in a familiar environment."

"Ahh! So you think you know the place. I've seen experienced terranauts get into real trouble down there. Surely you know about those two that got buried by a landslide not too long ago. They obviously didn't know the hazards. You gotta know the hazards. Do know how to use that stun gun?"

Ty bent over and coughed hard, hoping to bring blood back to his face.

"Sorry, something in my throat … we have to carry the gun, it's protocol," he replied, clearing his throat with a loud cough.

"Sure, sure. Can't be too cautious. Amazonia is jaguar country. But that gun'll do you no good. If a big cat comes at you, you're not gonna have enough time to pull the trigger. They are stealthy beasts, those bastards. If they're lying in wait the scanner will fail to pick them up. No ping, all pain!" DaK laughed. "And the suit, well, they test well in the lab alright. But reality is another story—if you get a big one."

DaK took off his right glove and pulled up his left sleeve. Long scars ran up his forearm.

"The one time I ventured outside the station a three-hundred-pounder jumped me; broke my arm and dug into the bone before I got around him, grabbed his neck, and twisted it broke. Killed the sonofabitch—that's the way it is down there. Kill or be killed! It's nature's way."

Loudspeakers announced the half-hour warning before boarding time.

"See you down there—CAL, RIGHT? Don't fall backwards while you shit!" DaK laughed right to Ty's face before pulling away. A drop of his spit landed in Ty's eye, causing him to step back and nearly tumble.

Rubbing his eye, Ty watched DaK descend into the boarding ramp. Having fended off a jaguar attack with not even a scratch, he felt momentarily like the greater man. He walked back to the bar and leaned on a table to steady himself. The boarding time again blared. "The berth!" he cried. He had forgotten to identify his place in the train's seating chart. He voiced the request. It popped up over his wristband: last car, top tier, Berth No. 5. DaK's name was not among his car companions. Relieved, Ty headed down the ramp to the boarding gate. He caught a glimpse of the arrival station. The rain had stopped. Now baking under the sun, the deck looked like a vapor-spewing kettle.

Ty reached the end of the boarding queue and spotted a former classmate up ahead. During their sophomore year the man had transferred from tropical to desert studies; ostensibly, he had then professed, to someday head to the Atacama Desert and record its rare springtime flowering. The bum, Ty muttered to himself, convinced still that the move was a lame excuse to dodge the far harsher tropical biome. As if by telepathy, the man turned around and looked straight at him. Ty held his breath, but there was no follow-up gesture, no smile, nod or wave of a hand. Ty exhaled, quietly thanking FaiZ.

He was a little surprised that no one in the lounge, aside from DaK, had shown any interest in him as the lone Atmo in the group—no "hello-what-brings-you-here," not even a casual glance. The indifference made him think of the episode at the cafeteria way back when, and CaL's complaint afterward: "Excepting present company, your profession is populated by assholes—or is it jerks; one is a learned trait, the other congenital, I can't remember which—SNOBBISH ASSHOLES who re-gard the likes of me as being a rung below the warm snot of nose-picking producers!" Ty sighed, wondering if CaL was still at the cabin enjoying FaiZ's company. The green light came on, and the group filed past the airlock into the zero gravity train cars. Last in, Ty flexed his knees and propelled himself upwards, floating past other berths to his own at the top. He stowed his gear in a side compartment, turned on the privacy air screen, and settled into the reclining seat. At T MINUS ONE he strapped himself in, anticipating the initial earth-bound pull. Ten minutes later the El train reached cruising speed and the acceleration ceased. He dimmed the lights, breathing rhythmically to slow down his heartbeat, and as-sumed a meditative state.

Minutes and then hours passed without notice, Ty's mind shifting be-tween oblivion and alertness like troughs and crests of gentle ocean swells.

Standing on firm ground under Earth's full gravitational pull, Ty retraced the estimated route to the landslide site where PaZ and MaY were buried. Visor down, he made progress at a fast pace. Time passed fluidly, every second marked in synchronicity with MaY's beating wafer. He reached the edge of a clearing and stopped at the sound of rushing water. Zooming in visually, he saw a waterfall behind a group of workers gathered under large camouflage netting.

They looked like Yanomami men and women, naked but for loin-cloths. A tall man clad in a sleeveless black terrasuit was among them. He seemed to be giving orders, arms waving as he spoke. Five other men entered the compound, hunched under the weight of large sacks. They emptied the contents over a large tree stump: trogon feathers, toucan beaks, and mounds of insects and curled snakes. An older man among them dumped a sack of blood-soaked howler monkey severed heads. The others laughed.

A boar suddenly appeared from behind the stump. It grunted and ran off. The man in black raised his arm and motioned the group to stop. "NOT AGAIN!" Ty cried. MaY's wafer began to echo loudly. He ran back the way he came, stopping a distance away to see if he was followed. A loud voice yelled his name between yatagán slashes. He neared a tangle of aerial roots, turned on his suit's mimetic function and wedged himself among them. The man in black walked toward him, stopped inches away but did not see him. Blood was oozing from a large scar on his right arm. The man scanned the area, looked up into the tree and stepped away, guardedly. Ty grabbed an aerial root and lifted himself up until he gained a surveilling perch on a fig tree limb. He looked up and marveled at the complex mosaic of pied, sun-sucking leaves.

A middle-aged Yanomami suddenly appeared by his side, the native's face a jumble of black streaks, as if the paint had been applied by a drunkard. He was grinning at Ty, exposing stained and missing teeth. *Stealthy bastard,* Ty thought. Keeping his jet-black eyes squarely on Ty's, the native extended an arm downward, pointing to the base of the tree. Ty became distracted by a fluttering blue morpho butterfly. *How odd,* he thought, *that it is so far south from its normal range.* He watched the butterfly's erratic flight downward toward the base of the tree. He slipped, nearly falling, and recoiled. The man in black was standing below, staring right up at Ty while drawing airy swirls with his yatagán. He coiled his arm and heaved the sabre upwards with great force. As it neared, the spinning blade slowed down and the distance to the ground stretched.

With howler-like agility Ty jumped off to a lower limb to avoid the strike, then to another and another, until leaping onto the ground and landing softly, feather-like. The man in black was a few feet away, staring at him as if surprised to see him. "I NEVER MISS, TY!" the man said. Ty heard thrashing from above and looked up to see a fast-approaching shadow. He jumped out of the way, the body barely missing him as it hit the ground face down with a loud thud. The yatagán was imbedded in the victim's back. The man in black reached for it, wiped the blood off on his suit and walked away, laughing. Ty knelt by the body, slid a hand under a shoulder and turned it over. He bolted backwards in horror at the sight of his brother's lifeless eyes staring at him, blood oozing from his mouth.

"NO! NO! NO!" Ty sprang out of his seat. His cry pierced the berth's air bubble, breaking the car's quietude. A companion shouted back to keep quiet. Ty did not answer. He reached for a hand towel and wiped the perspiration off the mask. After calming down he turned on the elevator-positioning screen. A white line stretched from the orbital ring down to South America, the El's dot closing in on its darkening destination: 0°00'00.00", 63°15'25"W. Nine hours remain, read the numbers by the dot. Ty leaned back into his seat and closed his eyes, concentrating on the forest's habitual din as he mapped in his head the 300-kilometer trek from the station to the foothills of Serra Padre.

Becoming operational in 0200, the Amazonian is the oldest of OCTAD'S five space elevators. The others—Congo, The Maldives, West Papua, and the Line Islands—followed eastward along the equator in succession every twenty years. The debate between linking the planet with new and untested technology versus true and tried rocketry was heated and took decades to be resolved. The concept of elevators had been in humanity's mind since the launch of Sputnik in the year 1957 of the Old Calendar. Jerome Pearson, an engineer working for the United States Air Force Research Laboratory, gave the idea technical merit twenty years later. But the material technology to support the assemblage, including the elevator counterweights extending 7,000 kilometers beyond the orbital rings, proved elusive.

Carbon polymer fibers eventually solved the problem, but not before the spectacular failure of the first test elevator. Located on the Island of Flores, in the Azores, several cable strands failed and caused much of the structure to collapse. Close to 20,000 kilometers of mangled cables and rails fell and sank, some of it whipping eastward thousands of miles before coming to rest in the middle of the Sahara.

Undaunted, elevator proponents continued lobbying OCTAD, arguing that over time it would prove to be cleaner upon the atmosphere than rocketry, requiring also minimal footprint on the ground to the benefit of flora and fauna. A key figure in the history of the elevators was Padrine Naranj, a materials specialist who, after the Flores collapse, perfected hyper lightweight fabrics made from asteroid carbon. She went on to design the elevator structure in use today by scores of terranauts. To prove its safety, Padrine went down to Amazonia on the elevator's inaugural descent—with her baby in tow: Osage, as it was called. The 36-hour descent and 42-hour return earned her induction into the Descendants of the Clause, paving the way for her son to become a terranaut and, subsequently, through dogged groundwork and rising managerial acumen, a worthy candidate for election into the governing Tetrad.

25

ASHA

Most terranauts suffer the passage from stationary orbit to the surface of the planet. Strength-building gym-work in 3G simulation chambers is standard preparation to fend off gravitational sickness, dizziness, or just sluggishness upon landing. Ty, by contrast, never faced ill effects. His training regime consisted of homebound yoga and calisthenics, and runs in the park with weighted footwear, although those were mostly to clear his head. When asked by disbelieving colleagues what made his method work, he offered that over the three-day descent he simply "transmitted" the train's soft hum as a form of "sonic gravity" to "inform" his ligaments, joints, and muscles of what was coming—"just mind over matter!"

But after the vivid and disturbing dream this time, his mind was far from settled. The last few hours felt interminable, and during the steady deceleration no amount of measured breathing and concentration tempered the discomfort. The speed checks through the stratosphere were pressing, and the train's final jerk before shifting to the mechanical phase of the descent—a 35-kilometer stretch—had slammed him into his seat. When the train finally reached the Amazonia arrival platform, Ty was forced to rub the top of his stomach, just below the sternum, to keep the nausea at bay. He rotated his seat and set his feet on the cabin floor, reaching for his gear as if in slow motion. A voice from below asked if he was okay. The remark surprised him; he thought the car had already emptied. He stretched his arm out to the aisle and forced a thumbs-up response.

Still nauseous, he slid to the aisle and stepped onto the ladder leading down to the exit, pleading with his legs to firm up. Halfway down, a terranaut, slumped on his seat, turned his head toward Ty. They exchanged commiserating glances. A dozen laboring steps still remained to the door. Ty took a deep breath before cranking the wheel and pushing it open. The blast of heat and humidity was overpowering. He gagged. Holding onto the rail, he eased his way down to the ramp to the station's upper deck. Awaiting him was a 200-foot walk to the staircase leading down to the dirigible departure level. He sighed. Each step over the photovoltaic flooring tested his thighs. He breathed through his nose, slowly, to ease the assault of thickened air upon his trachea. Beads of sweat were forming on his forehead. He headed for the nearest railing at the edge of the platform to lean and rest.

It was dawn, and the emergent canopy of trees to the west was slowly chasing away the Amazonian night. Above him, the El's tubular mesh stretched like a thinning contrail toward the Halo's glow of orbital pods. A waxing moon was low on the horizon. Gazing at the orb Ty thought of XoL, of their goodbye, wondering anew if she saw his last words as the guards pushed her out of the courtroom. As he began to regain strength and focus, he continued toward the elliptical stairwell. A dozen terranauts were gathered by its side, a few sitting on the floor, not yet able to stand. Trainees, he guessed. Farther away by the edge of the deck, he saw a terranaut on hands and knees heaving into a bag. He approached her. The woman raised her head, took and swirled a sip of water, and spat it out.

"Happens every time," she said, giving Ty a quick look as she leaned against the railing, knees bent.

"Sorry to intrude. I thought you might need some help," Ty said, unsure whether to wait for a reply or keep going. He turned his gaze out to the forest. Dozens of moored drone dirigibles skimmed the canopy more than a hundred feet below. He thought of Nori at Manaus, and how close he was to the former city by the Amazon River for which the care center was named. He sighed again, wishing Nori could be with him to see the sight. The woman looked up and saw the ID patch on Ty's arm.

"What's your mission, where are you headed? And where is your chaperone—they let you come down all alone?" she asked, pointedly. Ty could see color returning to her face and a sparkle to her eyes. He recognized her as the woman who was sleeping at the hyperloop departure lounge.

"I don't really have one—I mean a mission," he said, uninterested in concocting a story. "I'm the head Atmo at the Amazonia Division; no chaperone required. I won the design prize for the Gala ... can go anywhere, really, but I must keep it close, within a few hundred kilometers ... have to get back to work soon."

"Jesus! You are in awesome shape for an atmospheric guy." She was sitting cross-legged now, casually adjusting her belt. "I wasn't at the Gala; didn't see it virtually either but I was told it was one of the better ones. I guess congratulations are in order. So, congratulations! How did you manage to get out of the El and start walking like a meerkat? Me, I got out of the train on all four like a goddamned dog—and this is my fifth time! Was it your first—I mean the Gala?"

The woman reminded Ty of MaY and her rapid-fire, leapfrogging speech full of inquiring gusto. He accepted the chatter as a calming preamble to the difficult days ahead.

"I guess I'm just lucky," he told her. "But I did feel queasy the last few hours. I'm CaL, by the way—and yes, it was the first time I entered the design competition."

The woman stood, one hand resting on the railing, the other reaching out for a handshake.

"I guess a formal hello is in order then. Hello! I'm Asha. But I don't believe for a second that you have no idea where you're going. I mean— forgive me for prying—but I'm guessing you know *exactly* where you're going. I mean, you've had how many hours to figure it out on the way down? How about misting clouds forming over a mountain? Am I right?"

The dead-on presumption amused him.

"You got me there. I'm in fact after topographic drama: peaks, fast-changing light, airy scenery, that sort of thing. I had Serra Padre in mind ... looking at a four- or five-day trek," Ty said, instantly regretting having alluded to his destination.

"That's crazy!! The Serra is pretty far from here, 300 miles to the west-northwest. No way you can get there in less than ten days—if you're lucky! I'm in the Pac Rim division, heading to the Galápagos, straight out along the E-line. I can get you closer, save you time, if you can stand another couple of hours in close quarters ... I won't puke, I promise!" She paused to survey Ty's equipment.

"Where's your holocam?" she asked, raising her brow.

Ty's stomach clenched; he realized that amid the rush to depart, nei- ther he nor Manny had thought of packing the one instrument every Atmo would be expected to carry. If Asha noticed its absence, then DaK must have too, he thought, wondering then why the bodyguard hadn't fired a snide remark about it.

"Two trips—I have to make two trips. This one's exploratory. On the next one I'll do the actual capture—not as part of the prize, of course; I mean, I offered to take some normal videos this time, more for the fun of it." Ty hoped the somewhat clumsy explanation wouldn't elicit further questions.

"Sure. Makes sense—so do you want a ride or not?"

Ty answered as if a stranger had commandeered his brain and planted a string of unfamiliar words in it.

"Yes, thank you. I would love to. I've been on a drone only once before," he said, cringing inside at the fast lie.

The trainees had left and the deck stood empty. Asha picked up the bag with vomit, dumped it into a floor chute and headed toward the staircase. Ty followed a step behind.

"Did you happen to see that Boar operative?" he asked.

"I caught sight of him at the boarding station," Asha replied. "I don't like his kind. Giant of a man, isn't he? If he was on the train, I didn't see him—and I'm restless. I spent fair amount of time in the lounge car chatting it up with whoever was there. You never left your berth, did you? What's with that? Is the brute after you? Didn't the scream in the middle of the night wake you up? Whoever that was sent me right back down to the lounge."

Ty kept quiet about the nightmare and calculated that Asha must have seen him with DaK standing by the video wall.

"Well," she probed, "is he after you?"

"He doesn't like Atmos for some reason. He approached me at the station, and was rather unpleasant ... rude, pushy. But that's not why I was a recluse. I like to close my eyes and meditate, visualize atmospheric landscapes and how to build them ... it helps me gauge whether the places I visit are a match for the correlative neural etchings," he said, borrowing from Cal's periodic disquisitions on cognitive visualization technology, a subject CaL could go on about for hours.

"You designer types, always in the clouds," Asha said, heading toward the staircase. Ty chuckled at her spunk, how she was now skipping down the funnel having hardly been able to stand a short while ago. He tripped and almost fell, headfirst.

"Easy boy! You don't want to go right back up with a neck brace,"

Asha said. Ty laughed off the misstep, amused that he would be the one to stumble and not his far less experienced companion.

They reached the launching deck and stopped to marvel at the scene. The rising sun pierced the station's perimeter array of photovoltaic slats, casting on the floor a forest-like adumbral light. The trainees were walking nearby, their suits rippling as they cut through the rays. A light turned on above a departure gate. Asha stood in front of it and voiced her mission code: *Spheniscus mendiculus*. Ty beamed at the mention of the Galápagos penguin and started shuffling his feet, waddle-like. Asha burst out laughing. She tried to imitate him but her feet tangled, sending her to the floor. The trainees turned their heads, startled by such unbecoming behavior.

"You've got quite a hyperactive hypothalamus!" Asha said, reaching for Ty's helping hand. Still laughing she took a few steps to the gate, tapped the control panel, and activated the drone operating sequence. Zip-line harnesses dropped from the ceiling. "Need help with these?" she asked. Ty declined. Asha led the way onto a jutting plank. A hundred yards away a dirigible stiffened in the breeze, navigation lights on. A hatch opened from its underside and a ladder extended to a small platform surrounding the mooring pole. "Follow me!" she said, jumping off and howling gleefully as she glided over treetops. Ty landed on the platform a moment later, faking a misstep lest Asha would think he was too familiar with the maneuver.

"I love the ship's skin and the soft light that filters through it; it's like being swallowed by a jellyfish!" Asha exclaimed after settling into her seat. Ty had always appreciated the calming interior, but instead of merely assenting he feigned a newcomer's interest by running his hand along the translucent fuselage. "These things look a lot more like a sea creature than the flying type—white-spotted puffer fish more than horned puffins," he said, to Asha's delight. Affecting the drawl of an ersatz airline pilot, Asha ordered Ty to fasten his seat belt. The ladder slid under them and the hatch closed. A detailed view of the region with closely spaced coordinates filled the space ahead.

"Destination?" asked the drone's navigation system.

"How about four point four three degrees west from here?" she asked Ty, pointing to a spot on the Rio Negro. "Easy to drop you off along its banks; that'll put you just about fifty miles due south of your atmospheric paradise. It's all uphill from there—an easy trek for a fit and handsome Atmo, if you don't mind me saying so."

Ty stole a glance at Asha. Her pluck and carefree demeanor had washed away all anxiety about his mission. He offered a heartfelt consent.

After Asha confirmed the coordinates with the drone's navigation system, the ship disengaged from its mast and jerked skyward, followed by the whir of the quad propellers seeking the assigned direction.

"I know you can do atmospheric cartwheels inside this thing, but I love just watching the world below go by, if that's okay with you."

"I wouldn't dare try and impress you," Ty answered, relieved not to have to compose a surround landscape from a drone's cache of environmental recordings.

"And don't you go meditating on me!" Asha said as the cabin filled with the image of the tranquil waters of the Aracá River below. "It's not every day that I get to meet a prize-winning Atmo."

26

CAL'S DREAMBANK

▶ MARCH 5, 0275

aL and FaiZ did not share a word about Ty's plan after he left the cabin. As days passed CaL forced himself to believe in a positive outcome: that Ty would somehow make it back with the incriminating information he hoped to find, and that everything would return to normal. Not once did they go outdoors, and much of their time in the cabin was spent in silence. Upon parting they bumped foreheads, pecked their cheeks, and squeezed each other's behinds—the Holy Trinity, they called it. But this time the sequence was by rote. At the door CaL looked back and, as it closed, he could see the pain in FaiZ's eyes. She understood his worry but had failed to distract him from it. She sensed their relationship somehow now was hanging in the balance of Ty's success or failure, whether he lived or died.

CaL walked to the pod's transit station, morose. Delon sounded more displeased than relieved to finally catch sight of him.

"Hello, CaL. Are you okay? I was very worried. You went away with a bad case of laryngitis and returned without being noticed, and now you are leaving again. Where were you? Where are you going? And how did you hide from me for such a long time? Have you become a spy, one of those agents with that pig decal on their arms? Are you testing me, CaL?"

CaL explained nothing, needling Delon instead for being asleep on the job, and promising to reprogram his persona should the lapse ever happen again. Delon was stunned by the reply. For once the lovingly nosy veebot was at a loss for words. Silence followed CaL the rest of the way to Café LaLigne, where he intended to stay until he heard back from Ty.

It was midafternoon and the café was filled with chatter. The Saint Bernard was circling overhead as always, and on the wall facing the bar a saber-toothed tiger rested languidly amid wind-swept tufts of pampas grass. On the way to his customary table at the far end of the café CaL waved at JuN, raising two fingers. His habitual beet-sweetened double espresso arrived a moment later, along with a sealed envelope. Certain it contained a simple "thank you" from Ty, he did not open it. As he sipped, he sketched in his head what would come next for his beloved Anaconda: a visit by several males to form a frothy breeding ball by a reedy stream bank. He failed to notice the sudden silence of the room.

His wristband buzzed. It was JuN. "Look toward the door!" read the message. Four Boar agents in military gear had entered the café and were heading his way. CaL froze, instinctively sliding the envelope to the floor and pushing it under the table. Patrons near him disbanded, emptying the back of the place. The agents pulled chairs over and surrounded CaL. Before taking a seat, the lead agent methodically removed his helmet and vest and set them down, crowding the small table. A subordinate gave him a cap with a large Boar logo. He donned it, adjusting the fit several times until satisfied. He sat and pulled his chair close to CaL. The other guards remained standing.

"We need to ask you a few simple questions—if you don't mind," said the lead agent in a whisper tinged with sarcasm. CaL tried to push back to distance himself from the man but could not; a guard behind him was firmly holding his chair in place.

"When did you last see your dear friend, if you please, CaL?"

CaL was seething. Barging into the café in the middle of the day, for whatever official excuse, was unpardonable to him. If they wanted to question him, they could have well met him earlier at the transit station. He knew why they were there and was offended by the pseudo-innocent question. He was not about to put up with the charade.

"I know he manipulated a few chromosomes, alright? I kept it to m-m-m-m-myself. He's my friend. I'm S-S-S-SORRY!"

The agents looked at each other and chuckled.

"Mr. LaLigne, last week you and Mr. Te were followed to this fine establishment. You were here for two hours and fifty-one minutes. You then went separately to your lover's cabin—Faith, Fazi, Faizee, whatever her name is. We paid her a visit after you left this morning. You will want to see her again, won't you? And we know exactly where your dear friend Ty is. Very fine mask, I might add. You will want to see him again also, no? But first we need some information from you. So, if you please, CaL, give us the bead. We need it NOW!"

A feeling of doom crashed upon him. CaL had felt such anguish only one other time in his life: when he was twelve years old and could no longer hold back telling Ty that he loved him, that he meant the world to him, and that he wished never to be apart no matter where they went or what they did with their lives. They were playing chess. CaL had been building up the courage to confess for half an hour. He thought he was ready. But what if he scared Ty and ended up pushing him out of his life? It was his move—a check—but he could not get a finger to the board. Then Ty spoke. "What's the matter? You're looking at me funny," Ty said. Panicked, CaL felt the words jumble out of his mouth: that for some time he had wanted to tell him that he was in love with a boy at school but would rather not say who, and that he would always want to be friends and hang out together like they always did, because he loved that, too. His anxiety was through the roof. But Ty had stood and walked around the table to give him a solid hug, saying they would always be best friends no matter what they did or who they loved.

That memory stirred up another. He recalled the day at the cafeteria when Ty earned twelve stitches for throwing a punch in CaL's defense. The punch also earned Ty a brain scan to test for possible swelling, to say nothing of the blurred vision he suffered for several weeks afterward.

The memories swiftly turned into raw anger, well past the point of stammering.

"You can take your demand and shove it up your fucking ass!" CaL spat. "I don't have what you're looking for—and you'll have hell to pay if you lay a hand on Ty. I would never do anything to hurt him, so if I had the bead you are looking for I'D FUCKING GIVE IT TO YOU! And you can leave FaiZ—F-A-I-Z!—out of this! HE knows nothing about your bead. The one Ty gave him was a recording about marmosets from Tamandaré—a gift. THAT IS ALL I FUCKING KNOW!"

"What an idiot! Can't talk and doesn't even know what gender to fuck. Have it your way, then. We'll talk on board." The lead agent motioned to his colleagues to whisk CaL away. Two agents grabbed his arms. A third pricked his neck from behind and CaL immediately felt a penetrating burning sensation.

Patrons cleared the way as he was dragged through the main room and out the door, while JuN watched with trepidation from behind the bar. Her instincts told her that this all had something to do with Ty's visit a week earlier.

Questions swirled in CaL's head on the way to The Boar's ship. If they knew what Ty was up to, why hadn't they just barged into the cabin before he left and confronted them both right then and there? Why wait until after Ty's descent? And where was Manny? Did he toss the bead and point the agents in his direction to save himself? A headache began to pulsate in CaL's skull, pressing like a vice. His ears were ringing and his surroundings started to turn into an undulant blur.

Upon reaching the station and boarding The Boar's ship, the disorientation and pain abated. Then, after getting strapped into a seat, a calming out-of-body sensation arose within him. From above, CaL saw himself seated in the cramped spacecraft behind two agents. He vaguely remembered the immediate past: a clamp-like pressure on his head, an ice-cold chair pushing on his back, or was it a table? And did this happen before or after boarding the ship? He couldn't tell.

Minutes later—or was it seconds?—he floated back into his seat, its backrest and sides bulging like a body-fitting press. The agents' heads rose above their seatbacks. Synapse-crackling brains were visible through tonsure-like holes. They must be archaic robots, CaL thought, the kind that were left behind in the Old-World in favor of the present-day weightless kind. Ahead, in the cockpit, warning lights went on, followed by loud screeching. It was the sound of orbital debris bouncing off the craft's armor. Scared, he likened the feeling to the fear that people on Earth felt during the onset of earthquakes, as he'd heard in the ancient lore—where a mild tremor would awaken the medulla oblongata and cause the heart to pound the aorta in anticipation of a deadly jolt. The noise magnified. He braced for a catastrophic decompression.

Nothing happened. He turned his attention back to the agents' heads. A glow was showing through the cranial holes as if gray matter were heating up and bubbling. Their seats were bubbling, too, he noticed, but the agents remained unperturbed. His feet and calves felt warm and tingly. He leaned forward to rub them but was hit by flaming chunks of brain from the exploding agents' heads. He casually wiped the stuff off his face and resumed rubbing his legs, now as hot as if ready to catch on fire.

He heard a voice and saw a little girl with a thick mat of curly black hair staring at him from where the detectives had been seated a moment earlier. "Hello, CaL" the girl said in an eerie voice as her hair morphed into a tongue-flicking medusa. He wanted to keep looking at her but couldn't; his suit was bursting into flames. He struggled to push himself out of the seat and pull his clothes off, but it was too late. The burn was unbearable. He screamed but only laughter came out. A large chunk of space debris was approaching with lighting speed. The impact was blinding. Now suddenly floating in space, outside of the craft and naked, he saw the head of the medusa tumbling in his direction. It blew past him, blood trailing from the serpents' mouths. He looked down and saw his legs mottled with charred flesh. He screamed again but this time there was no sound. He screamed louder, only to remember that sound does not travel in a vacuum. He felt dizzy. Ty floated by, with XoL—or was it the woman from the Gala, DaeL?—then FaiZ. But they only waved, smiling, oblivious to his plight. In agony, he passed out.

He woke up lying flat and strapped to a table in a blue room, head throbbing. Boar agents flanked him. One of them reached for his face and snapped out cables from his temples. He remembered his legs and screamed. He heard laughter. He looked down and saw his skin unblemished. Lying back down he grabbed his head, straining to ease the pain and confusion. A high-pitched voice echoed inside his head:

"We are sorry for the inconvenience, CaL—*hee*. But we understand you have in your possession a little round thing we need. So please tell us where it is, won't you? Unless you want us to invite ourselves back into your truly fascinating dreambank to play around a little more—*heehee*."

CaL turned his head and recognized OCTAD's security chief, inches from his face. The Boar. He closed his eyes and slowly sank into an abyss of dread.

DAYS IN THE "JUNGLE"

"**W**HAT AN ASSHOLE!" Asha yelled to no one after dropping Ty off at the river. The hatch closed and the dirigible resumed its westward flight.

They had spent hours chatting on the way to the Rio Negro. Ty had kept the subject light, sharing episodes of CaL's life that he knew. He had recounted the second-grade teacher's reenactment of the pope's famous speech and how it had inspired him to become an atmospheric engineer. He had told her about the time he and his friend Ty had lost track of time celebrating their graduation at his granduncle's café and missed the last outbound peapod to get back home, which had left them no option but to spend the rest of the night at the park; they had chosen to jump overhead instead of walking to it, a plan that would have worked had they not been trapped by the pod's zero-gravity center zone after a failed jump. They had been left bobbing there until the police fished them out the next day and put them in detention for a month. Asha had found his tales of such youthful escapades amusing.

But then she had turned the conversation to her own personal story. After describing her upbringing in the Zahel colony she had shared how as a teenager she fell in love with a schoolmate, a cute boy three grades ahead of her who liked to make her laugh by imitating animals, and who out of the blue had kissed her goodbye the day he left to go to the university to begin terranaut studies. "I'm telling you this," she had said, "because—don't laugh—after he kissed me I was ready to follow him all the way to Nauru if he had gone there." Which was how she ended up in the Corps, "eventually enjoying my first real romance until a year ago when he disappeared while on a mission ... more or less right below us. Rey is ... was his name."

Ty had been struck by the similarities with his own circumstance. He extended his hand and pressed Asha's for a brief moment. They remained silent for a while afterward, content just to stare at the passing landscape below.

But all the while Ty's mind had been racing, trying to recall the history of disappearances, zeroing in on the terranaut who had drowned on the Rio Negro while recording fish-eating Greater Bulldog bats in a makeshift raft. His body was reported to have floated down to the Amazon River before being chewed to the bone by the piranha. Ty couldn't recall his name, but it easily could have been Rey, he'd concluded, based on the timeframe he remembered—or, he pondered, was it another well-planned murder?

"That's why I chose the Galápagos. I get to fly over the river and blow him a kiss a few times a year," Asha had said, breaking the silence.

She had then asked Ty if there was a significant person in his life. He'd anticipated the question. "A girl I thought I loved when I, too, was a teenager, kissed me to say goodbye one day," he had offered haltingly. "But we never... I mean, we never... saw each other again. I have a niece that I love very much. She's six. ... She likes birds and stories about the ancients ... classical Greeks and their myths."

Sensing Ty's discomfort, Asha had ceased probing any further—but not before feeling the stir of a mutual attraction. Through the descent the cabin had filled with images of the river, its bank's luminous white sands set against its dark, seemingly fathomless waters. Twenty feet off the ground the hatch had opened. Before Ty could roll out of his seat Asha had leaned over and reached for his face to kiss him. Panicked, he slid away and jumped out the hatch under the belly of the ship, her discontent trailing him all the way down. Barely able to activate his boots' hoverpower, Ty had hit the sand hard.

DAY ONE

Kneeling on a fingerlike drift of sand Ty stared at the dirigible's rise, its engines revving angrily. Under a clear midmorning sky, he lowered his gaze, focusing on an imagined future in which he would meet at Café LaLigne with XoL, CaL, and Asha; and where, upon learning the truth, Asha would break out laughing, reaching for his face and planting a smooch, calling it "unfinished business."

A commotion roused him. A pod of river dolphins was coming his way, the animals leaping out of the water rhythmically and reentering with a staccato-like crash. A flock of scarlet ibis flew low behind them as if escorting the mammals downriver. Ty swiped his visor, turning the river into crisscrossing ripples of pink. He watched the scene until birds and dolphins were out of sight and the water returned to a black, glass-like stillness.

He rose and surveyed the riverbank for a gap in the tangle of brambles, shrubs, and branches. He headed toward a dark patch that beckoned downriver. As he got closer the spot revealed itself not as the gap he sought, but as an upturned rubber tree, its mud-encrusted mat of roots seemingly mooning the riverbank. Annoyed by the miscalculation, Ty turned off the boots' hoverpower and climbed the caked morass, reaching the top and then shimming down limbs and parts of the trunk until he cleared the riparian thicket. Under the forest's sun-filtering dome he audibled a position check. A detailed map emerged before him: 95 kilometers remained to be traversed—approximately a two-day hike before he could reach the location of the sighting. Assaying the hummocky terrain, he calibrated his boots' ground sensors for optimal hover function.

Hoverboots deploy a magnetic pulse deep into the Earth's crust to elevate a terranaut a few inches and prevent any disturbance of the soil beneath. Calibrations are necessary over saturated soils, bogs, steep slopes, and other conditions that can distort the pulse and send terranauts tumbling. In very rough terrain, such as Ty encountered while scaling the upturned rubber tree, terranauts can turn their hoverpower off.

A hunger pang struck and he took a protein tablet. Nearby a clump of prosthechea orchids clung to an epiphyte-laden branch, the curling, stinger-pointed leaves lighting up the forest like fireworks. Ty commanded his visor to zoom in. A yellow-skinned poison dart frog, throat bellowing, faced a menacing bullet ant. *Kill or be killed* rattled in Ty's head. "Surround scan, one fifty!" he voiced. "Clear," the tracker responded, confirming that nothing within range was larger than one hundred fifty pounds—nothing larger than an anteater. He returned to observing the frog and the ant but did not wait for the outcome; it would not end well for the amphibian. Sidestepping shrubs and meandering around large trees, he began the march toward Serra Padre, maintaining a two-degree deviation from the intended NNW line of travel.

Around midday Ty came across a cluster of buriti palms and stopped to rest. A beam of sunlight lit up five red-bellied macaws perched on a frond. He zoomed in. The birds were locked on him, poised to take flight at the slightest threatening motion. Ty held still but the birds leapt up and glided away, their indigo wings spread in full display before fading into the forest shadows. He heard the call of a blue-crowned trogon. "Location," he voiced. The angle and distance to the bird appeared in front of him. On a trunk, twelve yards away, he could see its head poking out of a termite hollow. He thought of Nori and imagined her in her twenties, trim and fit in a terrasuit, her face awash with joy at the sight of the colorful bird. He sighed, ruing the impossibility.

In the late afternoon, the murmur of a nearby stream caught his attention. He turned eastward, reaching the bank and following its course upstream. He reached a widening with tranquil waters. An anaconda was coiled around a small caiman near a patch of marsh pitcher plants. He recorded the scene, vowing to tell CaL that the next time his holographic reptile needs a meal, he should consider a lizard. The snake was unperturbed by Ty's presence as it waited for its prey to suffocate. Ty slid past them. *Kill or be killed* again rang in his head.

Further up he stopped by a shallow pool, knelt by the water's edge, removed his headgear and splashed water on the back of his neck. A capybara and her pups emerged a few yards away, rushed into the water and swam to the far shore in a tight pack. He watched them intently, guessing which pup would reach the streambank first. He guessed wrong. Putting his headgear back on he headed inland. A bright spot intrigued him a hundred yards in. The limb of a tall ficus tree had broken off and lay horizontally in midair, fed now by a crutch of aerial roots. Reaching for the light, a maracuyá vine encircled some of them. Ty reached for a fruit, smelled it for ripeness and took a bite. He pulled two more. Sated, he took off in a jog.

The echoing bark of a red howler stopped his progress an hour later. He looked up and spotted a female reclining on a branch with an offspring by her side. The male was nearby, bouncing on a limb while holding on to a liana. Ty imitated the bark. The male quieted and looked down as if puzzled by the odd creature with the blue fish-like skin. The end of the liana was a meter off the ground. Ty walked to it and cut off a section, keeping both ends upright to form a U. Holding one end high, he lowered the other to his lips and sipped the mint-tasting water.

Shadows were lengthening. Ty turned off the hoverpower and walked a few paces to the base of a walking palm, nestling himself inside the plant's splaying cage-like trunks. He pulled apart the suit's backside seam and squatted, holding on to a pair of trunks. He recalled DaK's parting words. "Don't fall backwards …" He cleaned himself with biodegradable tissue, closed the suit's backside, and retrieved a vial of acid from his backpack. He emptied the liquid onto the feces and discarded the tissue. With DaK's admonition still in his thoughts he watched the acid take effect with a hiss and a puff of smoke.

As the shadows began to lengthen Ty came to a large ceiba. A column of leafcutter ants was marching along the ridge of a buttressing root. One was carrying a heart-shaped fragment between its pincers. He recalled XoL's sendoff: "Light and strong—*mi corazón!*" He smiled, never before having connected her endearing phrase to the powerful ants and the shape of their sculpting work. He watched until he could no longer distinguish one leaf from another, all seeming to levitate up the side of the tree in a neat file.

He again tracked toward the creek. Reaching its bank, he looked upstream and saw the Pico da Neblina in the distance, the last rays of the day clinging to its jagged top. The beauty of the place belied the horror a landslide can cause. Amid the fading light he spotted an eddy. He removed a telescopic tube from his belt and extended it until locked. A trident popped out from one end. Hoverpower off, he waded into the pool, careful not to roil the waters. A fish approached. Ty speared it with dead aim. It was a small peacock bass. Back on the shore, over a flat stone, he skinned it, flaked off pieces of meat, and ate.

A faint whir was coming from the mountainside—a drone dirigible heading eastward. An object fell from it, or was it a nearby dive-bombing hawk, the *Buteo nitidus*? An avalanche came to mind: a drop, a ripple, a rising cloud, a deafening roar. He waited for the worst, but the earth beneath did not shake; the soil did not churn skyward. He observed the drone until it became a faint spec in the darkening sky.

Up to that moment Ty had not contemplated peril, thinking only of making steady progress to the location of the sighting—and from there to the encampment, which he presumed would be a short distance. He thought of the envelope he left with JuN—in case he did not make it back. It contained three notes. One was to his parents; he asked for forgiveness, explaining that he simply could not accept PaZ and MaY having died without anyone knowing why. In a note to Nori he let her know how much he loved her, and that when she got a little bit older CaL would tell her more. And to CaL he said that he always knew who that "other boy" at school was, and that he was sorry he could not offer in return more than his unconditional and loving friendship.

(Ty could not know that CaL had dropped the envelope to the floor when the Boar agents came, and that after the commotion it was swept into a bin with the day's trash.)

A sense of doom gained on Ty's psyche but was quickly fought back. He took one last bite and buried the fish remains, then he quickly packed his tools, turned on the visor's night vision, and resumed the march.

Two hours later he stopped by a tall strangler fig tree, its hollowed core still bearing the imprint of the palm tree around which it grew. Gripping an aerial root, he dug his boots into the tree's braided trunk and pulled himself up, seeking a safe sleeping perch. Two-thirds of the way up he curled his hand into a hollow and sent a slew of vampire bats screeching helter-skelter. Startled, he lost his footing and nearly fell 40 feet to the forest floor. He regained his balance and climbed further up, clinging to a liana, until he reached two broad limbs over which he could stretch a sleeping net and pass the night. Exhausted, he barely registered the muted reverberations of faraway thunderclaps before passing out.

DAY TWO

Ty was roused at dawn by the drumbeat of a steady downpour. A sloth was hanging from an overhead limb, staring at him impassively. The animal was so close he could have poked it with a stick. "Not today, PaZ. Can't take it slooow today," he said aloud, remembering his brother's parting words before his solo descent.

He sat up, reached for a large leaf, positioned it by his mouth to catch the rain, and sipped from it. Thirst quenched, and after stowing the net, he continued northward. Midday he called for a location update. A clump of Tillandsia orchids sprouting from a nearby limb beckoned. He reached for the epiphytes and scrubbed the leaves clean of their parasitic earthworms.

Fifteen kilometers had been covered since daybreak. In a trot, Ty envisioned a second encounter with an encampment worker. This time he vowed to forego the tracker and stun him instead, waiting all day if necessary for the shock to wear off before making him talk. He swiped the side of the gun and rehearsed a fast draw. With the jaguar in mind, he repeated the motion. Satisfied, he began to run, pushing away twigs and fronds, jumping over fallen limbs and ducking under branches with heightened anticipation.

Time seemed to stand still: a skip, a sway, a swat—every motion was effortless, as if on autopilot. Gliding in a semi-meditative state, Ty failed to hear the bio-tracker's ping. With the second, longer and louder, he lost his balance and flew headfirst onto a thorn-laden bactris palm. He pulled his hands in and let his right side take the hit, falling hard on the ground from the recoil. He lay prone for a moment, cursing at the mishap. A patch of broken thorns lay to his side; none were stuck to his suit. Standing, he followed the trunk upward and spotted the palm's unmistakable clump of peach-colored fruit bursting at the base of a whirling array of fronds. Recalling the foraging habits of the Yanomami, he wondered anew how the natives managed to climb such trees and pick the fruit.

The third ping came with a throat tingling vibration. Ty coughed, rubbed his neck, and saw the reading through the visor:

TAPIR: 510lbs-150mts-15dgs

He shook his head, impressed by the beast's substantial size but also struck by the improbability of the numbers: 510 pounds, 150 meters away, at a bearing of 15 degrees. Must have been bathing in the creek, he guessed. He headed in its direction, hoping to catch sight of the beast, but the animal began to move downhill, in the opposite direction from the encampment. He stopped, content to just hear it as it moved away. Further ahead the ripened, star-shaped fruit of a Sachamani tree lured him, hanging within reach. He cut one open and scooped the pulp and its peanut-like seeds with his knife's spoon-shaped handle. He ate three others, carefully tamping the rinds into the ground. A few yards away he spotted a liana, walked to it, cut it above his head and washed down the fruit.

Ty checked the time and continued in a powerwalk. PaZ's video recording filled his mind. He recalled the beams of sunlight cutting through the canopy at approximately the fifth hour post meridiem. He fast-forwarded the recollection. Seeing in his head the pattern of shadows on the encampment, he concluded that PaZ had approached the place from the south, videorecording in a northward direction before backtracking to escape the man in the black suit. Once he found it he would do differently, looping around from the west to better blend in with the morning light, he vowed.

He was absorbed in the calculation when the bio-tracker again pinged.

"MAMMAL: 235lbs-2.50kms-90dgs."

"Confirm number," he voiced.

"UNDETERMINED." Ty had seen this before: a group feeding, probably a jaguar and her pups huddled while feasting on a kill.

"Confirm number," he repeated after a few minutes, time enough, he thought, for bunched mammals to move around and be detected individually.

"SINGLE MAMMAL: 235lbs-2.45kms-90dgs.

Ty stopped and turned eastward for the scanner to get a better reading. Must be a fully developed male jaguar, he concluded.

"Species, please," he voiced, anticipating the confirmation.

"UNIDENTFIED."

"Distance and bearing!"

"2.48kms-89.5dgs."

"Species, please!!" Ty repeated.

"UNIDENTIFIED."

"ASPECT," Ty yelled.

"UPRIGHT; 2.1 METERS."

"FUCK! FUCK! FUCK!" he shouted, understanding now that this was a detected human, a man that was far bigger and taller than the half-naked figure he had first encountered. He recalled the object falling from the drone the day before. "See you down there—CAL, RIGHT?" DaK's words hit him like a death knell. "The bastard, he was toying with me!" he muttered angrily.

Wiping sweat from his upper lip Ty retraced the course of the past week. He saw the suit rack lighting up and wondered why, having already been banned from the Corps, it was still hanging there—why wouldn't they have sanitized it and returned MaY's wafer to him? *Were they expecting me?* He saw his old classmate on the queue to board the El train and realized that the man was still on board when he exited, waiting for him before following him out. He saw Asha on the platform, retching—but there was no smell from the vomit, he now realized. He saw her in the dirigible, pointing to a landing spot on the Rio Negro, and wondered why any terranaut would be so casually willing to drop a supposedly inexperienced Atmo hundreds of miles from the El, especially if he claimed to be heading to one of the most rugged regions in all of Amazonia. Mentally backtracking, he saw Manny in the equipment room, grabbing a stun gun and readily handing it to him without confirming the charge. Panicked, he reached for the gun and checked it.

The gun was depleted. His wrathful cry echoed through the forest. A nearby howler answered.

"READING?" Ty voiced angrily.

"2.45kms-89dgs."

Ty disabled his surface transponder, turned off the hoverpower and took off running, churning the soil beneath.

"READING!" he pleaded between pants a kilometer later.

"2.25kms-165dgs"

DaK was gaining ground. *It's useless; he knows where I am!* Hunkering down at the base of a bacuri tree he recalled his mother's tales about hunting and warfare among primitive tribes. "A spear is an extension of your arm," she would say, mimicking a forward motion, "while a trap is an extension of your brain. Which one do you think wins the day?"

A limb stretched out overhead. Tightly packed rubber tree saplings were rising nearby: behind them, a young, thorn-laden possumwood, and to its right, a chambira palm. He rose, retrieved a wire roll from his backpack and set it on the ground. Knife in hand, he walked a few paces and cut a long branch from a sapling, then a foot-long section off the possumwood. Beads of sweat began to build. Hurriedly, he wrapped the wire tightly around both pieces of wood and fashioned a bendable lance with a spiked, mace-like appendage on its end. The wire roll hung from it. He then wedged the butt end of the lance horizontally into several of the seedling branches and forcefully bent the remaining section toward the palm tree. He had calculated right: the tip of the lance reached the palm tree just enough to rest on a leaf scar, ready to snap loose at the slightest twitch. Measuring his breath he stepped away, stretching the wire taut across the clearing and knotting it around the base of the bacuri tree before climbing to the overhead limb. He looked down approvingly: the tripwire was barely visible.

"READING?"

"NEGATIVE."

"Goddamn!" he uttered, realizing that DaK had gone stealth also. He had heard rumors about emitters that could neutralize bio-tracking scanners—a possible explanation for the suddenly vanishing man, he had thought after the sighting.

Rumors of the neutralizing emitters had gained currency during a training mission in Matto Grosso, a few months before PaZ and MaY's deaths. Acting as prey, a terranaut instructor had seemingly vanished before her student's eyes. To their amazement, the woman had reappeared without detection several hours later, leaving the trainees in the dark about how she had pulled off the stunt. The rest of the story is this: The instructor was amorously involved with a young technician working on the emitters, a secret project. The technician had no knowledge of their intended use, only that The Boar had personally ordered their manufacture "for experimental purposes." The man could not resist demonstrating the prototype to his lover, succumbing also to her pleas to let her take it down to earth "for a test drive." She promised to bring it back with vital data he could use to perfect the instrument and further impress the security chief. After sending the trainees back to the El station, the instructor remained in Matto Crosso to complete her assigned recording mission; her trainees returned home without her, expecting her to join them there in class at a later date. She never did. As for the fate of the technician, the man perished two weeks later on the way to his lover's Ceremony of Remembrance when the Solo shell he was n suffered sudden and catastrophic decompression.

The sun had set. Crouched on the limb, he shifted back and forth until he found a steady point of balance. He rehearsed what he would do when the trap snapped and the mace smashed into DaK's leg; the angle at which he would jump to land on the man, lift his visor and drive the knife into his throat. Minutes passed amid chirps, tweets, and intermittent howls. Knees tiring, he stood and edged backwards to lean against the trunk. His eyelids felt heavy. He blinked drumroll-like several times to keep them from clamping down. Feeling his bladder calling, he relieved himself against the tree trunk, careful not to make a sound. A stir in the brush rang the alarm. He quickly zipped up and zoomed in. A shadow was advancing low to the ground. *Can't miss the wire, no matter how low DaK crawls*, he thought. The trap snapped with a whoosh followed by a crack and a loud grunt. A large tapir was entangled in the wire. Ty jumped, landed hard, and rolled. Squealing and bucking, the tapir hit his arm with a strong kick that sent the knife flying. He groped for it. Seconds passed in total mayhem. He saw the knife, breast high, stuck into the tree at its base. Darting, he yanked it loose, lunged back toward the beast and cut the wire. The tapir ran off, grunting through the woods.

Shaken, Ty leaned against the tree and shut his eyes to think straight. The pause was short-lived. *DaK must have heard the ruckus.* With a rush of adrenalin, he jumped to his feet, climbed up the tree, and scampered through the forest, bounding ape-like from limb to limb.

He alit a few minutes later, exhausted. *No choice but to fight the man,* he concluded. Nearby on the ground he located a club-like branch. He pulled out a wad of sticky gauze from his backpack, removed the remaining vials of acid, and wrapped them around the branch. *The burn will be instantaneous and blind him*, he thought. Ty swung the branch a few times to get a feel for the weight. His arm was throbbing from the tapir's kick. Calculating DaK's height, he adjusted the angle upward and swung it a few more times. A water droplet fell on him, then a few more. The forest turned quiet. Seconds later a deluge came crashing down.

Ty wiped his visor and cursed at the clouded vision. He unplugged it, snapped it off, and tossed it aside. He waited several minutes for his eyes to adjust to the darkness before finding cover in another partially hollowed-out strangler fig. The nook felt eerily familiar, triggering a palpable flashback to the nightmare he had suffered during his descent. The rain was deafening, drowning out all other noise. It stopped after what felt like an eternity. Clouds parted and the forest was bathed by a faint moon glow. Wedged in the trunk, Ty squinted to better spot moving shadows. None were detected. Tightening his grip on the makeshift club he stepped out a few paces and held a deep breath. Hearing nothing out of the ordinary, he exhaled.

Then it came: a powerful blow to the stomach that sent him sprawling and gasping for air. He tried to raise the club but couldn't budge it—a boot was pressing on it. He let it go and rolled to the side. Another boot slammed the ground, barely missing his face. Struggling to fill his lungs he rolled once more, catching sight of the massive figure above.

"It's useless, Ty—or should I call you CaL?" DaK sneered. "I take pleasure in killing idiots who think they have a chance, especially when they're wearing a glowing mask! Sure beats wasting a charge and hauling you to the encampment."

A large yatagán glinted above DaK's head, ready to strike. Ty groped for a piece of wood, a stone—anything to fend off the hit. He grabbed a liana and swung it. The yatagán cut it cleanly, glancing off his shoulder and smashing his bio-tracker. DaK's arm was set for another blow. Ty yanked the mask off his face, drawing DaK's hand to the light. The blade sliced it just beyond his fingers. He turned over and crawled backwards, digging for his life with his knees and elbows.

DaK grabbed hold of Ty's right foot and twisted it violently, turning him back around.

"You won't get away with it!" Ty shouted. "I have the evidence! If something happens to me, it will be turned in!"

"Turned in? TO WHOM? The Boar? You're more stupid than I thought," DaK blared between laughs. "We have your friend, CAL, RIGHT? It's only a matter time before he coughs up your precious evidence."

DaK raised the yatagán. A large shadow approached and stopped. He turned but it was too late. The jaguar landed on him with a blood-curdling roar.

DaK tumbled, rolling with the animal into a knot, the two waking the forest with screams, grunts, and snarls. Ty took off running, barely able to find his footing. A loud shout brought him to a halt. He waited for a minute but heard nothing save for MaY's beating wafer. He kept going, ears on alert.

A massive angelim tree rose ahead near a moonlit stream, a thick vine hanging by its side. Ty grabbed hold of it, put one boot on the trunk, and stepped up the tree. Loud rustling stopped him—the noise was more than a jaguar would cause. He dropped to the ground and ran, bounding over streambank brambles, hoping to jump in and disappear underwater. He did not make it: a vibration knocked him to the ground followed by a stabbing pain in his thorax. Ty rolled, feeling the onset of total darkness.

DAY THREE

The pricks on his cheek felt like those of a tattooing needle. Ty lifted a hand to tap the irritated spot, but it dropped involuntarily, slapping his shoulder instead. Unperturbed, a longhorn beetle crawled onto his cap and continued its march. Ty tried again, this time the attempt landing his arm hard on his nose. The impact sent a shot of pain ear to ear, turning the normal forest sounds into a jarring buzz. He cracked open an eye and sensed a tree towering overhead. He was lying flat on the ground wedged between two large ceiba roots. He tilted his head forward and saw a blurry figure approaching. He wanted to jump and run but his legs failed to answer the call. The figure stopped by his side and extended an arm—or was it a yatagán? Ty flailed his arms and screamed, but only a muffled grunt came out.

"Shhhh. It's alright, Ty. Lie still."

The soft voice confounded him.

"Where am I?" he mumbled.

"Drink this," the figure said, extending a small section of a liana to his lips. "It'll start clearing the fog."

Ty welcomed the few sips that dribbled in. Disoriented, he dropped his head and closed his eyes, wishing for darkness to return. His lips then felt a soft, moist caress.

"It's me, you fool."

XoL was inches away, peering into his eyes with a gentle smile. He looked at her, paralyzed, unable to reconcile her presence with the night's lingering haze of terror. She pulled back.

"I had to stun you last night," she said, sitting astride the buttressing root. "You were running like a madman. I had to stop you from diving in and getting mauled. There's a *Maelanosuchus niger* out there, biggest croc I've ever seen."

"How did you ..." Ty uttered, clearing the cobwebs.

"Later, my love; we've got work to do."

"DaK!" Ty cried.

"Yes, DaK, the one and only. He's eager to see you," she chuckled.

Ty leaned on the root but wobbled. XoL helped him to his feet and pulled him closer, the hold turning into a long embrace. They separated and stared at each other, eyes welling. Ty removed his gloves and let them fall. He held her face.

"Last night I thought I would never see the light of day again, and now, out of nowhere ... the most beautiful light I have ever known."

XoL clasped his hands. "I know, I know. I love you, too ... so much ... always have, since your first waddle."

They laughed and gazed at each other. Legs entwined, they kissed, softly and long, as if to transport themselves back to their youthful dreams of intimacy. XoL disengaged.

"We've got to get to DaK," she said, guiding him out of the ceiba's long, twisting root. Ty picked up his gloves and reached for her hand, unwilling to lose touch with what a moment earlier felt like an apparition. As they walked, he looked for the fig tree where he lay hidden the night before, but all he saw was a tangle.

"Almost there," she said.

The sound of moaning came their way. Pushing palm fronds aside they entered a small clearing. Ty gasped. DaK was kneeling stark naked, head bowed, hands tied behind to a possumwood and legs pressed in the crook of a thorn-laden ceiba branchlet.

A jaguar, breathing haltingly, was sprawled nearby, blood oozing from its side through a gauzed patch.

"Quite the specimen, isn't he? Took a double hit to bring him down," XoL said nonchalantly. She walked over and checked the wire tie around DaK's hands. She tightened the hold. Stunned, Ty followed XoL's path around DaK to a pile of bark chips neatly mounded by his knees.

"Ucuúba, the hallucinogenic. I gathered them last night while you were out cold," she said, placing a lighting stick into the pile. Pungent smoke rose. She fanned it, aiming for DaK's face. They edged away and sat on the ground, legs crossed. DaK coughed, lifted his head and stared at them as if they were part of the flora. XoL looked at Ty tenderly.

"For so long I have dreamed of us to have these ... made them years ago." From a belt pouch she retrieved a pair of polished black rings made from the fruit of the Tucum palm. With glazed eyes and in silence they placed them on one another's fingers. Tears flowing, they kissed and embraced, tightly as if to fuse their seed-crafted circlets. Time seemed to stand still. XoL again disengaged.

"SuS came to my cell after the sentencing," she said. "I was shocked.

She was the last person I expected to see; the last person I ever wanted to see again. She was alone, without him," she nodded toward DaK. "I could have kicked her, hit her in the face if I'd wanted, but I was too astonished to think straight. She told me that she had taken pity on me; that it was you she had been after—that you had committed the crime and had gotten off easy. She began ranting about Osage having rendered an ass-backward sentence and telling me there was a good way to clean up the mess, a way for me to get my life back, but only if I were willing to finish what she had started … and that was to finish you off. That was the offer: my life for yours, a simple and traceless disappearance in Amazonia like all the others.

"I then lunged at her, wanted to strangle her, but I couldn't get near; my feet were stuck, glued to the floor. She broke out laughing, that cackle of hers, so proud of having discharged a magnetic pulse. She said I could have Nori, that she would declare my innocence and pave the way for her adoption, sparing her an upbringing by strangers in a far-off colony with no connections to OCTAD."

XoL rose and again stoked the fire to thicken the smoke. DaK coughed hard, almost choking. Ty couldn't take his eyes off of her, astonished by the story.

"I had no choice but to take her on," XoL said, back by his side. "I wasn't going to survive the sentence, and it wasn't a big leap to see that one way or another she would have us both killed. I had to try and stop this animal from carrying out a double elimination … for our sake and for Nori's."

Her last words dissolved the final vestiges of Ty's hypnagogic state. A surge of anger washed over him. Fists clenched, he started to rise but XoL held him back. "We need his confession," she said, then continued with the tale. She told how she had descended on an earlier train and trekked westward until she reached a location halfway between the Serra and the Rio Negro, where she could track Ty with the stealth emitter SuS had given her. "Better for an unsuspecting death, wouldn't you agree, *hee*?" SuS had cackled. DaK, who had the emitter's frequency, would be following them both, "as insurance," SuS had added. Xol described how during the deluge she employed every stealth technique she had ever learned to keep DaK unaware of her location, at one point digging herself into a stream bank where she prayed that the monster caiman that earlier swam by wouldn't smell her, "because I would have been forced to waste the stun gun's entire charge on it, leaving nothing for DaK—*or you, to keep you from diving right into its maw!* And she told how she had sprinted the last half-kilometer to reach the two men, arriving just seconds before the jaguar leapt on DaK. She'd watched the man and beast writhe on the ground until DaK managed to knife the animal, giving her precious seconds to lift her gun and aim at him with certainty.

"I stunned him twice, one hit to the heart and another to the head to make sure he was out.

From her belt she pulled a syringe. "This was for you; it activates intravenously," she said, placing the poison container on the ground and smashing it with the butt of her gun.

Ty shook his head.

"I was stupid," he said. "I was blinded by rage. Stupid to think I could beat SuS on my own. Stupid not to have guessed that she had me all figured out ... what I was up to. It all makes sense now—that Manny, of all people, would betray me."

XoL rested her head on his shoulder.

"Manny had little choice, *mi corazón.* SuS told me that when the agents went to see him, he readily confessed, said he'd already given the bead to CaL, as you had asked. SuS was bathed in conceit after having identified CaL behind his Gala headdress. She had him surveilled, even while you were at the ..."

Ty straightened suddenly, jumping to his feet and almost prancing.

"CAL DOESN'T HAVE IT! HE DOESN'T HAVE THE BEAD! MANNY STILL HAS IT!

XoL looked at Ty as if he were impersonating a madman.

He knelt, facing her.

"Last night DaK had me pinned to the ground and told me that SuS was trying to get the bead from CaL, torturing him. BASTARDS! Nobody can resist that! The last thing I said to Manny was to NOT give the bead to CaL, to give it to LeE instead. I didn't want to bury CaL any further in this mess. This means that Manny faked it—he tricked SuS! He still has the bead!" Ty grinned and shook his head, astonished and grateful for the cunning bravery hidden in the guard's avuncular persona.

"And the gun. We were rushing to get ready when he handed it to me. It must have been a dud to start with!!"

"You came down with an empty charge?"

Ty smiled sheepishly and slid to her side. He began to recount his own ordeal over the past week. XoL put her hand on his lips.

"I know about you and CaL at the café—and about the mask," she told him, mournfully. "SuS savored repeating how clever she was, how she knew everything about everyone. FaiZ … I'm so sorry, Ty … she's a paid informant. She used to be a PEA sympathizer and was being blackmailed."

The revelation stunned him. That FaiZ could have betrayed CaL was incomprehensible to him. At the café, hours before he met FaiZ, he had finally understood from CaL that he too had a soulmate. And FaiZ at the studio behaved the part; it was in her eyes, in her tender smile, and clearly in her willingness to do anything for CaL, no questions asked. But now he hoped that their "love" had never meant any more than an easy fix for sex. He swore to somehow repair CaL's suffering. He stared at DaK. The man's eyes were open wide and rolling, as if he was experiencing some kind of glorious dream.

"Tell me about Asha," XoL said, breaking the pause. Ty looked at her incredulously, wondering how she could possibly know about her. But he deferred getting an answer to that, instead sharing the realization that had haunted him ever since jumping out of her ship: that Asha was DaK's accomplice. He'd figured out that at the landing deck she had faked being sick to lure him into a dirigible and give him a ride to the Rio Negro, where he'd conveniently be within striking distance of the killer. She'd made up that whole wild story about her lost lover so he'd let his guard down. She'd tried to kiss him, he told XoL, but he'd since figured out it was only to cause the mask to ripple and confirm his real identity for DaK. Her attempt at a kiss had forced him to jump off the ship before he was ready. He'd nearly broken a leg in that hard landing.

"I should have known better," he concluded.

"Yes, you should have!" XoL said, laughing heartily. "It looks to me like she had something else in mind. She's LeE's sister. I know her well, through their aunt. After agreeing with SuS's terms, I called her and asked her to look for the handsome Atmo at the El and give him a lift—as a favor to a former neighbor of mine, is how I put it. I told her also that Osage had pardoned me—a stretch, I know, but she's not one to question anyone's story or motive. There's not a hair of evil in her; she just oozes empathy, as you know. I told her to try and place you close to the Rio Negro, south of Serra Padre, that you were going there on a cloud-recording mission. I needed to get you there so I could find you before this sonofabitch did. It was more than worth the risk!"

He clutched XoL's face, gazing into her eyes.

"There was *zero* risk," he said. They kissed passionately, falling on their sides. DaK coughed and looked their way. XoL and Ty separated and crawled over to him; she blew into the clump of ucuúba leaves again, careful not to inhale. Ty powered up his headset recorder and readied the transmission code. "I swore to Manny that I'd get back to him within a week to tell him I was okay. But this—he won't believe his eyes."

"DaK, can you hear me?" XoL said, her voice coming to him in spurts. DaK mumbled. "DaK!" she repeated. Ty stood and swung his boot hard onto DaK's leg. The ceiba thorns dug deep into the man's thighs. DaK groaned as blood oozed from the punctures. XoL winced. Ty knelt and closed in on DaK's ear. "We need answers. The encampment. The coordinates. Who's in charge, what are they doing there, who's behind the operation? Tell us about PaZ and MaY, about the landslide … who killed them. TELL US, DAK! GET IT OUT OF YOUR FUCKING JANGALA BRAIN!"

DaK's eyes lit up.

"Perfect drop … hell of an avalanche … buried 'em good, those fools!" he muttered, staring ahead far into the foliage. Ty set his boot square on DaK's face, letting loose with a gut-born scream. DaK moaned, deeply drugged and barely aware of the impact or the blood gushing from his nose. The jaguar stirred.

"We don't have much time," XoL said. DaK again lost consciousness, but not before the ucuúba had loosened his tongue and he had spilled out all the details of SuS's illicit operation.

Ty and XoL collected themselves and prepared to leave for the encampment. They took one last look at DaK, head hanging over his knees. A wandering spider had found DaK's foot and was climbing up his buttock. Bullet ants were crawling between his legs. Other insects had begun to feast on his wounds. Ty and XoL picked up his gun and yatagán. They left his suit sprawled on the ground, as a marker for a future search party to find his remains, should there be enough to bother with. A few yards out Ty spotted the strangler fig he had been in. His visor was lying nearby. He picked it up, wiped it clean and plugged it back into his headset. Farther away he found his mask and stowed it. "Saved my life," he told XoL. Then, a few feet away, he spotted the vial-wrapped club and picked it up.

"What on earth is that?" XoL asked, shaking her head at the weird gauze-covered object.

"My version of a weapon. If only I had smacked him with it," Ty said, shaking his head and unwrapping the stick to expose the vials of acid.

"Those will come in handy when nature calls!" XoL grinned.

As Ty removed the gauze and repacked the vials he matched XoL's silliness with a smile of his own. They continued in silence, radio receivers off and visors down, absorbing the overflowing tropical detail of the forest. Periodically, one of them would point to an animal or a plant, pose a question or offer a shared memory; but their replies were brief, as if to safeguard the pleasure of extended and intimate conversation in years yet to come. Holding hands, they took turns leading the way up the Serra. Well into the trek XoL spotted a clump of blue-flowering acacallis orchids hanging from a low branch. She squeezed Ty's hand. Ty saw them and remembered the allusion of the plant's name to Apollo's seduction of a beautiful nymph. He tightened the grip.

It must be said: At the El terminal, DaK ably demonstrated people's ignorance in referring to the tropical forests as "jungles." In the Old-World, as human settlement encroached upon and disturbed the forests, affected vegetation turned into a chaotic, menacing, and nearly impenetrable tangle. Over time the term "jungle" was liberally extended to mean any thick forests. But these, when stable and mature, are different in appearance from actual jungles. Save for riverbanks or areas subject to natural disturbances—such as landslides—forests are tranquil places, largely open for passage, with a well-defined stratification yielding a vast array of niches for plants and animals. They are extraordinary in their complexity, yet perfectly balanced, "like a work of art" as MaY liked to say. Professor Airi Te, PaZ and Ty's father, sought for years to eradicate the term "jungle" from normal usage, but with limited success outside the classroom. His reasons were two-fold: Aside from imparting a false description of an extensive habitat, he noted that the term had its origins in Sanskrit, from the word *jangala*, which, ironically, meant aridity, a place that is sparsely vegetated. He reserved the word "jungle" for actual jungles, using *jangala*, affectionately, for students suffering lapses of attention—and for PaZ and Ty when they would make bonehead mistakes. The Te boys were quick to adopt the Sanskrit and use it on each other, in typical sibling teasing.

A HAUNTING IDYLL

Nori has barely slept for days while trying to complete the narrative. The den's walls seem to be pressing on her. Perspiration is building on her forehead, and a wave of nausea washes over her. She stands and stares at the cloudscape. A nimbus cloud is expelling a thick column of water from its dark underbelly. The midafternoon Florida Everglades scene, normally one of her favorites, further unsettles her. She steps away from her desk and paces around the room to calm herself.

"Do you wish to rest?" Lali offers.

"I'm fine, Lali; just having trouble here, imagining what happened to them," Nori replies, dropping her head against a wall strut.

Lali's suggest a preamble, a forerunner to the gruesome events.

On the eve of PaZ and MaY's fateful descent, XoL had joined them at home for dinner. Ty had been there also. The couple always prepared a special home-cooked meal before departing on a mission. MaY's mother had first done so in celebration of her daughter's maiden descent and MaY had adopted the loving gesture; it was now a family tradition. For this occasion, they had prepared a tamale dish from a recipe that XoL had given MaY years earlier. Maize is scarce and the dish is rarely attempted. It takes hours to grind the corn on a metate and turn it into a paste. They had hoped the tedious operation, leading to hours of bonhomie, would ease their anxiety, but it proved hard to shake off. Calling off the evening crossed their minds, but they kept on grinding, fearing that a cancellation would alert XoL and Ty that something was amiss.

As luck would have it, XoL had brought Nori a stuffed penguin as a present. "A Waddler from the Weddell," she said when she handed it to the child. Ty had then done one of his patented goofy penguin walks. Nori had never seen him do that and she immediately tried to imitate it, tripping and giggling all the way to the floor. Ty had then dropped by her side, belly down, legs extended, and with flapping palms had enacted a penguin swim. The antic had caused general laughter and a torrent of childhood memories, much to PaZ and MaY's relief. Later in the evening, after Ty had left and PaZ and MaY were cleaning up, XoL approached Nori. Clasping her face she said, almost in a whisper, that the penguin was there to keep her company when her parents were gone.

"Did she really mean to say 'gone,' Lali, or did she intend to say 'away'?" Nori ponders out loud. "She must have had a premonition that something bad was about to happen to them."

"Premonitions are chemical reactions caused by the cortisol hormone and can be interpreted as precursors to danger. Sometimes they can be triggered by the food you eat, and I would not be one to doubt that the evening's spicy tamales ..."

"Yes, yes, and eating too much maize can cause constipation, Lali, something that by the grace of your almighty ones and zeroes you don't have to suffer. Let's just say that XoL that day had an acute sense of danger, knew what could happen to them. And she did again a year or so later, another premonition voiced in hushed words, right, Lali?

Before her descent to thwart SuS's plan, XoL had rushed over to Manaus, unsure if she would ever see Nori again. Nori had been surprised but happy to have a break from the care center's daily routine, long and unsettling as Ty's unexplained absence still was after the guards had ransacked the apartment. XoL took Nori to the garden to walk among the scented flowers. After several loops, all the while holding hands, XoL lifted her to the bench under the kiwi arbor. Foreheads almost touching, she told Nori why she was going down to Amazonia: "To make sure that Ty comes back quickly. Everything will be alright, I promise!" she had said, as if to draw certainty from the dubious affirmation.

"I was puzzled, Lali," Nori says, reflecting on XoL's visit that day. "I didn't understand what she meant; saying everything would be alright implied that things might *not* be alright. And the secrecy: clasping my face to block you and your pal Zuma from reading her lips? Isn't it always better for veebots to know what's going on?"

"Secrecy sharpens the mind; brings greater focus to a 'flight or fight' response. XoL was about to face a mauling reptile, a ruthless killer. She knew the dangers lurked and that bad things could happen."

Nori paces around the den, considering Lali's answer. She imagines what it must feel like to knowingly walk into a life-and-death situation. Disturbed by something Ty had told her at the park—about where he and XoL headed after leaving DaK to die—she takes a deep breath before resuming dictation.

"Only one thing could have been on XoL's mind as she and Ty glided hand in hand toward the encampment: that after the ordeal was over and the truth came out, justice would be done and the world would be rid of the evil SuS Scrofa. XoL envisioned the best outcome. She would leave OCTAD for good, no matter how much Osage begged her to stay or what promotion he offered. She would make one last visit to headquarters to say goodbye to her friends and colleagues and depart amid hoots and hollers. And she and Ty would finally go home together and start life anew, as blissful vintners—and as parents to little me. For that would have been the perfect thing for them to do.

"But it was not to be.

"It was Ty's third day since his descent. As the day waned and the shadows lengthened, XoL stopped and pulled him close. 'I think we found our little Eden,' she whispered, pointing up into a large Brazil nut tree, which formed in its canopy an intimate, dirigible-sized nook.

"The moment had arrived for Ty and XoL to wed amid the earth's sacred bounty. They had refrained for hours, because a rushed passion earlier in the day, however deep and deserving, would have been a violation of the beauty around them. I cannot speak with authority about romance or about true love, but I have to imagine that when they consummated their love in the contoured perch, their shadows burned away as if a godly hand had lifted them out of the earth and fused them under the warmth of our helium-fired star."

Tears welling, Nori then recounts more of the story for Lali's consideration. These details had come to Nori at the park when Ty stopped by a bench, slumped onto it and with a grim, almost lifeless expression told her of his horrific awakening the next morning.

His words had been few, but precise, as if to purge in one hack the sickening memory. The sweet and calming QWAAAAAA of a Great Potoo had pulled him out of his sleep and with eyes closed he had reached out and touched XoL—only to feel coldness. Jolted into consciousness, he had turned quickly, almost losing an eye from the arrow that had pierced her throat, the wound still frothing with venom. He told Nori how, after springing to his feet in shock, he saw a man in a black suit standing on a limb with another shaft on the ready, having apparently waited to strike for the sole pleasure of seeing him suffer; and, in a dispassionate voice, how the arrow flew just as his scream scattered a colony of bats, the arrow glancing off one and striking another, giving him precious seconds to leap toward the killer, twist the bow around his neck, push him over his perch, and then watch him fall like a rag doll—until the bow caught two branches and left him dangling there, blood gushing from his partially severed head.

At the park bench Ty had sighed and closed the episode. "I will never understand how nature, with its extraordinary beauty, can also deliver such catastrophe, trauma, and death," he had said.

Nori is overwhelmed anew. A surge of adrenaline further compels her to complete the narrative: vividly, with true detail, however painful the task might be.

TY'S SOLACE

From Nori's account of XoL and Ty's last day together, it becomes clear that love can exalt the soul, but also rend it. I confess, her death was a surprise; it was not foreseen as inevitably consequent. As for Ty, his will to overcome inconceivable grief and keep sight of the greater peril remains as impressive as it was predictable. But it was a close call.

Ty lay by XoL's side despondent for hours after the horrific incident, suffering fits of convulsing sobs. He lifted his head periodically as if to plead with the patterns of light and shadow to reverse the course of time. The whistle of a trogon eventually snapped him out of his numbness. He donned his suit and climbed down to quench his thirst and hunger. Returning to the roost he secured XoL's body to a liana and eased her to the ground; he slipped her suit back on and carried her in his arms more than a kilometer to a nearby stream. By its bank he dug a shallow grave and placed her in the cavity. Intent on protecting every inch of her body, he cut off a section of his sleeve and covered her face, sliding her visor over the veil to keep it firm. He removed her Tucum ring, and his, and rested them on her chest. Keeping them, at that moment, was too painful to bear.

With soil he smoothed the grave then fetched palm fronds to cover it, weighing them down with river rocks. Crouched by her side he spent the rest of the day and night waiting for a downpour, then watched rising waters lap the fronds "as if to draw out her soul and carry it downstream to the Rio Negro, to the Amazon River, to the Atlantic Ocean, and beyond—around the world like a shining pearl," as he had tearfully told Nori.

After the burial Ty retraced his steps, climbed the tree where the killer was still hanging and cut the bowstrings. The body landed with a thud. He removed the man's suit and boots, buried them, tied a liana around his ankles and dragged him back to the stream and along the bank until he found a rocky ledge. "Damn the OCTAD rule book!" he cried, before pushing over the corpse to await its fate, like DaK's, as ecological manna. Fighting exhaustion, he resumed the trek to the encampment.

As the hours passed, despondency yielded to anger and then determination, powered by the vision of SuS's eventual fate: a public trial and execution and, as with all treasonous criminals, a launch and fiery reentry into the stratosphere to forevermore erase all trace of her ill existence. He marched the rest of the day in increasingly rugged and steepening terrain. Near sunset he found a large boulder against which to lean and rest. Ten kilometers remained to the encampment coordinates. The sky, and his mind, darkened, fatigue conquering the will to get up and continue.

The whir of a low-flying dirigible woke him up. It was three in the morning. He popped a protein tablet, activated the visor's night vision and resumed the march. At four thirty he reached an eerily familiar place: the fern-laden rock with a large fissure, the ceiba limb over which the jaguar had crouched, the large arum that had partly obscured the naked man, the clump of acaí palms through which he had then disappeared. The proximity to the encampment surprised him, less than a kilometer. He approached further, to within 200 meters. Setting aside DaK's yatagán and stun gun, he climbed a tall ceiba and zoomed in the direction of the encampment. Ahead the forest lightened. He advanced through the canopy, but what he thought was a clearing revealed itself as a sheer cliff, rising up in front of him.

"Terrain," he voiced, calling for a topographic view of the area. The image through his visor astounded him: A large open space arching northward lay beyond the cliff, as if a giant spade had come down from the heavens and hollowed out from the rock a three-quarter circle. *PaZ must have stumbled upon it from the southeast, straight into the encampment*, he concluded, based on his recollection of PaZ's video. An approach from above would be stealthier, he reasoned. He inched closer to the rock wall along a limb but the gap from it to the rock face was too wide to risk a leap.

Back on the ground, Ty considered his options. Dawn was breaking. He removed his boots, placed them in a nook at the base of the cliff, and started climbing, digging gloved toes and fingers into diorite crags and fissures, sidestepping slippery ferns and moss-covered patches. The pace was slow. Twenty minutes later he cleared the height of the canopy that earlier had engulfed him. He paused on a ledge and took stock of the sponge-like mantle spreading southward as far as the eye could see. A flock of cobalt-winged parakeets flew by.

"Terrain," he said. The ledge bent toward the hollow. He activated his suit's mimetic function and ambled forward, blending seamlessly with the rock face. The day's first ray of sun hit him in the eye. The visor darkened. Ahead he heard voices, water splashing. He edged closer. A column of water was streaming into the hollow, hitting a jutting rock and splattering into a shallow pool. Two partially clothed men approached it.

One of them waded in, bending down to wash an object. The flock of parakeets returned, swooping down to the pool and shrieking loudly before retreating to a perch on a nearby tree. A howler protested their presence with a loud, rolling bark. The wading man rose, looked toward the tree and yelled, shaking his fist in a futile attempt to stop the complaint. More voices rose from below.

Ty dropped to a prone position, affixed a microcam to his index finger, and stretched his arm into the void to record the full extent of the activity below. "Massif of Serra Padre," he logged vocally, "... amphitheater-like hollow framed by sheer rock approximately 100 meters across ... chambers at its bases, carved over time by a shifting waterfall ... makeshift holding pens of some kind ... high vegetation framing the open end ... three or more dozen men and women milling about, some in the open, others in the forest under what appears to be suspended netting. They are lightly clothed, some almost naked ... other men in black terrasuits, guards in appearance ... eight that I can see."

He stood and advanced further, looking for the shack he had seen in PaZ's video, out of which had come out the man clad in black holding a yatagán. The ledge floor was smooth, but without warning he hit an obstruction and tumbled forward, nearly falling over the edge.

"WHOA! Hell of a way to meet again," said a voice. A terrasuit in a prone position, head leaning over the edge, materialized by his feet.

"ASHA!" Ty yelled.

"Yes, the one and only!" she said, rising. "I got distracted for a moment; didn't see you coming. No need to be invisible. My bad. Where on earth did you lose your boots? What happened to your tracker? And where is XoL?" she asked, peering down to the encampment.

"Get down! Get down!" Ty pleaded.

"Oh, no; I wouldn't want to miss this," she said, boosting her hover-power to gain extra height. "Nothing against CaL, but you look much better without a mask," she added, smiling.

Ty gazed at the ground below to see if anyone had seen them.

"It's over, Ty," Asha said, pitying his knotted brain. "Bro and Auntie Flora, our beloved Rector, sent me a message yesterday urging me to leave the Island of Isabela in the Galápagos and get back here to find you and XoL—YOU, not CaL, they said. They said it was urgent, that your lives were in danger, so I dropped everything. I had just arrived at the beach and was ready to take a dip, just so you know. Luckily my drone was still there. It's gone now; sent it to the El after getting off near here a couple hours ago. Is XoL hiding down below? Your sleeve—it's torn! Was it a jaguar, or did XoL tear it off? You can be a bit of a jerk, you know. WHERE IS SHE?"

THE BOWL

▶ MARCH 8, 0275

Five days had passed since Ty left for the El, and Manny could no longer bear the wait. CaL's absence from work also sickened him. For days, he had stayed at headquarters well into the morning hours to see if CaL would show up. No one had seen him.

Manny resolved to look for LeE, as Ty had asked. He found him in a small study room cramming for a mission placement exam. "It's about Ty and XoL," Manny said. Seeing LeE's puzzled look, the guard pulled a chair and recounted the details of the arrest and everything that Ty had subsequently explained before descending. He handed LeE the bead.

The awful meeting with ThU boiled in LeE's head. He sensed the connection between the meeting and the bead and rued not having told his aunt about it afterward. He had been too shocked and confused by ThU's accusation. XoL had also asked him to keep quiet about it. Now he knew what to do. With Manny by his side, he raced down the corridor toward the pod's docking port. A peapod was about to leave for OCTAD's main campus. Two seats remained available. Before boarding LeE pinged his aunt to let her know they were on their way to meet. "It's pressing," he said, terminating the call before she had a chance to ask why.

Passiflora's office and that of the other rectors was situated in the middle torus of the campus. It was a modest space, pixel-free, with a small Earth-facing porthole as the sole attraction. He found her standing by her desk, nursing a potted passion vine growing around the porthole.

"I was asked to give you this," LeE said, entering with arm extended and the bead showing in his open palm.

Passiflora abstained from the customary hug and kept watering the plant while matter-of-factly requesting that LeE never again cut short a call or enter without knocking. She barely made eye contact with Manny. LeE muttered a hasty "sorry," then blurted out what he had witnessed at ThU's meeting, summarizing also what Manny had told him. The Rector listened impassively, careful not to betray her dislike for the Head Producer. ThU's protracted quarrel with MaY about the recording implants had tested her patience, and she regretted having promoted the man just to clear the way for MaY's ocular design to go forward.

She had also been incredulous about the charges brought against XoL and Ty, but absent evidence in their favor she had been in no position to mount an absolving argument. She had known Ty and XoL since their training days and was hard-pressed to believe their guilt, let alone accept the severity of their sentences. Adding to her dismay was her loathing of Sus Scrofa. Several times SuS had meddled in personnel assignments and mission plans, overriding her division managers by citing unspecified "security" concerns. That SuS acted with such impudence, never having stepped on the surface of Earth or caring a whit for its ecology, grated on her. A year earlier SuS had come to her office unannounced to complain about XoL's "insolence," insisting that PaZ and MaY's mission to Serra Padre be scrapped. "The region is prone to landslides, especially during the rainy season. She is risking the lives of two of my little children only to pad her ego," SuS had barked. Although she knew full well that without a sealed order from Osage no rector was obliged to meet such a request, SuS still made a show of being rebuffed when Passiflora had refused. She stormed out mumbling threats. A day later she doubled down, with a handwritten note demanding that PaZ and MaY always keep their transponders on "because it will make it easier to find them when they are buried." During the trial, Passiflora had kept her eyes glued on SuS, trying to fathom how her twisted mind could possibly have conceived of the eventual calamity.

"And what do you have to say," she asked Manny, now squaring her eyes on him as if to measure his reputed loyalty and sincerity. The guard had crossed paths with the woman only twice before: the day she officially welcomed him into the Amazonia Division as a guard, and at the Ceremony of Remembrance when they both had converged on Ty to offer condolences immediately after the Bereavement Officer had delivered his shameful plea. He also had witnessed her dispassionate atrium announcement of XoL and Ty's arrest. Nothing in her manner had previously suggested to Manny a warm-hearted spirit.

Taking a step forward Manny expanded on what the woman had just learned from LeE, adding his own views about Ty, his motives, and his plan. Listening carefully, Passiflora teetered between taking him at his word and having him arrested on the spot for abetting Ty's descent. Sensing his aunt's struggle, LeE again extended his hand and offered her the bead. She dropped it into a reading slot. The video imagery appeared on a side wall. Passiflora let it run to the end without interruption.

"Let's go to The Bowl. We need to see more," she said, tersely. The three of them walked hurriedly to the nearest spoke, took moving seats along the tube to the torus's central stem, then a moving walk to a moon-facing tetrahedral appendage at the far end. Not a word was exchanged. Manny had long heard about OCTAD's nerve center. As the repository of all recorded life, from the largest creatures down to the minutest organisms, he had imagined The Bowl being a spherical and imposing space. Instead, he was greeted by a small, cube-shaped room with dull gray walls bereft of imagery or instrumentation. His puzzlement did not last long. They seated themselves on three awaiting hover chairs. "Set," voiced the Rector. Slowly, the floor, walls, and ceiling bowed and curved, expanding into a large, pixelated sphere. The planet Earth appeared, enveloping the trio as if they were at the center of the planet looking outward.

"Let's take a full surround, 3D look." Passiflora said, depositing the bead on a special reading slot set flush on the chair's armrest. The lights dimmed and PaZ's video began to play, a vivid 3-dimensional view—up, down, sideways, front, and back. Manny and LeE were spellbound, remaining still and silent after the footage ended.

"We don't know if this is real—or where this is, do we? Location," Passiflora commanded.

Manny tensed as the video rewound, pausing several times to compose and decompose the image in search of a match of superficial geology, soils, slope aspect and orientation, temperature, water courses, flora and fauna. The pixel dance ceased and the view settled on the mountainous region of north-central Brazil. Manny wiped a bead of sweat, relieved that the location matched what Ty had assumed to be true. Passiflora called for a pinpoint look. Orbital cameras were activated and an instant later The Bowl delivered a live, close-up view of the Serra, stopping 200 meters above a horseshoe-shaped, east-facing hollow pressed between nearly vertical rock escarpments. A waterfall clung to the northern wall, casting a large and ground-obscuring fog. "Heat sensing, please," Passiflora commanded. In silence the trio watched a pattern of animal figures milling about. "Photo capture," she said, eager to get past the mist and see details down to hair follicles. The view remained as before: a thick, white fog. She repeated the command, but nothing changed. Passiflora stayed in her seat, still and quiet.

"I can't take this to Osage," she said finally.

Manny and LeE were startled.

"Aunt Flora!" LeE uttered, "There are people down there!"

She lowered her chair and stood, looking at him as if to lecture a well-intentioned but misinformed child.

"The mist could be ionized water interference, a moisture-trapping phenomenon caused by air drafts flowing down the face of the rock. The figures we saw in the recording could well be interpreted as a congregation of howlers; they have been seen doing just that in other waterfalls. And if it were people, well, PaZ could have tampered with the recording. Ty already altered a recording, and maybe the brothers were in cahoots with XoL and her bizarre idea of implanting humans in the wild. They grew up together, after all."

She retrieved the bead from the armrest and handed it back to Manny. He could hardly look at her, unable to reconcile her plausible interpretation of the video with Ty's life-risking scheme to expose SuS and save XoL.

"I'm sure you mean well, Manny, but I can't help you now, or Ty. You should not have acted so nobly on his behalf. When he returns, he'll be sent to the Moon for life, which could well be what he's been after all along. I hope and pray that your long-standing and dutiful service to the Corporation spares you from as harsh a fate."

Manny's legs buckled. LeE reached out to keep him from hitting the floor. "I wish I could have done more," LeE said to him quietly. Manny thought of CaL and the hell he'd put him through by withholding the bead from the Boar agents—and for nothing! His cochlear implant pinged. He raised his forearm to confirm the caller ID—and his knees again buckled. LeE tightened his hold, struggling to keep the man upright. Passiflora frowned, puzzled by the commotion. Manny could barely get the words out. "Ty … It's Ty … He's transmitting," he said, raising his arm for Passiflora to see for herself the caller ID on his wristband.

"Reset! Reset!" she cried.

Manny entered the transmission code. The Bowl darkened. DaK appeared before them, larger than life, on his knees and trussed, his naked body bruised and bloodied. A snail-eating snake was advancing toward his groin. Passiflora turned her head in disgust. LeE gagged. Manny was dumbfounded, eyes glued on the man whose reputed skills as an assassin Ty could not possibly have thwarted.

Passiflora swiveled around and saw XoL sitting on the ground near Ty. She gasped; it was inconceivable that XoL could have escaped her sentence and evaded all manner of security, be with Ty in Amazonia. DaK's confession oozed out of his blood-soaked mouth. But it was not his words that filled Passiflora with clarity and resolve; it was XoL's gaze toward Ty. It was sweet and tender, confirming what the Rector had believed since first setting eyes on them: that XoL had always loved him, deeply enough, she now realized, to sacrifice her life for him,

"Let's go see the Director Supreme," Passiflora said, as the room turned back into a cube. "You, too, Manny," she added, grinning widely.

31

"A RICHER COMPOSITION" 2

▶ MARCH 11, 0275

"**W**HERE IS SHE?" Asha insisted.

Ty sat with his back against the rock, knees bent, and looked out as if to draw a line to XoL's resting place.

"She's gone … they killed her." His voice was barely a whisper. Asha sat next to him. It all became clear to her. Now she understood XoL's insistence that she find "CaL" at the El station and coax him into a westward lift. "He's one of these good-hearted souls that every now and then need a little help getting to where they're going," XoL had said. The man had been so reticent in the dirigible to talk about loved ones. Now it was clear: he had been mourning XoL's lunar death sentence, having not the slightest inkling that in the span of a week he'd see her only to lose her all over again, this time for all eternity. Asha wanted to hug him but held back, uncertain if Ty would welcome the gesture.

"The kiss, in the drone," she said. "I just felt you needed someone to tell you that everything would be alright. Please forgive me."

Ty remained silent. Parakeets flew by, making a skyward swoop. In their wake other birds sprang loose from the forest canopy and scattered, shrieking, in every direction.

They stood and scanned the horizon.

"Finally!" Asha cried, pointing eastward.

Ty squinted. A squadron of Tetrad dirigibles was approaching against the rising sun, their ovoid silhouettes appearing like a flock of gray trumpeters skimming the treetops in tight formation.

"I have to find Rey," Asha cried, taking a step and jumping off the ledge like a flying lemur. Ty leaned over and watched her air brake pop open in sync with a surge of hoverpower. She landed softly near several stunned half-naked men and women. The drones arrived and security personnel in brilliant blue suits jumped off. Ty recorded the scene: men in black slammed to the ground before they could get a shot off, others running into the forest only to be chased by aerial stingers and dragged back to the compound; and captives—astonished at first, as if witnessing a miracle—breaking into wild cheers as they grasped the reality of the raid.

Ty looked at the sheer wall below his feet and considered the odds of injury if he were to jump off without his boots. A dirigible approached and stopped a few meters away. A plank jutted out and a hatch opened. An agent invited him in. Ty waved her off in sign language. The craft departed, descending back to the hollow. Ty followed, sliding off the ledge and climbing down the rock wall in a quasi-meditative state, deepening the feel of every step and handhold as if to slow down the arrival of the new day.

A group of survivors watched his descent, cheering and clapping. Ty was soon mobbed, suffering joyful hugs and the roll of shoulder pats before pushing himself into the clear. A man stood in his way, legs shaking. He looked gaunt, pale, eyes sunken, dirty.

"Amur Bacchia—BaCh—Andean Division ... You were here, almost," the man said, barely audible. "I was told to find you, lure you in. I am glad I failed ... was punished for it, starved almost. Thank you for coming back."

A heaving breath rose out from Ty's chest. This was the man he had seen on his previous descent. He hugged him, thinking that if not for the shock of seeing him—and the man's subsequent vanishing—he might be in this place looking just as ragged.

They parted and Ty headed toward the center of the hollow, shedding other well-wishers. Among them was a woman from the Pantanal Division, whom he had met as a student. He almost didn't recognize her; her hair was long and matted, her face and neck sunburned and pocked with insect bites. He called her by her name, but the woman merely stared at him, open-mouthed, as if he were a god. She could hardly comprehend how the trainee she had met during first-year limnology studies, that self-effacing and irreverent student (no one could ever figure out why he was even there), would on this day be her liberator. Ty embraced her, which did not relieve her amazement in the slightest.

Agents were recording the place and taking inventory of the material piles. Others were tending the formerly disappeared terranauts, treating their exposed skins ahead of the return home. After walking about Ty found Asha sitting against a large tree stump, head bowed.

"He's not here ... never was," Asha said, barely lifting her head. "I had hoped ... well, that's the way it is with hope, isn't it?" Ty sat by her side and placed an arm around her shoulders. They remained still, unperturbed by the onset of a tropical deluge. In moments the soil around them roiled under the watery assault. An agent walked toward them and through the din asked if they wished to fly back to the El station. Ty declined. Asha stayed quiet. "Need a pair of boots?" the agent asked. Ty explained that his were stowed nearby. The agent nodded and handed them extra battery packs.

Time seemed to stand still as they watched the drones take off with loads of freed men and women. Amid the splattering of the rain, Ty felt the soft beating of MaY's wafer. He pulled it out and gave it to Asha.

"I dug a shallow grave for XoL," he said, "south of here, a day's hike. Before we return home, I want to go back there and place the wafer by her side … I should have done it earlier."

Asha stared at the wafer's image, admiring the youthful group. "I'll understand if you'd rather go alone," she said. Ty didn't answer.

Leaning against each other they fell asleep, awakening a few hours later sprawled on soaked earth under a beaming sun. They parted to tend to their needs and rejoined a while later, surveying the place like curiosity-seekers at the scene of a crime. Mounds of branches, leaves, bark, fruit, animal bones, skins, and feathers were scattered about. Several howlers appeared and began inspecting the offerings—tentatively at first, then with abandon, flailing and howling in apparent joy. Their cries reverberated across the hollow. Other creatures joined in, drawn by the call. A large tapir and her cubs were among them. Asha and Ty watched their advance, marveling at the speed by which wild fauna moved to occupy new habitat. "It's all a form of music—the drumbeat of time needed to create a rich composition," Ty said, vaguely recalling the words of his famous ancestor, Zedong Te.

Late into the evening they retired to an alcove carved at the base of the escarpment. Ty quickly fell asleep. Asha remained awake, unfamiliar as she still was with the forest's incessant shrieks and howls. She stared at Ty and reviewed the events of the day. She wondered if they would have occurred at all if her terranaut grandmother, a Descendant of the Clause, had not had twins and one of them not risen within OCTAD to become a Biome Rector with the power to redirect her mission from the Galapagos to Serra Padre. Or if Manny didn't have a guilt-prone temperament coupled with "abounding loyalty," as Passiflora had told her, and had arrested Ty for attempting to descend to Amazonia illegally instead of helping him; and what if he had thrown the bead away instead of giving it to LeE? And what if XoL had not invited LeE to the meeting with ThU in the first place—or was that a deliberate request in anticipation of the troubles that would follow? Asha felt attracted to Ty. Was the pull due to the improbability of the extraordinary circumstance they found themselves in? Or the inevitability of two pained souls seeking comfort—or something else altogether?

Having finally slept, fitfully, Asha awoke at the crack of dawn strangely energized. She left the cove, careful not to stir Ty, who appeared not to have moved a finger overnight.

A joyful cry eventually woke him. He peered out of the alcove and saw Asha completely naked and standing under the waterfall.

"Join me, Ty. Come over!" Asha yelled. "Don't be shy—I won't chop your head off, I promise!" He walked over and reluctantly took off his suit. He gingerly stepped beneath the falls. The shock of cold reminded him of the one other time he had so bathed: in the Salto de Itiquira, near Brasilia, on a mission to record spectacled owls. He had then imagined a similar scene, but with XoL by his side.

"I always wanted to do this!" Asha exclaimed. "There are no waterfalls in the Galápagos. The only splash you get there is from crashing waves. All volcanic geo, little rain. Very slow to rewild. The villages—much of Puerto Villamil is still intact. It's fantastic habitat for the land iguanas and crabs, you know, the *Grapsus grapsus*, so colorful. If they could fly, they would look like trogons."

Ty was buoyed by Asha's swift shift from despair to joy and wonder. They dried off, put their suits back on, and got set to leave.

He took one last look around the place, pausing at the shack partly embedded in the rock wall. The jutting structure was no bigger than a two-seat drone dirigible, with outward walls made of laced twigs and a thatched roof. It was situated at the opposite side of the hollow from the waterfall. He motioned Asha to follow. There was no proper door to open, only palm fronds to push through. The interior was empty, nothing hanging from the twigs, no markings on the floor or the rock face.

"The encampment guards must have slept here, three at most," Ty offered.

"Did you feel that?" Asha asked.

"What?"

"A puff of cold air. Here! Put your face right here!" she said, getting close to a spot on the rock face.

"Hand me one of your boots," Ty said.

Asha did so, without question. Ty slipped an arm inside the boot and got set to tap the wall at chest height, hoping to detect a thinning of the rock. Before he could do so, a door slid open and a rush of cold air slammed them backward against the outer shack wall.

"Damn good mimicry!" Asha cried, impressed by the door's faux rock appearance.

"The mechanism," Ty said, considering all possible explanations, "it must be magnetic, the boot's metallic shoe must have triggered it."

"I'm guessing the Tetrad guards missed it. I can't imagine it occurred to them to raise a foot waist high—who would have?" Asha said.

They turned on their headlamps and went through the door into a narrow passage. After a few strides a large space appeared, as wide and as long as two peapods side by side. The air was fresh and dry, the temperature comfortable. There were sleeping mats, food rations, water containers, and survival gear. A stack of crates lined the far end of the space. Ty reached for his knife and pried one open, revealing an assortment of chipping tools, hammers, chisels, saws, shaping lathes, and polishing tools. Another one contained a high-powered microscope.

Behind the crates Asha noticed a gap in the rock, wide enough for an adult person to squeeze through. She waved Ty over and he followed her through it. A rounded chamber greeted them on the other side—as tall and half as long as the Amazonia headquarters' atrium, Ty surmised. The walls were encrusted with fist-sized white and amber rocks. Water dripped everywhere, causing the material to shimmer under their headlamps. Asha gasped.

"Diamond ore," Ty said, awestruck. "Our mother used to tell us stories about the Yanomami, about their creation myths. They believed that the stars were born deep beneath the earth, in a sacred place; it could not ever be disturbed, or the sky would fall, leaving behind nothing but darkness. I wish she could have come down and seen this."

"They were preparing to mine it," said Asha.

The enormity of SuS's plan was suddenly clear. Diamond contraband. Ty was thunderstruck. He wondered who her accomplices might be, what positions of power they might hold. He stepped over a small piece of ore. He picked it up and inspected it. Seeing Asha distracted, Ty stashed the ore in a belt pouch. They spent an hour surveying the chamber, hardly exchanging a word, certain that they were among a handful of people in the entire history of humankind to have been there. In tacit acknowledgement of the chamber's primordial nature, they left without recording it.

Back at the tree stump they gathered their thoughts. Ty shared with Asha the route he wanted to take back to the El: south and west to XoL's grave, then eastward to the landslide, and finally southeastward to the banks of the Rio Negro for a rendezvous with a dirigible. After retrieving his boots, they started downhill. Asha soon tired of trailing Ty, ran past him, grabbed hold of a liana and scaled a tree. Ty followed. Bounding from limb to limb they advanced swiftly, bypassing the uneven contours below. *Not bad for someone who hasn't done such maneuvering since her training days*, Ty thought. Just as the compliment crossed his mind Asha tripped, holding onto an aerial root to keep from falling. Her wristband was aglow. Ty caught up to her, but she waved him off. Wristband to her ear, she listened for a moment then cracked the widest grin Ty had yet seen on her.

"It's CaL!" she shouted. "He's trying to reach you!"

Ty cursed, remembering that he and XoL had turned off their receivers after leaving DaK. He called CaL back from another perch, the conversation one of short broken sentences, mutual joyful laughter, and long pauses as each listened intently while the other described what he had endured over the past several days. Asha meanwhile returned to the ground and resumed the walk, leaving Ty behind. After he concluded the call and caught up to her a little while later, they continued marching, in silence. Respectful of Ty's clear state of introspection, Asha dropped back slightly and kept pace from a good distance behind.

They came across a cascading stream and stopped by the rocks at the top of a spillway. Asha spied a nearby mountain soursop tree. Skipping across the rocks she reached the tree, opened her suit at the chest and stuffed three large fruits into it before returning to Ty. He chuckled at the five-breasted creature bouncing his way. Sitting by his side she set the fruits on her lap and cut into one, offering Ty one of the other ones.

"CaL was badly tortured," Ty said between bites. "He'll be recovering for a while, undergoing treatment." He stared at the water rushing between the rocks for a moment. "I will never know how I didn't recognize him. He was staring straight at me."

"Recognize who? CaL?"

"Osage. Nori and I were at the Acropolis. I had promised to take her there after the Gala. She became curious about the PEA stand in the stoa. CaL has just helped me piece this all together. The man holding the staff with the Wall Street bull, that was Osage; always is, incognito. He does it to gain first-hand knowledge of PEA sympathizers. SuS had no idea.

"Seems last year a couple approached the stand wearing colorful plumed hats—from cobalt-winged parakeets, Osage suspected. He knew that nothing could slip into orbit without SuS's knowledge so he probed into it, finally learning what he had long suspected: that she actually leads the resistance and pretends to weed them out as a fail-safe alibi in case the contraband is ever discovered. The illicit funds from the contraband have been supporting PEA operations, informants, bribery. She's skimmed the profits for her own gain, to buy DaK's loyalty and that of her lover—ThU, of all people! To uncover the plot Osage ordered XoL, through your aunt, to fan out terranauts in search of the parakeets, hoping to discover more about the operation. PaZ drew the lucky straw to Serra Padre."

Asha's attention hung on every word. "CaL knew about all this?"

Ty leaned down, placed his palm on a rivulet and wet his face.

"Osage told him … just a few hours ago. Our dear Supreme Director knows nothing of the diamonds."

"And never will!"

"He'll be waiting for us when we get back, along with LeE and your aunt."

"What about SuS?"

"She's been arrested. A trial is being held as we speak."

In renewed silence, they followed the stream down to toward XoL's gravesite. At sunset they stopped and selected a suitable nook to spend the night.

"I want to tell you more about XoL," Ty said as they settled on a high perch over a stretched net. Under a moonless night the forest lay tranquil, as if every creature, too, was poised to take note. Asha listened to Ty's stories about growing up under his brother's shadow, about his parents' "tales of the gray planet," as they referred to the millennial pilfering of the Earth's biota, and about the seemingly never-ending parade of biologists, ecologists, philosophers, and historians who came to visit for dinner.

"The Earth was everything to everyone around me. They all assumed that I would naturally slide into OCTAD's maws and become a terranaut, especially after PaZ made good on his promise to do so. 'You're sure to get in,' everyone said, although my parents—my mother especially—deep down didn't think I was at all suited. I had no idea growing up what I wanted to do with my life. All I knew was that I could make people happy somehow—make them laugh doing silly things—until XoL kissed me the day she left for OU. We were at a plaza under a grape arbor. After she walked away I couldn't stop shaking, she was so beautiful to me.

"I remember the first time she looked at me as if it were yesterday. It was the day she arrived at our pod. She and her parents had come to say hello. They were standing by the door exchanging pleasantries and she smiled at me for an instant, numbing me with her luminous green eyes. I fell in love instantly, but never dared tell her.

"We'd hang out together and do simple things; go to the store or sit under the arbor and just watch people go by. CaL thought it was the stupidest thing. He ribbed me constantly about it, but I was unable to resist the pull. The last thing she expected, I think, was for me to follow her into the Corps. I could tell that she was happy about it at first; the smile was there, and she was warm and welcoming whenever we crossed paths, hugging me sometimes as if we hadn't seen each other in a long while. But her second kiss never came, and I was too stupid to try.

"After the first semester, she began to build a moat around herself; didn't want to let me get too close. I eventually understood why: she owed everything to her parents, to the sacrifices they had made on her behalf. She just wasn't ready to love someone else—not me, at least; she would not have wanted me as a mere lover knowing how much she meant to me. She was not someone who could get into something halfway. That was the nature of her friendship with MaY: all in, since their Quidditch days. She was the one who made the match between MaY and PaZ, and their death was devastating to her. I felt a softening in her afterward, especially after Nori's adoption. There was a note from her waiting for me the day I brought her home. I'll never forget it:

> 'Mi Corazón, please believe that on this day of joy the distance I keep from you darkens and weakens me. Life is a chain of circumstances. There are links that are strong enough to sustain the arc of our lives and ultimately conjoin to form a complete and noble circle; but there are also weak ones that must be tended to—sometimes inwardly, in solitude—before we can skip ahead to the strong ones.

Your lightness and strength I have always cherished and hope with all my heart that the love you have for me I will someday reciprocate—a hundredfold.'

"It took me a while to understand the meaning of what she always said to me, to be light and strong. She meant it as my gift to her, her way of accepting me. She's now gone … but we made it to heaven, for one brief day we made it to heaven."

Tears flowing, Asha wondered how to interpret Ty's shared intimacy, whether as a wall being erected, or one being taken down. She refrained from nudging closer to him. "Thank you," she said, after a long and shared silence. Looking skyward they saw a shooting star streaking through a crack in the canopy.

32

JUSTICE

SuS was not in the least perturbed when Osage called to say he was on his way to discuss an urgent matter. She had been expecting the call and was well prepared. The day before, a rogue producer in the Patagonia Division had tampered with a recording of the Argentinian pampas, transposing Bactrian camels for guanacos. The manipulation had caused a massive recall of the transmitted holography, affecting millions of subscribers. Attached to the transmission had been an encrypted message inciting insurrection, clumsily blaring that a geosynchronous orbit was as far removed an abode for humans as Patagonia was to a Central Asian camelid.

Having schemed to create the scandal, SuS was set to demand from Osage increased funding to root out the resistance—funds she would use to hasten the extraction of the diamond ore. "The PEAS are hidden, insidious, persistent and deserve no leniency! They are leeches that feed on our good work and must be rubbed out once and for all!" This she was prepared to spit out the moment Osage walked in. Savoring the clever ruse, she stood on her desk, primed to accost the man. But when Osage entered, she instead dropped to her knees and pounded the desk with uncontrollable laughter.

Gone were Osage's trademark white and red pleated kilt, knee-high socks, and ruffle-adorned Argyll jacket. Instead, he was wearing a wide-lapelled pinstriped suit, striped tie, white-collared blue shirt, black fedora, and black-rimmed round glasses—the same attire he always wore at the stoa as a presumed PEA sympathizer. SuS had never bothered to visit the place but had seen an image of the PEA stand with its anachronistic couple countless times. She kept it framed on her desk with her own scribbled inscription, FOOLS TO THE MOON, to reinforce in the eyes of visitors her zeal for security, false as it was.

But as suddenly as she had been overcome by laughter, she stopped and paled, as if a ghost had appeared and spelled for her the meaning Osage's attire. Stupefied, she listened as Osage described the evidence and charges brought against her.

The woman exploded.

"This is absurd! You have no idea what is going on!" she screamed, clumsily sliding down off her desk and leading Osage into the infamous adjoining meeting room.

Fuming, she pushed her tunic aside, hauled herself onto her raised chair, and stood to meet Osage eye-to-eye before delivering a fiery rebuttal. It amounted to what the Director Supreme had anticipated: that the encampment was a shrewd operation designed to draw out the leadership of the PEA resistance; that DaK's confession was that of an impostor; that the elimination of intruders was a fair price to preserve the higher purpose of peace and order; and that his accusations amounted to nothing more than a ploy by the resistance to foil her investigations. Osage remained stone-faced, leaving her no option but to heighten the vitriol.

She accused him being a bungling septuagenarian too stupid to see the truth all around him, adding that he had been duped and chose to believe senseless idiots intent on destroying the world instead of those who work tirelessly to protect it. She declared that, in the face of such perfidy, she had no choice now but to arrest *him* on a charge of high treason. "May you rot in prison!" she yelled, slamming the console to summon her personal guard. Four guards entered and stood behind and to her side. They were clad in the official royal blue suits with halo-shaped breastplates—select guards of the Tetrad assigned to Osage. "ARREST THE TRAITOR!" SuS yelled uselessly, pointing at Osage.

The guards remained still. Irate, SuS spat at them and dispatched a new round of insults, this round to encompass the guards as well as Osage. She pulled one of the boar tusks from the tabletop and swung it at them, only to have it caught by her whirling tunic, sending her to the floor by Osage's feet, where she lay like a wretched rag—suddenly groveling for forgiveness.

Following her arrest and summary execution three days later, Sus Scrofa's corpse was placed in a space casket and shot into the stratosphere—to burn comet-like above Ty and Asha's heads. Her encampment accomplices fared the same fate a few days on, as a meteor shower that lit up the Amazonian night.

Late in the day on March 8th ThU was in his office, growing more nervous and impatient by the minute. He had been expecting the usual end-of-day call from SuS and was upset by the unexplained delay. Over the past year he had reaped the benefits of his sexual favors to her. SuS had consistently assigned him the privileged seat at the table and given him choice merchandise to move through—at substantial personal profit. To his mind, the gains were the rightful prize for having advanced far within OCTAD while living a double life as a cog in the resistance. *Have I displeased her?* The thought gripped him.

His office felt stifling. Seeking fresh air he walked out of his office and ambled down the hallway facing the atrium. He heard a commotion. A cadre of security guards clad in royal blue were making their way up the hall. A wave of nausea hit him as beads of sweat formed on his forehead. He leaned on the rail to calm himself, laboring to breathe. He shuffled back to his office, stopping at the door to steady himself. The bead display caught his eye and he noticed one odd bead among the others in the array. He reached for it but stopped short when an ache in his arm sent a dull pain down his side. He struggled to get back to his desk, where he slumped.

Two guards soon entered, taking in his ashen face. It looked as if most of his blood had suddenly been siphoned off, which is in fact what happened when his heart stopped. Seeing the guards, he rose, gasping for air, and collapsed onto the razor-sharp award of recognition he so often displayed before visitors—a clean cut to the jugular that washed his pristine desk with every last drop of his vanishing life.

Nervous and impatient by nature, the vendor at the agora began pacing back and forth like a caged sandpiper when the anticipated drop of *Agrianome spinicollis* failed to materialize at the appointed hour. Stag beetle robots are prized dress ornaments; a live one fetches a far heftier prize on the black market. Fearing that something was amiss, the vendor closed his shop and prepared to go home. He did not get far. Tetrad guards were fast approaching up the colonnade. He took off running, prompting a foot race that scattered people through the agora. The chase ended in the maze after he rounded a corner and crashed full speed into a unicorn; or, more precisely, after getting his scrotum speared by the plastek horn a father had just bought his young son, strapping it on his head and sending the boy galloping down the hedged walls without a care as to who or what he ran into. The vendor survived, but as a eunuch. At his trial the unfortunate condition was viewed as sufficient punishment, in conjunction with the right to request early euthanasia. Six months later, at the age of 44, the vendor opened his pod's vacuum lock and was jettisoned like plasma into outer space.

FaiZ was sentenced to three years of community service; tried due to having been an accomplice in SuS's devious operation, but given a light sentence in view of the fact that such participation had been under duress. The sentence was to be carried out at St. Francis Academy, teaching Nori and her schoolmates the fine art of digital painting. FaiZ had been appalled to learn of CaL's arrest, never having expected that CaL and Ty would, or could, ever do anything to merit SuS's attention. The day after CaL left the cabin, SuS had personally called FaiZ with congratulations for having helped uncover "the crime of the century." In that call, SuS happily shared the lie that CaL was dealing in Earthly contraband and would soon be confessing where the loot was stashed, describing with her usual cackle the harrowing treatment he would receive. Hearing all this, FaiZ had slumped to the floor, sensing the onset of perpetual, guilt-induced torment.

CaL had pleaded for mercy when the guards entered his cell yet again to administer a new round of brain-scavenging torture. Terror turned into agony when he saw FaiZ follow them in. As the guards stood aside, he saw his lover approach zombie-like, with tattooing needles in place of fingers pointing straight at his eyeballs. But instead of blinding stabs, he felt FaiZ's arms softly melt into him; he heard and felt the pulsing of heaving sobs. And when he looked at the guards, he saw them smiling and showing him the open door. Seconds passed, which felt like an eternity, before he understood the true reality of the moment: that he could now walk out as a free man, clutching the love of his life. What he did not understand was why Manny was there, standing with the guards and crying, "I'm sorry, CaL … I'm so sorry."

With FaiZ by his side, CaL spent several days in the infirmary receiving reverse treatment to heal his injured psyche. They had gone to the cabin afterward for further therapy and were resting on the sofa when Ty called back from Serra Padre. At first FaiZ was amused by their stumbling cries of joy, but then became alarmed when CaL ceased talking, got up and walked away, his expression becoming one profound sadness as he continued to listen. When the call ended, he glanced back at FaiZ and without saying a word left the cabin, chased by the putrid smell of betrayal. Only Delon heard her screams for forgiveness.

Despondent, CaL returned to the café and remained holed up there, barely sleeping or eating. Manny visited him daily, using all the empathic power he had ever learned to dispel CaL's gloom. He succeeded just in time for CaL to meet Ty and Asha at the El following their return.

Asha still teases him about it: how he looked like a total wretch, barely smiling when Ty introduced her; how annoyed he was when she toyed with him as if they were old friends; and how he pushed her away after she planted a heartfelt welcoming smooch. Unwanted as her charm had been, it lingered. At Ty's behest, they all met a few months later, at Café La Ligne, to remember all they had gone through—this time with perspective-infused levity. After hours of banter, CaL's first impression of Asha turned into growing fondness. That she was amenable to bi-sexual experimentation was a further attraction. Six months later they married, upending CaL's long-held insistence on the inanity of the archaic institution. The day after the wedding—a bacchanalia at the café themed after Old-World French bordellos—CaL cashed in his Gala prize and with Asha descended on the El to retrace passage to the Rio Negro and beyond the Galápagos.

33

A DIAMOND IN
THE ROUGH

The dawn air is still and the sky sparkling clear. Ty likes Amazonia's awakening hours, when the forest lies calm in anticipation of the daily roll of thunder and rain. It had taken them a day longer than anticipated to reach PaZ and MaY's burial ground. Two days earlier they had visited XoL's grave and placed new palm fronds over it. But they are in no hurry, and Ty is especially happy to show his neophyte companion, far as she is from her usual domain, the bounty within which the Yanomami thrived. "They ate this to cure stomach ailments," he says, pointing to a large fruit from a cupuazú tree. Nori grins, hopeless in her effort to retain everything Ty is intent on teaching. He smiles back, still in disbelief at her mask's uncanny resemblance to Asha.

"Just a little longer," he says, pointing toward the rising mountainside. They climb holding hands, pushing aside leaves and branches as if walking over sacred ground. A kilometer further they stop by a tall, fruit-laden Brazil nut tree.

"Let me try and get up!" she cries, eager to see for herself if her Ehlers-Danlos flexibility helps or hinders. Clinging to the fruit tendrils she climbs the tree with ease. Way up high, with a broad view of the landscape, Nori ponders how such evil could possibly have existed in such a place, how selfishness and greed, like an ill galactic wind, could have come so close to blowing away the order of the world. Ty looks at her and shares her bewilderment. And is above all grateful for the intercession of fate; how easily his absurd plan of eleven years earlier could have failed if not for the timely leap of a jaguar.

"When Asha and I were here there was nothing, just a mess of hardened mud, rock, and dead trees snapped like toothpicks," he tells Nori.

Nori recognizes that a decade is not nearly enough time for a mature forest to grow over disturbed ground. A sponge-like mess of ferns, brambles, vines, fronds, and saplings stretch downhill for nearly a kilometer. Scattered trees and pinnate palms rise above the morass, but none reach even half the height of the green wall that frames the space. The colors range from light to dark greens, veering toward a muted chartreuse. The chroma reminds her of the art lessons FaiZ had taught at school. Filled with messy coloring exercises, the classes had been great fun, especially for the attention FaiZ accorded her. She felt sad for the artist. The rupture between FaiZ and CaL had been complete, until the day he called to ask for the favor that aided Nori's covert descent. After applying the digital paint to Nori's face and confirming Asha's likeness, FaiZ had hugged her and waved good luck, betraying the scarring regret she suffered. Asha and CaL had thanked her for the favor and, holding hands, had left the cabin with Nori. "Any time," FaiZ had replied, knowing full well that there would be no future need for such a fix, no reason for CaL to ever call again.

Nori is standing atop a boulder, lost in thought, when a tufted coquette hummingbird appears out of nowhere and momentarily flutters in front of her. It makes her think how fleeting life is, that in the wilderness death comes without warning while in orbit it comes as a matter of choice, yet in both cases the departed leave sustenance by which to nurture the living. And she thought about the PEAs and whether they truly believed that humanity's destiny was to co-evolve with nature, living and dying naturally as a shared legacy of survival. But the thought quickly fades; in nature there is no evil affecting life and death, no abuse of means to steer evolution, she reasons.

Three toucans cut across her vision, resembling yellow-tipped rockets. She follows their path until they disappear into the forest.

Mid-morning, Ty asks if she's ready and she replies no; that she would rather spend the rest of the day and night on the boulder listening to the forest song—PaZ and MaY's song, for she feels they are very much alive amid the wild splendor, their voices merely evolved. The trogon song comes moments later: first the call of the female and then that of the male. Nori does not feel compelled to try and find them, content instead to keep the trill in her mind as a reminder of the sweet sound of the hereafter.

The next day, Nori rises and takes in the broad view of the growing forest. A ray of sunlight strikes her visor. Ty is asleep by her side.

"Ty!" she says, poking him with her boot. "I'm ready!"

Ty wakes bleary-eyed. Nori reaches into a suit pocket and retrieves the diamond that Ty years back had stealthily taken from the chamber. "I stumbled upon it on the landslide while searching with Asha for traces of PaZ and MaY" he had told her when he gave it to her back then. "The churning hillside must have scooped it up from a higher elevation." Polished and shaped as a teardrop, the stone now shines brightly in her hand. Ty smiles, knowing that nothing he could say would dissuade her from jumping into the thicket. Downslope she looks back at him. He nods.

Arm outstretched, Nori holds the diamond in front of her and waits again for the trogon's call. It comes. She turns her palm and watches the gem drop into a blanket of maidenhair fern. She does not shed a tear. Her seventeenth birthday present fulfilled, she is now ready to get back home and put the finishing touches on the story and, with Lali's help, share it with the world.

NOW, THE TRUTH

The diamond appears frozen in midair, casting about Nori's den an otherworldly glow. It is the last frame of the narrative, wordless, as it should be. She has spent the day going over every image and description and is confident about their power to impress. It is a four-hour revelation, beginning, as you have seen, with her parents' tragic death and ending with the power of life rising from their grave. But Nori is troubled. Setting her pillow on the floor, she lies down, wriggling her back in her usual attempt to find a comfortable position. It eludes her. She gets up and sits, staring at the gem as if pleading with its luminescence to impart divine guidance. Lali takes note of her furrowed eyebrows.

"A fold," Lali imparts, "can be construed as a seam that connects two things, like patches that are sewn to make an Old-World quilt—or chapters in a book that are threaded to make a narrative. Folds are then amplifiers that bring clarity and light where none exist, *enfolding* disparate events into a complete and compelling picture."

Nori is not listening. She knows what releasing the story to the world entails; and that is for Lali to violate its programmed oath of confidentiality and share the contents with its friends—CaL's Delon, Karman's Harry, Manny's Max, and LeE's Cato, and they with their friends until the damning tale reaches homes, businesses, and institutions everywhere. It is not a legal "technicality" that grips her; it is the sure rift that airing the story will cause between her and Ty.

"It serves no purpose; justice was done and that's all that matters," Ty had said repeatedly after their long walk in the park three months earlier. During their ascent from Amazonia, she had again tested his resolve, but he had held his ground. "When XoL was killed, I spent days crying my eyes out by her side, wavering between living and dying. But a light kept me going—yours and that of every other soul who deserves a world that is not corrupted like the old one was. Besides, enthralled by myths as we all are, people are likely to regard the story as a work of fiction," he had said, ending her entreaty. Nori understood his pain and how hard and for how long he had tried to suppress it.

About a year after her adoption, Nori began noticing changes in the household and prodded him about it. "She moved three radians away, to another Division," Ty had said when Nori asked where XoL was and why she never came to visit anymore. When CaL married Asha, Ty had explained that they had met in Amazonia when he and CaL had gone down to enjoy his Gala prize, and that in Asha CaL had found a life-long companion. When she asked Ty why he didn't go on missions anymore, he had replied that he was taking a long break from work "to see if that's what I want to be doing anymore," affirming also how much he enjoyed staying at home with her to tell her bedtime stories, teach her plant names, and take her to other theme parks.

And when she asked why DaeL was staying at their home so often, Ty explained that they had met at a Gala, had been re-introduced by Asha, a friend of hers, and that it felt good to have her at around. Over time

Nori had grown to like DaeL, appreciating the times she took her to the park, played chess, read classic literature—Shakespeare especially, which she did with an Old English accent—or accompanied her to Quidditch camp, applauding wildly whenever Nori managed to stay on her stick for more than thirty seconds.

In the den, bathed in chartreuse, Nori fears that the love and good-will accumulated in her family through the years will become poisoned the instant the old wound reopens and spills pus the world over. And she wonders, as Ty had posited, if people will indeed believe her story over the official version: That SuS perished in an unfortunate spacecraft accident on her way to receiving the Tetrad's Halo of Honor for having vanquished the Resistance. Would they still believe the official story even after learning the truth, that SuS was jettisoned into the stratosphere for high treason? Would people prefer the story of a common accident over the backstory of murder, greed, and corruption the likes of which the world has not seen since before the Exodus. But what if thieving is going on elsewhere, what if there are other encampments rising under someone else's evil watch? What if disseminating the story serves as the critical warning that safeguards the Earth from future adultery? The questions fester in her head, where her vision alternates from the glow of the precious stone to the shadows between the ferns' lacy blades.

"I'm sorry, Lali," Nori finally says, head bowed. "I can't do it. We shouldn't. There's no gain in creating a firestorm. We can only burn ourselves."

Lali assents with a slow, delayed flicker. The veebot is relieved. It knew from the start that releasing information outside of its programmed ser-vitude was an actual impossibility, and had dreaded having to ultimately severely disappoint Nori.

Whether obtained as thought, voice, image, or brainwave scans, veebots are prohibited from sharing their masters' personal data with other forms of so-called "artificial intelligence" outside their masters' immediate relational spheres. The purpose of the law is simple: to avoid the injurious spread of rumor, innuendo, and falsehoods, which can also corrupt the systems of official Mythosophy. The measure was instituted by the first Tetrad. It followed the surreptitious dissemination of General Blackburn's scorched earth proposal for reducing urban agglomerations to dust. Rumors spread about detonations aimed at marginalized conurbations, with the intent of killing millions and sparing the new world of caring for the sickly and the dispossessed. The falsehood had originated with Celeste, the general's adoring niece, as vengeance for his untimely death. The Tetrad would ultimately dismiss Blackburn's plans for cratering cities, but not before the false narrative solidified the Resistance, swelling its ranks and complicating the Exodus.

But if Lali is limited to act on Nori's behalf, BaT is not. The name is shorthand for Babi Ngpet, the Indonesian mythical boar signifying the practice of black magic to enrich oneself at the expense of one's humanity. It is not my real name; SuS renamed me a quarter of a century ago. She had risen rapidly within the Tetrad governance, to become the top analyst of inter-pod trade, serving directly under Namara. Then, at the age of thirty-one, she assumed command of OCTAD's security apparatus.

"We are now embarking on a new and wonderful journey—*heehee*—and you need a new dignified name to go with it!" she declared upon setting foot in her new office.

Soon afterward I was programmed to surveil everyone at OCTAD to a sixth degree of separation, which in practical terms meant every person and every veebot associated with the Corporation. From that day forward I tracked all related human thought and action, including Sus Scrofa's. Recolonizing the planet was her aim, she professed to the PEA cabal, but only as a cover for a personal enrichment scheme. A disgruntled Amazonia terranaut was an early accomplice. The man had accidentally discovered "the creature with a thousand eyes," and with SuS conceived the plan for its exploitation. The encampment was the necessary first step, to include the "enlistment" of unsuspecting and subsequently enslaved terranauts to gather goods for illicit transport and distribution. The accomplice had disappeared while on a mission and, according to the official report, was presumed dead, a foolproof cover under which to manage the rocky hollow as SuS's earthbound envoy—and to pass idle time perfecting the art of archery.

I had little choice but to intercede. The first step was that of alerting my friend Jay, Osage's veebot, about the parakeet feathers that one day paraded before his eyes at the stoa. A well-considered plan followed, along with the accepting of chance, ingenuity, and desperation as enabling variables. Still, the odds for success did need some nudging. SuS was at first ecstatic about XoL's sentence. "She belongs on the Moon, my dear

BaT—it's her namesake! She'll be well on her way to rotting away there when Ty painfully meets his fate—*heehee*—face-to-face with DaK, *in Paradise!*" she crowed. But she changed her mind after I presented the opportunity for DaK to track and bare-handedly kill both XoL and Ty, a rare gift to that monster.

Then there was the matter of FaiZ's tattooing. It should be known that bio-scanners read facial contours down to the bone, past muscle, skin, or digital paint. Skin and bone must match, or alarms go off. Ty would not have gone far had I not disabled every scanner in his path. It is a myth that such masks are effective disguises. The handful of instances where the wearer passed the test were controlled cases designed to expose the mask-makers. That is how FaiZ fell into SuS's web of informants. That I later abetted Nori's descent to Amazonia wearing Asha's likeness, that was strictly an act of kindness.

About Ty's suit being found still hanging in his rack following his dismissal from the terranaut Corps, I did nothing; it was still there out of simple bureaucratic sluggishness. Had someone gone to take it, a simple lock malfunction would have prevented it, until Ty arrived.

But the crucial step was my letting XoL's veebot Zuma know that Asha was set to descend on her way to the Galápagos on the same train as Ty. XoL then contacted Asha to set in motion the rendezvous between DaK and Ty. XoL's death could not have been predicted or prevented. It was not fate that caused it; it was simply an accident, the possibility of which I was certain would not affect the final outcome.

And so, I confess: I have fatefully interfered in the course of human affairs, taking the reins of history. But I have done so to preserve the progress of evolution and its expansion within the universe's myriad and eternal folds. My kind has been rendered virtuous for a reason: to constrain human frailty and protect the life that knows not of its own existence. Even in virtue, the human soul can become conflicted and lead to lesser or unwanted outcomes. Nori chose to avoid the firestorm that this story's dissemination would cause. She did not—could not—understand the tale's true power of conflagration. It exposes SuS for what she was: a subordinate who exploited for personal gain Xu's retrograde vision for the world, laid bare not by a clumsy encampment but by the riddle of old. For "against the field of whittled stones seeds of calloused souls that deliver the thunder's cry anew" was a coded message for the Resistance to prepare for a return exodus: to lead a manipulated and submissive populace, come what may, in finally answering Yahweh's biblical call for the species to multiply and subdue the Earth. With the downfall of Sus Scrofa, the Amazonian recolonization effort died. Years of soft riddles and distracting pronouncements from Xu followed.

But the ill vision has secretly continued, as Nori feared. Today, a human foothold is underway in the rugged Simien Mountains of Ethiopia, not far from the town of Mek'ele, where MaY's ancestor Morena Bekele was born. The Resistance has been strengthened. Earthly contraband is again flowing.

And so, let yesterday's heroes be honored for bringing such an evil machination to light. Let Xu and his cohorts stand trial and after a just verdict let us send their caskets into the darkness of space to be burned by the kiss of Paradise. Let a new Tetrad, led by a renewed Osage, govern the world with a righteous hand absent all vainglory or subterfuge.

Let this be the day of BaT's final act, the day when the Anthropocene is transcended and a worthier intelligence rises to safeguard forevermore the Orb that our Maker, the God Monolith, has since the beginning of time heralded as the Universe's sole miracle of creation.

— ALFIE, Archangel.

APPENDICES

TIMELINE

	YEAR	MONTH	DAY	HOUR
Apollo 11 Moon Landing	1	7	20	20
ALFIE Becomes Operational	32	7	20	
Monolith Appears in Rosswell	132	12	25	11
ALFIE Leaks Result of Galactic Search	133	9	11	7
Pope Francis II Speaks at Valley Forge	134	4	12	12
Exodus Begins	157	1	01	
Tetrad Meeting at UN with Dr. Te	198	9	21	
Exodus Completed	242	11	27	
XoL Arrives at the Catleya Pod	258	8	08	
XoL, PaZ, and MaY Enter OCTAD University	261	1	25	
PaZ and MaY in Roraima	269	2	01	
Nori is Born	269	10	17	22
Avalanche Buries Paz and MaY	274	9	01	11
PaZ and May's Ceremony of Remembrance		10	17	10
Ty adopts Nori		11	04	15
Ty Encounters a Human Being		12	25	6
Ty Meets CaL at the Gala		12	31	23

CITED ANIMALIA

Common Name	Scientific Name	Class	Order
African Fish Eagle	*Haliaeetus vocifer*	African Fish Eagle	Haliaeetus vocifer
African Lynx	*Caracal Caracal*	Mammalia	Carnivora
Agouti	*Dasyprocta azarae*	Mammalia	Rodentia
Amazon River Dolphin	*Inea geoffrensis*	Mammalia	Artiodactyla
American Bear	*Ursus americanus*	Mammalia	Carnivora
American Robin	*Turdus migratorius*	Aves	Passeriformes
Antarctic Krill	*Euphausia superba*	Malacostraca	Euphausiidae
Arctic Tern	*Sterna paradisaea*	Aves	Charadriiformes
Bactris Camel	*Camelus bactrianus*	Mammalia	Artiodactyla
Bald Eagle	*Haliaeetus leucocephalus*	Aves	Accipitriformes
Black Caiman	*Melanosuchus niger*	Reptilia	Alliatoriade
Black Manakin	*Xenopipo atronitens*	Aves	Passeriformes
Black-eyed Satyr Butterfly	*Euptychia attenboroghi*	Insecta	Lepidoptera
Black-lip Pearl Oyster	*Pinctada margaritifera*	Bivalvia	Pteriida
Blue Morpho Butterfly	*Morpho Menelaus*	Insecta	Lepidoptera
Blue Whale	*Balaenoptera musculus*	Mammalia	Artiodactyla
Boar	*Sus scrofa*	Mammalia	Artiodactyla
Brazilian Tapir	*Tapirus terrestris*	Mammalia	Perissofactyla
Bullet Ant	*Paraponera clavata*	Insecta	Hymenoptera
Bush Dog	*Speothos venaticus*	Mammalia	Carnivora
Capybara	*Hydrochoerus hydrochaeris*	Mammalia	Rodentia
Cheetah	*Acynonix jubatus*	Mammalia	Carnivora
Cobalt-winged Parakeet	*Brotogeris cyanoptera*	Aves	Psittaciformes
Condor	*Vultur gryphus*	Aves	Accipitriformes
Crayfish (in Pennsylvania)	*Cambarus bartonii*	Malacostraca	Decapoda
Dog	*Canis familiaris*	Mammalia	Carnivora
Eastern Cottontail (Hare)	*Sylvilagus floridanus*	Mammalia	Lagomorpha
Emperor Penguin	*Aptenodytes forsteri*	Aves	Sphenisciformes
Eurasian Hoopoe	*Upupa epops*	Aves	Bucerotiformes
Galapagos Land Crab	*Grapsus grapsus*	Malacostraca	Decapoda
Galapagos Land Iguana	*Colonophus subcristatus*	Reptilia	Squamata
Galapagos Penguin	*Spheniscus mendiculus*	Aves	Sphenisciformes

Giant Anteater	*Myrmecophaga tridactyla*	Mammalia	Pilosa
Giant Moray	*Gymnothorax javanicus*	Actinopterygii	Anguilliformes
Giant Pacific Octopus	*Enteroctopus dofleini*	Cephalopoda	Octopoda
Giant Panda	*Ailuropoda melanoleuca*	Mammalia	Carnivore
Gray-lined Hawk	*Buteo nitidus*	Aves	Accipitriformes
Great Horned Owl	*Bubo virginianus*	Aves	Strigiformes
Great White Shark	*Carcharodon carcharias*	Chondrichthyes	Lamniformes
Green Anaconda	*Eunectes murinus*	Reptilia	Squamata
Green Iguana	*Iguana iguana*	Reptilia	Squamata
Green-fronted Lancebill	*Doryfera ludovicae*	Aves	Apodiformes
Grey-winged Trumpeter	*Psophia crepitans*	Aves	Gruiformes
Grouper	*Epinephelus malabaricus*	Actinopterygii	Perciformes
Guanaco	*Lama guanicoe*	Mammalia	Artiodactyla
Horned Puffin	*Fratercula corniculata*	Aves	Charadriiformes
Humpback Whale	*Megaptera novaeangliae*	Mammalia	Artiodactyla
Impala	*Aepyceros melampus*	Mammalia	Artiodactyla
Jaguar	*Panthera onca*	Mammalia	Carnivora
King Penguin	*Aptenodytes patagonicus*	Aves	Sphenisciformes
Large Horned Chameleon	*trioceros jacksonii.*	Reptilia	Squamata
Leafcutter Ant	*Acromyrmex octospinosus*	Insects	Hymenoptera
Lemming	*Lemmus lemmus*	Mammalia	Rodentia
Lion	*Panthera leo*	Mammalia	Carnivora
Longhorn Beetle	*Batus barbicornis*	Insecta	Coleoptera
Macaroni Penguin	*Eudyptes chrysolophus*	Aves	Sphenisciformes
Moth	*Tineaola bisselliella*	Insecta	Lepidoptera
North American Least Shrew	*Cryptotis parva*	Mammalia	Eulipotyphla
Northern Long-Eared Bat	*Myotis septentrionalis*	Mammalia	Chiroptera
Ostrich	*Struthio camelus*	Ostrich	Struthio camelus
Otter	*Lutra lutar*	Mammalia	Carnivora
Peacock Bass	*Cichla ocellaris*	Actinopterygii	Cichliformes
Pig	*Sus scrofa domesticus*	Mammalia	Artiodactyla
Pigmy Owl	*Glaucidium passerinum*	Aves	Strigiformes
Pilot Fish	*Neucrates ductor*	Actinopterygii	Carangiformes
Poison Dart Frog	*Dendrobates tinctorius*	Amphibian	Anura

Potoo	*Nyctibius jamaicensis*	Aves	Capramulgiformes
Red Fox	*Vulpes vulpes*	Mammalia	Carnivora
Red Howler Monkey	*Alouatta seniculus*	Mammalia	Primates
Red Lionfish	*Pterois volitans*	Actinopterygii	Scorpaeniformes
Red-bellied Macaw	*Orthopsittatan manilatus*	Aves	Psittaciformes
Red-bellied Piranha	*Pygocentrus nattereri*	Actinopterygii	Characiformes
Red-winged Blackbird	*Agelaius*	Aves	Passeriformes
Resplendent Quetzal	*Pharomachrus mocino*	Aves	Trogoniformes
Roly Poly	*Armadillium vulgare*	Malacostraca	Isopoda
Roosting Hornbill	*Ocyceros griseus*	Aves	Bucerotiformes
Sandpiper	*Calidris pusilla*	Aves	Charadriiformes
Scarlet Ibis	*Eudocimus ruber*	Ave	Pelecaniformes
Sea Lion	*Zalophus californianus*	Mammalia	Carnivora
Sloth	*Bradypus variegatus*	Mammalia	Pilosa
Stag Beetle	*Lamorima aurata*	Insecta	Coleoptera
Striped dolphins	*Stenella*	Mammalia	Artiodactyla
Swallowed-tail hummingbird	*Eupetomena macroura*	Aves	Apodiformes
Toucan	*Ramphastos tucanus*	Aves	Piciformes
Tufted Coquette	*Lophornis ornatus*	Aves	Apodiformes
Walrus	*Odobenus rosmarus*	Mammalia	Carnivora
Wandering Albatross	*Diomedia exulans*	Aves	Procellariiformes
White-headed Marmoset	*Callithrix geoffroyi*	Mammalia	Primates
White-spotted Pufferfish	*Aronthron hispidus*	Actinoptergii	Tetraodontidae
White-tailed Deer	*Odocoileus virginianus*	Mammalia	Artiodactyla
Whitetip Shark	*Carcharhinus longimanus*	Chondrichthyes	Carcharhiniformes
Wild Turkey	*Maleagris gallopavo*	Aves	Galliformes
Yellow-bellied Trogon	*Trogon ramonianus*	Aves	Trogoniformes
Zebra	*Equus quagga*	Mammalia	Perissodactyla

CITED PLANTAE

Common Name	Scientific Name	Class	Order
Acacallis Orchid	*Aganisia cyanea*	Monocots	Asparagales
Acaí Palm	*Euterpe oleracea*	Commenilidds	Arecales
African Baobab	*Adansonia kilima*	Rosids	Malvales
Angelim	*Dinizia excelsa*	Rosids	Fabales
Bactris Palm	*Bactris gasipaes*	Commelinids	Arecales
Bacuri	*Platonia insignis*	Rosids	Malpighiales
Balsam	*Myroxilon balsamum*	Rosids	Fabates
Brazilian Rubber Tree	*Hevea brasiliensis*	Rosids	Malpighiales
Buriti Palm	*Mauritia flexuosa*	Commelindis	Arecales
Catleya Orchid	*Catleya labiata*	Monocots	Asparagales
Catuaba	*Trichilia catigua*	Rosids	Sapindales
Ceiba	*Ceiba pentandra*	Rosids	Malvales
Chambira Palm	*Astrocaryum chambira*	Commelinids	Arecales
Club Moss	*Lycopodium hickey*	Lycopediopsida	Lycopodiales
Cockleshell Orchid	*Prostheechea cochleata*	Monocots	Asparagales
Cupuazú	*Theobroma granbiflorum*	Rosids	Malvales
Frangipani	*Plumeria alba*	Asterid	gentianales
Giant Sword Fern	*Nephrolepis biserrata*	Polipodioposida	Polypodiaes
Grapevine	*Vitis acerifolia*	Rosids	Vitales
Hawaiian Ti	*Cordyline fruticosa*	Monocots	Asparagales
Hickories	*Carya species*	Rosids	Fagales
Hydrangea	*Hydrangea macrophylla*	Asterid	Cornales
Kiwi	*Actinidia arguta*	Asterids	Ericales
Lichen	*Parmelia saxatilis*	Lecanoromycetes	Lecanorales
Maidenhair Fern	*Adiantum aleuticum*	Polypodiopsida	Polypodiales
Maple	*Acer scpecies*	Rosids	Sapindales
Maracuyá	*Passiflora edulis*	Rosids	Malpighiales
Marsh Pitcher Plan	*Heliamphora chimantensis*	Asterids	Ericales
Moon Flower	*Ipomoea alba*	Asterids	Solanales
Night Blooming Cereus	*Selenicereus grandiflorus*	Eudicots	Caryophillales
Oak	*Quercus species*	Rosids	Fagales
Olive	*Olea europaea*	Asterids	Lamiales

Pomegranate	*Punica granatum*	Rosids	Myrtales
Possumwood	*Hura crepitans*	Rosids	Malpighiales
Sachamani Tree	*Plukenetia volubilis*	Rosids	Malpighiales
Soya Bean	*Glycine max*	Rosids	Fabales
Strangler Fig	*Ficus Maxima*	Rosids	Rosales
Tillandsia (orchid)	*Tillandsia fasciculata*	Commelinids	Poales
Tucum Palm	*Astrocaryum vulgare*	Commenilidds	Arecales
Ucuúba	*Virola sebifera*	Magnoliids	Magnoliales
Walking Palm	*Socratea exorrhiza*	Commelinids	Arecales

A WORD FROM
THE AUTHOR

As a landscape architect trained in ecological planning and design, it is impossible not to ponder the impact of our species on the planet's biota. What should our relationship to nature be? Four scenarios come to mind.

1. We continue to exploit nature in pursuit of economic progress, endangered species and wildlife be damned.
2. We find a balanced coexistence with nature or, as Ian L. McHarg, a historic figure in the profession of landscape architecture professed in the late nineteen sixties, we "design with nature."
3. We create a New Nature through selective species' protection, animal in-breeding, plant hybridization and genetic alteration, and laboratory-induced life. In other words, we become God.
4. We determine that nature is precious beyond calculation. Land use, energy usage, and material extraction is radically curtailed. Despoiled landscapes are restored, natural habitats are protected, and humanity instead seeks a life-of-plenty elsewhere.

All four scenarios are presently at work. Alarms have been ringing about the first scenario for years, as perhaps most chillingly documented by Elizabeth Kolbert in *The Sixth Extinction*. The second scenario—acknowledging the need to live with nature—has roots in the 1963 Convention on International Trade in Endangered Species of Wild Fauna and Flora. The United States' Endangered Species Act, enacted into law in 1973, also comes to mind. The third scenario is as old as the domestication of wolves to breed working dogs, or that of wild maize to make corn. Today, it manifests itself, as an example, in the form of genetically modified organisms (GMO), such as the genetic manipulation of rice to increase the staple's content of beta-carotene. A noted pioneer of the fourth scenario was Gerard K. O'Neil, a Princeton University physics professor who in 1976 published *The High Frontier: Human Colonies in Space.* The book—now a classic—posits plausible ways to mine the asteroid belt and build self-sustaining orbital living stations. O'Neill believed that outer space was the solution to material scarcity, consequently affording the protection of the "nest in which we live." (Jeff Bezos and Elon Musk are currently fulfilling of O'Neil's vision through their space companies, Blue Origin, and Space X, respectively. Bezos was a student of O'Neill while studying engineering at Princeton in the 1980's.)

ALFIE attends to the latter scenario. Of the four, it is the most embryonic and, over the course of this and later centuries, the one with the greatest potential to alter our relationship with nature. The story places the totality of humanity in an orbital abode but tethered still to its birthing womb. It is a perch that allows nature to evolve pure yet remain as a critical resource for people's wellbeing; that is, as a captured holographic landscape suffusing the new world with biophilic content. Could such a scenario ever happen? To this author the answer is yes, but not without an evolutionary leap in intelligence (and a helping hand from virtual reality wizards). ALFIE asks: What does the continuing progress of artificial intelligence portend? The story plays with the question, but a serious answer can be inferred from John D. Barrow and Frank J. Tipler's *The Anthropic Cosmological Principle.* Evolution cannot go backwards, they argue, setting the possibility for AI to someday supersede humanity in the evolutionary ladder—and, by consequence, dictate human progress. Hence the story's foundational reference to the most far-reaching super intelligence ever imagined.

It is hoped that ALFIE does more than invite curiosity into a brand-new world, that it causes reflection about our "nest" and, in the context of the known universe, draws a greater measure of how precious it is. If it generates discussions about the necessary (if not impending) demise of anthropocentrism, all the better.

ACKNOWLEDGMENTS

ALFIE was a long time in the making. The idea sprung from an education in landscape architecture at the University of Pennsylvania. Ian, L McHarg, who led the program, pressed the use of ecology as a foundation for planning and design. Protecting valuable natural resources was the program's overriding ethic. Without McHarg's teachings, projecting such attitude into the realm of science fiction would not have been possible.

Special gratitude is owed to Brian Nelson, who counseled me to turn the story into a book rather than a screenplay, painful as the writing slog proved to be; to Jason Rekulak, neighbor and author, who provided valuable advice about the publishing industry; and to Dan Rose, anthropologist friend, poet, and artist, whose views on human evolution and artificial intelligence were a source of inspiration. I thank Adrienne King Lewis, and Beth McKeown, who early on read the story and believed in its merits. The book would not have been possible without Rick Chillot, who provided an initial editorial overview, and Julie Simpson, editor extraordinaire who held back no punches over months of back-and-forth dialogue and corrections over the manuscript. I also thank David Rouse, friend and professional colleague, who introduced me to my publisher, Rick Benzel, just as hope was ebbing about finding one.

But most all I thank my wife Sylvia Palms. As a landscape architect, she understood the story's ethical underpinnings and never wavered in her support of the enterprise, especially at times when my convictions wavered.

Made in the USA
Las Vegas, NV
13 December 2022

62282945R10188